HATHAWAY HEIRS

BOOKS 1-4

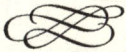

SUZANNA MEDEIROS

HATHAWAY HEIRS

BOOKS 1-4

Suzanna Medeiros

The complete series now available in one volume.

LADY HATHAWAY'S PROPOSAL

She will do anything for a few nights in his arms.

Twelve years have passed since Miranda Hathaway ended her courtship with Andrew Osborne and married the older, but much wealthier, Viscount Hathaway. It is only one week after her husband's death and Miranda cannot ignore the temptation to have a taste of what she threw away all those years ago when she followed her parents' wishes. But to entice the man she never stopped loving, she will have to act quickly.

Now the Earl of Sanderson, Andrew is no longer the same man who once believed in love. When Miranda asks him to help her conceive a child—one whom she means to pass off as the next Hathaway heir—he sees her deceit as proof that she is not the same woman he once knew. However, he cannot ignore the temptation to finally have her in his bed.

Miranda knows she is infertile, but her deception gives Her three weeks with Andrew. He plans to use that time to finally consign Miranda Hathaway to the past, while she hopes to build memories that will last her a lifetime.

LORD HATHAWAY'S BRIDE

If he can't have her love, he'll have her passion.

A marriage of convenience…
Sarah Mapleton has already had her heart broken once. When she finds herself compelled to marry the intriguing new Viscount Hathaway, she vows to protect her heart at all costs.

He has her hand…
After unexpectedly inheriting his uncle's title, James Hathaway discovers that the one thing he wants above all else is Sarah. He hopes to win her love, but until that happens, he vows to have her passion.

But can he win her heart?
Sarah is surprised that her new husband can wring unexpected pleasure from her body. But she realizes too late that his kindness has also torn down her emotional barriers. Her determination to protect herself from being hurt again might have pushed James away permanently.

CAPTAIN HATHAWAY'S DILEMMA

To fulfill his duty, he must forsake his chance at happiness.

When the man who saves his life during the Battle of Waterloo dies from wounds that were meant for him, Captain Edward Hathaway must live with the guilt of having survived and is determined to fulfill that man's dying wish.

Grace Kent only accepted her childhood friend's proposal of marriage so he wouldn't go off to war with a broken heart. But while she still grieves for her friend after learning of his death, she cannot resist her attraction to the handsome Captain Hathaway.

He is determined to discharge his duty at the expense of his own happiness. She wants only one taste of true passion. Together, can they overcome the guilt that continues to haunt them both?

MISS HATHAWAY'S WISH

Emily Hathaway makes a special wish this Christmas...

Emily Hathaway wants to marry for love, but after three unsuccessful seasons she's given up on finding the same happiness her brothers found in their marriages.

Sir Jonah Stanton has returned to England after ten years abroad. A Christmas party at Hathaway Manor provides the perfect opportunity to ease back into English society. But one thing has changed since Jonah's been away. His friend's little sister is now a young woman, and he finds himself appreciating her in ways he'd never imagined possible.

As Emily becomes reacquainted with Jonah, she discovers the feelings she'd attributed to friendship run far deeper. Is it possible Jonah might be the man she's been looking for all along?

To learn about Suzanna Medeiros's future books, you can sign up for her newsletter at https://www.suzannamedeiros.com/newsletter/

Hathaway Heirs: Books 1-4

First digital edition, January 2021

ISBN: 9781988223100

LADY HATHAWAY'S PROPOSAL © 2013 Saozinha Medeiros

Original title: Lady Hathaway's Indecent Proposal

LORD HATHAWAY'S BRIDE © 2018 Saozinha Medeiros

Original title: Lord Hathaway's New Bride

CAPTAIN HATHAWAY'S DILEMMA © 2015 Saozinha Medeiros

Original title: The Captain's Heart

MISS HATHAWAY'S WISH © 2019 Saozinha Medeiros

LADY HATHAWAY'S PROPOSAL

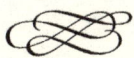

HATHAWAY HEIRS ~ BOOK 1

Twelve years have passed since Miranda Hathaway ended her courtship with Andrew Osborne and married the older, but much wealthier, Viscount Hathaway. It is only one week after her husband's death and Miranda cannot ignore the temptation to have a taste of what she threw away all those years ago when she followed her parents' wishes. But to entice the man she never stopped loving, she will have to act quickly.

Now the Earl of Sanderson, Andrew is no longer the same man who once believed in love. When Miranda asks him to help her conceive a child—one whom she means to pass off as the next Hathaway heir—he sees her deceit as proof that she is not the same woman he once knew. However, he cannot ignore the temptation to finally have her in his bed.

Miranda knows she is infertile, but her deception gives her three weeks with Andrew. He plans to use that time to finally consign Miranda Hathaway to the past, while she hopes to build memories that will last her a lifetime.

DEDICATION

To all my writing friends, who are too numerous to list.
Thank you for your inspiration and support over the years.

CHAPTER 1

$\mathcal{U}$NTIL THAT MORNING the Earl of Sanderson would have said he was long past making a fool of himself for Miranda Hathaway, yet here he was, following her butler into the drawing room of her London town house. He told himself it was only curiosity that led him to accept her request for a meeting. After all, they hadn't seen one another in twelve years, so why on earth would she want to see him now?

He took in the room's ornate furnishings as the butler bowed and left to fetch his mistress. Viscount Hathaway had always made a point of displaying his vast wealth at every opportunity, as was evidenced by the amount of gilt in the room. He wondered if Miranda approved of the decor, or if she, too, found it lacking in taste. The old Miranda would have believed the latter. Or so he'd thought at the time, but that was before she'd broken it off with him to marry the much wealthier older man.

Unease settled in the pit of his stomach, and annoyed at the sign of weakness, he moved to the window and looked out onto the fashionable Mayfair neighborhood. It was early for a social call and the road was quiet. No doubt most of Miranda's neighbors were still abed, recovering from whatever entertainments had kept them up the evening before. He would have been sleeping as well if Miranda's message hadn't arrived last night before he'd left for his club.

He resisted the urge to turn around and leave, just as she had done that last time they'd seen one another. Once again, he was at a disadvantage with her. In her house, at her summons, no knowledge of what this meeting was about. He was not, however, the same untried youth he'd been back then. If Miranda assumed so, she would be more than a little surprised.

He sensed her approach and turned in time to see her enter the room. He couldn't help but notice she still moved with the same grace she'd possessed as a young woman, setting the *ton* ablaze during her first season with her beauty and unaffected charm. It had been inevitable that she'd captured his interest as well. But the new widow standing across the room from him now, clad in stark black, was far different from the girl of eighteen who'd worn only pale colors.

That was a lifetime ago.

"My lord," she said, executing a fluid curtsey. Her expression gave no hint as to why she had sent for him.

He inclined his head in acknowledgement and watched in silence as she sat on one end of the ornate settee. A chair was positioned at an angle from her and it was clear she expected him to use it.

6

A need to ruffle her impassive bearing had him remaining silent and ignoring the chair. He moved past her and sat, instead, beside her on the settee. He left a respectable distance between them, but the way she stiffened told him she hadn't expected him to sit so close. It was self-indulgent, but he felt a small measure of triumph at her discomfort.

He watched, more than a little surprised, as she collected herself, smoothing away all signs of discomfort. Her body relaxed, her expression becoming one of polite cordiality as she held herself with an almost unnatural stillness. It appeared Miranda Hathaway had learned to control the youthful exuberance she'd once possessed. He wasn't sure whether to applaud her for her newfound reserve or mourn the loss of that once vibrant, impetuous young woman.

Silence stretched between them for several seconds before she turned to face him. He was struck once again, as he had been all those years ago, by her beauty. Her dark brown hair and the unrelieved black of her dress called attention to her pale coloring, making it seem as though she were carved from ivory. Her gray eyes were larger than he remembered, but she was also much thinner than when he'd known her. Almost painfully so. He almost asked if she was well but resisted the impulse. He had no desire to hear about how much she mourned the loss of the husband whose funeral had been only the week before.

The curve of her breasts and her unfashionably plump mouth were the only things about her that were still full. His eyes flickered downward and he remembered with unexpected vividness just how those full lips had felt under his. He'd been with many other women since they'd parted ways, but he'd never enjoyed kissing anyone as much as he had Miranda. Thoughts of how she could put that mouth to another use sent a wave of unwelcome heat through him.

He'd miscalculated. He'd wanted to set Miranda off balance, but being this close to her was having an unwanted effect on him.

"Thank you for accepting my invitation," she said, cutting through the uncomfortable silence. "I know it is early, but I can ring for tea if you haven't eaten yet this morning."

His wayward thoughts under control, he met her emotionless gaze with one of his own. "I think we can dispense with the niceties. We both know this isn't a social call."

Those luscious lips tilted ever so slightly at the corners. "I see you are still as direct as always."

"And I can see you've taken to hiding behind social conventions. You were never one to dance around a subject. You asked me to visit and, despite my reservations, I came. You clearly have something you wish to discuss with me."

He was surprised when she stood.

"This was a mistake." She took a step toward the doorway. "Forgive me for inconveniencing you."

After a brief moment of hesitation, he rose from the settee and moved to block her path. She stopped but kept her eyes averted.

"Miranda."

She didn't move. Against his better judgment, he placed a hand under her chin and tilted her face up to his. They stood that way for several long moments, during which he was painfully aware of the small woman before him. The woman who, he now knew, still had the power to make him want her.

8

She, on the other hand, had the appearance of a cornered, frightened animal.

He dropped his hand and kept his voice even, sensing she was a hairsbreadth away from bolting. "Why did you wish to see me?"

She hesitated and then he saw the resolve form in her eyes.

"Very well," she said before taking a step back.

She moved around him to the door, and this time he didn't stop her—he knew she wouldn't attempt to escape again. He expected her to ring for the tea she'd offered him and was taken aback when she closed the door and turned to face him again.

He raised an eyebrow in question but said nothing. She leaned back against the door for a moment before straightening and looking at him directly. Just as she used to do.

"You are aware my husband passed away last week."

"Yes," he said simply. "Please accept my condolences."

He should have offered them when she'd first come into the room, but after a nod of acknowledgment, she continued as though she hadn't noticed his breach in manners.

"The reason I asked you here has to do with his passing."

"Oh? I'll admit I have no idea why you'd want to see me."

Her smile was fleeting. "No, of course not."

She moved back to the settee and lowered herself onto it. This time when he followed, he didn't repeat his mistake of sitting next to her. But if she guessed at his reason for choosing the chair, she showed no sign of it.

"There is no delicate way to say this, so I must be blunt."

Her words, as well as her resolute manner, sent every one of his senses into high alert. He wasn't sure if she was aware she'd used those same words all those years ago when she'd told him she was marrying someone else. He was starting to regret preventing her from leaving the room.

"With my husband's nephew due to inherit the entirety of his estate, I will have to rely on his generosity in future."

Andrew had stayed as far away as possible from Hathaway —had tried not to think about him outside of those times he'd had to see him in the House of Lords—so he had no way of knowing if he'd ever met the man's heir.

"Given how important Hathaway's wealth was to you and your parents, surely you don't expect me to believe provisions for your future weren't made before your marriage."

She didn't react to the sarcasm in his tone. "I won't need to resort to begging in the street. But no one imagined I wouldn't provide my husband with an heir, so the settlement outlined for that eventuality is a small one." She hesitated and her eyes slid away from his before she continued. "I have spoken to our solicitor and he informs me that in cases where the widow is still of childbearing years, it is customary to wait a few months to ensure there is no heir on the way."

He couldn't stop his gaze from moving to her abdomen, but given the loose fit of her gown, it was impossible to see if it concealed a small bump. The wave of bitterness that rose at her words caught him off guard.

"I fail to see what this has to do with me."

He started to stand, but she reached across the small space that separated them and laid a hand on his knee. Her touch froze him to the spot and his awareness of the intimacy of their current situation intensified.

She moved back and clasped her hands sedately in her lap,

but she hadn't been quick enough to keep him from seeing the telltale tremble in her fingers. "I am not with child," she said as though nothing of import had just happened, "but I am hoping that will not be the case for long."

His mind was still on the unwanted rush of desire her touch had elicited, and so it took him several seconds before he realized what she was suggesting. Air rushed out of his lungs as the full implication of her words hit him. Why she'd summoned him here so early when no one would be about in the street to see his arrival. Why she'd closed the door to make sure the servants wouldn't overhear their conversation.

He welcomed the anger that rose swiftly within him, but he refused to let her see it. He wouldn't give her the satisfaction of knowing she could command more than polite curiosity from him.

"I am afraid I still do not know what any of this has to do with me. I am sure your solicitor would be able to advise you much better than I."

A hint of frustration crossed her face before she masked it. Despite her attempt to appear detached and businesslike, the revealing expression told him she was more emotionally invested in their conversation than she wanted him to know.

"You were never one to be so obtuse, Andrew."

"You will excuse me, Lady Hathaway, if I ask for some of that bluntness you promised me."

Her control was slipping, for this time he clearly saw her wince when he'd used her title. The narrowing of her eyes was minute, but she hadn't been able to hide it. She didn't speak for several long moments, long enough for him to think he had won. He was surprised, therefore, when she straightened, drew back her shoulders and met his gaze squarely.

"I want to have a child and I would like you to be the father of that child."

Disbelief almost robbed him of words. When he opened his mouth to tell her exactly what he thought of her proposal, she continued, forestalling him.

"I am under no illusion that we can continue our former relationship. I will make no demands of you and no one will know the child is yours."

Disappointment tinged the anger burning within him as she spoke. The deceitful, conniving woman sitting before him now, the one who would blithely make plans to defraud the heir to her husband's estate of his rightful inheritance, bore no resemblance whatsoever to the woman he'd once known and loved.

And with that realization came the certainty that he was well and truly free of the hold she had once held over him.

He started to refuse, but something held him back. He might no longer love Miranda, but he couldn't deny that he was still very attracted to her. And despite everything, this new woman sitting before him was a mystery he found himself longing to unravel.

"Can you have children? In twelve years you should have already had more than one."

She didn't hesitate before replying. "Robert was older. Our marriage was not a physical one."

He scoffed at that. "I hope you're not about to tell me you're a virgin."

She closed her eyes for a moment and it seemed as though

his question had embarrassed her. Given her former bravado and what she had just asked of him, her reluctance to discuss the details surrounding her outrageous plan was more than a little out of place.

"No. In the beginning he visited me, but it was not long before he stopped."

"Why?"

Annoyance flashed across her face.

"How would I know why? I assumed he had a mistress, but I was not about to ask him."

He couldn't keep himself from asking the obvious question. "How long has it been?"

She looked back at him. "Long enough that I am certain I am not carrying his child."

Her answer was far from satisfactory, but since he didn't want to hear the intimate details of her marriage, he didn't press her further.

They sat there for some time, holding each other's gaze, but neither one willing to make the next move. As the silence lengthened, his awareness of Miranda grew. Images of the two of them in bed, his hands sliding over every inch of her body, her face contorted in ecstasy as she found release, crowded his mind.

He didn't love Miranda, but he still wanted her. Perhaps he wanted to punish her as well. Give her a taste of all she had cast aside when she'd casually dismissed him for a larger fortune.

His lust for her wrestled with his conscience, but in the end it was his desire that won out, and he knew he would give her the affair she wanted. It would, of necessity, be of brief duration if she wanted to pass off his bastard as Hathaway's heir. And God help his black soul, but the thought gave him a sense of grim satisfaction. He'd have his revenge on Miranda, ruin her for any other man, and even the score with Hathaway for stealing the woman he'd so desperately wanted all those years ago.

If she wanted him to do this, however, she would have to work for it. She might have had everything she'd ever wanted fall neatly into her lap, but he was no longer willing to exert himself just because she crooked a finger in his direction.

"Satisfy my curiosity about something," he said, breaking the now oppressive silence. "Why me? I'm sure there are any number of men who would be willing to lie between your legs."

Her face heated at his deliberate crudeness, but he had to admire the fact that she didn't lose her composure.

"I know most men have no problem bedding whichever woman happens to be near at hand at the moment. I was young when I married, however, and have spent most of the last few years at our estate in Northampton. I never learned to be as casual as some women are about their bed partners. And..."

For a moment Andrew would have sworn she looked uncertain. Vulnerable. But clearly that could never be said about a woman who planned to pass off another man's child as the heir to a well-established title.

"And what?" he prompted when she showed no signs of continuing.

"You were once kind to me."

That was a vast understatement if ever he'd heard one. "Yes, well, kindness is the very last thing I feel for you now."

She said nothing to that. What was there to say?

"Did you want to start here or should we go up to your bedroom?"

That got a reaction. Her hand fluttered to her chest. "I'm not sure. Do you think it would be wise?"

She licked her lips, a gesture, he remembered, that always indicated she was nervous. His groin tightened. He'd been trying to shock her, but it appeared she was quite willing to carry through with her proposition, and his body responded eagerly.

Irritated she could still so easily rouse his desire, he lashed out at her. "Tell me, Miranda, did Hathaway kiss you and caress you before fucking you? Or did he simply raise your nightgown and grunt away on top of you while you congratulated yourself on the excellent match you'd made?"

She didn't try to hide the anger his words had roused. Good, he thought. This was the Miranda he wanted. The calculating, aggressive Miranda. He wanted no reminders of how young and innocent she'd once been.

In reply, she stood. His innate manners had him beginning to stand, but she placed her hands on his shoulders to stop him. He leaned back in the chair and waited to see what she would do next. He wasn't disappointed.

She lowered herself onto his lap, leaned into him, and raised her hands to frame his face. He could feel the rapid rise and fall of her breasts against his chest and, in anticipation, his own breath quickened to match hers. She placed her mouth against his, and in that moment he wanted nothing more than to crush her against him and take what she so freely offered. Instead, he willed himself to remain still, letting her take the lead. She moved her mouth against his, but it soon became clear she'd acted out of bravado and not experience.

When she drew back again, frustration had etched little lines above her nose. Despite the fact she had given him little more than a chaste kiss, she was not unaffected. Her gray eyes had darkened and her breathing was ragged. Aside from confirming the type of marital relations she'd shared with her husband, her kiss had given him another piece of vital information. He needed more, and he needed it now.

When he stood, taking her with him, she gave a surprised gasp and wrapped her arms around his neck. He moved the two steps to the settee and lowered the two of them onto it. She remained on his lap, but now his arms were around her. Her eyes widened when she felt his erection pressing against her hip.

"Right, no kissing," he said, surprised to find his voice hoarse with his effort at controlling himself. "Let me show you how it's done."

He claimed her mouth slowly at first. Touching his lips to hers and brushing them against hers in slow, tantalizing movements aimed at gaining her trust. It was not too dissimilar from the way she had kissed him, but she obviously took comfort from the fact he was now participating. She relaxed against him and the heat of her body, pressed against his, fueled his desire.

He'd been all too innocent and eager to prove himself worthy of her when he'd courted her as a youth and so hadn't kissed her the way he'd longed to. But now, with the confidence that came from experience, he intended to make up for his former restraint. When she sighed, he took advantage of the opportunity to deepen the kiss, tracing his tongue first against her lips and then entering her mouth. She stiffened, but only for a moment before matching his movement.

The notion entered his mind that perhaps she'd been acting the innocent earlier, but he dismissed the notion as inconsequential. Did it really matter? He leaned back against the cushions and she followed, draping her body over his. He groaned as the kiss became more urgent, their tongues and mouths dueling for dominance. Blind to everything but the lust sweeping through him, he placed one hand on her backside and ground his erection against her hip. He lifted his other hand to cup her breast. She moaned low, arching into his touch as he covered her full breast and teased the hardened nipple with his thumb. She moved now, writhing against him. Without conscious thought, he shifted, reversing their positions so that she lay under him on the settee.

When he had her exactly where he wanted, he started to raise her skirts so he could settle between her legs. It took him a few moments to realize that her hands had moved from clinging to his shoulders to trying to push him away.

He lifted his head and looked down at her. Her lips were swollen from their heated kiss and a flush stained her cheeks and upper chest a rosy pink. She was clearly aroused. Behind the heat in her eyes, however, he detected a hint of uncertainty. Damn. How had he lost control so quickly? He closed his eyes, and took a deep breath before pushing himself away from her. He watched in silence as she struggled with her skirts before rising to sit on the other end of the settee. One hand moved to touch her bottom lip and he knew with certainty that neither her husband, nor any other man, had ever kissed her that way.

"Are you…" Flustered, she stopped before starting again. "Does this mean you agree to my request?"

Mere agreement was laughable when compared to the feelings warring within him. Desire. Lust. An almost desperate need to throw her back down and finish what they'd started. Oh yes, he would most definitely give her what she wanted. And at the same time he'd finally get Miranda Hathaway out of his system and be done with her. And if a child resulted… Well, he wouldn't be the first man with a bastard. And in his case he knew his son would be well provided for as the next Viscount Hathaway. And a daughter would also ensure Miranda had claims to the next Viscount's generosity.

Schooling his features to mask his anticipation, he rose and moved to the door. With one hand on the knob he turned back to face her.

"I'll send word of where and when."

At her nod he opened the door and, anxious to be away from Miranda and his newly aroused need for her, showed himself out.

CHAPTER 2

ANDREW'S NOTE CAME the following morning. It contained simply an address and a time later that evening and was signed with an *S* for his title—Sanderson. That formality told her everything. He wanted her to know that despite the heated kiss they had shared the previous morning, there was to be no real intimacy between them.

That kiss had haunted her the rest of the day and had led to a night of passionate dreams. It had also served to make her feel like a fraud when acquaintances and family friends called on her to offer their condolences and see how she was faring. While she appreciated their show of support, the very last thing she needed was to be forced to act the part of the grieving widow when all she could think about was the fact she would soon be physically intimate with Andrew.

The hours crawled by and when evening finally arrived, a swarm of butterflies had taken up permanent residence low in her belly. But despite her nerves, she could hardly wait for the appointed hour to arrive. Her brief meeting with Andrew had told her what she had always suspected—there was more to the intimate relations between a man and a woman than what she had experienced in her marriage. She knew men took great pleasure in that physical act, and if the way she'd felt when Andrew had touched her was any indication, she suspected there could also be great pleasure for a woman.

When it was time to prepare for their encounter, she took great care to dress to her best advantage, choosing an outfit that would give her the confidence she'd need. Given the illicit nature of the errand she was on, she couldn't bring herself to wear one of her mourning gowns. She chose, instead, a satin gown of deep red that had a simple row of buttons up the back that she could reach herself with a little effort.

Her maid had been surprised when Miranda dismissed her after the woman had laced her corset, but it was vital that the servants believe she was going out to have a quiet dinner at the home of a family friend. If gossip started to spread about her activities, she would not be able to carry out her supposed ruse and Andrew would have no reason to see her. If that happened, she would never find another reason to entice him to make love with her.

She left her hair in the simple knot her maid had created that morning and concealed her outfit with a black cloak before stepping out into the street. Her butler had been aghast when she'd told him she planned to walk, alone, to her destination, but it was only a few minutes away and he'd had no choice but to acquiesce to her insistence that she be alone. She'd felt a stab of guilt knowing he'd only backed down because he hadn't wanted to upset her further during what was supposed to be a very painful time for her.

To ensure no one would discover her true destination, she hired her first carriage a few blocks from her home and changed hansoms twice during her journey. When the third cab finally stopped at the address Andrew had provided, she was relieved to find herself at a small house on the outskirts of London.

She paid the driver and stepped down from the carriage. Despite her nerves, she thought she'd managed to push aside the last of her misgivings. But standing before the front door of the nondescript house, she couldn't help but wonder if she was making a mistake.

Her husband had been ill for some time, but his illness hadn't been a fatal one. After the shock of Robert's unexpected death the week before had worn off, she'd been taken aback by how quickly the idea for her current plan had come to her. She'd tried to ignore it at first, but the need to see Andrew again, to recapture the emotions she'd once experienced when they had courted, wouldn't leave her.

Their courtship hadn't ended well and it had been her fault. He'd been so young and earnest then, only a year older than her own eighteen years. They'd been in love. She might have been young and inexperienced, but she'd known he would never leave her and she'd felt the same devotion to him. Her confidence that they could have a future together had withered under her parents' displeasure. Andrew had been next in line to be the Earl of Sanderson, but theirs was not a wealthy estate and everyone had expected it would be many years before he came into his modest inheritance. Her parents had, therefore, taken it upon themselves to promise her hand in marriage to the much older Viscount Hathaway.

She couldn't blame them for all that followed. They'd acted in what they considered to be her best interests and she'd relented. She knew in Andrew's eyes it did not speak well to her character that she'd so easily acquiesced to her parents' desires.

And it hadn't been a horrible marriage. She'd been content enough over the years despite the fact theirs had not been a marriage based on love. Robert had treated her like a pet he doted upon, and she'd done her best not to dwell on what might have been. Andrew had left for Europe just before her marriage had taken place, and she'd been grateful she didn't need to worry about running into him in Town. And when she'd learned of his return a few years later, she'd fled, retiring to spend the majority of her time at Hathaway's estate in Northampton.

Over the years she'd managed to accept her lot in life, but she'd never forgotten him. When her solicitor had asked her if it was possible she was with child, she'd known she wasn't. Robert had been eager to conceive a child with her and had visited her regularly over the years, but had stopped a few short months ago when he fell ill.

That question, though, had sparked a ridiculous idea that wouldn't leave her. Especially when she realized she now had an excuse to approach Andrew and attempt to fill the emptiness that had grown inside her since she'd let her parents convince her to give him up.

She had no illusions that he'd been pining for her all these years, just as she was also under no illusion about her likelihood of falling with child from their time together. She hadn't been able to conceive a child in the twelve years of her marriage, and since Robert already had an illegitimate daughter when they married, she knew the fault lay with her. Her courses had never come regularly, not like they did with other women, and as the years passed she had no other option than to accept the fact she was barren.

But now she had an opportunity—an opportunity she would not so easily throw away as she'd done when she was a foolish girl of eighteen. She would finally learn what it was like to be physically intimate with the man she loved.

She tested the door and, finding it unlocked, let herself in. Two oil lamps lit the hallway, but other than that the house seemed empty. In the unnerving quiet, her heart sounded loud to her own ears. She took an inventory of her surroundings and saw right away the rooms on the main floor were dark, but light beckoned from the second level. Unnerved by the silence and the gloom surrounding her, she made her way upstairs, the light serving as a beacon.

The door to the room at the top of the stairs was ajar, and when she pushed it open, she wasn't surprised to find herself in a bedroom. Most of the furniture was simple but for one notable exception—the bed. It dominated the small space, appearing a good deal larger than any she'd ever seen. The curtains at the windows were closed, the light from the fireplace and an oil lamp on the sole bedside table making the room seem cozy and welcoming. Miranda moved to the fire blazing in the hearth and held out her hands to warm them. It was still early enough in the spring that evenings were much cooler than during the day.

Questions rose, unbidden, about just how many other women Andrew had brought here over the years, but she pushed the unwanted thoughts from her mind. She had no right to begrudge him the companionship of other women. Not after she had denied him her own.

She spun around at the sound of a floorboard creaking behind her and found herself face-to-face with Andrew. He stood several feet away, his features in shadow, which somehow made the effect of his presence more intimate since it high-lighted what they were both here to do.

She had a moment of doubt, wondering if the now mature Earl of Sanderson could live up to her memories of the young Andrew Osborne she'd met and fallen in love with twelve years before. He was different, harder, but the years had been good to him. The attractive, charming young man had blossomed into a man of account.

He wore his hair short now. She remembered how, when it was longer, the brown had been threaded through with blond high-lights that had given him a tousled, almost boyish appearance. In its current close-cropped style, his hair looked much darker than its medium brown. His face had also lost its youthful appearance, the slight roundness gone. It was more angled than she remem-bered, his square jaw and cheekbones more prominent.

His eyes, however, were the same. A medium green unlike any she had ever seen before or since. She used to adore gazing into them when they danced at those many balls that one season they'd had together. But now they mocked her. Gone was the warmth she'd once found in their depths.

Her heart was racing… whether from fear or anticipation,

she wasn't sure. Probably a little of both. She did her best to keep her breathing even, however. Having made such an outrageous proposition as asking him to help her conceive a child, she could hardly act the part of a shy virgin. At any rate, she was far from being that.

It seemed Andrew planned to just stand there, probably hoping to make her nervous, so she broke the silence. "I find it hard to believe we are both here, about to do this thing."

He raised a brow. "You cannot possibly be more surprised than I."

He bridged the last few steps that separated them, stopping only when their bodies were almost touching. She knew then he wanted to intimidate her. Gain the upper hand. She wouldn't allow her nervousness to show, but she did feel at a disadvantage when she had to tilt her head back to look up at him.

For one horrible moment she feared he expected her to act first. Relief flooded through her, therefore, when he took her hands in his much larger ones and brought them up, around his neck. He was so much taller than her that in this position her body was flush against his.

Everything else faded away as they stood like that, she pressed against him, their eyes locked and the air of anticipation swirling around them. Gone were the memories of the many unsatisfactory couplings she'd shared with her husband. The panic she'd undergone when he'd died and she realized she was now truly alone in the world, for she would never again go back to her family and allow them to control her life. Even the desperation that had led her to proposition the Earl of Sanderson so she could finally feel, if only for a little while, what it was like to be happy again.

For she was happy just being here with him. She hadn't expected that.

"I'm not going to ask if you're still sure you want to do this," he said.

She had no second thoughts, but his statement surprised her. The Andrew she'd known had always been considerate to a fault.

She spoke around a mouth that had suddenly gone dry. "Why not?"

"Because I don't want to know if you've changed your mind. You made your offer and I accepted. There's no turning back now."

He'd lowered his head and his last words were spoken against her lips. When she opened her mouth to reply—she couldn't say with what—he took it as an invitation to kiss her. This time there was no gradual buildup. The kiss was hot and hungry, and she dove into it without hesitation.

Yes, this was what she wanted. Andrew holding her, kissing her as though he wanted to devour her. His hands moved to her backside and pressed her more firmly against his impressive erection. She realized she was making mewling sounds low in her throat. Perhaps she should have been embarrassed in case he believed her wanton, but she couldn't bring herself to care. With this man only, she *felt* wanton. Deliciously so.

He must have taken her physical response as the answer to the question he hadn't wanted to ask and walked her backward until her legs bumped against the edge of that enormous bed. He moved away from her then, but only a fraction so he could lift her into his arms and deposit her in the center. He joined her there, covering her with the heat of his body, and she shivered with need. This was nothing like the rushed, emotionless couplings she'd shared with her husband.

She expected him to raise her skirts and bury himself inside her, so was confused when he levered himself away to kneel on the bed beside her.

"Is something the matter?" She was shocked at how hoarse her voice sounded to her own ears.

"You're wearing too many clothes."

She didn't protest when he pulled her into a kneeling position before him and removed the cloak she'd only just realized she was still wearing. He made a strangled sound when he saw the red gown she wore with its very low bodice. She'd been uncertain whether to be so brazen when dressing, but now she was glad she'd chosen the provocative dress.

"I promise to take time to appreciate you in that dress later, but for now, it has to go."

He shifted until he was behind her and started to work his way down the row of buttons. Her mind blanked. Surely he didn't mean to actually disrobe her? Never, in all her years of marriage, had Hathaway removed her clothing. Then again, she'd always worn her nightdress when he came to her, so perhaps Andrew would stop when she was down to her chemise.

Her wayward thoughts scattered when he loosened her stays. When the undergarment was held up only by the loosened bodice of her gown, he placed his warm hands on her shoulders and lowered her dress. She moved to take her arms out of the sleeves, but he pulled the garment tight around her again, stilling her movement. She remained that way, her arms trapped, her breathing quickening, while he drew the stays from her body. He pulled her back against him and cupped her breasts through her chemise.

He groaned and the sound echoed deep within her. He completely surrounded her. The coolness of his satin waistcoat chilled her back through her thin chemise while his warm hands squeezed and played with her breasts. Not caring what he might think of her, knowing only that she needed more of what he was doing to her, she let her head fall back against his shoulder and thrust her breasts more firmly into his hands. When he tweaked her nipple between his thumb and forefinger, she moaned. Heat spread from his hands and traveled though her body, moving across her belly and settling lower, between her legs.

She struggled against the constraints of her dress and he relented, moving away and helping her to remove her arms and allowing the dress to fall to the bed around her. She tried to turn and reach for him, but he wouldn't allow it. He untied the tape at the top of her chemise and before she realized his intention, he'd dragged her undergarment down as well. She should have been embarrassed, kneeling on the bed, all her clothes pooled around her, but at that point she was far from caring about her modesty. She craved the touch of his hands on her body again, and the idea of lying bare-skinned with him was more exciting than she could have imagined.

She expected him to touch her breasts again, waited almost breathlessly for it. With a low curse, he moved from the bed and started removing his own clothing. She watched, her attention riveted on his quick, efficient movements as he cast aside his topcoat and waistcoat, untied his cravat, and drew his shirt over his head.

She'd known his chest was broader now—assumed it had happened when he'd shaken off the last of his youthful appearance—but she hadn't realized he was so muscular. He looked back at her then and, catching her staring at him, let out a sound she could only describe as a growl.

He made quick work of his shoes, trousers, and small-clothes, then stood there, fully erect before her, as though waiting for her to comment.

"When you marry one day, your wife will be most fortunate."

At his scowl she realized it was the wrong thing to say, but she didn't have time to examine why. He climbed back onto the bed, and when he eased her onto her back, she went willingly. He slid an arm under her hips, lifting her so he could strip her gown and chemise from where it had tangled against her legs. She could only stare at him, her breathing heavy, as he removed first one slipper, tracing his fingers along the high arch of her foot, then the other. He repeated the caress before smoothing his hands along her calves. When he reached her knees, she feared she'd stop breathing, but he continued until he reached her garters. They were red, like her dress.

"Did you wear these for me?" he asked, stroking the skin above them.

His eyes, when they met hers again, were a dark green, and the emotion she saw reflected there told her he was just as affected as she.

In truth, she hadn't expected him to see the garters, but she nodded in response. He rewarded her with quick kisses,

SUZANNA MEDEIROS

high on each thigh, through her drawers, and she almost jumped out of her skin. He rolled the garters and stockings from her legs and cast the flimsy garments away. His smooth movements told her more than anything else that this was far from the first time he had performed such an intimate action with a woman.

When he started to remove her drawers, panic surged through her. She grabbed his forearms, halting him.

"Must you?"

She'd barely managed the words as she felt the first real twinges of alarm.

"All or nothing, Miranda."

She hesitated only a moment longer before nodding. She squeezed her eyes closed and lifted her hips while he removed the garment, unbearably self-conscious. She knew he was staring at her body, taking in the sight of her hips, which were as slender as a boy's, and her most intimate of places. Not even her husband had seen her completely in the nude.

He eased himself over her, and she moaned at the feel of his hot, hard body, pressing her into the mattress, his erection branding the outside of her thigh. She fought the urge to run her hands all over the smooth expanse of his skin.

"Open your eyes," he said, his voice rough. "When I take you, I want you to know who you're with."

She could hardly mistake this man for her husband. The two did not even appear to belong to the same species. She opened her eyes and they stayed like that for what seemed a lifetime, his eyes ensnaring hers and their bodies touching from chest to thigh. She wasn't sure who moved first, but their mouths met in a hot, urgent kiss.

She brought her hands up to encircle his neck, her fingers weaving into his short hair and keeping his head right where she wanted it. Her mouth opened wide, allowing him full access. He took advantage, but she didn't remain passive. Her tongue tangled with his and she gave as good as he.

She allowed herself to explore him then, running her hands across his shoulders and down the muscles of his arms. When she snaked her arms around his waist, he made an almost-strangled sound and tore his mouth from hers.

The next time his head dipped, it was lower than she'd expected. He placed his mouth on her neck, trailing warm kisses along its length. The heat of his breath caused an almost unbearable yearning within her. He didn't stop there but moved even lower, nibbling playfully on her shoulder before proceeding to rain kisses down to her breast. He kneaded one breast while he trailed his tongue across the slope of the other. When he took the nipple into his mouth and sucked hard, she arched off the bed. He held her down, continuing to torture her with his mouth and hands as pleasure speared through her.

She needed to have him inside her and opened her legs. The tip of his shaft slid along her wet folds and she moaned.

"Shh. Not yet." The words were softly spoken, but they seemed to echo in the room.

He trailed more kisses down her abdomen, startling her. When he continued his downward path, she tried to close her legs. His hands on her knees easily prevented the movement.

"Andrew, don't..."

She jumped when he slid his hands high up on her thighs

and held her there, his thumbs almost touching her opening. "What are you doing?"

He looked up and the naked lust in his eyes stole the rest of her protest.

"You proposed this arrangement—it's all or nothing. I want to do this."

He waited for her assent. She was uncomfortable with him seeing her so intimately, but at that moment she knew she would do anything for him. She also knew that despite what had happened in the past and how he had changed, she trusted him. If she hadn't, she never would have approached him.

She nodded and started to close her eyes but then, remembering what he'd said about giving him everything, kept her gaze on him. She had difficulty holding still when he placed a kiss high on the inside of her thigh. He stared at her there, between her legs, and she fought the urge to turn away from him. With his thumbs he held her open, which confused her. Why would he want to look at her down there?

"I've imagined doing this to you."

Before she could ask what he meant, his mouth covered her intimately and she jerked in shock.

His tongue swept along the place where she knew her center of her pleasure rested. Her husband had never touched her there—she'd had to discover it on her own. Having Andrew between her legs now, his tongue stroking her along that spot, was almost too much to bear. She was wetter than she had ever been, and the heat of his mouth, his tongue… Oh God, he entered her with two fingers and moved them in rhythm with his tongue.

She could no longer bear it. She closed her eyes and light exploded behind her lids, her hips bowing up off the bed. She might have yelled, but she was too overcome, and too astonished, to be sure.

He covered her in a flash. His manhood pressed against her and she opened her legs wider to welcome him. When he surged inside in a sudden, smooth thrust, she gasped in surprise. Surprise because there was no pain, only pleasure at finally being filled.

"Look at me, Miranda."

And she did. He moved, his thrusts deep and steady at first. She panted but never broke eye contact. This she knew. She'd experienced this thrusting with her husband far too many times over the years. It had never been like this, however. With Hathaway she had only wanted it to be over quickly. But now she wanted it to go on forever.

Instinctively, she wrapped her legs around his lean hips and arched up to meet each of his thrusts. Her breathing quickened. Staring deep into Andrew's eyes, she almost felt as though she could touch his soul. What she saw there scared her a little. Desire, certainly, but also satisfaction. He knew she had never experienced such pleasure with her husband, and he reveled in the knowledge that he was showing her everything she had missed over the years by choosing Hathaway over him.

She allowed him that satisfaction, for he'd more than earned it. Her entire world centered on Andrew in that moment. All that mattered was him.

She climbed toward that same peak again and could no longer maintain eye contact. She threw her head back and panted each time he drove into her. His pace increased and he pressed his lips against her throat and murmured words she could not understand.

"Now, Miranda," he said, lifting his head again to look down at her.

Unable to resist the command, she came apart in his arms. He continued to move inside her, drawing out the moment of ecstasy until, with a groan, he buried himself deep inside her and joined her with his release.

He collapsed against her and they lay like that for some time. His heavy weight against her comforted her and she wished they could stay like that forever. But even as she tried to draw comfort from his warmth, bone-deep regret began to spread through her. She'd been a fool to let herself be so easily swayed all those years ago. She never should have allowed her parents to convince her to give up Andrew.

CHAPTER 3

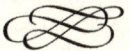

*H*E NEEDED TO MOVE. To get off her, get dressed, and leave. Instead, he rolled onto his side and drew her to him. She snuggled against him, hiding her face in his chest, and he hated how good it felt.

Miranda had gotten what she'd wanted from him. No, she'd gotten more. He could tell she hadn't expected to orgasm. He shouldn't ask the question—he already knew the answer—but he couldn't help himself. "Was it like that with Hathaway?"

A full minute passed and he didn't think she was going to reply.

"No," she said finally. Simply.

Satisfaction filled him, along with a hint of relief that she hadn't volunteered further details. He'd needed to know that at least in this one thing he'd surpassed her expectations. Lord knew, he hadn't been enough for her in the past. He didn't want to think about her in another man's bed, however, so the less she said, the better for his peace of mind.

They stayed like that for some minutes as their breathing slowed and their bodies cooled. Only when he began to harden again did he push her away. Without speaking, he gathered her clothes and tossed them onto the bed. The sight of her, hair disheveled, face flushed, and lips full, partially open… his eyes moved lower. Her slight body remained on display and he was sorely tempted to tie her to the bed and keep her there for a week.

He had to call on his considerable self-discipline to turn his back and begin dressing. He heard her moving behind him, heard the rustle of fabric, but steeled himself not to turn around.

"Andrew?"

God, he had to get out of here. Now.

"What?" His tone was more abrupt than he'd intended.

"I require assistance."

He took a deep breath and, gathering all his reserve, turned to face her. She stood there in her chemise, her drawers and stockings back in place. He could see her nipples, the dark triangle of hair, and those damn red garters through the thin material of her chemise. His head started to pound and it took him a few moments to realize she was holding up her stays.

"Turn around," he said, the words almost strangling in his throat. She did, holding the corset against her front. He stared at her back, wanting nothing more than to strip the flimsy chemise from her body again and throw her back onto the bed. Somehow he kept himself from cursing aloud as he moved behind her and began lacing the strings of her stays.

"You've done this before."

Did he detect a tremor in her voice? No, probably not. She appeared to be collected while he was a mass of desire and emotion.

Anxious to be away from her, he didn't reply. He gave the garment one last sharp tug, finished tying the knot, and went back to his own dressing.

When he was done, more than ready by then to put distance between himself and Miranda Hathaway, he turned around. She'd donned her gown, but it gaped open and she was struggling to do up the buttons herself. This time he didn't hold back his curse, and she looked up, startled.

They stared at each other for several long moments before she turned and waited for his assistance, the very picture of patience. A hint of anger slithered though him. How dare she remain so unaffected while he could barely contain himself? Needing to ruffle her calm demeanor, he moved behind her and placed his hands on her waist. She stood almost unnaturally still.

"What are you doing?"

He smiled with satisfaction when he heard the unmistakable quiver in her voice. That was better.

"Nothing. I was just wondering when you wanted to do this again. One time without precautions only suffices when one doesn't wish to be with child."

His hands moved to the row of buttons and she waited until he had finished before turning to him. Her flush had deepened. Knowing she'd never been one to color with embarrassment, he could only surmise it was from desire and his body stirred.

"What do you suggest? I don't want to be an imposition."

He gave a bark of laughter at that. "Sweet, making love to a beautiful woman is never an imposition."

He froze when he realized he'd used his old endearment for her. If she noticed, though, she gave no indication. When she seemed at a loss as to how to answer, he continued.

"When did you last have your monthly courses? And are they regular?"

She looked away, clearly disconcerted by the question.

"We are both adults here, Miranda. These things are natural, and when one is intimate with another the subject will arise."

She couldn't conceal her surprise. "If you insist. I can tell you that in my experience, the subject was never once raised in my marriage."

He wondered at that. It was clear Miranda's marriage hadn't been a passionate one, but surely there must have been a time when Hathaway wanted his rights as a husband and she'd had to put him off.

"You are evading the question."

She hesitated before replying. "My first day of bleeding was one week ago, the same day my husband died. How is that for a morbid twist of fate? And before you ask, I don't expect it again for at least three and a half weeks."

He didn't show it, but the news sent a surge of anticipation through him. Three weeks, at least. Surely he could slake his lust for Miranda Hathaway in that time and finally consign all thoughts of her and what might have been to the past, once and for all.

"In that case, I suggest we meet daily for the next three

weeks." She balked, but he spoke over her protests. "You don't have the luxury of trying for months on end. If you want others to believe the baby you carry belongs to your husband, you need to do everything within your power to conceive this month."

She took a shaky breath and licked her lips before replying, and he held back a groan, hoping she wouldn't look down and notice he was already hard again.

"Very well," she said with a small nod.

"Good. My carriage is waiting for me not too far away. I'll arrange to have another carriage come to the house for you. There's an extra key on the fireplace mantel so you can lock up when you leave." He strode to the door, already anticipating what he would do to her the following evening. "Oh, and Miranda," he said, turning when he'd reached the threshold, "fancy dresses really aren't needed. I won't care what you're wearing since your clothing will be removed as soon as you arrive."

CHAPTER 4

*M*IRANDA TOOK ANDREW at his word and wore something simple the next night. She chose a sky-blue day gown to wear under her dark cloak, not having it in her to wear mourning colors. Despite the fact that she hadn't been in love with Robert and the fact that theirs had not been a passionate marriage, she'd still cared for him. And he'd always been good to her.

She tried not to think about how disappointed he'd be with her if he could see what she was doing. Her actions were the height of selfishness, but she knew that without the excuse of asking Andrew to help her sire an heir, she would never have had the courage to approach him for a traditional affair. Worse, she feared he would have laughed in her face. He'd been shocked by her proposal, but she'd counted on him wanting revenge against her husband. She'd hurt Andrew and it was human nature to want to lash back at the person who'd caused that hurt. Some might say she was being naïve, but she trusted that he wouldn't hurt her, but he could strike back at the memory of her husband.

The fact that he'd shown her passion beyond her wildest imaginings was something she hadn't expected. After twelve years of marriage, and the increasingly frantic and frustrated couplings she'd been subjected to by Robert when she failed to fall pregnant month after month, who would have thought she'd be so ignorant about the business of lovemaking?

After arriving home the night before, she'd taken out the slim volume of erotic art she'd found in her husband's bedroom after his death. She hadn't been able to make herself look through it before, but did so then with the hope of learning how to give Andrew the same pleasure he had shown her. She knew he'd been satisfied, she'd felt him finish, but she hated the idea that he might soon become bored with her. It was clear he didn't lack for female companionship, and for the short time they would be together she didn't want him sliding into boredom brought on by her obvious lack of carnal knowledge.

Filled with anticipation for the evening to come, she unlocked the front door and entered the house. Just as it had been the night before, the first floor was in darkness save for the light of the two lamps. She climbed the stairs, the bedroom on the second floor her destination. This time, Andrew was waiting for her in the room. On the bed. He'd already removed his boots and coat, and his relaxed posture made her ache to join him.

At her entrance he looked up from the book he'd been reading, a sensual smile forming on his wicked lips. He closed the book and placed it on the nightstand.

"I've always appreciated the fact that you're never late," he said, leaning back against the headboard. He folded his arms across his chest and watched her.

Feeling self-conscious, she removed her cloak and draped it over a chair. When she turned back to face him, he remained motionless, watching her intently. The way he seemed to devour her with his eyes should have embarrassed her. Before last night, it would have. Now, however, the heat in his eyes only served to heighten her desire.

Since he showed no sign of moving, she raised her hand to undo the dress's hook at the nape of her neck. The movement caused her breasts to thrust forward, and the appreciation in Andrew's eyes spurred her to continue.

She'd made sure to choose a dress that would be easy for her to remove on her own. She lowered her arms and bent them behind her back to undo the second hook in the middle of her back and the one at her waist. That was all it took to loosen the bodice. With a simple movement of her shoulders, it slid down her arms. Andrew lifted a brow in surprise when he realized she wasn't wearing a chemise.

She stepped out of the dress and bent to retrieve it, and her breasts threatened to spill out from the short corset she'd worn. She knew Andrew waited to see if they'd succeed, and when she straightened he let out a sound of disappointment. She placed her dress over her cloak on the chair and stepped out of her shoes before turning back to stand before him in her short corset, stockings, and drawers. This bravado was new to her and her resolve not to show how nervous she felt slipped a notch when Andrew didn't move, his eyes half-lidded with desire, waiting to see what she was going to do next.

When the silence stretched on, she realized he was making a statement. He'd been willing to take the upper hand yesterday, but now he was letting her know if she wanted to make love, she was going to have to take the initiative. Fine. If that was how he wanted the evening to proceed, she was up for the challenge. She straightened her shoulders and approached the bed. Climbing onto it, she kneeled sideways beside him.

His nostrils flared, and from the rigidness of his posture she could tell his restraint was costing him dearly. She held back a smile of satisfaction. His eyes remained fixed on her breasts when she leaned forward to unbutton his waistcoat. He shifted toward her when she reached the last button so she could draw the garment off his shoulders and down his arms. She started to rise from the bed, to bring the garment to the chair, when he clamped a hand around her wrist to stop her.

She froze. Their eyes caught and held, and the very air thickened around them. He released her arm but held her in place, instead, by gripping her waist. His warm hands burned into the bare skin between her corset and drawers, where he stroked her in maddeningly slow circles. Reminding herself to breathe, she laid the waistcoat on the bed beside them and raised her hands to untie the knot in his cravat. She unwound it and tossed the rumpled piece of fabric next to the waistcoat.

She couldn't resist touching the skin that showed above the open neck of his shirt. His flesh was hot, and a few hairs peeked out from beneath the bottom of the opening. His pulse beat an erratic rhythm under her caress.

"You're killing me," he said, his voice tense.

This time she didn't hide her smile. In a swift movement, she tugged his shirt from the waist of his trousers and, with his help, lifted it over his head. She placed her hands over his chest and elicited a sharp intake of breath from him when she ran her hands over its broad expanse. Gathering the rest of her nerve, she lowered her hands and traced the muscles of his abdomen before following the line of hair down to where it disappeared into his trousers. She'd never performed such an intimate act for her husband, so her hands weren't steady when she reached for the fall of his trousers and undid the buttons. She could feel his erection straining against the barrier and a shiver of anticipation raced through her.

Tension fairly vibrated from Andrew and she knew he warred between allowing her to continue and taking control. When she pulled the fall aside and reached in to stroke the hard length of his arousal through his smallclothes, he lost the battle. Before she realized what was happening, he'd reversed their positions and pushed her down onto the bed amid the pile of his clothing.

"Your clothes…"

"I could not possibly care less about whether my waistcoat will be wrinkled," he said through gritted teeth. To underscore his words, he shifted her aside to grab the offending articles of clothing and tossed them onto the floor.

Miranda remembered how much Hathaway had hated to be seen less than impeccably dressed. The fact that Andrew did not share the same concern—that he seemed only to care about being with her—sent another thrill of excitement through her.

He quickly stood to remove his last remaining garments and joined her, again, on the bed. This time, however, he straddled her. In this position she couldn't ignore his erection, which jutted out proudly from its thatch of dark hair. Venturing into territory about which she knew nothing, but anxious to learn more, she reached out to touch him.

"Like this," he said, taking her hand and wrapping it around his erection and showing her how to slide her hand up and down. She marveled at the softness of his skin that covered his hard length.

Remembering one of the drawings she had seen in her husband's book, she gave his shaft one final squeeze before releasing him.

"I would like to try something," she said, her voice husky with arousal. "If you would…"

She placed her hands on his thighs and pushed. She wouldn't have been able to move him if curiosity hadn't gotten the better of him. He hesitated only a moment before moving off her. He kneeled at her side as she rose to a sitting position.

"On your back."

He raised a brow at her command but complied. He lay, sprawled on the bed, every masculine inch of him on display. She drank in the sight. The perfection of his body almost overwhelmed her and she couldn't help but wonder how many other women had seen him this way over the years. For that matter, she didn't even know if he currently had a mistress.

The jealousy that swept over her was overwhelming and decidedly unwelcome. Andrew wasn't married and he'd never said she would be his only lover. She hated the idea that he might be sharing these same intimacies with another woman but tried to push aside the images that rose in her mind at the thought. She needed to concentrate on the present and the moments she could steal with Andrew Osborne.

Remembering the way he had touched her the night before and the heightened pleasure it had aroused, she leaned over him and explored his body with her hands and mouth. When she flicked her tongue over his nipple, he jerked.

"If you're going somewhere with this, you'd better hurry. I won't be able to restrain myself much longer." His voice was rough and she knew it was testing the very limits of his self-control to hold back. Even at the young age of nineteen, he'd been a man of action—rarely content to sit and wait, and certainly not one to let others take the lead.

She ran a trail of hot, openmouthed kisses down his abdomen. When she reached his manhood, every muscle in his body was taut.

"Miranda…" His voice held a hint of warning.

Not sure what she was doing, relying only on that drawing she had seen, she wrapped her right hand around the base of his erection and took him into her mouth. He almost jumped off the bed and the groan that escaped him filled the room.

Remembering how he'd wanted her to stroke him with her hand, she began to move her mouth up and down on him. He tangled his hands in her hair, helping her with the rhythm. She'd imagined this act would be distasteful and had wanted only to show him the same pleasure he had shown her the night before when he had used his mouth on her intimately. But having him fill her mouth now, the taste and smell of him overwhelming her senses, excited her and she felt a rush of wetness between her thighs. His obvious enthusiasm for her ministrations let her know that he, too, enjoyed what she was doing. She was surprised, therefore, when his hands tightened around her head and he pulled her away from him.

Worried she'd done something wrong, she stared at him for a moment before saying, "I thought you were enjoying it."

"I was—too much—but you won't conceive a child if I spill inside your mouth."

Flustered, she looked away. For those few short moments, she'd actually forgotten they weren't really lovers. She'd had to lie to him so they could have this brief liaison. She might have gotten carried away, but it was clear he hadn't.

She remained kneeling beside him while he rose onto his elbows.

"Take off your drawers," he said.

She'd been so engrossed in what she was doing she'd forgotten she still wore her undergarments, and it was clear Andrew liked to make love without any barriers between them.

She moved to the side of the bed and removed her drawers. She still had on her corset and stockings, but when she started to remove her garters, he told her to stop. Confused, she glanced at him over her shoulder.

"Leave them on and come here."

She hesitated. Somehow, wearing only stockings and a corset, bare in between and the latter pushing her breasts up so they almost spilled over the top, made her feel more exposed than she had yesterday when he'd stripped her of all her clothing.

"Come over here," he repeated.

Doing her best not to show her unease, she moved back onto the bed and sat beside him. It was more than a little ridiculous, given everything that had already happened between them, but she covered her mons with her hands. She expected him to laugh at her belated modesty, but instead his expression was tense.

"On my lap," he said, sitting now.

Evidently she was no longer the one in control of this encounter, so she did what he asked. Taking a deep breath, she moved to sit sideways on his lap, very conscious of his jutting arousal. He placed his hands on her hips, surprising her, and moved her so she was on her knees. He brought her down over him, spreading her legs so she was straddling his thighs, his arousal between them.

He kissed her then, for the first time since she'd entered the room. Unlike the kisses they'd shared the evening before, this kiss was softer, like the start of the first one they'd shared just two days before in her town house when he'd come at her invitation. He spread featherlight kisses on her cheeks, the lids of her closed eyes, even her nose. When he reached her mouth again, he kept the kiss light, brushing his lips over hers. Frustrated, she tried to deepen the kiss, but he held her at bay. When he dragged her lower lip between his teeth, she heaved a sigh of frustration and ground herself against his hard erection, now trapped between them.

That spurred him on because he stopped teasing and opened his mouth to allow her entrance. Almost desperate for another taste of him at that point, she took the lead, exploring his mouth as she had his body. He tangled his tongue with hers and the nature of the kiss deepened. Darkened. They were both panting for breath now.

His hands tightened on her backside, urging her on as she writhed against his erection.

He drew back slightly and spoke against her mouth, the

49

words coming out between harsh breaths as she continued to rub herself against him. "Now, Miranda. Take me inside you."

His desperation inflamed her further and she knew what he wanted her to do. She'd also seen an illustration of this in Hathaway's book. She rose up on her knees until the blunt tip of his manhood was pressed against her entrance, where she was almost impossibly wet. Using one hand to hold him in place, she impaled herself on his hard length.

Her breath huffed out on a long moan when he was finally where she needed him most, deep inside her. In this position, he was deeper than before. She swayed against him and lowered her head onto his shoulder, enjoying the way he filled her.

"You're still killing me," he said in a hoarse voice, his hands flexing on her hips.

He lifted her until just the tip of him was inside her, then dragged her back down. She released her breath on a shaky sigh but followed his lead and started to move up and down over him.

When she had found her rhythm, Andrew turned his attention elsewhere. It took little effort for him to scoop her breasts out from the top of her corset, and she arched into his hot hands while continuing to move over his hard length.

He fondled her, squeezing her breasts as he knew she liked and flicking his thumbs over their stiff points before covering one with his mouth and suckling hard. Shafts of liquid heat shot straight through her to where they were joined.

Her movements became quicker, less elegant, as her heart raced and her breaths came out in pants. He reached between them to touch her right where she needed him, and she exploded around him, his name mixed with another moan.

She sagged against him, spent. He simply held her while her heartbeat slowed. It took her a full minute to realize he was still hard. She lifted her head to look at him.

"You didn't finish."

His green eyes were dark with unfulfilled desire.

"No, but I will."

He lifted her again and slammed her down against him. She was too wrung out to help him, and when he realized that he flipped them over so she was now beneath him, his hard-ness never leaving her. His face showed signs of strain.

"I can't wait, Miranda."

She lifted a hand and cupped his cheek. "Don't."

He closed his eyes for a moment and moved his face deeper into the caress. But he indulged himself only for a moment before starting to move again. Each thrust was hard, desperate, and before long a similar desperation rose within her. Again. She clung to his shoulders and wrapped her legs around him, meeting each slam of his body against hers.

He didn't last long before arching his back and burying himself deeply one last time. With a guttural sound, he exploded. The rush of his hot seed inside her triggered another orgasm, and she had to bury her mouth against his neck to keep from screaming.

CHAPTER 5

MIRANDA HAD BEEN EXPECTING James Hathaway for days now, ever since her meeting with the solicitor earlier in the week. She'd been the one to initiate that meeting, but the fact that her husband's nephew was now at the town house caused a wave of sadness, almost suffocating in its intensity, to sweep through her. She'd known this day would come but was still unprepared for the final sign that this phase of her life was over. She wouldn't miss the town house and its ever-present reminder of her marriage, however. What she'd miss most was Andrew.

While she would love nothing more than to remain in town and see if they could have more together, she wasn't foolish enough to believe he wanted the same thing. Andrew hadn't said or done anything in the almost three weeks they'd been together to lead her to believe he would have any difficulty moving on after their affair was over. And she had no doubt

SUZANNA MEDEIROS

there were many other women who would willingly step into her place once she was gone.

She gave her head a small shake, as if doing so could somehow dispel her melancholy thoughts. Nothing would come from delaying the inevitable, so she took a deep breath, collected the cloak of reserve around her that she'd managed to perfect over the years, and made her way to the drawing room.

In the twelve years of her marriage, she had never met her husband's heir. Taking in his appearance as she entered the room and he rose, she could see immediately why Robert had been so distraught at the knowledge that this man would be the next viscount. The long row of portraits of the numerous viscounts that was prominently displayed at the Hathaway estate depicted men who were similar in appearance to her husband—fair-haired and fine-boned. James Hathaway, however, did not fit into that mold.

What struck her first was his size. The man standing before her now could never be confused with the other men who had held the Hathaway title. He stood well over six feet in height and his build... Andrew was muscular, but this man was even broader. In fact, he had the appearance more of a brawler than a peer of the realm. The slight curve in his nose, indicating it had been broken at least once, underscored that perception. And his hair, slightly longer than was fashionable, was black as night.

Miranda couldn't miss the wariness in his expression as he rose. Given that he had never been made to feel welcome by his uncle, she could well understand his reticence.

After a rather awkward greeting, she offered to ring for tea,

54

but he refused. She took a seat on the settee and watched while her nephew lowered himself onto the chair opposite her. As they often did when she was in the drawing room, her thoughts went immediately to Andrew and the first kiss they had shared on that very settee, and she had to force herself to concentrate on the present.

"I am so glad you accepted my invitation," she said, meaning it. She'd always hated the distance that her husband had placed between them and his younger brother's family.

She could almost see the tension easing from the man's body when he realized she wouldn't be treating him with the same disdain her husband has shown him.

"I must admit I was more than a little surprised to receive the letter from your solicitor. After a lifetime of assurances that I would never inherit the title, I find it impossible to believe I am sitting here with you."

He was referring, of course, to her inability to conceive an heir and the fact she was not carrying a child now.

Hoping to reassure him that she bore him no ill will, she gave a small shrug. "Sometimes these things answer to a higher authority."

Her reply seemed to surprise him. He leaned back and examined her closely for several moments before saying, "May I be candid with you?"

"By all means," Miranda said. "Despite what Robert may have chosen to believe, we are family."

A brief flicker of emotion crossed his face at the mention of his uncle, but when he spoke, Miranda was relieved that he clearly didn't wish to address the acrimony between the two families.

"You are not at all what I expected."

She tilted her head to one side, amused at his obvious confusion. "You thought I would be throwing a fit right now? Or that I would be pleading with you for a larger settlement?"

"Frankly, yes. I've seen the terms of the will and your marriage contract. My uncle was less than generous in the eventuality that you did not give birth to the next viscount."

She shrugged. "One cannot predict these things. My parents were very happy with the marriage settlement, and one always assumes that in time children will come."

He hesitated before saying, "It's no secret that the Hath-away estate is a very prosperous one. You should know that I intend to increase the amount of your allowance."

"No!" Guilt had caused her to speak more loudly than she'd intended, and from the expression on James's face she could see he was taken aback by the vehemence of her response. But she could not entertain the idea of seeking a larger income from the Hathaway estate, not after the way her actions were dishonoring her husband's memory even now.

"I would argue that after twelve years of marriage, it is no less than your due."

"Perhaps," she said, careful to keep further emotion from her voice. "But I am content to live modestly. I have learned over the years that having money does not always mean one will be happy."

The pity on James Hathaway's face told her that she had said too much, and another wave of guilt at tarnishing Robert's memory swept through her. She knew better than to argue that her marriage had not been as bad as he might be thinking. There was no love lost between James and his uncle and he was unlikely to want to hear her defense of him.

"So it is all settled," she continued. "I only ask that you grant me a few days to make preparations to retire to the country."

She knew he would assume that she would move to the dowager house on the Hathaway estate, but chose not to correct that assumption since it served her own plans.

"I want you to know it is not my intention to force you from town. I realize that you cannot socialize until you are out of mourning, but you are welcome to remain here. Or if you'd like, I can help you find a new house."

Miranda realized she liked James Hathaway and was glad she had finally gotten a chance to meet him, but there was no way she could remain in London after her affair with Andrew ended.

She stood and he rose to his feet as well.

"I thank you for your generosity, but I would prefer the quiet of the countryside right now. I am not removing from town because of you."

He gave her a small nod of acknowledgment. "Very well. I will leave my address with your butler. And if there is anything you need, please know I am at your service."

She remained standing as he left, but her legs gave out as soon as she heard the front door close. Pain lanced through her as she realized it was almost over. Within days she would leave the Hathaway town house and London, and she would never see Andrew again.

CHAPTER 6

$\mathcal{H}$E WAS LATE, caught up in a particularly heated debate in the House of Lords. As the hours ticked by into the evening, he grew increasingly more bad-tempered. At several points it occurred to him that he should arrange to have his driver deliver a note to Miranda before she left for the house he'd rented, but he couldn't bring himself to cancel the evening. Not while there remained a glimmer of a chance one side might cool down enough for the matter to be resolved.

When it became clear that wouldn't happen, he could have arranged to have a note delivered to her at the house, but still he held off and that annoyed him more than anything else. He needed to see Miranda. Craved her with a desperation that alarmed him, and with that realization his mood darkened even further.

As the hours passed, curious glances were cast his way as those around him began to sense his dangerous mood. No one approached him until Viscount Morrison was foolish enough to intercept him when the session had finally ended for the night.

"I don't suppose we'll see you at Brooks tonight," the man said with a knowing smirk.

Andrew barely resisted the urge to wipe the smile from the man's face and started to turn away, but Morrison's next words halted him in his tracks.

"There have been a few wagers placed as to the identity of the woman who has captured your interest to the exclusion of all else. I'll admit to more than a small curiosity myself. I don't suppose you'd care to enlighten me?"

The look he aimed at the slight man would have been enough to keep another from continuing. Morrision, however, had never been known to possess much good sense.

"She must be very good. Perhaps I can give her a go."

Peripherally he became aware that their conversation was drawing the attention of others, but Andrew's attention remained focused on the man before him. Every muscle in his body had tensed at Morrison's last statement, but somehow he managed to keep from planting his fist into Morrison's thin face.

"I don't share." Andrew's words were clipped, his anger barely contained at that point, but the fool continued.

"Oh no, neither do I. I meant when you tire of her, of course."

Morrison paled when Andrew took a step closer and allowed his hands to curl into fists at his side. One more word along the same vein would have been enough to destroy the little control still within his grasp.

Morrison opened his mouth but must have thought better of it, because he closed it again right away. With a quick nod, he turned and fled. Andrew's gaze swung to the group of men that had stood by, watching the scene as it took place. They, too, wisely chose to turn away and pretend nothing had happened.

Without another word to anyone else, Andrew made his way from Westminster and headed straight for the house. It was already nine and he expected Miranda had long since returned home, no doubt thinking he had tired of her and was seeking other pursuits for the night. His pride had balked at the notion of showing any weakness, but now he regretted he hadn't sent her a note telling her he would be late and asking her to wait for him. He didn't want to analyze the part of him that feared she would have received the note and decided to go home anyway.

He didn't realize his heart was racing until he found her in the bedroom. She had fallen asleep waiting for him, and as he took in her slender figure lying beneath the covers, it hit him like a fist to the gut that he still loved her. And they had only three more days until her monthly courses were due. After that, whether or not they had been successful, their affair would be over. It should have been over already, but neither of them had wanted to say the words that would end it, so they waited for nature to end it for them.

His need for her was a bone-deep ache. Refusing to acknowledge the unwelcome emotions going through him, he undressed and slid into bed bedside her. She woke when he drew her into his arms and the sleepy smile on her face made his heart turn over. Damn. It appeared he wasn't going to

remain unscathed when his relationship with Miranda ended
—again.

∼

HE'D BEEN INSATIABLE, making love to her several times. The
last time he'd been particularly forceful, and she sighed,
remembering the things he had done. Her body ached, but she
relished the sensation. Relished lying beside him now as he
slept.

Andrew had always taken great pains to make sure she
knew his interest in her was merely physical, so he must have
been exhausted to allow himself to fall asleep. And she,
desperate to know whatever modicum of closeness he chose to
share, even if it was only physical, was content to accept their
alliance for what it was. Now, watching him as he slept, she felt
she'd been given a gift she'd never expected to receive.

His features were softer, making him look younger than his
one and thirty years. In some ways, watching him sleep was
more intimate than making love to him and her heart yearned
for the closeness they had once shared.

She cursed herself for being a fool twice over. First for
having denied her feelings for him all those years ago and
allowing her parents to sway her into accepting Hathaway's
marriage proposal. But her second, and greater, mistake was
the foolishness of her scheme to find a way to be close to
him now.

She'd known almost from the start that their physical relationship was full of risks not just to her reputation, but also to
her peace of mind. She'd never stopped loving Andrew, but at

that moment she couldn't hold back her regret as bitterness threatened to engulf her. A large part of her wished she had never started out to learn what it was like to make love to Andrew Osborne. Now, along with the memories she'd hoped to cling to during the coming years, she'd also have to live with the knowledge of what she could have had if she'd stood firm against her parents' wishes. If she had, he would have asked her to marry him and they would still be together. She'd always known that to be true, but the full import of what she had lost had never been more clear to her.

Panic, remorse, regret... all swam within her and threatened to consume her. Stifling a sob, she rose from the bed and dressed with shaking hands. She allowed herself one more quick glance at the bed.

"Good-bye, Andrew," she whispered before turning and escaping from the stifling confines of that unassuming house. She'd made her plans well and had no need to return to the Hathaway town house. She would simply disappear.

CHAPTER 7

*W*HEN ANDREW WOKE the next morning and found himself alone in bed, disgust swept through him. Disgust that he had let down his guard and allowed himself to enjoy the comfort of holding Miranda as he fell asleep, for enjoy it he had. He'd clung to her the night before like a drowning man clinging to a lifeline.

Hoping to fix the damage he'd caused by spending the night, he dressed and went in search of Miranda so he could take his leave. He expected to find her in another room, perhaps the kitchen, but the annoyance he felt at his unwelcome sentimentality the night before changed to disbelief when he realized she wasn't in the house. She hadn't even left a note. A dark sense of foreboding settled over him like a shroud as he made his way from the house.

Not caring who took note of his visit, he called on her later that afternoon. The very last thing he'd expected to learn was that Hathaway's heir had taken up residence.

Andrew was shown to the library and was taken aback by the tall, dark-haired man who joined him a few minutes later. The new Viscount Hathaway bore no resemblance whatsoever to the old one.

After making their introductions, they settled into armchairs across from one another.

Hathaway spoke first. "To what do I owe this honor?"

Andrew was careful to keep his expression neutral. "I heard you were in town and wanted to pay my respects regarding your uncle's passing."

Hathaway leaned back in his chair and gave a short, disbelieving shake of his head. "It will never cease to amaze me how quickly gossip spreads in a place as large as London. I only took up residence this morning." He frowned before continuing. "But why, then, did you ask for my aunt?"

Andrew wondered if Hathaway had learned of his previous visit and decided it would be best to acknowledge that meeting in case he had.

"I've already expressed my condolences to Lady Hathaway, but I wanted to see how she was faring. Hers was, after all, the greater loss."

Hathaway was silent for a moment, as though considering his next words carefully. "I wasn't aware that you and my uncle were friends."

Andrew shrugged. "We weren't. We saw each other often in the Chamber, but usually from opposing sides of far too many bills."

"Ah, so that's why you're here. You want to sound me out on my political leanings."

Andrew grasped at the excuse. "You can hardly blame me

for wondering. We had a horrible evening yesterday, and it never hurts to have an additional vote on your side."

Hathaway seemed to accept the excuse. "To be honest, I haven't given it much thought. I do have my personal leanings, of course, but…" He shrugged. "Uncle hated the fact I was his heir, and the few times we saw one another, we never discussed politics. In fact, the few discussions we had centered on how he was going to make sure I didn't inherit. Perhaps if he'd chosen another bride he would have succeeded, but he chose one who couldn't give him what he wanted most."

Considering what Miranda had told him about how her husband had stopped visiting her bed early in their marriage, he found the younger Hathaway's assertions difficult to believe.

"When does the title go to you? I know it's customary to wait to make sure the widow isn't with child."

"She isn't," he said with a wave of his hand. "Lady Hathaway told the family solicitor that my uncle wasn't up to the task for several months, if you catch my meaning."

Andrew's head began to swim with the realization that Miranda hadn't told him the truth. She'd told him her husband hadn't bedded her in years. And was she really barren, or did the fault lie with the elder Hathaway? He knew sometimes it was the man who was at fault and not the woman. Was she so desperate to hold on to her current wealth that she didn't care if everyone knew that any child she might be carrying wasn't fathered by her husband?

He didn't know what to think anymore. He did, however, know that he had to see Miranda and ask her himself, but he couldn't insist on seeing her right now.

"Yes, well, I'm sorry to have met you under such circumstances." He said the words despite the fact that it was clear James Hathaway was far from mourning. He stood before continuing. "If you would let your aunt know I called and asked after her well-being, I would be grateful." He turned and started to leave, letting Hathaway know that the call was over.

Hathaway followed him to the door. "She's no longer here."

Andrew stopped and turned to face him, anger rising swift and hot. He didn't bother to conceal it. "Tell me you didn't cast her out. That she has somewhere to go."

Hathaway's jaw tightened. When he replied, his words were clipped. "She chose to leave. Her maid, whom she didn't take with her, informed me that she'd had her personal belongings moved out, one trunk at a time, over the past week. I was surprised to learn she'd left behind all her jewelry—even the pieces my uncle had purchased for her."

Dread settled deep in his belly. Andrew needed to speak to Hathaway's servants, to find out what exactly had happened, but he couldn't make such a request without revealing his more-than-casual interest in the new Viscount's aunt.

"I suppose she wanted the comfort of her home on the estate until she can make other arrangements for herself."

"She's a damned strange woman, if you must know, Sanderson. She left a note saying she wasn't returning to the estate or to her parents' home. I've questioned the servants and no one knows where she's gone." He ran his hand through his hair. "What a disaster. Everyone will say I had her cast out into the streets without a penny to her name."

The blood had frozen in Andrew's veins. Miranda had left

and no one knew where she was. He wanted to curse, to rail against her foolishness, but somehow he managed to hold himself together and keep from revealing himself.

"It is clear from your worry that is not the case. No doubt she was too deeply affected by her husband's death to think clearly. I'm sure she just needed some time alone and will send word shortly."

"I hope so," Hathaway said.

Andrew made his way from the house. His thoughts kept coming back to one seemingly unalterable fact—Miranda had lied to him. Her husband had never given up trying to beget an heir. He tried not to think about what it must have been like for her to suffer his attentions over the last twelve years. She'd been surprised that first time he'd brought her to fulfillment and he knew she'd never before reached that peak.

He suspected now that she'd never intended to pass off a child of his as the heir to the Hathaway title and fortunes since it appeared everyone involved already knew it wasn't possible that she was with child. And she certainly wouldn't have disappeared if she'd hoped to blatantly pass off a bastard as the heir.

It had all been a lie.

CHAPTER 8

*I*T TOOK ANDREW almost one month to find Miranda after she disappeared that last night they were together, much longer than he'd expected. He'd hired Bow Street's finest to investigate, but she had covered her tracks well. Finally, when he started to fear they might never find her, one of the agents learned she'd traveled to a small village in Yorkshire where she was renting a small cottage.

The man who'd discovered her whereabouts assured Andrew that when he'd seen her in the village she'd looked well. That should have been the end of it. When he'd hired the Runners, he'd reasoned that he only wanted to make sure no harm had befallen her, but deep down he'd known he was only lying to himself. Their three weeks together should have been more than long enough to get her out of his system, but somehow she'd managed to burrow deeper under his skin. Damn him for a fool, but he was still in love with Miranda Hathaway.

Now that he knew where she was hiding, he had to see her again. Aside from his unwelcome feelings for her, there were too many questions to which he needed answers.

It took him two more days to reach her. When he finally arrived at the village where she'd last been seen, it was almost evening, and he stopped at the posting inn to leave his horse and ask for directions. He was hot and dirty, and politeness dictated that he rent a room and bathe first before calling on Miranda. He was too close, though. A small, irrational part of him feared that if he delayed further, she might slip away yet again and he would lose his opportunity to see her.

By the time he reached the small cottage twenty minutes later, the sun had almost set. As he stood before the modest home, he couldn't deny the irony that it was, in appearance, very similar to the house he'd rented so he and Miranda could meet in private.

He rapped on the door and didn't have to wait long before a stout woman he assumed to be the housekeeper answered.

"I am here to see Lady Hathaway."

The woman was clearly surprised that a gentleman, alone, would be paying a call on her mistress, but she didn't comment as she showed him into a small sitting room. Miranda sat by the fire, working on a small square of needlepoint, and he took a moment to drink in the sight of her. He enjoyed the way the golden light of the fire gilded her skin and reflected the chestnut highlights in her dark brown hair.

"Who was it, Mrs. Evers?" She looked up then and paled when she saw him standing in the doorway. "I see. Thank you, Mrs. Evers," she said in what was clearly meant as a dismissal.

Andrew didn't miss the way the older woman glanced

between the two of them, a speculative gleam in her eye, before inclining her head and turning to leave.

Miranda placed her needlework on a small table and stood. She smoothed her hands over her black skirts in a nervous gesture, and he was alarmed to see she'd grown even thinner over the last few weeks. Seeing the wariness in her expression, he held back the almost overwhelming need to start demanding answers.

"Good evening, Miranda."

She licked her lips before replying, and his groin tightened in response.

"Andrew," she said, allowing him the briefest of curtseys. "I'm surprised to see you here."

"I can imagine," he said, unable to keep the note of bitterness from his voice.

She sat again. "Are you hungry? It is late, but I can ring for tea and refreshments."

He lowered himself into the chair opposite her. "I see we're back to social conventions."

She looked away without replying.

"I thought," he continued, "that after everything we'd shared, we could have parted on better terms. A farewell, perhaps, or a small wave as you ran away from me again."

She raised her shoulders in a small shrug, but he could tell from how stiffly she held herself that the casual movement was far from indicative of how she truly felt. His presence here had rattled her.

"I didn't see the point," she said, meeting his gaze. "You were tired and needed to sleep. And when I returned home I discovered my courses had arrived. Since I'd failed to conceive a child, I saw no point in remaining."

"Tell me, Miranda. When did James Hathaway move into the house?"

Her lips tightened before she said, "If you're implying that there was anything untoward between us—"

He cut her off with a wave of his hand. "Don't be ridiculous. Even if he was tempted, Hathaway's heir would hardly be foolish enough to do anything to risk the line of succession at this point. He certainly wouldn't want you to fall pregnant."

Her breath blew out in an offended hiss and he didn't know what he'd said wrong.

"Meaning it was James's ambition that kept him from accepting my wanton advances?"

"No, of course not. You are hardly that type of woman."

She was silent for a moment before replying. "I was with you."

How well he remembered. "I find it most curious your husband didn't try harder to produce an heir."

It took her a moment to adjust to the abrupt change in subject. "I think he took comfort in the knowledge that James was such a capable young man."

She held herself almost unnaturally still when she replied, just as she had when he'd first seen her again in her drawing room almost two months before. He'd been watching her closely and it didn't escape his notice that she couldn't meet his eyes when she spoke the lie. How had he not noticed that telltale giveaway during his first visit when she'd laid out her ridiculous proposal? He'd been so astonished by her suggestion that he hadn't been paying attention to the signs that revealed what was now obvious to him—Miranda was lying.

"That may be true, but a man still wants to have his own son inherit. Nephews and such are never a first choice."

She met his eyes then and he couldn't tell at first what he was seeing in her expression. Defeat? His conscience pricked at him. He'd have preferred her anger. But damn it, he wasn't the one who'd lied.

"It is late and I am tired. I don't have the energy to play these games with you."

He suspected she'd lied, as well, about having received her monthly courses that last night they were together, but he didn't think she was with child. Not after all those years of trying if Hathaway's nephew was to be believed. Despite that knowledge, his eyes moved down to her midsection. She noticed and stiffened.

"What is it you want to hear, Andrew?"

"The truth would be a pleasant change."

She glanced away and considered her response for several seconds before finally saying, "I was wrong to leave without a word to you. I felt awkward after everything we'd done together. I knew we'd failed, and I was a little ashamed at my attempt at deception."

"Liar."

The accusation was softly spoken, but echoed in the room.

"Excuse me?" she managed when she overcame her surprise.

"I'm tired of your lies, Miranda. Tell me, truthfully, why did you leave?"

"I told you everything. I'm sorry if it's not what you want to hear—"

"Do you want to know what I think?" The room was small, their chairs placed close together, and when he leaned forward Miranda had to lean back to maintain the distance between them.

"No" she said, but the words, again, were obviously a lie.

"I think you ran away because you were overwhelmed. I think you knew from the beginning that you couldn't have children, but you latched on to this mad scheme as an excuse to lure me into your bed."

She laughed, the sound brittle. "You have a very high opinion of yourself."

But he'd seen her shock before she'd attempted to conceal it behind false levity.

"I know it's the truth."

"It's clear to me that you wouldn't recognize the truth if it walked right up to you and introduced itself."

"Enough, Miranda." His voice was louder than he'd intended and a stab of guilt went through him when he saw her flinch. He continued in a softer tone. "I spoke to James Hathaway. According to him, his uncle was quite desperate up until the end to ensure he never inherited. A man in that situation would never leave his wife alone year after year. No, a man who wanted to secure his succession would keep trying. I know you lied about that."

She couldn't meet his eyes and silence stretched between them for what seemed an eternity before she finally looked at him.

"You are correct. My husband wasn't at all happy when I

failed to fall pregnant each month." She must have seen the anger that surged through him at her admission, because she hastened to add, "He didn't treat me badly, but he was very disappointed in me."

He didn't want to hear the details. Twelve years, and in all that time she'd never known pleasure in the bedroom until she started her affair with him.

"Would you care to know what else I believe to be true?"

She lifted her shoulders in a shrug that was meant to seem indifferent. He could tell she'd guessed he knew everything, but she wasn't about to betray herself.

"I think you still care for me. Why else would you go to such lengths and concoct such a lie to be with me?" He was bluffing, but a man could hope, and hope was all he had to go on at the moment. "But what I don't know is why you ran away."

She laughed at that, a small, self-deprecating sound. "I propositioned you one week after my husband's death and betrayed his memory in the worst possible manner. Do you honestly believe I could go on pretending to be the respectable Dowager Viscountess?"

Now it was his turn to tread carefully. Miranda was as tense as a doe he'd once stumbled upon in a field, and he didn't want to frighten her away by being too aggressive.

"I never would have called at your town house if you hadn't left without a word. Never would have had a reason to question James Hathaway and learn that you'd lied."

She shook her head. "I couldn't."

He reached out and took her right hand in his. She tried to draw it back, but he wouldn't let go.

"Why not?"

He didn't think she was going to reply, but when she did she met his gaze straight on.

"Because you are right. I still care for you, but I know you no longer feel that way about me."

"Miranda—"

"Yes, you agreed to bed me, but I know I was no different to you than the other women you've been with."

"Do you really believe that?"

She swallowed visibly and nodded. "I don't blame you. I know I hurt you when I accepted Hathaway's suit. I could try to lay the blame on my parents, tell you they were relentless in pressing me to agree. Which is true, but it doesn't change the fact that I was weak. Too worried about disappointing them. So, instead, I disappointed you. I have no excuses, nor do I deserve your forgiveness."

In the face of her misery, he kept his growing good cheer in check. "You're right," he said softly.

She merely nodded again, but her eyes appeared over-bright.

"We seem to have a problem, then," he continued.

"A problem?"

"Yes. In the beginning, I told myself I could do what you asked. Get you with child, then leave, all the while congratulating myself on having bested Hathaway in the end. And I could finally satisfy my curiosity about what it would be like to have you under me, screaming out my name."

She looked away, saying nothing.

"It did not take me long to realize I was wrong. I could

never have left you to raise our child alone, let alone allow you to pass him off as another man's son."

She swallowed. "Yes, well, you needn't worry about any of that now."

"Perhaps not, but what about my discovery that I can't let you go a second time?"

When her eyes met his again, they were wide with disbelief. "What are you saying?"

He clasped her hand between both of his and prepared to bare his soul. "I love you, Miranda. I've always loved you and I know now that will never change. I want you for my own."

"As your mistress?" The words were barely above a whisper.

"No, Miranda, as my wife."

Her choked sob was not the reaction he'd expected. He'd hoped to see joy at his declaration, but instead a tear escaped and trailed down her cheek. She brushed it away with her free hand and he noticed that it shook. His heart squeezed painfully as she tried to pull away again, but he wouldn't release his grip on her hand.

"You deserve to marry someone who can give you children."

"We still don't know that you can't."

"Robert has a daughter," she said, her voice flat. "She was born to a mistress years before he married me, so the fault for my never falling pregnant did not lie with him."

He'd already come to terms with the possibility he would never have children before he'd set out after Miranda. But now he had to make her believe that.

"These last few weeks without you have shown me that I

cannot bear to live without you. I barely survived the first time. Don't ask me to go through that again."

"You'll come to resent me. After all, a man still wants to have his own son inherit. Nephews and such are never a first choice."

Her mimicry of the words he'd used when he was trying to draw the truth from her sent a surge of anger through him.

"I'm not Hathaway, damn it, so don't tar me with the same brush. Do I want you to have my children? I won't lie and say no." This time he allowed her to pull her hand away, but he followed and kneeled before her, grasping her thighs in a vain effort to keep her anchored, because he was suddenly afraid she would disappear from his life again. "Unlike your husband, I love my sisters and their many children. Given a choice between Jane's eldest inheriting and marrying some other woman just to procure an heir…" His grip tightened. "I'd much rather have you."

She closed her eyes and a spasm of pain crossed her face.

He didn't bother to hide his hurt when he continued. "Why is it so easy for you to cast me aside?"

She opened her eyes and looked down at him. "You think this is easy for me? I've barely eaten or slept since I left you. I could think of nothing else but how much I wanted to go back and beg you to allow me some small part of your life. But marriage…" She shook her head. "I can't do that to you. You deserve better."

"What I deserve is the woman I love."

She started to reply but instead burst into sobs. Horrified, he pulled her from her chair until she kneeled on the floor with him and drew her into his arms. He was afraid she'd resist, but instead she clung to him until her tears began to slow.

"I am so ridiculous," she said, the words muffled against his shoulder.

He pulled back so he could see her face. "I refuse to allow you to insult the woman I love."

The smile she gave him was tremulous, but it made his heart lighten.

"What am I going to do with you?"

He raised a brow and gave her an exaggerated leer. "I can think of a thing or two."

She laughed—a genuine sound of joy this time—and he'd never heard anything so wonderful in his life.

"I'm still in mourning and will be for the next ten months."

"I can wait if I know you'll marry me at the end of it."

"Then I suppose we're waiting."

He gave a whoop of joy and sprang to his feet, drawing her up with him so he could swing her around. She gave a small squeak of surprise and wrapped her arms around his neck.

"But I refuse to wait a moment longer before making love to you again."

This time when she smiled her tears were gone, as was her uncertainty.

"Then you should put me down so I can tell Mrs. Evers she can go home now."

His eyes followed her as she left the room to find her housekeeper. It would be hard to wait until he could claim her as his own, but he'd do it. Miranda was worth it.

EPILOGUE

THEY WAITED ONLY eleven more months to announce their engagement—one month after Miranda's period of mourning had officially ended. Miranda returned to town after Andrew found her and they were careful to keep their relationship a secret from everyone until she was out of mourning. Shortly after the announcement was made, they were married in a private ceremony with only their family as witnesses at the chapel on Andrew's estate.

"I'm worried about James," Miranda said.

The wedding breakfast had ended a short time before, and she and Andrew had left their guests to escape to the bedroom.

"Perhaps we can talk about your nephew another time," Andrew said, frowning down at her.

She ignored him and continued. "He's so aloof around Sarah. I don't think he's happy."

Andrew snorted. "Hathaway adores his wife."

He tried to draw her to the bed, but she held her ground.

"How can you say that? The two of them barely looked at one another during breakfast."

"Only a man in love can see the signs in another. He was trying too hard to make it appear as though he was barely aware of her presence. A man does that when he cares too much and doesn't believe his affections are returned."

Miranda frowned. "Is that what you did?"

"Of course. After being tossed aside once by you, I wasn't going to let you know how much you still affected me."

She allowed him to turn her around and begin undoing the row of buttons down the back of her wedding dress while she went over the meal they'd just shared in her mind.

"Why do you think he doesn't want her to know he cares about her?"

"I can't imagine. Perhaps the fact that she can barely bring herself to even look at him?"

Miranda had noticed that as well. "It could be she's shy. I've known a few women who were that quiet, and yes, even with their husbands."

Andrew laughed. "The new Lady Hathaway is not shy."

He'd finished the buttons and was working now on untying her corset.

"How do you know that?"

"Because I've been to a few social events when her parents were trying to marry her off. She could flirt with the best of them."

He drew her dress down her arms and removed her corset and she turned to face him again. His eyes were hungry as he took in her shape beneath the near-transparent chemise. Her blood heated in response, but she held him back with a hand to his chest.

"Do you think her parents forced the marriage?"

He shrugged. "They would hardly be the first set of parents to set their cap for the Hathaway fortunes."

Miranda frowned at the reminder that her parents had done just that. "But if she cares for him and he cares for her, why would they need to be so formal with one another?"

Andrew exhaled, the sound impatient. "I think your romantic imagination is running away from you. I saw no indication that she cares for him."

"She does. You didn't see the look in her eyes when we were talking about him earlier."

"I'll have to take your word for it. But perhaps it wouldn't be remiss if she showed him she cared."

"The way he shows her?" She laughed and sat on the edge of the bed. "Oh, what a pair. I wonder if we should make them aware of their feelings since they seem to be so oblivious."

Andrew lowered himself onto the bed beside her. "In cases like this, it's best to come to such a realization on your own. I would have flattened anyone who'd so much as hinted that I was still in love with you, and I have no wish to be on the receiving end of your nephew's fists."

"I could talk to him——"

"Absolutely not," he said, lowering her onto the bed and shifting so he was atop her. "They need to figure this out for themselves. We could both be mistaken."

She was finding it difficult to concentrate on the subject, but was about to insist when he placed a finger over her lips.

"Promise me, Miranda. Meddling will only make it worse."

She drew his finger into her mouth and watched as his eyes darkened before releasing it.

"Just a small nudge?"

Andrew didn't bother to hide his impatience to be done with the conversation. "They are already married and there is nothing more we can do."

"You're right, of course," she said, remembering the look of misery on Sarah's face during the wedding breakfast.

That was her last coherent thought before Andrew made her forget everything else but him.

LORD HATHAWAY'S BRIDE

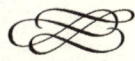

HATHAWAY HEIRS ~ BOOK 2

If he can't have her love, he'll have her passion.

A marriage of convenience…
Sarah Mapleton has already had her heart broken once. When
she finds herself compelled to marry the intriguing new
Viscount Hathaway, she vows to protect her heart at all costs.

He has her hand…
After unexpectedly inheriting his uncle's title, James Hathaway
discovers that the one thing he wants above all else is Sarah.
He hopes to win her love, but until that happens, he vows to
have her passion.

But can he win her heart?
Sarah is surprised that her new husband can wring unexpected

pleasure from her body. But she realizes too late that his kindness has also torn down her emotional barriers. Her determination to protect herself from being hurt again might have pushed James away permanently.

DEDICATION

To Jolly Mark, LC Alleyne, Lenore Providence, Lorraine Harding, and
Pearl Toy,
for all your inspiration and support over the years.

CHAPTER 1

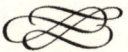

November 1812

 AS SHE REALLY going to do this? Marry a man she barely knew… a man who intimidated her more than she cared to admit?

After a lifetime spent witnessing her parents' unhappy marriage, Sarah Mapleton had vowed never to enter a loveless marriage herself. Yet here she was, about to marry a man she'd spoken with on only a handful of occasions.

As she moved into place at the foot of the aisle by her father's side, her gaze centered on her husband-to-be standing at the front of the small church. His back was to the congregation—to her—but she knew what she'd see when he turned around. Triumph. He'd won after all. After initially spurning his suit, here she stood, poised to marry him.

She tried to calm her racing heart, struggled against the urge to turn and flee. Her father's grip covered her hand like a vise where it rested in the crook of his arm, anchoring her to his side. Panic bubbled up within her when the organ began to play, and following her father's unrelenting lead, she took her first step down the aisle.

Her gaze settled on her mother and younger brother, who were seated in the first pew. Her mother turned to look back at her, and their eyes met. Her mother looked happier than Sarah had seen her in years, and her thoughts began to clear as she remembered why she had finally accepted James Hathaway's proposal of marriage.

After the stress and worry her mother had borne over the past year, stress brought on by how horribly her father had mismanaged their modest estate, Sarah had no choice but to relieve some of that stress by marrying well. She'd agreed to marry the new Viscount Hathaway for her mother's and younger brother's sake. And in doing so had doomed herself.

Welcoming the numbness that descended over her, she forced her feet to move, telling herself that to get through the day, she needed to force down her emotions. But with each step she took, she had to struggle to keep her doubts from surfacing.

Her only consolation was the fact that her instincts about people were rarely wrong, and her instincts told her that the viscount was not a cruel man. No, it wasn't that she was afraid of him, certainly not the way her mother was intimidated by her father. But he was an unknown quantity. A man who exuded confidence and who wouldn't be easily controlled.

She'd learned this past year that she couldn't count on love when the man she'd expected to wed, someone she had known her whole life, had tossed her aside. After that heartbreak,

Sarah decided that if she did marry, it would be to someone who'd give her everything she wanted—comfort and security. Someone who wouldn't demand too much of her time and attention. Instead, she was marrying a man who was giving her father everything he desired—his debts repaid and a titled husband for his daughter.

She reached the top of the aisle, and Lord Hathaway turned to face her. She was struck again, as she normally was, by the sheer force of his presence. He was tall—much taller than anyone she knew—and much broader. Some men went to the trouble of padding their coats, but it wasn't even a possibility that the breadth of Hathaway's shoulders was the result of extra material.

The man standing next to her didn't spare her father a glance as he took her hand in his. Instead of the triumph she'd expected to see in his expression, there was heat in his gaze as his dark eyes caught and held hers. For a moment she felt as though she'd been seared, both from the inside and from the touch of his hand through their gloves.

She'd caught glimpses of that expression before, although he usually masked his emotions behind a wall of civility. It came as a surprise that a small part of her, hidden so deep she hadn't even known it existed, responded to that heated glance.

While they stood like that, her hand in his much larger one as they continued to stare at one another, she found herself beginning to lean toward him. Embarrassed by her unexpected and unwelcome reaction to her future husband, she looked away and gently pulled on her hand. She feared he wasn't going to release it, but after a moment he did and they both turned to face Reverend Meeks.

Sarah found it impossible to concentrate on the wedding service. She was trapped inside her own thoughts, chief among them disbelief that she was actually getting married and not to the man she'd hoped to wed. Time and again she tried to force herself to pay attention to what the minister was saying, but the task proved to be beyond her ability.

She lost track of time, and when Hathaway reached for her hand again, she jumped. Something flared in his eyes, but he didn't betray any annoyance as he recited his vows and slipped a ring onto her finger. She stared down at her hand and hesitated before finally collecting herself and repeating her own vows. Somehow she managed to keep her voice even.

When the minister declared them husband and wife, it was impossible to miss the satisfaction on Hathaway's face. In that moment she had to struggle against the constraining feeling that the door of a cage had closed behind her.

THE MORNING OF James Hathaway's wedding should have been a happy one. After all, he now had everything a man could desire.

Despite his uncle's best attempts to sire a son, he had died without an heir. Upon his death, the title of Viscount Hathaway had passed to James, and with it had come a great deal of land and wealth.

He hadn't expected to inherit, and so he'd never given more than a passing thought to the title and all that would come with it before his uncle's passing. But the title had gained him the one thing he'd recently discovered he desired beyond all else—his new wife.

Her father, a baronet living near Hathaway Park in Northampton, had paid James a call when he'd taken up residence. Sir Henry Mapleton had made not-so-subtle references to his daughter during that visit, but by that point James had already become accustomed to the seemingly unending parade of mothers and fathers who made no pretense about throwing their unmarried daughters at him. Daughters whom he had no intention of courting.

Then he'd met Sarah Mapleton.

He'd done everything in his power to try to engage her regard, but she'd barely even looked at him whenever their paths crossed—and her father had taken every opportunity to ensure that happened often.

James knew she'd only accepted his suit because her father had pressed her to. He hoped that with time and patience she would come to accept him fully, but as he watched her during the wedding breakfast, it was clear to him that it would not be that day.

The wedding ceremony had been an intimate affair. From his side, there was only his mother and younger sister, his uncle's widow and the man he knew would be her husband when her official mourning period was over. He wished Edward were there, but having recently been promoted to the rank of captain in the British army, his brother was engaged on the continent.

Sarah's immediate family was equally small—her parents and a younger brother, George, who'd come down from Eton for the day. But the wedding breakfast was a different matter.

They'd opened the house to friends and neighbors in Northampton, which meant that strangers, few of whom he'd even met before that morning, now flooded several rooms on the main floor of the manor.

Sarah sat next to him during the actual meal, but she'd spoken only a few words. In fact, she'd hardly glanced at him, doing so only when he forced her attention by addressing her directly. From her demeanor when he'd begun to court her, he'd originally thought her shy. He'd since witnessed her several times in other company and had come to realize that she was only reserved with him.

Leaning against one wall of the large dining room, he watched her flit from guest to guest, showing them the outgoing side of her personality that she kept hidden from him. Despite her efforts, he saw enough to realize she was acting a part for their guests. His wife certainly looked the picture of a beautiful, happy bride. Her silk dress of white seemed to shimmer as she moved about the room, her blond curls bouncing as if they, too, had been ordered to appear happy and confident. But he couldn't help noticing that she laughed just a little too loudly, smiled a little too stiffly. He wondered if it was as obvious to everyone else that his new bride would rather be anywhere else than here, celebrating their marriage.

He also didn't miss the way one young man kept looking at Sarah, trying to find opportunities to speak to her, and how she went out of her way to avoid him. Robert Vaughan. James had made it his mission to learn his identity, and it hadn't comforted him to discover that many had once thought he and Sarah would make a love match.

His thoughts were diverted by yet another person demanding his attention. Never good with names under even the best of circumstances, James could have told the portly older man that his effort at currying favor while he was surrounded by so many new faces was unlikely to bear fruit.

After ten minutes of tedious conversation about politics and current happenings on the continent that served only to make him worry more about his brother, James made some vague excuse about being needed elsewhere and went in search of his wife, who had disappeared. Leaving the dining room, he made his way through the other open rooms on the main floor.

He found Sarah in the drawing room, seated on the settee next to a young woman he didn't know. His wife's posture was stiff, her brows drawn together in a slight frown. Feeling the need to rescue her, he crossed to where they sat on the far side of the room. He was almost upon the pair when the other woman's whispered words reached his ears.

"…can't believe you were actually forced to marry someone so common. He may have inherited the title, but there can be no mistaking that he doesn't come from the same noble stock as the old viscount. How can you stand it?"

He froze in place, waiting to hear his wife defend him. But instead she looked down at her hands, which were clasped tightly in her lap, and shrugged. Disappointment surged within him.

The other woman looked up then and made a strangled noise of dismay. James didn't even glance at her, all his attention focused instead on Sarah. His wife looked up at that moment to see what had alarmed her companion. Their gazes met and clashed.

"It was so nice to have a few minutes to talk to you," the woman said, stumbling over her words and rising with unseemly haste. He didn't look at her as she fled from the room.

Sarah tore her gaze from his and rose as well. He supposed he should have been angry, but given how tense things were between the two of them, he wasn't surprised. He couldn't think of anything to say that wouldn't make the situation worse, and since the room had become more crowded since he'd entered—were people actually following him?—he murmured something about wanting to introduce her to his mother and sister. She nodded, managing a small, tense smile for the benefit of those who were unabashedly watching them, and took his arm.

CHAPTER 2

*I*T WAS MIDAFTERNOON when the last of the guests finally departed. With them, it appeared her new husband had also disappeared. Even his mother and sister had left, insisting that they were comfortably settled in the dower house. She found it odd that they hadn't taken up residence in the manor. Heaven knew it was more than large enough. If she hadn't seen for herself the affectionate manner with which her husband treated his family, she would have assumed a familial rift existed between them. But watching them interact, there clearly was no such conflict.

Sarah was grateful for the time alone as she struggled to come to terms with the fact that her life had completely changed. It hadn't helped to see Robert at the wedding breakfast. She had no idea why he'd chosen to attend, but she hoped he hadn't realized she wasn't happy. She didn't want him to know that her heart still hurt when she looked at him.

Avoiding her bedroom lest Lord Hathaway decide to join

her there before evening, she decided to explore the house. It was much larger than her parents' modest home. As she made her way to the second floor, she was amazed by the signs of wealth on display everywhere she looked. She'd never been inside the Hathaway manor house before but had expected it to be dark, its walls lined with rich woodwork. Instead, she was surprised to find the house was almost unnaturally light. Pale walls were set off by accents heavy with marble and gilt. The great number of candle sconces everywhere told her the effect would carry over well into the evening.

She'd heard others speak of the former viscount's great wealth, but even though his heir had paid off her father's not-inconsiderable debts, she hadn't quite believed it. She did now.

A footman had told her that the master suites were in the east wing, so at the landing she turned right and headed in the opposite direction. She wandered past many closed doors but ignored them, assuming they were bedrooms that were closed off.

Curiosity led her toward the open door at the end of the hall where light spilled out into the hallway. When she crossed the threshold, she could see why. Tall windows lined one entire wall, and there were no curtains to block the sunlight. The room was long and wide, the wall opposite the windows lined with paintings. Not just paintings—portraits.

She was in the gallery. She knew that manor houses of the nobility often possessed such rooms dedicated to showcasing the family's lineage, but she'd never actually been in one.

Her interest captured, Sarah moved toward the first painting. An inscription below proclaimed it to be a portrait of the first Viscount Hathaway. She was surprised to see that he'd been granted the title less than 150 years earlier. The previous viscount, her husband's uncle, had always seemed so imperious, as though countless centuries of noble blood ran through his veins.

As she examined each of the portraits, she couldn't help but notice the marked similarity in the appearance of the various viscounts over the generations. Every single one of them possessed fair hair and a slim build. There wasn't a painting of her husband, but he was so different that it was almost impossible to believe he belonged to the same family.

JAMES FOUND HER in the gallery, frowning at the row of portraits of the previous men who had held his title. His stomach clenched. He knew exactly what she was thinking. He'd hoped never to have this conversation with her, and especially not on his wedding day. But no one had ever accused him of being a coward, and he wouldn't shy away from the truth now.

"I see you've discovered the family's deepest shame."

He winced as the words left his mouth, realizing that they sounded bitter. He'd been aiming for levity.

She turned and waited for him to reach her before replying. "It is a shame to be fair-haired?"

"No, it is an embarrassment that I am not. Something that my uncle never let me forget on those few occasions he deigned to speak to me."

He could almost see her mind ticking away, weighing the implications of his words. His new wife was a clever woman. If she hadn't suspected the truth before, she'd know now. He only hoped she wouldn't be too scandalized.

She licked her lips before she spoke, and he almost groaned at the slight movement. He'd wanted Sarah for his own since first setting eyes on her. It was killing him to exercise restraint and keep his distance in the face of her obvious unease in his presence.

"I was of the belief that illegitimate children couldn't inherit."

He inclined his head. "And you would be correct. My father wasn't illegitimate, but I don't think anyone had any doubt that he and my uncle did not share the same father."

She nodded, apparently accepting his words without censure.

"Your grandmother would hardly be the first woman to bear a child from a lover and raise him together with her other children."

She spoke so calmly that for several moments he was speechless as he wrestled with the implications of her acceptance. Was it possible she was already with child? Or perhaps she was thinking of the day when she, too, would take a lover. Her ready acceptance of his familial history would certainly explain why she'd agreed to marry him despite the fact that she could hardly seem to stand being in his presence.

Jealousy speared through him at the thought, the emotion so intense and unexpected that he almost recoiled.

"Tell me you're not already increasing."

Color drained from her face at his words, and for a moment, he feared it was due to guilt at his having discovered her secret. The roar of blood pounded in his head. When color seeped back into her face, there was no mistaking that her shock had now turned to anger.

"How dare you accuse me of such a thing." Her lips were pressed together, her chest heaving with indignation as she finished.

It was a struggle to keep his tone even. "You would hardly be the first woman to marry another man after finding yourself in such a condition." He'd deliberately echoed her words, telling her that it was her own fault that he'd come to that conclusion.

Her brown eyes narrowed as she glared at him. "I may live in the country, but I am not a simpleton. Just because I've seen other women behave in such a manner does not mean I come by my knowledge from personal experience."

"So you are not increasing?" The relief coursing through him was immense.

"No," she managed between clenched teeth.

Their tentative camaraderie was now gone, and it was obvious to him that she wouldn't soon forget this conversation. He'd misstepped. Badly. He was supposed to woo Sarah, gain her acceptance of him since he'd never force himself on a woman. Not even his own his wife.

Judging it best to retreat and allow her temper time to cool, he made a swift change of subject.

"I've arranged for you to meet with Mrs. Phillips, the housekeeper. She's waiting for you now if it isn't too inconvenient."

She released a breath, and he couldn't tell if she was trying to dispel her anger or exhibiting her relief that she would no longer have to bear his company.

"Now is fine." She looked down and must have realized she was still wearing her wedding dress. "I'd like to change first."

He nodded and took his leave. She didn't move until he'd left the room, no doubt anxious to ensure he wouldn't follow her to her bedroom.

CHAPTER 3

S ARAH DIDN'T KNOW what to do with herself as she
waited for her husband to join her. She had never
even kissed the man and now she was about to lie with him.
She couldn't help but remember the kisses she'd shared with
Robert. She'd believed that he cared for her, but given how
casually he'd broken her heart, it was clear she'd been wrong.

The Vaughans were respected within their corner of
Northampton, so there had never been any doubt they'd be
invited to the wedding breakfast. Incredulity had filled her,
though, when she'd seen Robert. Her disbelief had quickly
turned to anger, and she'd been tempted to ask a footman to
escort him from the house.

In the end, she'd been grateful for the reminder that men
couldn't be trusted. The conversation she'd had with Hathaway in the gallery that afternoon had shown her that he felt
the same way about her sex. She still found it difficult to
believe he'd actually asked her if she was with child. That one

question told her that he had a very low opinion of her—perhaps of all women given his family's history. The fact that he'd essentially bought her by agreeing to pay off her father's numerous debts no doubt solidified his low opinion. But then again, their union was no different than that of any other member of the *ton*.

After that brief, uncomfortable meeting in the gallery, she'd spent the rest of the afternoon with the very efficient Mrs. Phillips, who had wasted no time in going over the menus and discussing the running of the household.

She had found it almost impossible to concentrate, her fear of what that night would hold growing by the second as the housekeeper went on about household matters. Sarah hadn't made a good impression with the older woman, but honestly, what had she expected? It was no secret that her marriage wasn't a love match, and she'd wager that any new bride in similar circumstances would be nervous about their upcoming wedding night.

James had seemed content to leave her to her own devices, something for which she was more than a little grateful. Whenever he entered a room, he seemed to take up all the space and she had to keep reminding herself to breathe. She was constantly on edge in his presence. She went to great pains to hide the fact that he made her nervous, but she couldn't tell if her efforts were successful.

When he'd sent word that he wouldn't be joining her for dinner, she'd taken the opportunity to have a tray sent to her room, hoping the time alone would allow her to settle her nerves. It hadn't worked.

She cringed again as she remembered that he'd overheard

her cousin offering condolences on her marriage, a sentiment she knew had sprung from her cousin's jealousy and not from true concern. The flash of disappointment she'd seen on his face still haunted her. Of course she hadn't been successful in hiding her reservations from him. She didn't think anyone else had seen through her attempt at a content, if not entirely happy, facade. The fact that he had seen below that surface had unnerved her and served as yet another reminder of how much his mere presence unbalanced her.

When her maid finally left after spending an absurd amount of time fussing over her, Sarah turned toward her new bed. She considered pretending to be asleep, but such a ruse would only gain her an extra day. Perhaps. It was entirely possible Hathaway would wake her.

She started to pace as she considered what was about to happen. In what had been an extremely awkward conversation, her mother had told her that the first night would be the worst. It might be better for her nerves to just get it out of the way. Maybe he'd leave her alone once their marriage was consummated. And if not, she might be lucky and conceive right away. Surely he wouldn't continue to demand his marital rights when she was carrying his child.

She tried not to dwell on his joining her. Much as she had wanted to avoid the conversation, her mother had gone out of her way to ensure she knew the mechanics of what would happen on her wedding night. Sarah had heard innuendos from some of the staff when they hadn't realized she could overhear them but hadn't been able to piece together herself just what was involved. How was she supposed to bear having a virtual stranger take such personal liberties with her body?

Her only hope was that the ordeal would be brief and that he'd return to his own bed after it was over.

Determined not to let fear overwhelm her, she forced herself to stop pacing. She took several deep breaths and tried to push back her racing thoughts.

After her meeting with Mrs. Phillips, Sarah had headed straight to the library to find a book to read. She piled the pillows on the bed and settled against the headboard. Despite her resolve, when she opened the book she could barely concentrate on the words before her. She forced herself to continue, however, determined not to allow her fear free rein.

A shared dressing room connected her bedroom to her husband's. When the soft knock on her door finally came, she lowered the book to her lap with exaggerated care and bade him enter. She gave herself a mental pat on the back when her voice didn't waver.

When he strode into the room, she experienced again the odd sensation that he had taken up all the available space. He still wore the clothes he was attired in that morning for their wedding, but he'd removed the topcoat and cravat. In his shirt and waistcoat, the former open at the throat, the evidence of her husband's muscular physique was undeniable. A strange sensation stirred deep within her at the sight.

Trying to retain her composure, she looked away from him and realized she was holding her book so tightly her knuckles were white. She forced her fingers to relax and made a great show of marking the place in her book before setting it on her bedside table.

Tense silence stretched between them as she searched for something to say. Something that wouldn't reveal just how nervous her husband made her. Even worse, she had no idea what she was supposed to do. Did he expect her to lie there while he joined her? But he'd need to undress first, and if she stayed as she was, she'd witness every moment of it.

Heat rose to her cheeks at the thought, spurring her to scramble from the bed and face him. She would turn around if he started to remove his clothing. She glanced at her bedside table. Should she snuff out the lamp she'd left on so she could read?

When she looked again at Hathaway, she saw his eyes travel down the length of her night rail, lingering on her breasts, then lower. His eyes seemed to burn into her, and embarrassment coursed through her as she looked down to see that the thin garment clung to her uncorseted breasts and wrapped around her thighs. Shocked, she looked up and met his gaze. Hunger shone in his eyes, threatening to steal her breath.

Turning away from him, she came up against her reflection in the mirror of her dressing table. Was that…? She squinted at her reflection. Dear Lord, how had she not realized this garment was quite so sheer? Surely the modiste who'd created it for her wedding night should have said something to her—she could almost see right through it. She covered her face with her hands, mortified that she was virtually naked in front of this man who was little more than a stranger to her.

She heard him move behind her and tensed when the weight of his hands settled on her shoulders.

"You're afraid." She could hear the concern in his voice. "I won't hurt you."

She lowered her hands and crossed them over her breasts,

her hands settling just below his on her shoulders. Their eyes met in the mirror.

"We barely know one another. It seems unbelievable that I'm here with you, like this. And I don't know what I should be doing."

"You hate the fact that you're not in control."

She was going to deny it but then realized he was correct. Yes, she was nervous, and yes, she was embarrassed, but what she struggled with most was exactly what he'd pointed out. It was the first night of their marriage together, and she feared that by ceding control to him now, she would find herself on even shakier ground in the future.

His hands covered hers, making her aware of the ring he'd placed on her finger just that morning. Slowly he dragged her hands down to her sides and held them there while his gaze traveled over the reflection of her body.

"You are very beautiful," he said, his voice thick.

She knew she was pretty, but the way he spoke, his voice almost reverential, gave the words extra weight. He wasn't just paying her a compliment... The words sounded as though they had been torn from his very soul. She stared at him in the mirror, unable to look away. When he moved his hands to her waist, she drew in a deep breath. His hands were so hot they seemed to burn right through the thin fabric of her night rail. She might as well have been wearing nothing.

She could only watch in silence, holding her breath and bracing herself for the touch of his mouth as his dark head descended toward the side of her neck. Robert had never done this to her, and she felt powerless, unsure what to do. When her husband's lips touched her skin, she closed her eyes, unable to watch. She was taken aback by his gentleness, his mouth resting against her throat, the heat of his breath causing a shiver to go through her.

When she opened her eyes again, she saw that his eyes were trained on her face in the mirror. He started to inch his hands upward. His palms settled over her breasts, his thumbs toying with the hardened peaks through the fabric, and she let out a shaky breath. The intimacy of his touch was almost unbearable.

"Please," she said, feeling suddenly shy. "I can't watch… It's too much."

He stilled, and for a moment she thought he was going to deny her, but then with a curt nod he shifted their bodies so she was no longer standing in front of her dressing table.

Without the embarrassment of having to watch herself while he touched her, there was only him. Her husband. His large body pressed against her from behind, his hands holding her, one on her breast, the other on her stomach. And oh God, he'd lowered his mouth to her neck again and was doing something wicked with his lips and tongue that caused her to moan and tilt her head farther to the side.

She could feel his hardness pressing into her lower back, and she should have been afraid. She knew what was going to come next, and while her mind tried to prepare her for the pain of his impending penetration, her body seemed to revel under his touch. Without conscious thought, she pressed back into him and a thrill of satisfaction went through her when she heard his groan. He had completely unbalanced her, giving her pleasure when she'd expected none, but she was also having a similar effect on him.

His hands bunched the fabric at her hips, and when he started to drag the material up, she was almost breathless with anticipation at the thought of feeling his warm touch on her skin.

Was this normal? Was she supposed to be enjoying his touch so much?

When he caressed her now-bared thighs and swept one hand between them, she opened for him without having to be asked. His other arm gripped her around the waist, keeping her back pressed against his front.

A soft whimper escaped her lips when he touched her there—the most private part of her.

He made a soft shushing sound. "Let me show you how much pleasure I can bring you."

And he did. He brought her more bliss than she had ever thought possible as his fingers stroked her. His other hand moved up to cup her breast again. Almost delirious from the sensations he coaxed from her, her head fell back against him. He pressed the side of his face against her cheek as he caressed her breast and continued his wicked movements below.

She couldn't think, could barely remember to breathe as pleasure overwhelmed her, just like he'd promised. And when it reached a point that she didn't think she'd be able to stand it any longer, her whole body seemed to convulse. His grip on her breast tightened briefly and he exhaled harshly, but the fingers of his other hand continued to move, prolonging the moment. Finally he stopped and released the fabric of her night rail so it fell around her, covering her once more.

They stood like that for at least a minute. His hand still on her breast, his cheek pressed against hers, and he wrapped his other arm around her waist, securing her to him as they both tried to regain control of their breathing.

As she came back to herself, she realized that he was still hard where he pressed into her back. Her thoughts were reeling… What had just happened? How had he affected her in such a way? And surely now he would take his own pleasure.

He released her and took a step back. She turned to face him, but he was already moving away. She stood, stunned, as he walked to the door that separated her room from his and crossed through it, closing the door behind him with almost exaggerated care.

JAMES HAD KNOWN his plan to introduce Sarah slowly to the physical side of marriage would prove difficult, but it had been harder than he'd imagined to keep from taking his new bride after she'd fallen apart so gloriously in his arms. He was hard and aching. It went against his nature to deny himself something he wanted so badly, especially when it was clear Sarah had been prepared to carry out her duty.

But if that day's events had shown him anything, it was that his new bride had not fully accepted their marriage. She'd been unfailingly polite when he'd courted her, but she hadn't encouraged his suit. Perhaps he should have given her more time to come to know him, but he'd known from the first time they met that he wanted her for his wife. He hadn't wanted to risk losing her to someone else. He couldn't say why, exactly, but she affected him in a way no other woman ever had.

He was well aware of his shortcomings and knew it would

SUZANNA MEDEIROS

take time for Sarah to accept him fully. He wasn't classically handsome… certainly not as handsome as Vaughan. His mouth twisted in distaste just thinking of the man.

Physically, James had more in common with dockworkers than his fellow members of the aristocracy, but he'd never wanted for female companionship. Those liaisons had been with women who were willing to engage in a little bed sport, but none of them had wanted to marry him. Not until he'd inherited his title. Then, overnight, he'd become a desirable catch.

But not for Sarah. She hadn't had a dowry and he hadn't cared. He had more money now than he could ever imagine spending. Still, she hadn't hidden her reluctance to marry him, and his conscience wouldn't allow him to forget that her parents had pressed her to accept him.

He paced the length of his room, unable to bear the thought of getting into his cold, lonely bed. He vowed silently that he would have Sarah. If her reaction to his touch that evening was any indication, it might even be as soon as the following night.

His palms itched with the need to touch her again, and his cock refused to go back down. It didn't help that he could still feel the warmth of her skin, could still smell her desire on his hands.

Cursing, he unbuttoned his trousers and set about giving himself some relief.

CHAPTER 4

WHEN SARAH WOKE the next morning, she was no less confused about the events that had taken place the previous evening. She'd expected Hathaway to climb over her and sate his desires within her body and had tried to prepare herself for that scenario. What happened instead had left her shaken. Instead of caring about his own pleasure, he'd thought only of her. And to her surprise, the desire he'd wrung from her had been more than she could ever have imagined.

And then he'd left.

She'd felt the evidence of his desire pressed against her back, so knew he'd wanted to go further. He hadn't, and she couldn't understand why. He'd wanted her, she was his wife and he could have had her, but instead he'd walked away.

But most confusing of all was the fact that she hadn't wanted him to leave. During those last few seconds, when she'd been certain he was about to remove her nightgown, she'd wanted him to do it.

It had occurred to her that in order to get through her wedding night she might have to pretend it was Robert who was touching her. In reality, her entire world had centered only on her husband. As she'd come apart in his arms, it was his face she saw, imagining the way he'd looked at her in the mirror. Everything about him was larger-than-life. How could any other man, even the memory of one she'd once loved, hope to compete when he was near? And for that reason, he posed a danger to her mental well-being.

Was he playing a game with her? In the light of day, she could see only one reason for his actions the previous night. He sought to unbalance her, to keep the upper hand in their relationship.

She wouldn't be able to avoid Hathaway forever, so she gathered her courage about her, imagining it was a cloak that safely shielded her, and made her way downstairs to the break-fast room.

He was already seated, and she had to endure having his eyes on her as she murmured a quiet greeting and moved to the sideboard where a wide variety of dishes was laid out. It was far more lavish than the breakfasts she'd had at home. Butterflies rioting in her belly, she helped herself to eggs and toast before returning to the table.

Self-consciousness threatened to overwhelm her as she gazed at her husband seated opposite her.

"How did you sleep last night, my lord?" She was aiming for polite conversation but realized her mistake as soon as the words were out.

He gazed at her with mild amusement, one eyebrow quirked. "Horribly," he said. "But I trust your night was quite satisfactory."

At the reminder of the pleasure he had shown her, she glanced away, embarrassment causing her cheeks to heat.

"And don't you think it's time, Sarah, that you call me by my name?"

The way he uttered her name, as though he were relishing the sound of it on his tongue, did nothing to ease her embarrassment.

"Hathaway?" she asked, confused. Surely she'd already called him by his title. That was how she thought of him.

He shook his head. "No. James. I never expected to inherit, and I find I dislike having my wife call me by my uncle's title."

He'd mentioned a rift between him and the former viscount when they'd spoken in the gallery, and she could understand why the constant reminder of his uncle was unbearable.

She inclined her head in agreement. "I'll try… James."

His face lit with satisfaction and something else she couldn't name. When she found herself wanting to draw closer to him, she had to look away to break whatever spell he was casting over her.

She took a forkful of egg and had just managed to swallow it when Hathaway—no, James—indicated that the footman leave the room. Then he brought up that which had been uppermost on her mind since he'd left the previous evening.

"We should talk about what happened last night."

Her fork clattered to the plate and she cast a furtive look at

117

the door to see if the footman had overheard. She was relieved to find he was nowhere in sight. If he was waiting in the hallway, however, he might be able to hear their conversation.

She kept her voice low when she replied. "Must we?"

He appeared amused by her embarrassment. "Yes, we must. Especially since we are not legally married until the marriage is consummated."

She closed her eyes, hating that he wanted to talk about the physical side of their union. When she opened them again, his brows were drawn together in concern.

If they were going to talk about the previous night, she might as well take this opportunity to see if she could discover his true motivation for leaving her the night before. Had he been trying to manipulate her, or had he left for another reason?

"Why didn't you…" She waved a hand between them, asking without saying the actual words why he hadn't taken his own pleasure. And, as he'd rightly pointed out, made their marriage legal.

"Because I know you didn't want this marriage and you were afraid. I'm not the type of man to force myself on a woman, not even my own wife. But I did want to show you there was pleasure to be found in the marriage bed."

A new flood of heat crept into her cheeks as she remembered, again, just how he had touched her. "I think you already know that you succeeded in your goal."

He was silent for several moments as he stared intently at her. She could feel him examining her as though trying to read her thoughts. "Do you think you'll be afraid tonight?"

She looked away and tried to imagine him coming into her room after dinner. Remembering the anxiety she had felt as she waited for him last night, she expected some of that feeling to return. Instead, she had to face the truth. She was looking forward to seeing what else her husband could show her.

For a moment she considered putting him off but decided there was nothing to be gained. In fact, the opposite was true. By delaying the inevitable and denying the truth, she risked angering her husband and making things much worse between them.

She shook her head. "I don't believe so."

He closed his eyes briefly. "Thank God."

She could see, in that moment, just how much his consideration of her feelings had cost him. And she realized that perhaps their marriage wouldn't be the hardship she'd imagined.

It was not yet midday when Sarah was informed that her mother was waiting for her in the drawing room. Her mother hadn't said anything about planning to visit when she and her father had left the day before, and Sarah couldn't help but brace herself for bad news.

When she made her way to the drawing room, she found her mother unabashedly admiring the furnishings. The house had an inordinate amount of gold accents and gilded trim, and not just in the accessories or on the frames of the paintings. Sarah considered the decor more than a little ostentatious and wouldn't be surprised to learn that the arms of the settee were not merely covered with gold leaf but made from solid gold. The way James's uncle had thrown money about was almost shocking.

Her mother turned when Sarah entered and greeted her with a warm hug. Sarah exhaled in relief and lowered herself onto the settee, inviting her mother to join her.

"This is a surprise, Mama. I didn't expect you to visit quite so soon."

Her mother made a fluttering motion with her hand. "I know you're still on your honeymoon, but surely a mother can be excused for caring about her daughter's happiness."

Sarah bit back a sharp retort about how her mother hadn't seemed concerned about her happiness when she and her father had forced her to accept Lord Hathaway's proposal of marriage. Instead, she said, "I'm as well as can be expected."

Her mother pressed her lips together and looked away. "Was last night so terrible?"

Sarah could have kicked herself for her words. She'd consoled herself that in marrying Hathaway... no, James... and having him settle Papa's debts, she'd at least be able to lessen some of her mother's worries. And here she was adding to them.

"Last night was..." What could she say? That her wedding night had been wonderful, more amazing than she'd thought possible? That her new husband had been incredibly generous and had thought only of her pleasure? "He was gentle with me," she said finally. The words were inadequate, but she was reluctant to discuss the details of what had transpired between her and James. Especially since it was clear from her mother's warnings that the physical side of her own marriage was far from satisfying.

Her mother cast her eyes upward. "Thank heavens. I couldn't stop thinking about how you'd fare."

Sarah laid a hand over her mother's, which were clenched in her lap. "Can we talk about something else? I love you, Mama, but one conversation about what happens between a husband and a wife was already more than enough for me."

Her mother gave a small laugh, her relief obvious, and turned a hand over to squeeze Sarah's before releasing it. "I understand. It's not something I enjoy, but it is a burden all wives bear."

Trying hard not to think of her parents sharing similar intimacies to what she had experienced, Sarah changed the subject. "How is Papa today? I imagine he's quite satisfied with himself."

Her mother made a soft tsking sound at the peevish tone Sarah was unable to conceal. "He is happy, yes, but you can hardly expect him to feel otherwise. Your match was more than he could have hoped for."

"Because he gambled away my dowry?"

"Must we talk about this?" Her mother stiffened and looked away again.

What was the matter with her? Why must she insist on bringing up subjects that would only make her mother anxious again? Papa's selfishness meant that her mother was as much a victim of his excesses as she and her brother.

"I'm sorry, Mama. Please tell me, how is George? He almost didn't arrive in time for my wedding, and I barely spoke to him yesterday."

"You know your brother. He was anxious about missing school and is already on his way back to Eton. He left early this morning." Her mother lifted one shoulder in an attempt to appear indifferent, but Sarah could tell that her brother's haste to escape his family had hurt her. If Papa had celebrated her marriage last night in his usual manner—by imbibing just a little too much and becoming bitter and melancholy—she couldn't blame him. Now fifteen, at least her brother could escape their father's outbursts by spending as much time as possible at school.

"I always envied him, you know. That he was able to escape Papa's moods for most of the year."

A ghost of a smile touched her mother's lips, but it didn't reach her eyes. "I daresay he might say the same of you now."

Her mother's statement made Sarah sad beyond words. For her mother there would be no escape from her father's angry moods when he gambled and lost far more than they could afford. The one time Sarah had raised the subject directly with her mother, she'd replied that she would gladly take hurtful words over physical violence. Something in her mother's eyes had led her to believe that she'd experienced the latter, or at least been witness to it, but Sarah hadn't pursued the conversation. She was sure that made her weak, but she hadn't wanted to know.

"Enough of this grim subject," Sarah said. "Now that Papa's debts are settled, I'm sure he'll be content. Would you like me to show you the rest of the house?"

Her mother couldn't hide her hopeful expression even as she shook her head. "I fear I've already taken up too much of your time…"

Sarah waved her hand in dismissal of her mother's reservations. "Nonsense. Besides, it will help me to refresh my own memory. This house is so large I fear I've already forgotten much from the tour the housekeeper took me on yesterday." She stood and held her arm out to her mother. "Shall we?"

CHAPTER 5

T̲O SAY THAT DINNER was a stilted affair would have been a vast understatement. It was just the two of them, and his new wife had informed the staff to serve their meal in the breakfast room instead of the much larger dining room.

In that moment, when he'd stood to welcome her as she entered the room, he realized just how much they had in common. As the only brother to the former Viscount Hathaway, there was no question that his father would be accepted by the *ton*. But his family almost never ventured out into society, and the formal trappings of that world—his world now—felt unnatural to him. He was more comfortable raising horses in the stables his father had founded than negotiating the ballroom, and he struggled with what to say and what was expected of him in this new life.

Given the modest means by which her family lived, Sarah's simple request to have their meal served in the smaller room spoke volumes as to her character. He'd expected his new wife to revel in the wealth that came with her new position. He had no doubt that she could hold her own in even the most imposing of dining rooms. The fact that she'd sought out comfort over formality gave him hope for their relationship.

The tension in the room was almost palpable, and James struggled for a way to ease it. From the way Sarah avoided his gaze as the first course was served, he knew she was thinking about their conversation that morning. He'd asked her if he could make love to her tonight and she had agreed.

He'd thought of little else all day.

He'd tried to distract himself, somehow managing to stay away from the house so he wouldn't drag Sarah up to his bedroom to make up for the wedding night he'd denied himself. He'd gone first to the dower house to visit his mother and sister. His mother tended toward self-sacrifice, and he wanted to ensure his family didn't want for anything. After leaving them, he'd headed to the stables.

Inheriting the viscountcy had affected his entire family. James's father had received only a modest inheritance that consisted of a small, unentailed property in Newmarket. He'd taken that inheritance and founded a stable that had gone on to become one of the best in all of England.

James had continued his father's legacy when the stables had passed down to him and his brother Edward. His passion for raising horses hadn't ended now that he was the viscount. For all his uncle's excesses, the stables at Hathaway Park were unexceptional, and James had only been able to bring a handful of horses with him to Northampton. But work was currently underway to construct new, larger stables. He hoped when his brother retired from the military that together they'd be able to expand the business.

Despite managing to fill the hours until it was time for dinner, it had been next to impossible to stop his thoughts from drifting to his wife and everything he wanted to do when he finally had her alone again. She probably wouldn't enjoy their first coupling, but he'd make it up to her in other ways.

He shifted in his seat as he began to grow hard. Again. He'd been half hard for most of the day.

So lost was he in thoughts of the coming night he almost didn't realize Sarah was speaking to him.

"Mrs. Phillips mentioned that you went to visit your mother and sister. They are more than welcome to stay here."

"Emily would like nothing better, but mother is finding her change in station a little overwhelming. I tried to convince her to move into the manor, but she prefers the smaller dower house. It reminds her of our former home."

Her brow furrowed, and she was silent for several seconds before saying, "I hope you're not saying that to spare my feelings. I imagine any mother would want more for her son than to marry the daughter of a man who'd gambled away everything that wasn't entailed."

Her words took him by surprise. He never imagined that she'd believe she wasn't good enough for him. The thought was laughable.

"To be completely honest, Uncle was horrible to us. The rest of us paid no attention to his snide comments about our branch of the family, but his belief that he was our superior in every way bothered my mother more than a little. I fear it has tainted her enjoyment of her new situation. She's here only as a show of support to me. If she had her preference, she'd be returning home." He scowled as he remembered just how much the old viscount had upset his mother.

"Well then, I'd say we're evenly matched. I know for a fact your uncle never approved of my family. I daresay he's turning over in his grave even as we speak."

The corners of his mouth lifted in amusement. His wife had wit and spirit. He liked that about her.

"To upsetting my uncle's plans," he said, raising a glass.

With a small laugh, she raised her own glass, and they shared an unexpected moment of quiet camaraderie.

They fell into silence again as they finished their meal. Minutes ticked by and he could sense Sarah growing more tense. Much to his chagrin, he found himself considering if the best course of action would be to continue in the same vein as the previous evening. But he honestly didn't think he had it in him to show such restraint a second time, which meant he might just have to absent himself altogether after dinner.

When dessert was served and he had to endure watching his wife close her eyes as she enjoyed the syllabub, his control almost snapped. He barely restrained himself from taking her hand and leading her upstairs right then.

Finally, after what was surely an eternity, the meal was finished and the last plate whisked away. When Sarah looked at him, there was no missing the fact that her nerves were back in full force.

"I am at a loss as to what happens now," she said. "Normally my mother and I withdraw to the drawing room after dinner and I read while she sews. My brother joins us when he's home. On those rare occasions that he doesn't go to the tavern, my father buries himself in his study."

She licked her lips, and he was powerless to keep his eyes from following the motion of her small tongue as it flicked across her top lip. He almost groaned aloud.

"I don't suppose you wish to retire to your study now?"

He met her gaze, and reflected in her eyes he could see that she knew very well what he wanted. Relief filled him when he realized that while she might be nervous, he couldn't detect even a hint of the fear he'd seen the night before.

He pushed back his chair as he rose and held his hand out to her. She hesitated only a moment before placing her hand in his. He pulled her to her feet.

She tried to draw away, but he didn't release her.

"I'd like to retire now, but not to the study."

She swallowed and gave a small nod. "I'll ring for my maid and prepare for… bed."

He should let her go—it was the civilized, courteous thing to do—but he was incapable of letting her out of his sight. "I don't think you'll need her tonight."

She stared at him, uncomprehending, for several seconds. He could see the moment she realized his meaning when color swept into her cheeks. He released her hand then but held out his arm for her to take. He almost expected her to step away from him, but instead she took a deep breath and placed her hand on his arm.

A heady mixture of relief and desire filled him as he turned toward the door. She didn't lean against him. Their only point of contact was the touch of her hand, but his body vibrated with tension at her proximity. It seemed almost impossible that this was going to happen. That he'd finally have Sarah in his bed. When he'd first met her a scant few months before after taking up residence at the Hathaway family seat, he wasn't sure he'd ever see this day. And the fear in her eyes yesterday whenever they were alone together had only increased that doubt.

He was almost afraid to look at her as they made their way upstairs, afraid that if he did, he'd see that her fear had returned. But as long as he restrained himself, giving her time to remember what it had felt like to come apart in his arms, she would be his. He'd never lain with a chaste woman before, but he would be gentle. It might kill him, but he wouldn't push her until she was prepared to accept him.

He slowed when they reached the door of his bedroom but then moved past it to hers, reasoning that she would feel more comfortable in familiar surroundings. It would also help her to remember the pleasure he had already shown her in that room.

When they reached her door, she took her hand from his arm. He felt the loss keenly and almost snatched it back.

"Alice will wonder why I didn't ring for her," she said as she fumbled with the doorknob before finally opening the door.

Afraid she was about to leave him standing in the hallway, he pushed his way into the room behind her. "If she does, I'm sure one of the other servants will explain it to her."

She blushed, and he found himself aching to see that color spread over her chest again as it had the night before when he'd brought her to her peak. He closed the door before facing her again.

She swallowed, clearly nervous, but he knew he could make those nerves disappear. If there was one thing he'd learned over the years, it was how to please a woman.

"Are you afraid?" He didn't think she was, but he needed to be certain.

"No," she said with a shake of her head. "But I don't know what I'm supposed to do now."

He leaned toward her and spoke in a conspiratorial whisper. "Well, since I've deprived you of your maid this evening, you can consider me her replacement."

Taking her cue from him, she surveyed him from head to foot, paying particular attention to his hands before replying. "The buttons on my dress are quite small. I'm not sure you'll be able to manage them."

He smiled, relieved that she appeared to be softening to him. "I accept your challenge," he said, placing his hands on her shoulders and turning her away from him.

And a challenge it was. Halfway down the long row of buttons, he had to force himself to continue with what were probably the smallest buttons known to man. He tamped down on the temptation to yank apart the rest of the dress and send the buttons scattering.

When he finally reached the end, he spread the material apart and, without a word, began to unlace her corset. Her breathing quickened, and when he dropped a kiss onto her shoulder, he felt the tremor that ran through her body.

"I never imagined being undressed could be quite so stimulating," she said.

He lowered the dress from her shoulders. "You should feel free to press me into service whenever you'd like."

He released the dress and watched as it fell to the floor around her. When she stepped out of the pile of fabric, he pulled away her corset and cast it aside.

Like he had the night before, he pulled her body against his—her back to his front—and raised his hands to cover her breasts through her chemise. She released a soft sigh and dropped her head back against his shoulder, enjoying the way he was stroking her. Tearing himself from her side the previous evening had been one of the most difficult things he'd ever had to do, and he was glad he'd restrained himself, but tonight there would be no stopping.

He breathed against the side of her throat and felt another shiver of awareness go through her as he dropped a kiss there, then against her jaw and her cheek.

"Do you want me to continue?" His voice was rough and he knew the question was a gamble. He didn't think he'd be able to stop—the unspoken signals Sarah was giving him told him that she didn't want that either—but it was important to him that she realize she was a willing participant in their marriage. Her parents might have compelled her to marry him, but she did want him. Even if that want was only physical, he needed her to acknowledge it.

She made an inarticulate sound, but her eyes were still closed. He stilled his caresses and repeated the question. When she nodded in reply, he hesitated, considering whether he should press her for the words. He decided against it, knowing that he'd already risked too much by giving her the opportunity to say no. But before this night was over, he vowed that she'd have no doubt she craved his touch as much as he did hers.

He turned her to face him. When she gazed up at him, her warm brown eyes were slightly dazed. Lust, hot and swift, stole his voice. He lowered his head, determined to show her that she would not regret placing her trust in him.

He hadn't kissed her last night, and when she opened her mouth without prodding, he realized he wasn't the first man to kiss her this way. Jealousy speared through him, but he pushed it aside and dedicated himself to making her forget whoever had gone before him.

His need to take her was so great his hands were almost shaking. He pulled back to remove his tailcoat and tossed it onto a chair. Her eyes were riveted on him as he did so. He might not be conventionally handsome, but women had always appreciated his body. He sincerely hoped his wife would be one of those women. He was not unaccustomed to hard work, and it showed in his physique, but as a gently bred woman Sarah would be used to men who weren't quite so muscular.

He watched her carefully for any sign of fear as he undid the buttons of his waistcoat. Seeing none, he removed the garment, tossed it on top of his coat, and proceeded to untie his cravat.

Her eyes moved to the exposed skin at his throat before she looked away.

She started to turn, but he wouldn't let her shy away from him now.

He reached for her hand and stopped her. "Have you changed your mind?"

"No, my lord." She wet her lips before saying, "No, James."

He frowned and almost groaned at the gesture. "Then why are you running away?"

She searched for a reply and he waited, knowing it was difficult for her to talk about their intimate life so openly.

"I thought... I was told..." She closed her eyes and took a deep breath before rushing on. "Isn't that what happens now? I lie on the bed and you... take your marital rights." As she reached the end of her statement, her voice was barely audible.

"I don't want a martyr, Sarah. I mean to show you that there can be great pleasure between a man and a woman."

Color bloomed on her skin, extending down beyond the edge of her chemise. It was with great difficulty that he kept his eyes on her face.

"I already know that. But tonight it is your turn."

"And you think that means you must be brave and suffer my touch while I seek my own pleasure?"

She raised a hand to rub the back of her neck. "I was told that was what to expect."

"By whom?"

If his wife had had the power to make herself disappear, he could tell she would have done so in that moment.

"My mother."

He winced as he tried to envision just how such a conversation would go. "I won't lie, the first time will probably be uncomfortable." He hoped it would only be that—he hated the idea of hurting her. "But I will do my best to make up for that initial pain."

She didn't appear convinced.

"Let's try this." Threading his fingers through hers, he led her to the bed.

He sat on the edge and pulled her into his lap. She inhaled deeply but didn't balk at the intimacy.

"For our first time together, I thought that you might prefer to take the lead."

Right now his wife was like one of his skittish colts who needed a gentle hand so he could gain its trust. That meant letting her control the pace to an extent.

When he saw her confusion, he had to hold back his smile. His wife truly was an innocent and the thought did nothing to stem his arousal. In fact, the opposite was true.

She was sitting primly on his lap, her body angled away from his. He pulled her closer, and when she settled against him, he nuzzled the side of her neck, inhaling deeply. She smelled of some flower he couldn't name, but the scent wasn't overwhelming. He kissed her neck and she melted against him with a soft sigh, gripping his upper arms. He didn't think it possible to get any harder, but the proof of her desire and the fact that she seemed to trust him made a heady aphrodisiac.

She pulled back and turned her face toward him, initiating a kiss. His heart soared as he allowed her to take her time. It wasn't long, however, until he was taking control, turning her soft exploration of his mouth into something deeper.

When she tugged his shirt from his trousers and burrowed her hands underneath the hem, he couldn't hold back his groan of pleasure.

"Am I doing this right?" she murmured against his mouth.

His hands tightened on her waist, and he lifted her to straddle his lap. Her chemise bunched at her hips, and her eyes widened with shock when he pulled her core against his hard-ness. Barely restraining a curse of impatience, he lifted his shirt up and off before tossing it onto the floor.

Somehow he remained still when she leaned back to look at him. She skimmed her hands up his arms to his shoulders and then trailed them down his chest.

"You're so hard," she said with wonder.

"And you"—he cupped her breasts in his hands—"are delightfully soft."

"I'm a little *too* soft."

"For which I am eternally grateful." He brushed his thumbs across her nipples and watched as they hardened against her chemise. "You're wearing far too much," he muttered as he lifted her chemise away. She was now naked in his arms, save for her stockings, and straddling his hips while he wore only his trousers. He wanted nothing more than to strip them off, but they served as a much-needed barrier to help him keep the pace slow.

She made a small sound of dismay, but her protest died when he brought her fully against him. Her breasts pillowing against his bare chest, he took her mouth again. He couldn't say who initiated the movement, but his hands gripped her hips, and she was rocking against his covered erection, soft mewling sounds coming from the back of her throat.

When she stiffened, he tore his mouth from hers and looked down at her impassioned face. Her eyes were closed, her face flushed, and her mouth rounded in surprise. He held her like that, tight against him, while he struggled not to embarrass himself.

She came to herself slowly, and when she opened her eyes

she must have seen how much his restraint was costing him. "Show me what to do for you."

His voice thick, he managed to say, "Unbutton my trousers and take me out."

She didn't hesitate, and his heart beat a heavy rhythm in his chest. When she'd slipped the last button through its housing, she reached past his smalls and touched him. He covered her hand with his, showing her how to hold him, how he liked to be stroked. Knowing he wouldn't last much longer, he grasped her wrist after several seconds and pulled her hand away.

"Am I doing it wrong?" Her brows were drawn together in concern.

"You're perfect, but right now I need to be inside you."

He saw the brief flicker of fear in her eyes before she straightened her shoulders and nodded. He couldn't stop now —he only hoped this first time wouldn't be too painful for her.

He rose just enough to pull his trousers and smallclothes down before sitting back on the bed, enjoying the way she gripped his shoulders so he wouldn't unseat her. When he brought her womanhood against his bare erection, they moaned in unison.

He forced himself to slow down and enjoy the feel of her slick heat against him.

"I had no idea this would feel so good."

And with those words his hard-won control snapped. He gripped her hips and lifted her so the blunt edge of his manhood pressed against her opening.

"You need to take control," he managed to grind out.

Her eyes widened, but whatever reservations she'd had were clearly gone. "I don't know how."

He closed his eyes, struggling not to move. "Lower yourself onto me."

When she took her lower lip between her teeth, he hissed out a breath. Brow furled, she started to drop over him. Fortunately, her climax had prepared her body to accept him. After an initial moment of hesitation, she bore down on him and he slid in easily. She stiffened and lowered her head onto his shoulder, and he forced himself not to move.

He trailed his hands up and down her back. "All will be well now. The most difficult part is behind you."

"You're so big," she said, and he groaned.

"When you think you're ready, rise and then lower yourself onto me again."

She was still for what felt like an eternity before tentatively lifting herself. He was half afraid she would slide off him completely, but then she reversed and sank onto him. Her breath shuddered out, and he could tell she was surprised that this time there was no pain.

He helped her then, guiding her movements with his hands on her hips while he captured her little sounds of pleasure with his mouth.

He wasn't going to last long. He pressed a thumb against her, right above where they were joined, and she whimpered. Her movements were almost frantic now, mirroring his own desperation as they both reached for that peak. He reached it first and brought her hard against him. Harder than he'd intended. When she cried out, he feared he'd hurt her, but the telltale shudder of her body as she tightened around him told him otherwise.

He struggled to catch his breath, his relief profound that she had been with him the whole time. He fell onto his back and she followed, draping herself over him.

They lay like that, their bodies still entwined, for several minutes. When he felt himself begin to harden again, he knew he had to return to his own bedroom. Sarah would be too sore to enjoy a second round of lovemaking, and he didn't trust himself not to press the issue.

Sarah had already fallen asleep, so he shifted slowly, careful not to wake her as he rolled her away from him. Every part of him screamed in protest when he stood, covered her with the blankets, and returned to his room and his cold bed.

CHAPTER 6

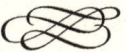

SARAH WOULD HAVE THOUGHT it impossible that a man she barely knew, and for whom she had no romantic feelings, could bring her pleasure in the marriage bed. Yet that is exactly what had happened and she was at a loss to understand why.

After the intimacies they'd shared, she wasn't sure she'd be able to face James in the morning. She'd been told that her husband would take the lead in consummating their marriage and had thought all she'd have to do was lie back, endure, and pray it would soon be over. She should have realized James Hathaway wouldn't be content to behave in the expected manner. He had actually allowed her to take charge, and in the heat of passion, she'd done so with great enthusiasm.

He'd unbalanced her so thoroughly that she'd woken several times during the night from heated dreams of James making love to her over and over. So intense were those dreams that she could almost feel the weight of his hands on her. She'd been disappointed when he left her and chided herself for that sentimentality. Had she expected him to stay the whole night? There was a reason, after all, that married couples kept separate bedrooms.

She had to live now with the knowledge that her husband had firmly taken the upper hand in their marriage. She might have been innocent before marrying James Hathaway, but she wasn't a fool. It was obvious he was very experienced. She was woefully out of her depth and couldn't hope to have the same hold over her husband that he had gained over her.

It took her longer than normal to dress before venturing downstairs for breakfast, but her nerves instantly calmed when she learned that James had already eaten and gone out to meet with the builders for the new stables he was having constructed. She hated the fact that she was behaving like a coward, but she desperately needed time away from her husband if she hoped to maintain her composure in his presence.

She ate quickly, deciding she would get to know her husband's family that day. She'd been completely over-whelmed on the day of her wedding, most of her thoughts centering on how she would survive what she'd thought would be the ordeal of her wedding night. She'd concentrated mainly on smiling, trying to appear the happy bride, and hadn't spoken to James's mother or sister beyond their formal intro-ductions. That would change today since his family was now hers.

After breakfast, she penned a note informing them that she planned to visit and arranged for a footman to deliver it. It was already midmorning, but she wanted to wait for a reply before descending on them. Perhaps one day they'd grow close enough that such formalities wouldn't be required, but until that happened she didn't want to presume on the relationship.

It was a cool morning, so she donned a cloak and sturdy walking shoes before venturing outside to explore the gardens as she waited for the footman to return. They were, of course, as formal and rigid in design as the former viscount. From what she knew of the viscount's widow, she seemed very friendly, so Sarah could only imagine that she hadn't been given leave to show any of her personality in either the house's furnishings or the garden.

As she walked amid the immaculately trimmed hedges, she wondered if she'd be allowed to make any changes. Excitement filled her at the thought. Perhaps James would allow her to curb some of the excesses in the house. The furnishings were unquestionably beautiful, but the formality of the decor made it difficult to feel truly at home.

She was mentally redesigning the drawing room—starting with the removal of the impractical gold settee that seemed designed to be admired rather than used—when the footman returned. Instead of the note she'd expected, the footman informed her that James's mother would be happy to receive her at any time.

The dower house was only a mile from the manor, a distance she covered quickly on foot. Upon arriving, Sarah was ushered inside and shown into the drawing room where James's mother and sister were already waiting for her.

She could see immediately why her new mother-in-law preferred to live here rather than stay at the manor house with her son. The house was considerably smaller, but what it lacked in size, it made up for in warmth. Instead of delicate, ornate chairs that looked as though they would collapse under a person's weight, the furniture was made from deep mahogany and upholstered in rich green fabric. And the walls —she'd only seen the entryway and the drawing room, but there was actual color on the walls. Whereas the manor was furnished to impress visitors with the owner's wealth, this house was designed to be welcoming and warm. Given the choice, Sarah thought she'd prefer to live here as well.

James's mother was a petite woman, and it was difficult to believe that her husband had come from such a small person. Given his height and the breadth of his shoulders, she imagined that he took after his father in appearance. Mrs. Hathaway—who asked that Sarah not refer to her as "my lady" or "Lady Hathaway" as it made her uncomfortable, having only earned the title when her son inherited—couldn't be older than fifty. Gray streaked her dark hair, but she was still a beautiful woman. That beauty was reflected in her daughter, Emily.

Mrs. Hathaway was a quiet woman, but Sarah's sister-in-law more than made up for her mother's reserve.

"I'm so happy you decided to visit," Emily said, linking her arm through Sarah's and leading her to the overstuffed settee. "I wanted to visit, but Mama said it was too soon. That you and James needed time alone together."

Sarah's thoughts immediately went to the things she and her husband had done the previous evening, and she felt the telltale heat of embarrassment color her cheeks. A quick glance at Mrs. Hathaway, who was attempting to hide her amusement, was sufficient to tell her that James's mother knew exactly what she was thinking.

"I've always wanted a sister," Emily said, oblivious to the knowing look that had passed between the two other women. "It's dreadfully dull having two older brothers. Though, with Edward gone, I will admit that I miss him. At least we still have James… and it was so kind of you to allow us to live here. I'd hoped to stay in the main house—it's very grand, is it not? —but Mama wanted to stay here. Not that I don't like this house. It's very pretty too."

Sarah stared at Emily, amused and charmed by her enthusiasm. "Goodness, I can see now why James is a man of few words. After you were born, he probably rarely had the opportunity to speak!"

As soon as the words were out, she feared Emily would take them the wrong way, but the young woman's breathless laugh told her she was not so easily offended.

Mrs. Hathaway took advantage of the break in Emily's chatter to speak. "Perhaps you should give Sarah the opportunity to tell us why she is here."

Emily waved an impatient hand. "Sarah is family now. We needn't stand on ceremony with her."

It was clear to Sarah that James's mother was not yet comfortable in her presence, but the woman couldn't find a way to repeat her rebuke without appearing impolite.

Sarah rushed to reassure her. "James is overlooking the plans for the construction of the new stables, so I thought today would be a good time for us to become better acquainted." She turned then to face Emily. "You already know I only have one brother, and I, too, have always longed for a sister. I think we will get on quite well. I suspect you wouldn't have it any other way," she said with her own laugh.

"See, Mama? I told you that James had chosen well."

Mrs. Hathaway shook her head in defeat, but the relaxed slope of her shoulders told Sarah that her words had put the woman at ease.

As they exchanged pleasantries, Sarah found it almost impossible to keep up with Emily's effusiveness, and she was happy to find that her original hope was proving to be true. Despite the fact that Emily was only sixteen—six years younger than Sarah—it was already clear to her that they would become close. It was impossible not to be captivated by Emily's guileless charm. Mrs. Hathaway, on the other hand, was harder to draw out, but her initial reticence at the beginning of Sarah's visit seemed to have disappeared.

The soft chime of the clock over the mantel told her that almost an hour had passed. Content with the way the morning had gone, she stood to take her leave, but not before inviting James's mother and sister to join them for dinner that evening.

Emily's eyes lit up at the invitation, and she turned to her mother. "Can we go? Sarah wouldn't have invited us if she felt we'd be an imposition."

Mrs. Hathaway turned her eyes skyward for a second before letting out a soft sigh. When she met Sarah's gaze, however, it was amusement Sarah saw in her eyes.

"Thank you. As Emily has made clear, we would love to join you."

Emily must have been afraid that any further show of eagerness on her part might cause her mother to change her mind, for she said nothing more about the invitation, but Sarah could see her enthusiasm bubbling just below the surface. Her new sister-in-law might be able to hold still when the need arose, but she couldn't disguise the excitement dancing in her eyes.

Sarah was smiling when she left the dower house. She liked James's family very much, and it was clear that she was already beginning to like her husband as well. Perhaps too much. He still overwhelmed her, but he'd been nothing but kind to her so far. How was it possible that he was so much larger-than-life when his family was so down-to-earth?

She was starting to question whether she'd be able to keep her emotions from becoming involved with respect to her new husband, and that thought scared her to death.

CHAPTER 7

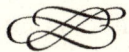

December 1812

$\mathcal{W}$ ITH THE ASSISTANCE of the efficient Mrs. Phillips, Sarah acquainted herself with the running of Hathaway Park over the next few weeks. She still lost her way on occasion when she decided to venture into an unfamiliar part of the house, but those instances were finally occurring less frequently.

All too soon it was mid-December. Every year as Christmas approached, the Vaughans hosted a party. Some years, when the snow was heavy, only the families that lived closest to their estate attended. The Mapletons were included in that group. But since they'd yet to see any snow that year, Sarah knew that every family within a few hours' drive would be present.

As much as she'd wanted to, Sarah didn't protest when James mentioned receiving their invitation. As the new

Viscount Hathaway, it was important that he become further acquainted with the families in the area, many of whom he hadn't seen since the wedding day. She only hoped she'd be able to avoid Robert Vaughan, the man she'd once thought she would marry.

The carriage ride took just over an hour, but that hour flew by thanks to Emily's excited chatter. Since her sister-in-law wouldn't be out for another two years, this would be the largest social event Emily had ever attended. Her enthusiasm helped ease the dread Sarah felt about the evening ahead.

Even James's normally reserved mother seemed to be looking forward to the evening. Her husband's demeanor, on the other hand, could only be described as stoic. He hadn't said as much to her, but she suspected he wasn't yet comfortable with his new title.

A small part of her wondered if some of his unease stemmed from the knowledge that she'd once had an understanding with Robert. But if James had learned of their former courtship, he hadn't mentioned it to her.

As the carriage drew nearer to the Vaughans' estate, Sarah couldn't stop thinking about the Christmas party the previous year, when she'd expected that this year she and Robert would either be betrothed or already married. She expected that memory to cause her pain. Instead, she was surprised to find that her grief at having lost the man she loved and being forced to marry someone she barely knew was no longer as acute as it had once been. She could only attribute that to her new husband. She didn't love James—after Robert's casual dismissal of her feelings, she would never again give a man that much power to hurt her—but she appreciated the fact that he went out of his way to ensure she would have no cause to fear him.

In fact, the opposite was true. She never would have thought it possible, but she found herself looking forward to their nightly lovemaking sessions. Her thoughts drifted to the previous night and, without realizing it, her eyes came to rest on James, who was seated opposite her.

He met her gaze, and she could tell he was either remembering last night as well or thinking about what would happen later in the evening. Her stomach dipped at the fire in his eyes, and a corresponding heat began to spread through her. They stared at each other for several long moments before she tore her gaze away. A quick glance at their companions assured her they hadn't noticed that James had the power to fluster her with merely a look.

The moon was out and the night clear, so she turned to stare at the bleak scenery outside the carriage window, thinking about how pretty it would look when the snow began to fall. She murmured responses to Emily's inquiries when they were required as she struggled to maintain her composure.

It was impossible to keep her thoughts from centering on the first month of her marriage. James had visited her every night, initiating her into a world of pleasure she'd never expected to experience with him. He was always gentle with her, ensuring she found pleasure before he returned to his own bedroom. But she suspected that he was holding back.

Their marriage was still so new and her husband still an unknown quantity. He was so big, so overwhelming. The fact that he seemed to hold himself so tightly leashed made her anxious about the day he finally lost that control. She'd seen all too well how her own father could change from one moment to the next, especially when he'd been drinking. The slightest transgression could change him from the kind country squire most people thought him to be to a man filled with rage and bitterness. He never physically hurt them, something for which her mother informed her and George that they should all be grateful, but that didn't change the fact that his words could cut as deep as a knife.

Much as she wanted to believe that her own marriage was vastly different from that of her parents, she went through her days feeling as though she were in limbo. On the surface, things were pleasant and certainly more than she could have hoped for, especially after her own dashed hopes with respect to Robert. But her husband was being far too circumspect in his treatment of her. She couldn't shake the feeling that the emotions bubbling beneath the surface would one day break free. She only hoped that when they did, they would be the gentle popping of bubbles reaching the surface when a kettle began to simmer and not the violent explosions that burst forth during a full boil.

Until that happened, she could only take comfort in witnessing how he treated his family. She'd watched James with his mother and sister, when he didn't have that air of caution that was so evident when he interacted with her, and she had yet to see any evidence of a temper. But she also hadn't seen him when he was in his cups. Would his personality change then, like her father's did?

While her feelings toward her husband were conflicted, the same couldn't be said about her relationship with his mother and sister. After her initial wariness, Mrs. Hathaway had warmed to her, no longer seeming to fear that she would say something wrong or make a blunder. And Emily… in the short time Sarah had known her, Emily had become like a sister.

Since James was occupied with overseeing the planned expansion to the stables—hoping to make considerable progress before it got too cold or began to snow—and becoming acquainted with the running of an estate as large as the one he'd inherited, she was left to her own devices most days. Meeting with the housekeeper to go over the meals and the running of the household didn't take that much time out of her day. Sarah loved to draw, spending hours working on pencil sketches and watercolors. And Emily had taken to visiting her almost daily, but she only stayed for dinner twice a week on the evenings when her mother joined them.

When their carriage pulled to a stop before the Vaughan estate, James didn't wait for a footman to open the door. He leaped down from the carriage and turned, holding out a hand to assist the others.

She couldn't avoid the knowing look in his eyes when she placed her hand in his. The way his eyes traveled over her figure caused heat to rise in her cheeks again. She was wearing a cloak, but she knew him well enough to know he was already envisioning divesting her of the gown she wore beneath it.

"Behave," she whispered. She needn't have wasted her breath, for instead of being chastised, he lifted the corner of his mouth in a knowing smile that made her insides tingle before he released her hand and turned to assist his mother and sister.

While no longer painful, entering the house she knew almost as well as the one in which she'd been raised—and which she'd expected to one day become her home—made her more than a little uncomfortable. Her family and the Vaughans had once been very close, and she couldn't remember a time when she hadn't known Robert. But after he'd told her that her father was too steeped in debt to make a marriage between them possible, she'd never expected to cross this house's threshold again.

She held her breath as she did so now, taking comfort from James's solid presence at her side. She must have squeezed his arm because he looked down at her, one brow raised in question.

Before she could manufacture an excuse for her nerves, Emily claimed his other arm. "I'm so excited," she said with a smile that fairly beamed. Sarah wouldn't have been surprised if her sister-in-law started bouncing on her toes.

"The house looks lovely," Sarah said, acutely aware that James was watching her closely. And it did. As always, the Vaughans had spared no detail in decorating the house for the holiday.

While the butler took their outer garments, enlisting the aid of a footman, she took in the familiar home. Greenery spilled from containers that lined the entrance, and boughs were wrapped around the stair rail. Sarah didn't miss the mistletoe that hung from the doorways.

"Is that… It is, isn't it? That's mistletoe," Emily exclaimed, gazing up at the archway they were about to pass under.

Sarah could have kissed her sister-in-law at that moment, for her exclamation was enough to draw her husband's attention away from her.

"If anyone even contemplates kissing you, they'll live to

regret it." James's tone was light, but Sarah could tell he spoke in earnest.

Emily frowned at her brother. "Who would I want to kiss? I don't even know anyone." She turned to look at Sarah. "How well do you know the Vaughans? Am I correct that your parents don't live far from here? You must know them well."

And there it was, out in the open—the question she'd been hoping to avoid. "My parents are friends with Mr. and Mrs. Vaughan. We've been coming to their Christmas party for as long as I can remember." She didn't dare meet James's eyes as she replied. He was far too perceptive, and she feared he'd sense that she wasn't being entirely truthful.

They passed under the archway, following the butler to the small ballroom at the back of the house. It was a modest-sized room, but Sarah knew how proud Mrs. Vaughan was that their house was large enough to have a ballroom. Sarah's parents couldn't boast as much despite the fact that her father was a baronet.

When the butler announced their arrival, every eye in the room turned their way. The room was full to overflowing. She couldn't remember there ever being so many guests in previous years and realized most of the partygoers must be here to see the new viscount and viscountess.

She shook off her slight unease at being the center of so much attention as they greeted Mr. and Mrs. Vaughan. Robert was there as well. Fortunately, he was off to one side, speaking to one of their neighbors. It was bad enough having to see him at all, but she wouldn't have been able to bear having to greet him under the watchful eyes of his parents.

"We're honored that you chose to attend," Mrs. Vaughan

said. "Your uncle never had time... I'm sure he was very busy."

Sarah glanced at her husband, wondering what he was thinking as he murmured a few words in greeting and turned the subject to the unseasonably warm weather. Everyone knew that his uncle had thought himself above everyone there.

Mrs. Vaughan turned to her next. "We are so pleased to see you again, Sarah. It was a pleasant surprise to receive the invitation to your wedding."

Sarah smiled, hoping that her unease wasn't evident. "I'm glad you and Mr. Vaughan were able to attend."

The fact that she hadn't mentioned Robert didn't go unnoticed. The look of compassion on Mrs. Vaughan's face almost killed her, and she had a frantic moment of worry that her husband would realize the other woman was trying to communicate her sympathy. She might not love James, but she did respect him, and she wouldn't allow anyone to disparage him. Not like she had on their wedding day when he'd overheard one of her cousins extending sympathy on her marriage.

She was prevented from responding when the butler announced another arrival and James drew them away. Her husband was almost immediately swept away by a group of men eager for the opportunity to befriend the new Viscount Hathaway.

As she watched James walk away, she couldn't help but compare him to Robert, struck anew by their differences. James was tall, broad across the chest and shoulders and dark haired, while Robert was the complete opposite in nearly every way. The only thing they had in common was their height, but James was still a few inches taller.

Robert was more like the old viscount in appearance—fair-haired and slim. She'd once thought him the most handsome man of her acquaintance, but somehow his appeal had dimmed. When she looked at him now, the yearning she'd expected to feel was absent. She could only attribute it to the fact that her eyes had been opened as to his selfishness in the most blunt manner possible when he'd casually dismissed her feelings for him because of her lack of fortune.

She refused to believe there was another reason for her lack of emotion toward the man she'd once expected to wed.

Sarah introduced Emily and Mrs. Hathaway to several of their neighbors. Emily was in her element, unable to hide her enthusiasm at attending her first ball, and Mrs. Hathaway seemed to overcome her shyness with every person who greeted her warmly. But Sarah didn't miss the way her mother-in-law frowned whenever she happened to glance at their hostess, confirming that she had caught the other woman's slight toward James.

THE MOMENT HE ENTERED the ballroom, awareness that he didn't belong settled over James. He didn't look like a typical gentleman, being both taller and broader than any other man in attendance. He could hide his work-roughened hands inside the gloves he wore, but could do nothing to conceal the fact that he'd spent countless hours toiling under the sun.

The awareness that everyone was sneaking glances at him, judging him, reminded him, yet again, that his uncle had thought him unworthy of inheriting his title. James did his best to push those negative thoughts to the back of his mind where they usually resided, but as he was discovering more and more lately, those doubts about his suitability were no longer content to remain buried.

It didn't help that the Vaughans and many of the other guests seemed to be going out of their way to impress him. He wasn't sure what they expected from him. He couldn't tell if they believed that he thought himself better than them. Certainly his uncle had held that belief, and from everything James had learned, the former viscount had rarely interacted with his neighbors. Or perhaps they saw through his facade, seeing him for the ordinary man he was, and were waiting for him to embarrass himself.

Whatever the case, he couldn't shake the sensation that he was on display. It certainly wouldn't be an exaggeration to say that every man present had approached him and attempted to monopolize his time.

The dull throbbing of his jaw made him aware that he was clenching his teeth, and he had to force himself yet again to relax. He wanted nothing more than to walk away from the incredibly dull duo that was bragging about improvements they'd recently made to their respective estates, each one trying to outdo the other by going on about how much money they had spent. He tried to feign interest even as he became aware that the small group of musicians playing in one corner of the room was coming to the end of yet another set. He'd made it a point to see if Sarah was dancing, but so far she'd remained by his mother's and sister's side. He'd hoped to dance with her that evening, to show her that she hadn't married someone who was completely without manners.

When the dinner bell rang, he made good his escape. He inclined his head to the two men and turned to the right, where he'd last seen Sarah. But before he could start toward her, Mrs. Vaughan commanded his attention. It took him a moment to realize that as the highest-ranked guest present, he would be seated next to her during dinner. That was just another of the annoyances that came with inheriting his title— he could no longer choose who he sat next to at dinner.

Instead of the curse that sprang to his lips, he greeted the older woman with a smile and offered her his arm. Again, he chafed under the realization that many of the guests were watching them as they made their way from the room.

When everyone was finally settled around the long dining table, he wasn't surprised to see that his wife was seated at the far end of the table, next to their host. Annoyance flared, however, when he saw that Robert Vaughan sat on her other side.

He found it almost impossible to keep his attention from drifting to the pair and was only half listening to what their hostess was saying. But finally her words penetrated his preoc-cupation.

"They make such a lovely pair, don't you agree?" He glanced at Mrs. Vaughan then and saw that she, too, was looking at Sarah and her son. "We were so disappointed that things didn't work out between them. Between you and me, I'm afraid that Robert broke Sarah's heart."

Her voice faltered when he swung his gaze back to the older woman, incredulity mixing with more than a hint of anger. Surely she didn't think it polite dinner conversation to tell someone that their wife was in love with another man.

"But of course," she rushed to add, "everything worked out in your favor."

He couldn't tell if she was referring to her son's thwarted relationship with Sarah or if she also included how much James had gained after his uncle's death. In the end, it didn't matter. He decided then and there that his uncle had the right idea in avoiding his neighbors. He wouldn't go so far as to ignore everyone, but he couldn't foresee a time when he would cross over the Vaughans' threshold again.

For now he chose to remain and act as though he wasn't the brute many no doubt thought him to be. While he wanted nothing more than to drag Sarah away from the slim young man who seemed intent on capturing his wife's attention, he wouldn't embarrass her by making a spectacle of himself.

But that didn't mean his temper wasn't boiling beneath the surface. He took a small measure of satisfaction in turning away from their hostess, focusing his attention on the older woman seated at his other side. Mrs. Vaughan's soft sound of distress when he continued to ignore her soothed his pride only a tiny fraction because he couldn't turn a blind eye to what was happening at the other end of the table.

The younger Vaughan made a great deal of effort at first to engage Sarah in conversation, but his wife demurred and seemed to concentrate on her food. James couldn't tell if she was trying to dissuade Vaughan from conversation or attempting to be coy.

James had just managed to convince himself that his wife didn't want the other man's attention when he saw her eyes narrow at the way Robert was speaking to Emily, who was seated next to them. Sarah continued to watch Robert carefully as he spoke to her sister-in-law, and James almost snapped the stem of the glass he raised to his lips.

He realized that he didn't know his wife very well… aside from the fact that she'd been vehemently against marrying him of course. It was true that she came alive in his arms at night, but their relationship outside the bedroom could only be considered cordial at best. Jealousy churned in his gut as he was presented with the very real possibility that his wife was still in love with another man.

CHAPTER 8

SUPPER HAD BEEN more uncomfortable than she'd feared. Sarah couldn't imagine what Robert's mother had been thinking to seat them together. He'd been charming and courteous to both her and Emily, which had made her more than a little uncomfortable. She was grateful, however, that Robert had acted as though they were merely acquaintances, treating her no differently than he did Emily.

But every time she'd spotted James looking their way, she couldn't help but feel a twinge of guilt. Guilt for doing nothing more than attempting to enjoy her meal. She hadn't been able to eat more than a few bites of every course. Mrs. Vaughan had outdone herself with the sheer amount of food they'd served, and it had all been delicious. But at some point near the start of the meal, she'd become aware of the fact that James was angry. She'd spent the remainder of the meal with her stomach in knots.

Now, standing at the side of the ballroom again with Mrs. Hathaway, she cringed as Robert approached. She sent up a silent prayer that he wouldn't invite her to dance.

He stopped before them and executed a deep bow. It took everything in her power not to roll her eyes when he straightened and smiled at them. It was always thus, though it had never bothered her before now. Robert was so used to everyone thinking the sun rose and set on his shoulders that he took it as his due that he had merely to smile at someone and they would fall at his feet.

He turned to Mrs. Hathaway, making a remark about the weather and asking her if she was enjoying the evening. In truth, Sarah was barely paying attention to him. Her eyes followed her husband as a group of men that included her father drew him away from the room. She knew her parent well, and since the Vaughans normally set up a card room, she imagined they'd enticed him to join them in a game.

She wasn't worried about James. From everything she'd learned, he could well afford to play and not worry about going into debt. And truthfully, from the successful horse-breeding business he'd run before inheriting, she imagined he was good with money and would never wager more than he could afford to lose.

Her father, however, was another matter. He'd already been on the verge of losing everything before bartering away her hand in marriage. Was he hoping that James would continue to finance his penchant for wagering money he didn't have?

She knew James had paid all her father's gambling debts

and that he hadn't cared that she'd come to the marriage with no dowry. She hadn't seen the actual marriage contract, however. How much money had James given her father? And how much more would he continue to give him?

She struggled with the unease that settled in the pit of her stomach. In truth, it wasn't just the money that concerned her. Her father always drank liberally when he played, and if he lost, it would put him in a foul mood. A mood that would have him heaping verbal abuse on her mother all the way home.

Robert caught her attention again when he said, "I know your daughter isn't out yet. This is just a small Christmas celebration, not even a country ball really. But I couldn't help being charmed by Miss Hathaway's enthusiasm over supper. I thought she might like to join me for the next dance."

"Emily is only sixteen," Sarah said.

Robert's smile remained in place as he glanced at her before turning his attention back to Mrs. Hathaway, but she hadn't missed the way his jaw tightened. *Good, let him be annoyed*, she thought.

Emily turned a look of pleading on her mother.

"I don't see the harm," Mrs. Hathaway said with a smile.

Sarah could only look at her in surprise. No harm? James would be angry. He was no longer in the room, however. Perhaps he wouldn't learn of Emily's dance with Robert. Almost as soon as that thought occurred to her, Sarah realized that Emily wouldn't be able to stop talking about her first dance. James would definitely find out about it.

Despite her misgivings, she said not a word as Robert smiled down at Emily and held out his arm. Emily didn't hesitate to take it, and Sarah was struck by just how pretty her sister-in-law looked tonight. Her stomach tightened further when Robert had the temerity to wink at her before leading Emily out.

"James won't be happy," Sarah said when the pair was no longer within hearing range. She wished he were here now to put a stop to what was happening. In that moment, she realized that she was also disappointed her husband hadn't stayed in the ballroom and asked her to dance.

Mrs. Hathaway made a small noise of impatience. "James is far too protective. Emily isn't the only girl not yet out who is dancing."

Her mother-in-law was correct of course. In fact, it didn't seem all that long ago when Sarah used to look forward to the Vaughans' annual Christmas gathering for just that reason.

The opening strains of a quadrille began to play, and she watched as Robert bowed to his partner. Emily's smile widened as she curtsied, and it occurred to Sarah to wonder just how large Emily's dowry would be. Worse, she realized Robert might be hoping to ensnare the girl's interest since it was almost certain Emily would come to her future marriage with a sizable settlement.

Her mother approached them then, and while Sarah managed to keep track of the conversation between her mother and Mrs. Hathaway, her gaze kept drifting back to Emily and Robert. The young woman moved with a grace that shouldn't have surprised Sarah. It might have been Emily's first ball, but it was clear she had practiced her dancing. What concerned Sarah most about their dance, however, was the way Emily was looking at Robert. She feared that James's sister was in danger of developing feelings for him.

"Sarah, you're distracted," her mother said, peering around Mrs. Hathaway to see what her daughter was looking at. When she spied Robert and Emily, she released a soft "Oh dear."

Mrs. Hathaway frowned. "What is the matter? I know Emily is still too young for a proper ball, but since we are informal here and there are others her age dancing, I didn't see the harm in allowing her the liberty."

Her mother looked at her, and Sarah gave a small shake of her head. The very last thing she needed was to have her mother discussing her past *disappointment*—how she hated that word—with James's mother.

"It is nothing. I was merely curious. Is there..." Her mother hesitated, and Sarah braced herself, unsure if her mother would reveal her past connection to Robert. "Is there something more between Emily and Robert?"

Mrs. Hathaway's brows lifted at the question. "Of course not. Why would you think there was?"

"No reason," her mother said before glancing over the other woman's shoulder. "Oh, I see Mrs. Henderson. If you'll excuse me, I must speak to her."

After watching Sarah's mother scurry away, Mrs. Hathaway turned to her. "Is there something I should know?"

Sarah waged an inner debate and, in the end, decided that she couldn't lie to the woman. But that didn't mean she'd tell her the entire truth. She certainly wouldn't tell her that Robert had broken her heart. "At one time, people thought that

Robert and I would make a match. But of course that never happened."

She'd meant to keep her words light, but the other woman must have detected the hint of anger she'd been unable to disguise.

"I see," she said simply.

If she wanted to know more, she was too polite to ask, something for which Sarah was more than a little grateful. The last thing she wanted to discuss with her current mother-in-law was her former feelings for Robert Vaughan. Fortunately, she didn't have to search for a way to change the subject. Her husband's attendance was the most exciting thing to happen at the Vaughans' Christmas ball in years, and that meant the company of his wife and mother would be sought out by all their neighbors.

When the current set came to an end and the pair she'd been unable to keep herself from watching returned, Emily's cheeks were flushed in a most becoming fashion. She kept glancing up at Robert with something akin to rapt adoration on her face. The way he looked down at Emily left Sarah with no doubt that he was doing everything in his power to encourage that feeling. It took a great deal of effort on Sarah's part to keep from frowning.

Instead of excusing himself, Robert stayed with their group, engaging her companions in light banter. With each passing minute, Sarah realized that her suspicions about his intentions toward Emily hadn't been an overreaction on her part.

"I'm quite thirsty," Sarah said when she couldn't stand it

any longer. She had to put an end to Robert's schemes. "Would you mind fetching a drink for me?"

Robert hesitated only a moment, but after meeting her gaze, he excused himself with the promise that he'd return shortly. They'd done that in past years when they'd wanted to spend some time together, inventing an excuse to meet for a few minutes of privacy. She watched his progress, and when she saw him slip from the ballroom, she knew he'd understood her intent.

The last thing she wanted was another secret meeting with him, but it couldn't be helped. She had to speak to him in private, convince him to turn his attention elsewhere. Emily was still two years away from coming out, and she could say with certainty that her husband wouldn't welcome any advances from potential suitors until that time.

She made a vague excuse to Emily and Mrs. Hathaway, whose attention had already been ensnared by another of their eager neighbors. As she slipped from the room, it only then occurred to her that it was possible Robert had misconstrued her intention. She quickly shook off that thought. Even if she were the kind of woman to betray her husband, Robert knew her well enough to realize that her pride would never allow her to make a fool of herself over any man. Especially not one who had so little regard for her feelings.

She moved past two rooms, grateful that she didn't have to pass the card room on her way to the library. Relief swept through her when she reached her destination without encountering anyone. She slipped into the room and closed the door behind her.

The lighting in the library was much dimmer than it had

been during their meetings in past years, a solitary lamp on a low table providing the only illumination. She realized in that moment that Robert had made a point to prepare the room ahead of time for one of their Christmas interludes. Clearly, he was hoping that tonight they would go much further than whispered words and a few kisses.

She turned when he moved out of the shadows to her right.

"This is a pleasant surprise," he said, his smile smug as he moved far too close for her comfort.

She took a step back and his smile faltered.

"I'm here only because I need to speak to you."

His easy smile returned, and she found herself wanting to wipe it from his face. She licked her lips as she tried to think about how best to approach the subject without coming out and accusing him of being a fortune hunter.

"I need to speak to you about Emily. She is still very young and impressionable."

"She's not any younger than you and I were when we first kissed."

She winced at the reminder. "And look at how well that ended."

He didn't try to hide his amusement. "I understand your disappointment. And I must say, I find your display of jealousy heartening."

"I'm not jealous," she said immediately. It was the truth— her only concern was for Emily—but she could tell he didn't believe her. She shrugged off her annoyance. After all, it didn't really matter what he believed. All that mattered was that he not take advantage of James's sister. "Just promise me that you won't encourage Emily. I don't want to see her hurt."

His mouth turned down at that, his eyes narrowing. "That's hardly fair, Sarah. You know very well I couldn't marry you when I learned your family was on the brink of financial ruin. But you've done very well for yourself. I don't understand why you'd deny me the same opportunity."

"This isn't about me or what happened between us in the past. My only motivation in speaking to you now is to ensure that you don't hurt Emily."

He continued on as though she hadn't spoken. "I regret that we couldn't wed. I hate the idea of that brute you married laying his hands on you. But that doesn't mean we can't still enjoy ourselves."

Her anger at the disparaging remark Robert made about her husband was quickly replaced by shock when she realized what he was saying. He didn't know her as well as she'd thought if he expected her to forgive him and agree to having an affair.

"I'm not here to talk about us. Not that there is anything between us anymore."

His smile could only be described as a smirk. "There could be. Don't pretend to be surprised. I always thought we were meant to be together. It's a pity your family's circumstances kept us apart, but you should know that my feelings for you remain unchanged."

Annoyance threatened to rob her of speech. "You made your feelings perfectly clear when you spurned me."

He made a soft tsking sound. "Still so bitter? I imagine your disappointment must have been great, especially when your parents forced you to wed that beast." His lips twisted in derision before he continued. "Oh yes, I know you very well, Sarah. How could I not? We've been friends for as long as I can remember. I could tell you wanted nothing more on your wedding day than to escape."

"Is that why you attended the breakfast? To make sure I was miserable without you?"

He shrugged. "You can hardly blame me for being curious about your new husband. But we both know you'll never care for him the same way you do for me."

Her stomach turned at Robert's overweening conceit. How had she never noticed his selfishness before now? And more importantly, how could she have imagined herself in love with him? She couldn't fathom that he expected her to believe he cared for her, not when it was evident that the only person he really cared about was himself.

She realized that he'd done her a great favor when he'd ended their courtship. She also recognized that this conversation was pointless. Robert Vaughan lived in his own world, one where he believed every member of the fairer sex would count themselves fortunate to receive even the smallest crumb of attention from him.

And, as always, he would do whatever he wanted. She'd just have to be vigilant about ensuring that Emily wasn't ensnared by him.

He moved so quickly she didn't realize his intentions until he'd pulled her into his arms. When his lips touched hers, anger galvanized her into action and she pushed him away.

"Don't say anything right now," he said, his hand against her mouth. She wanted to bite his fingers, but he pulled his hand away as soon as the thought entered her mind. "We'll speak again later."

Stunned into silence at his presumption, she could only stare after him as he sauntered from the room.

JAMES FINALLY MANAGED to extricate himself from the card room where his father-in-law had demonstrated that he lacked any skill at all in playing cards. He also lacked the control to keep from playing and losing money everyone knew he didn't have. He'd have to do something about that, but later. Right now he was intent on finding Sarah and inviting her to dance with him.

He stood just inside the ballroom doors, his eyes scanning the guests, but couldn't find her. She wasn't with his mother and sister, nor was she dancing.

He headed back into the hallway, wondering if the Vaughans had opened another room for their guests' entertainment. He had just moved past a closed door when it swung open.

He turned in time to see Robert Vaughan exit the room, a satisfied air about him. Something about his expression and the fact that his wife was nowhere to be found set his senses on high alert. He couldn't stop replaying Mrs. Vaughan's voice over in his mind when she'd mentioned their past.

He took a step backward into the shadow of another doorway, waiting until Vaughan returned to the ballroom before making his way to the room the man had exited. With each step, he tried to convince himself that he was seeing betrayal where none existed.

The door was still open and he saw her before she noticed him. She was sitting in an armchair, looking down at her hands and breathing deeply. Trying to steady her breathing, he realized.

He stepped into the room and closed the door behind him. Sarah's gaze flew to his as she stood.

"What is the matter? You seem upset. Has something happened?"

Anger surged as he realized she was trying to play him for a fool. "I'd say discovering that my wife is having a secret assignation with a former lover qualifies me to be angry."

She stiffened at his words. "Robert and I were not lovers— you know that for a fact."

Hearing her use the other man's Christian name was like adding tinder to a flame. "Tell me, Sarah. Would that still be the case after tonight? Or perhaps you were merely making arrangements for a future encounter?"

Her chin tilted upward in defiance. "If you're worried about your heir, you needn't be. I know my duty, and I'll make sure I am with child before I look elsewhere."

Her cheeks were red, her fists clenched at her side. He couldn't tell if she was upset he'd caught her out or angry at his accusation. His heart ached to believe it was the latter, but she'd never given him any reason to think she cared for him outside the pleasure he could give her in the bedroom. It wasn't inconceivable that she'd seek out that same intimacy with the man she'd once loved. Perhaps still loved.

He turned and locked the door to ensure they wouldn't be

interrupted. Sarah might still love Vaughan, but it was he who brought her to the heights of pleasure. She was his, and he wouldn't share her with anyone.

The sound of the lock clicking into place sounded unnaturally loud in the stillness that had descended after her declaration. He stalked toward his wife, satisfaction filling him when he saw the heat enter her eyes.

Well, at least she was no longer afraid of him.

CHAPTER 9

*W*HAT WAS THE MATTER with her? Why on earth had she suggested that she would look outside her marriage for the intimacies she shared with him? Even if she still had feelings for Robert—and their recent conversation had shown her that those feelings were gone—she would never betray her wedding vows. She might not love James, but she respected him enough to remain faithful.

He'd been more shocked than anything when he'd accused her of arranging a romantic rendezvous with Robert, but now he was angry. The way his body had stiffened when she'd made her ridiculous statement, and the careful, measured steps he took as he stalked toward her, told her that her words had hit their mark. Despite the dim lighting in the room, she could see him clearly.

A part of her recognized that she should be afraid right now. Her stubborn pride had led her to provoke him with the one thing a man would never accept from his wife. But for some reason, she wasn't scared of her husband. Her head might tell her that she was playing with fire and was in grave danger of being burned, but her heart wanted him to deliver the sensual punishment she could see burning brightly in his eyes.

He stopped only inches from her. Her mind was telling her to proceed with caution, but her body was responding to his nearness. As he stared down at her, she found herself struggling to breathe, her nostrils filled with the scent that was uniquely his. Her heart was racing, but it wasn't from fear.

"I don't share, so you can put all thoughts of Vaughan or anyone else from your mind."

His breathing was almost as ragged as hers, the words spoken in a low, but deadly tone. And God help her, she almost swooned.

She couldn't say who moved first... She reached out to grasp his upper arms just as they came around her. His head descended, and when his lips met hers, she made a breathless sound of excitement. Gone was the tentative exploration he normally employed when he kissed her. The movement of his mouth against hers, the way his tongue thrust into her mouth, was dark, urgent. A corresponding desperation swelled within her as she raised her hands to wrap them around his neck and tried to draw him into her very skin. Seeking to tell him with her body what she could never tell him with words—that only he would ever touch her this way.

James turned with her in his arms and moved her backward. She assumed he was going to seat her on the small desk in the corner of the room, remembering how he had once made love to her on her dressing room table. She was surprised, therefore, when her back met a wall. No, not a wall. The door he'd locked.

He raised his head and stared down at her, his eyes almost black. "You're mine." His voice was low, dark. She should have been shocked when he started to lift her skirts, but instead she felt shivery and hot at the same time.

She urged his head back down to hers, and he came willingly. His hands didn't stop their movement, however. He hiked her skirts up to her hips and pressed his arousal against her mound. He was hard and huge, and her hands clutched at his shoulders. She tried to press herself more firmly against him but couldn't get close enough.

She knew he could bring her to fulfillment like this, by rubbing himself against her. It wasn't what she wanted, but she didn't imagine he'd take it further than that.

She was very wrong.

His hands left her hips briefly and she made a small sound of disappointment until she realized he'd shifted away from her to unbutton the fall of his trousers. Her heart was pounding, her body already eager to accept him. She wondered briefly if she was going mad. Surely it wasn't normal to be so desperate for another person that she didn't care that she was in a house filled with other people. The door was locked, and all that mattered to Sarah was getting closer to James. She wanted him inside her... needed him inside her. If he didn't ease the ache building within her, she would surely die.

She brought her mouth to the side of his neck and licked him there, just below his ear where his pulse beat an erratic rhythm. She was rewarded when he shuddered against her.

Her arms moved to wrap around his neck when he lifted

her, and she made a soft sound of confusion when he kept her pressed against the door. She'd expected him to carry her to the desk.

His muscles bunched as he hooked one arm under her bottom and used the other to bring his hardness against her. He was poised at her entrance, the thick head brushing against her wetness, and she almost cried out in frustration when he raised his head to stare down at her.

"Who do you belong to, Sarah?"

He didn't have to ask her twice. She knew he sought her surrender, and she gave it willingly. Eagerly.

"You. Only to you."

He continued to stare down at her for several moments, some nameless emotion shifting behind his eyes. Captivating her. And then he pushed inside her, and she had to bury her head against his shoulder to keep from crying out at the delicious fullness.

He wasn't gentle, but gentleness was the last thing she needed. She needed the reminder that this was what their relationship was all about. She couldn't love her husband—she would never again allow another man to have that much power over her—but she could give him passion.

He thrust into her again and again, and some small part of her mind that wasn't swept away by James's lovemaking was grateful that the door was sturdy, making no sound as he drove into her.

Heat rose quickly, threatening to steal her breath as she raced toward release. When it came, she would have cried out if he hadn't taken her mouth in a kiss that lacked his normal finesse. He was continuing to thrust into her, his movements jerky, and as she rose to another peak, she was surprised that her desire had not been completely fulfilled.

She tore her mouth from his and leaned her forehead against his as he continued the onslaught. "What are you doing to me?" she murmured, her voice unsteady, their breath mingling.

He didn't reply, and her question was forgotten when she felt herself clenching against him again. This time she closed her eyes and pressed her teeth against her bottom lip to keep from crying out. Her breath hitched when he thrust into her one last time and released his seed deep within her.

They stayed like that for some time as their heartbeats slowed and their breathing returned to normal. When he pulled out of her and started putting his clothes back to rights, she almost moaned in disappointment. He handed her a handkerchief without a word. She took it, heat rising in her cheeks as she cleaned herself with quick, economical movements.

When she looked at him again, he was watching her, his arms folded across his massive chest. His expression was impossible to read. Their gazes held for several seconds before he spoke. "Will you be ready to return to the festivities soon?"

It took her a few seconds to realize what he'd just said, so great was her confusion. Surely he didn't expect her to return to the Christmas party after the heated encounter they'd just shared? A quick look down at herself told her that her dress was wrinkled, and she didn't even want to imagine the state of her hair. Everyone would know what had happened between them with just one look. James, however, looked as impeccable as ever.

"I don't think I can face everyone out there."

He scowled. "Everyone or Vaughan?"

This time she didn't allow her temper to goad her into saying something she didn't mean. "Everyone. I smell like you... They'll guess what we've been doing."

The corners of his mouth lifted in unmistakable satisfaction. "We're married, love. I think most people already know what goes on between a husband and a wife."

Normally his flippant attitude would have annoyed her, but his endearment unsettled her.

"Please, James."

He stared at her intently for several seconds before relenting. "I'll arrange to have the carriage brought around and then tell Mother and Emily that we're leaving. The carriage can return for them if they wish to stay a little longer."

She reached for his hand and squeezed it gently before releasing it again. The small gesture didn't change the way she'd jabbed at him, or the fact that they'd just been intimate in someone else's home—the Vaughans', no less—but she didn't miss the way his eyes softened.

"I fear I look a frightful mess. I need to visit the ladies' retiring room, after which I'll wait for you in the entryway."

He brushed the back of his fingers over her cheek, and an unsettling warmth spread through her as he said, "You could never be anything but beautiful."

CHAPTER 10

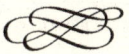

Christmas 1812

$\mathcal{A}$s James reached up to loosen his cravat, he realized he was nervous. Which was absurd, really, but it felt like he had more at stake that morning. He knew he could take his wife to the heights of pleasure physically. He had yet to discover whether he could please her in other ways.

He glanced around the breakfast table, taking in his family. Sarah sat opposite him, his mother and sister on each side. Later that morning, Sarah's parents and her brother would join them. The only person missing was his brother Edward. James had received a letter the week before that the British army had retreated to Portugal for the winter. When he'd received the missive, he'd hoped that it contained news his brother was returning home. He should have known better. Edward was committed to doing his part to defeat Napoleon, and aside from becoming injured, only victory would lead him to retire his commission.

Emily nudged his arm, bringing him back to the present. "If you're insisting we wait until after breakfast to open presents, the least you can do is actually eat." She glared at his untouched plate.

Sarah laughed, a sound that never failed to touch him. It warmed his heart to see how well she got along with his family.

"I'm afraid I'm going to have to agree with Emily," she said, smiling at him before glancing at Emily with affection.

"Never say I wouldn't do everything possible to please the women in my family," he said, taking a large forkful of eggs.

Sarah's eyes met his, and he almost choked at the heat he saw reflected there. His thoughts immediately went to the previous night, and he knew she was remembering it as well. She had just finished her monthly courses, and after being away from her for several days, he'd been insatiable.

He wasn't even embarrassed when his mother cleared her throat, breaking their connection, and changed the subject.

Emily dragged them into the drawing room as soon as the meal was over. He almost suggested they wait until Sarah's family arrived, but before he could open his mouth to do so, Sarah touched his arm.

"Mama said they would exchange presents before leaving. They won't expect us to wait for them."

He nodded, robbed of speech for a moment. Sarah was so beautiful that morning—her hair a riot of curls, a festive yellow morning dress reflecting the gold in her hair. He wanted to draw her into his arms, but since they weren't alone he settled for bringing her hand to his lips.

An odd expression crossed her face, and it took him a moment to realize it was tenderness. Directed at him, not at something amusing his sister had said. His heart stuttered.

"Come on, you two," Emily said, dragging him away from his wife. "I've waited long enough. Now sit while I hand out the presents."

A footman had brought in the gifts while the family was at breakfast, and Emily headed straight for the pile of brightly wrapped boxes that was carefully arranged on a table placed next to the fireplace.

James took a moment to gaze around the room—the mantel groaning under the weight of festive greenery, his mother seated next to Sarah on the settee while Emily searched for a particular gift. His heart felt almost full to over-flowing.

He was still nervous about his gift. He'd consulted Emily about it, wanting to ensure he gave Sarah something she'd enjoy. But now he wondered if it was enough. Perhaps he should have gotten her jewelry instead.

"I know you'll both appreciate the extreme sacrifice I'm making in waiting for the two of you to go first," Emily said, dropping colorfully wrapped packages in his and Sarah's laps. Her eyes glowed and she winked at him as she stepped back a few paces to wait. She was almost vibrating with excitement.

Sarah looked at him, but he waved his hand at the box in her lap. "I insist you go first."

It was the gentlemanly thing to do, but in reality he was beset by doubt. He'd placed so much importance on getting her something she would like, and now he worried that he'd failed. He needed to get her gift out of the way so he could enjoy the rest of the day.

As Sarah began to unwrap his present, his hands clenched involuntarily. He barely managed to keep from mangling the gift on his lap as he waited, suddenly certain that he hadn't done enough.

Unlike Emily, who usually tore the wrapping off her presents, Sarah carefully removed the paper, setting it aside before opening the wooden box. She stared at the contents for several long moments, and James's stomach dropped. She hated it.

When she looked up at him, her eyes were wide with wonder. "You got me oil paints."

"I know you love to draw and paint. Emily mentioned that you'd always wanted to try oil, but your parents insisted you limit yourself to watercolors. It seemed a shame that you not indulge your talent."

She stared at him, and he wondered if he'd misspoken.

Needing to fill the silence that had descended, he rushed on. "I've also arranged to have the room next to the gallery set up as your studio. It faces south and receives sunlight for a good portion of the day."

He stopped talking when she placed the box on the tea table and stood. He set aside his own gift and followed suit. "If you'd rather have jewels…"

She threw her arms around him and placed a kiss on his cheek. "They're perfect," she said after several seconds, leaning back to beam up at him.

"You're perfect," he replied, his voice low enough so only

she could hear. Color rose in her cheeks, and her smile made his heart feel a thousand times lighter.

He released her reluctantly, and she turned to lift the flat box he'd set aside. "Now it's your turn."

He accepted the gift again and waited for her to sit before lowering himself into his chair.

"You have everything a man could possibly want," Sarah said as he tore the paper on his gift. "I thought, perhaps, you might enjoy this. It isn't much."

James didn't really care what she'd given him. It was enough that he'd made her happy.

His grin widened when he realized that she'd given him a picture. Not a watercolor, but one she'd drawn with colored pencils. It was a striking likeness of Rakehell, the prize stallion he'd brought with him when he'd taken up residence at Hathaway Park.

When he glanced back at Sarah, he could tell she was nervous. "I knew you were talented, but I grossly underestimated your ability. I'll definitely be framing this."

Sarah's smile wobbled, and he lifted a brow in question.

"There's a second picture below that one."

If it was even half as good as the first, his wife had no reason to be concerned. Curious, he lifted the top page. When his gaze fell on the second picture, he froze. There, on the paper, was a drawing of him. He was at the stables, a hand on Rakehell's mane as he leaned close to speak to the animal.

His mind went back to the day it was drawn. Sarah and Emily had visited the stables, and he'd been very aware of her presence as he'd gone about his work. Emily had been chattering nonstop while Sarah drew, but he'd had no idea she was drawing him.

"So this is why you and Emily were out at the stables that day."

"I couldn't think of what to give one of the wealthiest men in all of England. Since I know how much you love your horses…" She shrugged.

It wasn't the horse in the picture that had captured his attention but the way she'd drawn him. There was a light in his eyes and a grin on his face that almost made him appear handsome. Was that how Sarah saw him? Or had she made him appear more handsome than he really was? As his eyes scanned the drawing, however, he saw that she'd accurately captured the slight bend in his nose from the time he'd broken it trying to tame a particularly stubborn stallion. And it didn't appear as though she'd altered any of his features for the better. Yet, somehow, she'd made him appear more handsome than he knew he was.

"I don't know what to say."

"Do you like it?" She was biting her lip, and he wanted nothing more at that moment than to draw her onto his lap and show her just how much he liked it. How much she'd taken away his breath with her thoughtfulness.

Their eyes met and held. "I will treasure this."

What he didn't tell Sarah was that looking at the drawing gave him hope that she would one day come to care for him. Perhaps even love him.

"Now it's our turn," Emily said, capturing his attention. He'd almost forgotten he and Sarah weren't alone. "Mama and I also got you presents, but if I don't open that large box over there with my name on it, I'm going to expire from curiosity."

James laughed, his heart feeling a hundred times lighter than when he'd entered the room. "By all means. I'd hate to be the cause of your distress."

Emily needed no more encouragement. She quickly handed out the rest of the gifts and then proceeded to tear open her present.

Before long, all the gifts were open and Emily was suggesting they head into the music room to sing Christmas carols.

They would be leaving for Christmas service later that morning, after Sarah's family arrived. James wanted to spirit Sarah away and thank her properly, but that would have to wait until later that evening when everyone had gone. James steeled himself for the long day ahead. Much as he loved his family, he looked forward to exploring whether Sarah's gift contained the hidden meaning he wanted to ascribe to it.

HAPPINESS SETTLED OVER SARAH as they proceeded to the music room. She hadn't wanted to admit to herself that she'd been worried about her husband's reaction to her small gift. What did one give someone, after all, who already had everything? He loved nothing better than his stables, and Emily had assured her that her brother would enjoy the drawings.

The way he'd looked at her after opening her gift had flustered her. It was the same look he gave her when he joined her in the bedroom. And while Emily and Mrs. Hathaway were opening their own presents, she'd glanced his way more than a few times to find him staring at her. She couldn't help but wonder what he was thinking.

Emily urged her to play the first song, and Sarah had to take a few deep breaths as she settled before the pianoforte. It wouldn't do to mangle the song she was about to play because she was distracted by thoughts of her husband.

"I hope you'll all join me," she said as she shifted over on the bench so Emily could sit next to her. "I can manage playing, but my voice is only passable at best."

"Oh, never fear," Emily said, giving her a small hug as she sat next to her. "Singing carols on Christmas morning is a family tradition. We'll all join in."

"Even James?" It had never occurred to her to wonder if her husband could sing. Her own brother and father loathed the activity, which was understandable given that neither could carry a tune.

"Oh yes," Mrs. Hathaway said, beaming with pride at her son. "He has a very nice singing voice. I admit that he puts Emily and me to shame."

"I shall be the judge of that," Sarah said with mock seriousness as she began to play "God Rest Ye Merry, Gentlemen," one of the few carols she knew well enough to play by memory.

She'd thought her mother-in-law was exaggerating her son's talents, but when James's smooth baritone joined in, she found herself gaping at him in shock, almost losing her place in the song. He winked at her, knowing full well that he had surprised her.

"Mama never lies," Emily said when they'd reached the end of the carol.

"I can see that," Sarah said, shifting over on the bench so Emily could play the next song.

They were interrupted by the soft murmur of voices coming from the hallway, indicating that Sarah's family had arrived. She rose and had just reached James's side when the footman announced them.

Sarah greeted her mother and brother with heartfelt hugs but hesitated when she saw the stern set of her father's jaw. She dropped into a brief curtsy in front of him, hating the relief that flooded through her when she didn't detect a hint of spirits. It embarrassed her that it wasn't outside the realm of possibility for her father to have already started drinking this early in the morning.

She watched James greet her parents and brother, the happiness of the day disappearing when she noticed the way her father glared at James.

Her eyes flew to George's, and her brother gave a short, abbreviated shake of his head, their signal to each other that their father was in a mood and would be quick to anger.

As usual, her mother attempted to make up for her father's rudeness by greeting everyone warmly and throwing herself into the activity they'd interrupted. Sarah didn't resume her seat at the pianoforte, choosing to sit next to her mother while Emily played.

She tried to concentrate on the next carol. She didn't expect her father and brother to join in, but James's rich voice seemed to wrap around her, giving her a measure of comfort.

That comfort was quickly ripped away when he stopped singing midway through the song.

She turned in time to see her father say something to him, then the two men stood and left the room. She looked at George, wondering if he knew what was happening, but he only shrugged in reply. Her mother gave no indication that she had noticed the men's departure, but Sarah knew that her calm demeanor was only a mask. Her mother was always one to avoid conflict, and she wouldn't want to draw attention to whatever it was that had upset her father.

For several moments, Sarah wrestled with what to do. When she stood, her mother reached out to grasp her hand, giving a small shake of her head. That small motion, however, convinced Sarah that she needed to learn what was happening. She wouldn't have admitted it, but she was suddenly worried for James.

She heard her father's raised voice the moment she stepped into the hallway and made sure to close the door to the music room behind her. She found the two men in the drawing room.

James was standing just inside the doorway, facing her father who was pacing as he ranted about something. When he noticed her, his shoulders stiffened.

"You should return to the music room," James said.

Her father spun around at his comment and pinned Sarah with an angry glare. "Do you know what your husband has done?"

"With all due respect, Sir Henry, I don't think Sarah needs to be present for this discussion."

Her father snorted with disgust. "So you've deceived her as you have me?"

"There was no deception," James replied, his voice calm despite the other man's anger. Sarah had detected the slight hesitation before he spoke, and she couldn't help but wonder what it was that James didn't want her to know.

"He's made it known that no one is to accept credit from me. Do you know what that means?"

Sarah knew exactly what it meant and silently applauded her husband's foresight.

"It means you can no longer drive your family into debt. I would prefer, of course, if you could manage your own money, but since it's clear that you cannot, I've had to take steps to ensure there's still an estate left to bequeath to your son."

Her father's face turned an alarming shade of red, and for a moment, she feared that James had pushed her father too far.

"It is Christmas Day, Papa. Surely this conversation can wait until another time."

Silence descended upon the room, and Sarah held her breath as she waited for her father's reply.

"You'll speak to your husband on my behalf, right, Sarah?" her father said, turning to face her.

"Of course," she said, relieved that her father was being reasonable. It didn't happen often, but he wasn't in his cups, which normally helped his mood.

He nodded stiffly, moving past her to leave the room. Sarah waited until she heard the music room door being opened, the festive music spilling out into the hallway momentarily before her father closed it again.

When she turned back to face James, she was surprised to see he was still tense. Confused, she placed a hand on his arm to set him at ease. "Thank you."

His brows drew together in a slight frown. "You're not upset with me?"

His demeanor made sense now. He'd expected her to censure him for his behavior.

"We both know my father has no self-control. I'll admit I've been worried for George. Once you'd paid all of Papa's debts, I expected him to run up new ones." She gave her head a slight shake. "He'll always hold a grudge against you for this though. And I'm sure he'll seek out ways to continue his gambling."

"I might be able to help with that. It seems that having a title—and the obscene wealth that comes with this one, in particular—actually gives me some influence with others. I've already let it be known that anyone who allows him to run up any future debts won't receive so much as a shilling from me. For some reason people care about my displeasure. I'll admit, it's an odd sensation."

Sarah smiled as she saw him wrestle with the notion before shaking it off. She almost told him that she cared about his feelings but held herself back at the last moment.

"We've only postponed your father's ire. He won't thank me when he learns I didn't allow my wife to cajole me from my decision."

"You don't have to shield me," Sarah said, oddly touched that her husband would take all the blame upon himself.

"Nonsense. Your father is already angry with me. I doubt he could be more so. There's no reason for him to turn that anger onto you." He held out his arm, and Sarah took it automatically. "What say you, should we try to enjoy the rest of this day?"

Warmth spread through Sarah, replacing the dread she'd felt when she entered the room. "I'd say that is an excellent suggestion."

CHAPTER 11

May 1813

SARAH SPENT THE NEXT few months waiting for her father to upset the peace that had settled over their household since Christmas. He was too set in his ways to change, and over the years she'd learned from her mother—who treated her more like a confidante than a child who needed to be sheltered from the realities of life—that he had a talent for finding people to lend him money. Money he would then proceed to lose at an alarming rate. James had put a halt to that temporarily, but she worried that her father would find a way to return to his old habits.

Instead, the disturbance came from an entirely unexpected quarter… her former suitor.

It was early afternoon when Sarah was told she had a caller. As he was most days now that the construction of the new stables was reaching an end, James was away from home.

Expecting her mother, Sarah made her way to the drawing room. When she entered the room, however, she was dismayed to find Robert waiting for her.

His audacity left her stunned for a moment as she remembered the last time she'd seen him and the impertinent suggestion he'd made. How had she forgotten that moment or the fact that he'd tried to kiss her? But then, given the vigorous and often inventive ways her husband had used to distract her since that evening, it wasn't surprising that Robert would be the last person on her mind.

Robert rose when she entered the room and she couldn't help but notice that he had taken great care with his appearance. But then Sarah had never seen him with so much as a hair out of place. She couldn't help but contrast his fastidiousness to her husband's more casual attitude toward fashion and was surprised to find that the man who stood before her now—his fair hair neatly swept back, his royal-blue coat carefully matched to the color of his eyes—no longer impressed her.

In the few short months of their marriage, she'd come to appreciate the confident ease with which her husband carried himself. James liked to loosen his cravat as the day progressed and never bothered to wear a tailcoat when they weren't expecting callers. He did start the day with a waistcoat, but even that concession to formality was often discarded at some point during the day.

Clearing her mind from the wayward thoughts that sprang to mind with the realization of just how much she enjoyed watching her husband loosen up as the day progressed, she forced a smile and inclined her head.

"Good afternoon," she said, pleased that she'd managed to keep her voice even.

A slight frown creased Robert's brow at her cool manner, but he bowed briefly and waited for her to take a seat on the settee. Instead of resuming his seat, he crossed the space between them and lowered himself onto the settee next to her. She had to stifle the impulse to stand and move to one of the chairs, knowing that Robert would take her action as proof she was still affected by his nearness when the opposite was true.

"I am surprised you are here."

He smiled at her, and a spark of alarm ignited within her when she saw the mischief in his eyes. "Aren't you going to offer me refreshments, Sarah? I think the company you've been keeping of late hasn't improved your manners."

Somehow she held back the rebuke that sprang to her lips. It wouldn't do to make an enemy of this man, not when she was already worried about the motivation for his visit. It was entirely possible, after all, that Robert was here because he was hoping to get closer to Emily.

But the last thing she would do was give him reason to stay longer than necessary and risk having James return to find them alone together. Again.

"I trust your parents are well?"

Robert pursed his lips in a moue of disappointment, and Sarah felt a stab of irritation at the affectation. "Come now, let us not pretend to be mere acquaintances exchanging polite pleasantries. I think you know why I am here."

She'd almost convinced herself that he was there to see Emily, but the way his eyes kept creeping down to her décolletage suggested otherwise. Much as she hated his presumption, she was relieved that she'd been mistaken. She could handle Robert. Emily, however, was far too young and innocent, and she feared it would take very little effort on Robert's part to cause her sister-in-law to fall in love with him.

"Don't be coy, Robert. You know I don't enjoy guessing games."

He made a soft tsking sound and gave her a meaningful look. "I'm here about my proposal."

She wasn't surprised. Robert always did think that the world revolved around him. Still, his audacity almost took away her breath. "You would actually approach me here, in my husband's home, to suggest I betray my wedding vows?"

Robert lifted a shoulder in a casual shrug. "Your husband's habits are very predictable. He's so enamored with the construction of his new stables—" The twist of his lips told her clearly what he thought of her husband's plans to continue breeding horses. "He won't even know I was here. But if you prefer, we can make arrangements to meet elsewhere. I know you'll be leaving for Town soon. It shouldn't be too difficult to arrange a meeting while you're there."

He ended with a broad wink, and Sarah was almost embarrassed for him. How could he be so delusional as to think she would fall into his arms after the way he had cast her aside? Clearly he thought himself so irresistible that she would be content to accept whatever scraps of attention he chose to give her.

"You would be mistaken." Her husband's voice came from the doorway, and with a gasp she turned to see him standing there, the breadth of his shoulders almost encompassing the whole opening. Sarah had never seen James's eyes so cold and hard. From the way he was clenching his fists, it was clear he'd heard enough of their conversation to know the reason for Robert's visit.

Robert leaped to his feet. "I'm not sure what you think you heard—"

"I heard you propositioning my wife." James moved into the room, his anger palpable in the tense atmosphere that settled over the room. Wisely, Robert took a step back, but he wasn't quick enough to escape her husband. James grabbed him roughly by the throat and bent Robert's right arm behind his back. The slighter man clutched at James's arm with his left hand, but he was powerless to move him.

Shocked at James's display of anger, Sarah stood on shaky legs and could only watch, frozen, as he yanked Robert closer to him.

"If you wish to live to see another day, you will put all thoughts of my wife behind you. If your paths should cross in public, you will acknowledge her as is befitting her station and then continue on your way." His face was now mere inches away from Robert's. "But if I ever find you alone with her again—or learn that you've been alone with her, and you can rest assured that I *will* hear about it—I will take great pleasure in making sure you regret that action. Do I make myself clear?"

A gurgle of sound emerged from Robert's throat, but he nodded his assent with a frantic, jerky movement, his eyes wild with terror.

For one heart-stopping moment, Sarah wasn't sure James would release Robert. When he finally did, he flung him away and Robert stumbled backward. Sarah cried out, visions of

Robert lying in a broken heap on the floor crowding her mind.

James cast her a look that threatened to steal her breath, for in it she saw hurt. He believed she would betray him. And why wouldn't he? She'd never told him what had actually taken place between her and Robert at the Vaughans' Christmas party. Instead, she'd allowed her husband to continue to believe the words that her foolish pride had spurred her to utter... that she would one day betray him.

He turned and glared at Robert as he scurried from the room. They remained frozen in place—James facing the doorway and Sarah staring at his back—as they listened to the sound of the front door opening and slamming closed.

When James turned to face her again, the hurt she'd glimpsed was gone. In its place there remained only anger.

"I need to explain—"

"Don't." The harshly spoken word stopped her in her tracks.

"But that wasn't what it seemed—"

His harsh laugh caused an odd shifting sensation some-where in the vicinity of her heart.

"I don't need your explanations. Your actions have spoken volumes."

With that, he turned and strode from the room.

As she watched him retreat from her, clarity entered her mind. She realized that she'd done the very thing she'd vowed never to allow—she'd fallen in love with her husband. Even worse, she'd led him to believe that she was the type of woman to whom he could never entrust his own heart.

Her legs gave way and she collapsed onto the settee. How

could she have allowed that to happen? And more importantly, how was she going to protect herself from this new heartbreak?

HAVING GROWN UP with a father who railed against any slight, whether real or imagined, Sarah thought she'd prefer the polite distance James now showed her. It came as a shock, therefore, to discover that his icy demeanor had an agonizing effect on her emotions.

She couldn't stop thinking about the hurt she'd seen in his eyes and hated herself for having caused it. She tried on several occasions to explain that she had no intention of betraying her marriage vows. After he cut her off for the third time, she realized the effort was futile and stopped trying to raise the subject. There was another subject she wanted to raise with James, but the distance between them made it impossible.

That week dragged by slowly, made even longer by the fact that James didn't visit her at night. She tried to occupy her time with preparations for their trip to London, but there wasn't a great deal for her to do. They'd only be staying a few days before heading to the Earl of Sanderson's estate just outside of Town to attend his wedding to James's aunt.

She attempted to escape into the little artist's studio James had set up for her but found that drawing or painting brought her no joy. Her heart ached each time she looked at the set of oil paints her husband had given her at Christmas. She could only hope that getting away from this house, away from reminders of what her husband thought he had witnessed, would ease the strain between them.

She counted on Emily and her mother-in-law's presence to help defuse the tension during the trip to London. When the date for the departure arrived, however, she was disappointed to learn that only she and James would be making the journey. Mrs. Hathaway had fallen ill with the grippe and Emily was to stay behind to care for her mother.

The trip to town was made in one day with a short, awkward break at an inn for a midday meal. If Sarah had thought the week leading up to that day was long, it was nothing to riding alone within the stifling interior of the Hathaway coach. Instead of keeping her company, James chose to spend the majority of the trip on horseback.

Sarah had hoped the enforced confinement of their trip would allow her to share the news she had received the day before. The doctor had visited while James was at the stables and confirmed her suspicion that she was with child. She wanted to tell James, but it was impossible when he went out of his way to avoid her company.

By the time the carriage arrived at James's town house—a residence that was much larger than the other houses in the very fashionable Mayfair neighborhood—dusk was falling and exhaustion pulled at her. She hadn't been able to sleep during the journey, her mind spinning as she tried to imagine how James would react upon hearing her news. A part of her wondered if he'd already learned of the doctor's visit. Did he already suspect she was with child and just not care?

She tried to push that horrible thought away, but it was impossible to keep from dwelling on the negative. Especially when James didn't take her arm after helping her down from the carriage.

The butler opened the front door just as they reached it. This was Sarah's first visit to the Hathaway town house, and she braced herself for the inevitable introduction to the staff. Fortunately, the servants weren't as numerous as at Hathaway Park and that formality was soon over.

Finally Sarah allowed her curiosity free rein and wandered into the drawing room. She could only stare, amazed that the decor was even more ostentatious than that of the estate. The marble floor was polished to a mirrorlike shine, and the walls were covered in a paper that, if she wasn't mistaken, actually had gold embossing. She tried to imagine what the rest of the house would look like and found that her imagination wasn't up to the task.

"I didn't think it was possible for any house to be more ornate than Hathaway Park."

"I thought you'd like it," James said, his eyes cold as he stared at her. "But you did agree to marry me for my money, after all."

It was the most he'd said to her in days, and she barely caught herself from flinching as the harsh words tore through her.

She didn't reply, needing desperately to get away from James before she broke down into tears. She turned to the butler, who was standing off to the side, pretending not to have heard James's insult.

"I'd like to see my room now. I find that I'm quite fatigued from the journey." She turned back to James, adding, "If you'll excuse me, I'll have a tray sent up to my room."

James frowned, but in that moment Sarah didn't care if he could see just how much his words had wounded her. As she followed the butler up the stairs to her bedroom, she could feel the weight of her husband's gaze on her back. She made sure to keep her spine straight and her head held high.

CHAPTER 12

TWO AGONIZING DAYS HAD dragged by since their arrival in London. Interminable days during which Sarah only saw her husband at dinner. She filled the time by becoming acquainted with the staff and the manner in which the town house was run. They wouldn't be staying long enough for her to impose any changes, but it soon became apparent that none were needed. She wasn't surprised since she knew how fastidious James's uncle had been. With her marriage, she might just have inherited one of the best staffs in all of London, rivaled only by the small army employed in the upkeep of Hathaway Park.

She tried to pass the time sketching but was acutely aware of every minute that passed without seeing her husband. At night she waited for him to join her but dropped, alone, into an exhausted sleep. Faced with James's cool demeanor at dinner, she still hadn't been able to bring herself to tell him that she was increasing.

When the morning of the wedding of the dowager Viscountess Hathaway finally arrived, Sarah found herself alone in the carriage with her husband. Unlike their journey to Town, James chose not to ride alongside the carriage. She knew him well enough now to realize he was self-conscious about how others perceived him. He wouldn't want to arrive at the wedding smelling like the stables.

She spent that hour-long drive buffeted by emotion. Wanting to reach out to her husband, tell him that she did not see him as wanting… that, in fact, she found him more noble than most of the men of her acquaintance. Yet fear that he'd scorn her outpouring of sentiment held her back.

Or worse, that he'd laugh at her for hoping that his feelings for her went beyond enjoying their time in bed together. She couldn't shake the suspicion that he didn't actually like her since she hadn't seen any indication that he wanted to know her outside of the bedroom.

Well, except for his behavior on Christmas morning. She hadn't even realized that he'd given any thought to her love for drawing and painting. Surely a man who'd gone to the effort to give her something so meaningful must care for her, even if just a little.

Their arrival at the Earl of Sanderson's estate brought an end to her internal turmoil. As the carriage drew to a halt, she glanced sideways at James, where he sat looking out the carriage window, and sighed. Even if she couldn't tell him about her emotions, she'd have to find the courage to breach the distance between them and tell him he would soon be a father.

James held himself stiffly, an indication that the trip had

been equally uncomfortable for him. Despite that, Sarah couldn't help but admire how handsome he was as she drank in his profile. Her fingers itched to explore the hard muscles that lay beneath the fabric of his waistcoat. She wanted to trail her hand upward, ease the stiffness of his jaw, see his mouth curve into that wicked smile he gave her when he was about to make love to her.

She ached from the need coursing through her in that moment.

Her heart fell when the carriage drew to a halt and James remained seated, waiting for a footman to open the carriage door and help her down instead of preceding her and handling that task himself. She hadn't realized until that moment how much she'd been looking forward to that small amount of physical contact from him.

As it was almost time for the marriage ceremony, they were greeted by one of the earl's sisters. After welcoming them, she summoned a footman to show them to their bedroom. She and James would be staying the night before returning to Hathaway Park in Northampton on the morrow.

James barely entered the room they were to share, remaining just inside the doorway when the footman left to collect the one trunk they'd packed for their brief stay and to summon a maid to help Sarah dress.

James cleared his throat before meeting her gaze. "The ceremony will begin in just over an hour. I'll leave you now to…" James faltered only momentarily, but it was enough to tell Sarah that her husband could hardly wait to quit her company. "I'll return to fetch you when it's time."

"You needn't put yourself out," she said, unable to hold

back her own annoyance. Really, was it so difficult for him to pretend that he could tolerate her presence? "I'm sure a footman will be able to show me the way to the chapel."

He offered her a curt nod before turning and leaving her alone. The sound of the door closing behind him sounded unnaturally loud in the still room. Sarah let out a silent scream of annoyance and flung herself onto the bed. Her waspishness toward her husband certainly wasn't helping the situation, but if he'd wanted a meek wife who would be content to have whatever scrap of attention he threw her way with nary a word or raised brow, he'd married the wrong woman.

An hour later, Sarah found herself following another footman to the chapel situated a short walk north of the Sanderson estate. She'd managed to steady her nerves, and she was determined to close the gap that had grown between her and James.

The maid who had been sent up to help her dress had teased her hair out from the practical knot she'd worn for the carriage ride. Thankfully, her natural curls didn't require a lot of attention, and now they framed her face in what she knew was a becoming manner. She'd chosen to wear a deep blue gown that was cut just low enough to showcase her breasts, and she knew the color complemented her fair coloring. She didn't bother trying to deny to herself that she was hoping to ensnare James's attention. They were sharing a room for the night, after all. Surely when they retired for the evening, he'd finally make love to her again. Afterward, she'd tell him about her condition.

James was waiting outside the chapel and when he saw her, his eyes dropped to her bodice. Instead of the desire she'd hoped to see when he lifted his gaze to hers again, his expression was carefully neutral. She squelched her disappointment and smiled at him when she took his arm, her heartbeat sounding unnaturally loud to her own ears as they entered the chapel.

IT WAS MADDENING how much he wanted the woman standing by his side, the warmth of her small hand on his arm seeming to burn a hole through his coat. James had to struggle against the almost overwhelming need to draw Sarah into his arms.

The ride down from London had been bad enough, the intimate interior of the carriage ensuring he was aware of her every breath, the scent of her filling his nostrils. It had taken every ounce of willpower he possessed to leave the bedroom the footman had shown them to. Only the memory of the horrified expression on his wife's face when he'd threatened the man she still loved had given him the strength to turn away from her.

But it was clear to him now that this woman would always be his weakness. How he could still desire her even though he knew she wanted nothing to do with him was a mystery—one he feared he would never solve.

James's uncle had married a woman quite a few years younger than himself, hoping she'd give him a son to inherit the Hathaway title. Their marriage had lasted twelve years, but the union had not resulted in any offspring. Now, just thirteen months after his passing, Miranda Hathaway was marrying a man she appeared to love. It was equally clear to him that Sanderson was just as enamored of his wife-to-be. James was happy for the pair, but he couldn't help feeling a pang of envy.

The actual wedding ceremony wasn't long. Seeing the way Miranda and Sanderson looked at each other, James couldn't help but contrast the event to his own wedding to Sarah. She had done an admirable job of hiding her discomfort, but he'd been aware of it nonetheless. He wondered how many other people had been aware of her reluctance to marry him.

Probably everyone.

Normally he tried not to think back to that day, but given his wife's recent behavior, it was impossible to ignore the fact that nothing had changed in the past six months of their marriage. Yes, she was a willing partner in the bedroom, but she hadn't given him any indication that her feelings for him had changed outside of that room. The hope he'd harbored after receiving her Christmas gift had only proven how much of a fool he was when it came to his wife.

He had to endure the walk back to the estate for the wedding breakfast with Sarah clinging to his arm. In contrast to the way she had ignored him during their carriage ride that morning or the way she had snapped at him after they'd arrived, she seemed to be going out of her way to be pleasant to him. Much as he wanted to take her new behavior at face value, he knew she was only putting on a show for the other guests. He supposed he should be grateful. Marriages of convenience were common among the *ton* but he was very aware that he didn't fit in. Anyone witnessing her cool behavior toward him would assume—correctly—that she was miserable in her marriage and laid the blame squarely at his feet.

When she smiled at him before taking her seat at the breakfast table, he had to hold back the urge to tell her that she needn't pretend quite so prettily for his sake. Instead, he told himself that at least here he wouldn't have to worry about finding his wife alone, yet again, with the man she loved.

CHAPTER 13

By the time Sarah retired for the night, her jaw ached from forcing herself to smile, and her head was pounding. The doctor had told her she would tire more easily because of her pregnancy, but she recognized that her fatigue stemmed from more than her physical condition.

As the maid helped her unbutton her dress and unlace her too-tight corset, she had to acknowledge that she was dejected by how the day had progressed. James had barely spoken to her during the wedding breakfast, and when it was over he'd taken his leave with a small bow. When the newly married couple had disappeared as well, she'd hoped to retire to their room and rest for a bit. But the earl's sisters had thwarted that plan, having scheduled several activities to occupy their guests.

She hadn't seen James again until dinner, which proved to be a dreadfully long affair. Worse, she'd had to sit opposite him and watch as another woman—a young widow to whom

Sarah had taken an instant dislike—all but offered herself up to him.

She was seated next to a middle-aged, talkative gentleman, so she couldn't overhear her husband's conversation, but whatever they were discussing seemed to amuse James. Really, the way the woman leaned into him, even having the nerve to place her hand on James's arm while she laughed at everything he said, made Sarah want to climb over the dining room table and claw out her eyes.

She wanted to believe that her husband was putting on a show for her benefit, paying her back in kind for what he believed to be her transgressions with Robert. But the fact that he never glanced in her direction caused her to doubt that was his motivation. Surely if he were trying to make her jealous, he would have glanced at her at least once to gauge her reaction to his performance.

No, her stomach had turned into a dark knot of despair at the realization that he simply didn't care how she was taking their intimate tête-à-tête. In fact, he seemed not to be aware of her presence at all.

As she dismissed the maid and crawled into bed, she couldn't help but worry that it might already be too late to repair their relationship, let alone win James's affection. Too much time had passed and she'd given him no indication about her true feelings. It was entirely possible that he had given up on her.

She sighed. Had he even wanted her affection? She had no reason to believe he'd ever wanted anything from her other than a legitimate heir. What she'd taken as his jealousy toward Robert was, in all likelihood, the behavior of someone trying to hold on to their pride. What man wanted to be cuckolded or to raise another man's child as his own? Certainly not James. He'd made that very clear on the day they'd wed.

She tried to remain awake, hoping that her husband would join her soon, but fatigue pulled her into a deep sleep almost at once. When she started awake the next morning, disappointment flooded through her.

She wasn't sure what she expected to find when she rose from the bed. Surely there would be some sign that her husband had spent the night in their shared bedroom even if he hadn't woken her. Rumpled sheets on the other side of the bed, a discarded cravat... something. Instead, she found the room as pristine as it had been when she'd retired. Had her husband returned to their room at all last night?

A suspicion, almost too horrible to contemplate, formed in her mind as she remembered the way James's dinner companion had blatantly flirted with him throughout the meal. Had James chosen, instead, to visit the widow's bedroom last night?

Pain lanced through her at the thought, so swift that it left her momentarily gasping for breath. Worse was the realization that when she told James she was carrying his child, he would no longer need to visit her bed. She'd hoped that would be the case when they'd first wed, but it hadn't taken long for her to become addicted to her husband's touch. More than that, she craved his attention. His love. But if the previous evening had shown her anything, it was that there were plenty of women willing to take her place.

She almost didn't hear the soft knock at the door so mired was she in fear that she had already been replaced. She had just enough time to turn away before the maid who had helped her the previous day entered the room. She quickly dashed the tears threatening to fall, took a deep breath, and turned to face the woman.

"I'm sorry to disturb you so early, my lady, but His Lordship left word that you would be departing early. A breakfast tray will be sent up shortly."

Sarah took small comfort from the thought that she'd be spared the sight of watching her husband pay court to another woman while she attempted to break her fast. Such a sight would have turned her stomach, not to mention what it would have done to her heart.

She tried to shake off her unease as the maid helped her dress. She'd have to face her husband soon, and she had no idea what she would say to him.

Another knock at the door just as the maid was leaving signaled the arrival of her meal. But instead of a footman, the tray was brought in by James's aunt.

"I hope you don't mind that I intercepted your breakfast. We haven't had the chance to get to know one another, and since you and James will be leaving shortly, I knew this would be my only opportunity to remedy that oversight."

"Not at all," Sarah said, taking the tray and carrying it to her dressing table. "I welcome the opportunity."

Miranda moved to the chaise and sat. James's aunt was only a few years older than him and still a very beautiful woman. Her dark hair was pulled up into a simple but elegant knot, her gray eyes almost too large for her face. Sarah could almost feel those eyes looking deep into her soul.

"There's only one cup," Sarah said. "I can ring for another one—"

Miranda shook her head. "I've already eaten this morning."

When Sarah hesitated, uncertain whether the other woman intended to watch her eat, Miranda let out a sigh.

"I'm sorry, it appears I've made you nervous. That wasn't my intention." She shifted on the chaise. "Come sit next to me. I'll only be a moment, then I'll leave you to finish your meal."

Sarah did as the other woman requested, feeling as though she was about to be brought to task for some transgression.

"Oh dear, I'm only making things worse. Excuse me for being blunt, but I have to ask. Do you care for my nephew?"

Sarah considered lying, her first instinct to protect her pride. But she was tired of pushing people away. If she hadn't been so determined to keep her husband at arm's length, she might not be in the sorry situation in which she now found herself.

"I didn't expect to, but much to my surprise, I do."

"Andrew told me not to get involved, but I couldn't help but notice that things are tense between you and James."

Sarah wanted nothing more than for the floor to open up and swallow her whole. What could she say that wasn't already evident to everyone who saw the two of them together?

"Does James know how you feel?"

Sarah hadn't expected this line of questioning. If she'd been asked, she would have said that she'd do everything in her power to ensure it never took place. But in that moment, she needed to speak to someone. She couldn't confide in his family, and she didn't want to burden her mother with the knowledge that she was so unhappy.

Sarah shook her head. "He believes that I care for someone else." She rushed to explain when she saw the frown on the other woman's face. "There was an unspoken understanding between myself and another, but that ended before my marriage. I'll admit, I entered the marriage not expecting to care for James, but somewhere along the way my feelings changed."

Miranda covered her hands, which she hadn't realized she was clutching together in her lap.

"Would you like me to speak to him on your behalf?"

Sarah hated the pity she saw on the other woman's face. "And say what? It is clear to everyone that you and Lord Sanderson care deeply for one another, but most marriages aren't love matches."

Miranda seemed to weigh her words before speaking. "Andrew believes that my nephew cares for you."

Sarah couldn't hold back her mirthless laugh at that bit of absurdity despite the fact that the other woman's words had caused her heart to clench. "Oh, he likes me well enough in bed. It's all the other times when he can't bear to even look at me."

Miranda would understand how such marriages worked. She, herself, had been in a similar marriage to the former Viscount Hathaway before his death had left her a widow.

Miranda squeezed Sarah's hand again before releasing it. "I really don't think that's true. Perhaps it's time for you to take a chance and tell him how you feel." Sarah was about to protest, but Miranda continued. "Would you really be more unhappy if you tried and failed than you are right now?"

Sarah honestly couldn't answer that question.

Miranda gave her a quick hug, then stood and took her leave.

Sarah sat there for several minutes, unable to banish Miranda's words from her mind. She wasn't sure if she could summon up the courage to tell James that she loved him, but it was time for him to learn that he might soon be getting his heir.

JAMES REGRETTED HIS DECISION to ride in the carriage with his wife almost as soon as they left Sanderson's estate. It wasn't so much Miranda's comment about how tedious the journey home would be for Sarah alone in the carriage that had him changing his mind but the look of disappointment on Miranda's face when he'd started to tell her that he would be riding alongside the carriage. He knew that his aunt and her new husband were in love, and it was clear that Miranda hoped the same was true of his marriage. For some reason he couldn't fathom, she seemed oddly insistent that James remain with his wife.

The carriage felt even more cramped than it had on their trip to Sanderson's estate the previous morning. He was acutely aware of his wife's presence, and he decided that he'd been away from her for too long. It was almost two weeks since they'd made love, something which he planned to correct that evening after their return.

Until then, thoughts of what he wanted to do with her plagued him.

Last night had been hell. He'd retired very late in order to avoid Sarah. She'd been going to bed earlier of late, and by the time he'd returned to their shared bedroom, she'd been asleep. He'd spent a miserable night on the chaise longue, battling the urge to crawl into bed with her. He'd finally given up trying to get any real rest at about five in the morning and had dressed quickly—thankful that he'd never had a valet until recently—and ventured downstairs.

He'd been successful in his aim to show Sarah that while she might not love him, he could bring her physical satisfaction. Now he couldn't help but worry that she would seek that satisfaction with another man. Vaughan. The thought of the other man's smug face had him clenching his hands.

The intimacy within the carriage was too much to bear and his nerves were on edge. Better that he spend the rest of the trip sitting next to the carriage driver outside. He raised a hand to rap on the roof of the carriage but stopped just short when his wife cleared her throat.

"Are you leaving?"

"I thought I'd get some air. I didn't get much sleep last night, and the morning air should keep me from falling asleep."

She looked away at his words, and for a brief moment he thought he could detect a hint of hurt on her face. It disappeared almost instantly, and he chided himself for thinking he could have any sway over her emotions.

"I have something important to tell you." Sarah met his

gaze and this time, by the way she clenched her hands together in her lap, he could tell she was worried.

He settled back in his seat and waited for her to continue. He wanted to ease her concern, but perhaps after the way he had been avoiding her lately, he would have to earn back her trust.

"I didn't want to say anything until I was certain, and after that you seemed to need some time to yourself…"

He tensed but said nothing as he waited. He wouldn't cut her off just yet, but heaven help him if she wanted to discuss Vaughan.

"I am with child. There is no question… the child is yours."

Mixed emotions battled within him. Sarah, the woman he cared for beyond anything or anyone else, was pregnant with his child. Elation rose within him like a swift tide. But that elation was inextricably mixed with more than a hint of dread. After all, she'd been up front in telling him that she would make sure he had his heir first before looking elsewhere for companionship.

"Say something," she said.

He realized that he must have been quiet for some time. Sarah was twisting her hands together in her lap, wrinkling the fabric of her dress.

He spoke carefully, not wanting to give voice to his doubts. "I'm pleased."

"You don't look happy. I thought you'd be overjoyed."

He remained silent, not wanting to ruin this moment with an argument. Sarah, however, had no qualms about continuing.

"I make you a solemn promise, James, that I won't be seeking the company of anyone else. I know you've come to expect the worst from me, but you should know that Robert's actions were entirely his own. He made overtures to me, but I no longer reciprocate his feelings."

His eyes met hers, words jamming in his throat.

When he didn't reply, she continued. "I intend to be faithful to my wedding vows. To you."

Relief, pure and blessed, poured through him. He didn't believe that his wife would lie just to ease his mind, not when she'd been so forthright with him before now. He wasn't sure what had caused her to change her mind but could no longer hold back his hope that Sarah was coming to care for him.

No longer content to wait, he moved to sit next to her. He didn't exactly pounce on her, but it was a near thing.

He dragged her onto his lap, his blood heating when she wrapped her arms around his neck and pressed her body against his. He took her mouth with his, and as always, she responded eagerly.

They spent the rest of the carriage ride home making up for having spent the previous two weeks apart. And, finally, Sarah fell asleep in his arms.

For the first time since he'd been forced to accept that his new bride loved someone else and hadn't wanted to marry him, James had hope for the future.

CHAPTER 14

S ARAH COULDN'T SAY if she was happy exactly, but she was certainly content with the new state of her marriage. A week had passed since their return to Hathaway Park, and she and James had settled into a new peace.

She hadn't told him that she loved him, but assuring him that she intended to remain faithful seemed to be all he required from her. There were even times when she could almost convince herself that James cared for her.

Yes, she was content with her marriage.

Her maid was hovering over her, having just stripped her down to her chemise, when Sarah froze. Turning away from the other woman, she lifted the fabric and gazed at her thighs in horror.

"Is something the matter, my lady?" Alice asked as she came around to face her. Her gaze followed Sarah's and she gasped. "I thought you were with child?"

"I am," Sarah said, releasing her chemise to hide the sight of the blood. "Call for Dr. Reynolds, quickly!"

She watched Alice flee the room, standing in place a full minute. She tried to calm her racing heart as she moved to the bed, tossing the dress she'd worn onto its surface so she wouldn't stain the bedclothes. She frowned down at it, remembering how much James seemed to like that dress.

James found her several minutes later, rummaging through drawers, trying to remember where Alice kept the towels.

"Your maid told me that you needed the doctor."

She threw her hands up in the air then, losing the battle to keep her tears at bay. "I'm bleeding," she said, hating the tremor in her voice. "And I can't find a towel to place on the bed so I don't ruin the sheets…"

James swore, ignoring his wife's gasp as he lifted her off her feet and carried her to the bed.

"I'll buy you a whole new bed if need be, but you are not going to move from that spot until the doctor arrives."

His gaze moved down her form and she saw the color drain from his face. She didn't have the courage to look down again, afraid of what she'd see.

"I'm so sorry," she said before breaking down into sobs, barely able to catch her breath as she wondered if she was being punished in some way. It had taken her months to conceive, and now… Her mind shied away from finishing that thought.

James said nothing. What was there to say, after all? But he lowered himself onto the side of the bed and pulled her against him, cradling her as she worked to control her fear.

She didn't know how long they stayed that way, but her

tears had stopped when they finally heard a soft knock at the door.

James left her then and went to answer the door. She couldn't make out the muffled voices before James returned to her side.

"I'll be right outside while the doctor examines you," he said, leaning down to place a soft kiss on her forehead.

She knew he meant the words to be comforting, but she could see the concern in his eyes when he straightened to leave and couldn't help but feel that she had failed him.

JAMES HADN'T BEEN WAITING LONG, but each minute that passed seemed like an hour as he paced outside Sarah's bedroom. Her sobs had torn his heart in two, and he'd never felt more powerless in his life.

Finally the doctor stepped into the hallway, closing the door softly behind him.

He lacked the voice to ask, but his heart lifted when he saw the smile on the older man's face.

"Your wife is well," he said.

"And the baby?"

"I won't lie to you," Dr. Reynolds said. "Your wife is at a very delicate time in her pregnancy. Some women have next to no symptoms during this time and are able to continue their routine with very little modification. But your wife is not one of them. For now, I see nothing to indicate that the pregnancy is in immediate danger. Some women bleed during these early months and reach the end of their confinement with no difficulty. But since we have no way of knowing whether that will be the case for Lady Hathaway, it is important that she rest as much as possible."

James felt as though a huge weight has been lifted from his chest. That feeling was short-lived, however, when the doctor continued.

"Lady Hathaway informed me that the two of you have been sharing a bed. Given the extra care your wife will need to ensure she carries this baby to term, I will have to insist that you forgo visiting her until we know that the health of her and her baby are no longer in danger."

The concern James had felt for his wife and unborn child was nothing compared to the guilt that settled over him now. His own selfish needs had caused this. If he had stayed away from Sarah, neither she nor the baby would be in danger now.

James hesitated outside his wife's bedroom door after the doctor had left. He didn't know what he was going to say to Sarah, but he had just steeled himself to face her when the door opened and her maid exited the room.

"My lord," she said with a quick curtsy before turning away.

"Wait," he said, stopping her. "How is she?"

"She's very tired. A good night's rest will do her wonders."

"Maybe I should leave her then."

"Oh no," she said with a quick shake of her head. "My lady is anxious to speak to you."

He gave her a curt nod and stepped through the door. Sarah was sitting upright in bed, and his remorse increased when he saw how pale and fragile she looked. He'd done that to her.

He approached the bed and lowered himself onto the edge, taking hold of one of her hands. It was so very cold.

"The doctor is optimistic," she said. "The bleeding has stopped, and he assured me that it looked more shocking than it actually was. Apparently some women are prone to bleeding early in their pregnancy—"

He silenced her with a soft kiss on her lips. He hated that she seemed to be blaming herself.

"It was my fault. I shouldn't have been so demanding of your attention. I assure you that it won't happen again."

Her shoulders slumped at his words. "I'm sorry."

He wanted to take her into his arms and just hold her, but they didn't have that type of relationship.

"Rest." Unable to resist, he placed a final kiss on her forehead and left the room.

CHAPTER 15

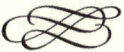

October 1813

FIVE MONTHS HAD PASSED since Sarah's one and only bleeding episode. Five months since her relationship with James had come to a screeching halt.

Dr. Reynolds conducted his examination that morning, peppering her with questions about her level of activity. By his side stood the local midwife, Mrs. Bryers, who had been visiting her often to check on her progress.

When the doctor was done, Mrs. Bryers helped her back into a seated position and draped a bedsheet over her. Together, they waited for the doctor's pronouncement.

"I've seen nothing in this, or in my previous examinations, that gives me cause for concern. In my opinion, you are the picture of health."

Sarah hadn't been aware she was holding her breath until that moment. Air rushed out of her lungs, and she gripped the midwife's hand. "You are quite certain there is no danger to the baby?"

"No more than any other pregnancy. There is always a risk when a woman is increasing, you understand, but whatever caused you to bleed that one time, it is clear the danger is now well past."

"It's as we've told you," Mrs. Bryers said. "Sometimes women bleed in the early months but go on to have healthy babies. I've seen it many times myself."

Dr. Reynolds nodded. "Just so."

Calm settled over her at their reassurances. Everything was going to be fine. After her initial panic, she'd been certain her baby would be born healthy—she still believed that—but she'd been trying to mentally prepare herself for the worst.

Her thoughts went immediately to James. The doctor had still advised caution during his previous examinations, but his concern seemed to have passed. "Can my husband and I...?" She was too embarrassed to say the words. And if truth be told, she felt almost greedy asking the question. Surely it was too much to hope that everything would now fall into place for her and James.

The doctor smiled benevolently at her. "Yes, you can resume marital relations. If you'd like to rest now, I'll see if I can find him to tell him the good news. He's been very concerned for your well-being."

"Thank you so much, Dr. Reynolds." The words seemed inadequate.

The doctor turned to leave, and she tried to be patient while Mrs. Bryers fussed over her for a bit.

When the midwife finally left, she made her way downstairs. Her skin tingled. She couldn't wait to find James. Surely their marriage would now go back to normal. She was larger, but she knew from their past lovemaking that there were ways for a man and woman to be together where her size wouldn't be a hindrance.

James wasn't in his study, and when she asked the butler about his whereabouts, she was dismayed to learn that he'd gone out. She returned to her room, wondering if the doctor had spoken to him.

NEEDING TO DISTRACT HERSELF as she waited for James to return, Sarah decided to visit the dower house. The doctor had lifted the physical restrictions under which he'd placed her, yet she made sure to keep a leisurely pace. The twenty-minute walk stretched to half an hour, and a footman followed in case she needed assistance. She arrived at the smaller house flushed from the unaccustomed exertion yet happy at her newfound freedom.

She did, however, ask for a carriage to fetch her at the end of her visit. She didn't want to risk overexerting herself on her first day away from home in months.

It was midafternoon when she arrived home, and she was excited to learn that James had also returned. She thanked the butler and proceeded to her bedroom, wanting to refresh her appearance before seeing him.

Nerves assailed her as she made her way upstairs. Their time apart had been a constant ache. At first she'd missed the physical side of their relationship most, but it didn't take her long to discover that what she really missed was *him*. All of him. The way he looked at her, how he went out of his way to check in with her throughout the day.

When she'd first started experimenting with the oil paints he'd given her at Christmas, he'd checked on her progress daily. He'd been there for her first few abysmal attempts, and when she'd finally started developing a feel for the new medium, the wonder on his face lifted her heart. She could almost feel his pride at those first modest accomplishments.

James was supremely confident most of the time, but now and again she'd caught a brief glimpse of uncertainty on his face. She hated that she'd caused that disquiet. She'd vowed to keep him at a distance, and for so long she'd succeeded. She wished now that she'd taken the advice of James's aunt and told him about her feelings. Because of her need to protect herself from being hurt, he'd withdrawn from her completely once they could no longer be intimate.

His absence had left a void in her heart. The only time she saw him now was over dinner, and more often than not his mother and sister were also present. He'd excuse himself once the meal was over, and she wouldn't see him again until the following evening.

She knew he wasn't sleeping in his bedroom, though she had heard him moving around during the day on occasion. It hadn't taken her long to start wondering if he was fulfilling his needs with another woman. Sharing the pleasures he used to share with her. He was, after all, a very physical man.

From there her thoughts had wandered into darker territory, imagining what would happen if another woman willingly shared more of herself than Sarah had been willing to give. It terrified her that he might come to love someone else.

Would James even want her now, given how large she'd become?

That thought had her hesitating outside her bedroom door, but only for a moment. Miranda Hathaway—no, she was Miranda Sanderson now—had been correct. She should have told James how she felt all those months ago. Now it might be too late.

Taking control of her wayward thoughts, Sarah straightened her shoulders and entered her bedroom. She would freshen up and then go in search of her husband.

She was reaching for the bellpull to summon her maid when the door to the dressing room that separated her bedroom from James's opened. Sarah spun around, her heart in her throat, expecting to see James. Instead, her maid rushed into the room. Startled, it took Sarah a few seconds to realize the importance of what she was seeing.

Alice was normally impeccable in her appearance, but at that moment she could only be described as disheveled. She was trying to straighten her loosened hair as she took a few steps into the room but froze when she spotted Sarah. Her cheeks were flushed, her uniform wrinkled.

Sarah's heart stuttered. She turned away quickly. Her vision swimming with unshed tears, she reached for a bedpost to steady herself.

Alice rushed to her side and grasped her around the waist. "My lady, are you unwell? Should I call for the doctor?"

A bubble of hysterical laughter threatened to erupt at the question. The doctor had just told her that everything was perfect with her, only it wasn't. Her life was as far from perfect as possible.

"I turned too quickly," she said, unable to keep the slight tremor from her voice. "I am feeling a little light-headed. Could you bring me something to eat?"

"Of course, my lady. What would you like?"

Sarah didn't think she'd be able to keep anything down just then, but she needed to get Alice out of the room. "Anything will do."

"I'll fetch something right away."

With a curtsy, her maid hurried from the room and Sarah let out a shaky breath. She tried to tell herself that she was jumping to conclusions and that Alice wouldn't betray her in that way. She knew her husband's sexual appetite was large, and it had been months since they'd last made love, but surely he wouldn't conduct an affair with her maid right under their roof.

She could try to find out.

Her gaze moved to the dressing room door, but she hesitated as she considered her next course of action. She could remain where she was, wait for Alice to return with something Sarah knew she wouldn't be able to eat. She could approach James another time, after her nerves had settled.

Or she could go through the dressing room to his bedroom and confront him.

Her head told her to take the first course of action, but her heart prevailed. She couldn't live with the uncertainty.

Her hands settled on her belly, and she took several deep breaths. Finally, her breathing somewhat steady, she dropped her hands, straightened her shoulders, and entered the dressing room.

It was empty, of course. Pressing forward lest she lose her nerve, she opened the second door and stepped into her husband's bedroom.

She'd been hoping to find it empty as well. Instead, her husband faced away from her while his valet stood behind him, a freshly starched cravat in his hands. On the bed lay a crumpled shirt and waistcoat.

He turned to face her, his freshly laundered shirt gaping open at the neck.

Her stomach dropped and her legs threatened to give way. Why would he be changing so early? Given the state her maid had been in when she'd exited the dressing room, Sarah could only think of one reason. Words fled and she could only stare at him in silence, her heart aching.

James frowned. He motioned for his valet to continue, and the other man draped the fabric he was holding around James's neck and proceeded to tie the simple knot she knew her husband preferred.

"Did you wish to say something or just gawk at me?"

She flinched at the harshness of his tone. "I need to speak to you in private."

He said nothing and she waited. Dread was now a living, breathing thing inside her, and she had to wrestle with the almost overwhelming urge to turn and flee.

Fenton finished tying the knot and James dismissed him. When they were alone, he turned to face her. The expression on his face could only be described as forbidding.

Sarah hesitated as she considered what to say. How did

one go about discussing the subject of resuming marital relations with one's husband? Despite what she now suspected to be true, she wanted… No, she needed to find a way back into her husband's affections. She told herself that Alice was merely a convenient diversion. If James was able to turn to his wife to satisfy his needs, he would have no use for the other woman.

She licked her lips, and he flinched before his scowl deepened. That small telltale sign that he wasn't immune to her gave her the courage to continue.

"The doctor was here this morning."

"I know."

"Did he… did he speak to you before he left?"

James hesitated, and for a moment she wasn't sure he was going to reply. Then he said simply, "Yes."

His admission surprised her. She'd assumed that the doctor hadn't had the opportunity to speak to him.

"So you know?"

He said nothing.

"You know that there is nothing to stop us from enjoying the relationship we had before he placed me on bed rest?"

"Yes, there is. Bedding you might hold only a small risk to our child's health, but it is a risk I am unwilling to take."

"But the doctor said there was no risk at all. I have been completely healthy since then. It's been months, and Dr. Reynolds said that if the baby was at risk, I would have continued to bleed."

He turned away from her, that small motion telling her more than words that he would not bend. And why should he? When faced with bedding his wife, who was as large as one of his horses, or his current mistress, what man wouldn't choose the latter?

Somehow she kept her voice from trembling when she continued. "I'm sorry to have disturbed you."

She managed to hold on to the shreds of her dignity as she exited the room through their shared dressing room. When her maid returned with something for her to eat, she feigned that she was asleep. She listened while the young woman placed the tray on her dressing table before quietly exiting the room. Only then did she allow her tears to fall.

HE'D MADE A HORRIBLE hash of things with Sarah, but James forced himself not to follow when she walked away from him. The only thing stopping him from plowing his hand into the wall was the knowledge that Sarah would hear it, and the last thing he wanted to do was to upset her even more than he'd already done.

Anger, directed mainly at himself, and frustration were his ever-present companions and he struggled daily to stay away from his wife. When he'd seen her standing in the dressing room doorway, he'd thought for a moment that he was dreaming.

It had taken every ounce of strength he possessed not to pull her into his arms and clutch her like a drowning man. Surely this was what it felt like to go insane. His nerves were frayed and his very skin felt too tight.

When she'd told him that she wanted to resume their love-making... He closed his eyes, feeling again the surge of lust that had risen within him. He'd been intentionally cold to her and hated himself for the hurt he'd seen in her eyes. But he'd needed to ensure she left before he caved and gave in to his baser urges. He vowed to make it up to her after their child was born. He only prayed it wouldn't be too late and that her feelings hadn't turned to hate before then.

CHAPTER 16

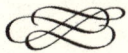

SARAH COULD BARELY stand to look at Alice, but she didn't confront the woman. What would she say? "By the way, are you sharing my husband's bed?" Nothing would be gained. After all, her husband wouldn't allow her to dismiss the woman who now warmed his bed.

It had been a week since she'd approached James, hoping to put an end to their estrangement. While it hardly seemed possible, she saw even less of him than before. She'd taken to having dinner in her room the past few days, unable to hide her low spirits from James's mother and sister while he remained absent.

A soft knock at the door signaled that her maid wished to collect her dinner tray. Sarah rose and steeled herself to betray none of her hurt.

Alice entered and dipped a brief curtsy before turning to remove the tray. She was so pretty it almost hurt Sarah to look at her. Tears began to sting her eyes, and she had to turn away.

Instead of leaving with the tray, she heard Alice move behind her.

"My lady?"

Sarah took a couple of deep breaths and turned to face her maid.

"I need to tell you something, and I'm afraid you'll be unhappy."

A kick to her stomach would have hurt less than those words. "Perhaps we can just continue as we have been." They were the words of a coward, but Sarah wasn't sure she possessed the strength to have this conversation.

Alice frowned. "His Lordship said you would understand."

Sarah's legs threatened to give way, and she sat heavily on the edge of the bed. "This concerns my husband?"

Alice shook her head. "Not directly, no, but he does know about it."

A tiny spark of hope flickered to life within her. "So what you wish to discuss… it isn't about James?"

There was no mistaking the confusion on Alice's face. "No, my lady. I know I should have told you that day you saw me leaving the dressing room, but I was in such a state, and I couldn't be sure how you would react."

Sarah looked down into her lap where her hands were resting and noticed that they were shaking. She clutched them together to stop the trembling and looked back at her maid. "What did you wish to discuss?"

Alice swallowed heavily before replying. "My relationship with Fenton."

Sarah had to remind herself to breathe. "My husband's valet?"

Alice nodded. "We've…" She hesitated, and Sarah wanted to shake the words from her. But she waited while her maid visibly gathered her courage. "He's asked me to marry him."

Her words came out in a rush, and for a moment, Sarah thought she'd misunderstood her.

"So last week when you rushed into the room from the dressing room…"

Alice clenched her hands before replying. "We were having a romantic moment. But it wasn't something we'd planned. We've been very careful to make sure our relationship doesn't affect our work. I was putting away the new dresses that had arrived for you, and I think he was arranging His Lordship's cravats…"

Sarah could picture the scene. "And my husband entered his room then."

Alice nodded, clearly embarrassed. "I rushed in here, which you saw, and Fenton went out to attend to Lord Hathaway."

Relief swept over her, so intense that for a moment she found it difficult to breathe.

"I was afraid we'd both be dismissed from our positions, but Fenton spoke to His Lordship recently and he gave us his blessing. But you've been so out of sorts lately. I was afraid you'd learned of our relationship and disapproved."

This time it was Sarah's turn to be embarrassed. She should have known that James wouldn't betray her with her maid.

"When you rushed out of the dressing room, disheveled, and I saw my husband was in his bedroom, I'm afraid I jumped to the wrong conclusion."

The look of horror on the young woman's face was almost comical. "Oh no, my lady. How could you think I would do something like that? I would never betray you in such a way."

It wasn't wise, but Sarah needed to speak to someone about her feelings even if that someone was her maid. No doubt the entire household staff already knew that she and her husband were estranged, so it wasn't as though she'd be revealing any secrets.

"My pregnancy has been hard on our marriage. We've had to be apart, and you know how men are. They will find their amusements elsewhere. I apologize for thinking the worst of you, but when you came out looking as you did…"

"His Lordship cares for you. He wouldn't betray you."

Sarah glanced away and took a deep breath before replying. "I wish I could believe you, but his absences every night lead me to think otherwise."

Alice shook her head, her expression earnest. "No, my lady. It doesn't mean what you think. I didn't say anything earlier because it wasn't my place to intrude, but I believe you need to know the truth. His Lordship has spent every evening at home. He stays up late in his study and then retires to a bedroom in the guest wing. Fenton told me that your husband is concerned only about your health and has decided it is best if he stays away while you are increasing."

So many conflicting emotions rioted within her, she had to close her eyes for a moment. "No," she breathed.

Alice nodded. "It is true. The entire staff knows that His Lordship is devoted to you."

Sarah resisted the urge to laugh, knowing the sound would only come out tinged with bitterness. It appeared that the fates had played a cruel joke on her. How could the entire staff know her husband better than she did?

"There is one more thing," her maid said.

"And what is that?" Sarah prompted when Alice hesitated.

"Fenton told me this in confidence. He must never learn that I told you, but I feel it is vital you know."

Sarah managed to breathe evenly. "I promise no one will know."

Alice nodded. "His Lordship doesn't believe he is worthy of you. He thinks you are too good for him and that he did you a disservice in convincing your parents to allow him to marry you."

Sarah had never hated herself more than she did in that moment. She had done that to him. James was everything a woman could ever want in a husband. Certainly he was more a man than Robert had ever been. Yet, to protect herself from being hurt, she'd hidden the fact that she'd loved him almost from the beginning of their marriage.

She stood and squared her shoulders, prepared to do battle with her stubborn, too-good-to-be-believed husband. "Where is Lord Hathaway right now?"

CHAPTER 17

*H*ER CONVERSATION WITH ALICE played over and over in her mind. She still couldn't believe she'd thought he was spending his nights with her maid when, in fact, he'd been hiding from her in a different part of the house. All because he cared for her and wanted to ensure her safety.

With the clarity of hindsight and with a light shone on all the dark, suspicious places in her mind, it all made sense to her now. She remembered just how stricken he'd been when she bled early in her pregnancy. Since that day, she'd convinced herself that he'd cared only about keeping his potential heir safe and that he'd decided to relieve his very healthy sexual appetite elsewhere. But she'd misjudged him in every way possible.

The fact that he believed himself unworthy of her was so far from the truth it almost hurt to contemplate. Her heart clenched as she acknowledged that she had been the cause of that. She'd convinced herself that all men were like her father and like Robert—selfish and only concerned about themselves. And in her zealous desire to protect herself from being hurt, she'd in turn hurt a man who had done nothing to deserve such treatment. In the end, she'd only succeeded in making both herself and her husband unhappy.

James… the man she loved.

She had to go to him, to tell him—and to show him—that she cared for and desired him above all other men. And God help her, she'd even bare her own heart and confess her love. It was more than she deserved that he'd love her, but she would learn to be content to have their relationship return to how it had been before everything had fallen apart.

She wrapped herself in her dressing gown and made her way down the dark hallways to his study. At six months of pregnancy, she feared she was beginning to waddle. But she'd occasionally caught the heated glances he cast her way when he hadn't started to avoid her completely, giving her hope that he still found her desirable. Her greatest problem, however, would be overcoming his reluctance to act on that desire.

Feeling more certain about her course of action than she'd ever been in her life, she knocked on his study door and waited for his permission to enter. When it came, she gathered her resolve about her like a cloak—knowing that her husband would do everything in his power to send her away—and entered the room.

James was sitting at his desk, his elbows on the surface and his head cradled in his hands. He looked the picture of defeat, and words failed her.

When she didn't speak, he looked up. His eyes widened in

surprise when he saw her. He rose swiftly, his eyes darting to her belly. "Is something amiss with the baby?"

"No, everything is fine," she said, rushing to reassure him. His shoulders sagged with relief and she took a moment to close the door behind her. "In fact, that is exactly what I wished to discuss with you."

His brows drew together. "I don't understand."

She crossed to his desk and skirted around it until she was standing next to him. She didn't miss the fact that his hands were clenched at his sides. Before that evening, she would have assumed he was annoyed with her, but given Alice's revelations, she now believed he was trying to keep himself in check. To keep from reaching out for her. That small proof of his emotions caused hope to surge within her.

"I haven't had a bleeding episode in months, and the doctor believes the danger to my pregnancy has passed."

He looked away from her and raised a hand to massage one temple. "We've already had this discussion. There is nothing more to be said."

She had to take a deep breath and gather her courage before she could continue. "I need to know why you haven't returned to my bed."

He dropped his hand and turned away from her.

"James?"

He shook his head. "I cannot discuss this with you."

"Cannot? Or will not?"

"Both."

She moved closer and reached for his hand. Placing it on her rounded belly, she watched as his expression softened. His hand curled over her middle, the warmth of his touch seeping through her nightdress and dressing gown.

"And what if I don't accept that?"

He lifted his face to gaze into her eyes and she saw, reflected in their depths, the pain he was suffering.

"I was selfish before and put our child's life at risk. Put *your* life at risk. I won't do that again."

She could tell by the tightness of his jaw and the determined glint in his eye that he wouldn't be swayed from his decision. But if James had taught her anything, it was that there were ways for a man and woman to be together that would pose no risk to her or to their baby.

"I miss you," she said.

He held her gaze, his eyes seeming to burrow straight through her, but he didn't reply. She would have to press the matter, and she knew just how to do it. She'd offer him the one thing she knew he'd wanted to experience with her but that she had always been too shy to even contemplate. Remembering again how selfless he had been on the first night of their marriage, she vowed to do the same for him now. She would show her husband that she placed his pleasure above her own.

But first she had to make sure he wouldn't pull away.

She feigned a swoon and he caught her upper arms, holding her steady. Sarah leaned into him, making sure to press her breasts against his chest. His sharp intake of breath gave her all the additional strength she needed to continue.

"I think I need to sit down." She didn't have to feign the breathlessness in her voice.

He led her the few steps to his study chair, released her,

and frowned down at her. "Have you eaten? Should I ring for your maid?"

Before he could escape, she reached for his hand and tugged him closer. He came, stopping when his legs brushed against hers, but didn't hide his reluctance. Somehow she managed to suppress the smile of satisfaction that threatened to undermine her plan.

"I know you feel strongly about this, so I won't try to change your mind."

He visibly relaxed, but she could tell he would like nothing better than for her to leave. He'd been avoiding her for months, but that was going to end tonight.

"I'll see you to your bed," he said. When she raised a brow, he squeezed his eyes shut and blew out a breath. "Not like that."

"I know, James. You are far too noble."

He released a snort of derision. She hated that he doubted his own worth.

"I want to give you pleasure like you did for me on the first night of our marriage and on so many other nights since then."

He couldn't hide the effect her words had on him as a shudder went through him. "You needn't make the sacrifice—"

She could see that he was already hard with desire. He was trying to act the gentleman, but his body betrayed him. She placed her hand over the solid length of his arousal and was gratified when she felt him twitch at her boldness.

He shook his head, but when she started to undo the buttons, he didn't stop her.

"I want to do this. I *need* to do this."

She pulled down the placket covering the front of his trousers and drew out his hard length. She'd missed this more than she'd thought possible. Missed being uninhibited with her husband, being able to touch him anywhere she wanted. And the way he looked down at her—a combination of disbelief and awe on his face—told her he felt the same way.

She stroked up and down his hard length just the way she knew he liked. Although he had proposed it on more than one occasion, she'd never taken him into her mouth, so he wouldn't expect her to do so now. And given their current estrangement, she knew he wouldn't suggest it.

He was standing before her while she remained seated, and she only had to shift forward a little to bring her mouth against him.

"Sarah." Her name was a ragged whisper, an unspoken plea that urged her to continue.

She wasn't sure if she was doing it correctly, but she knew how he liked her to run her hands up and down his hardness. She imagined that she needed to mirror that motion with her mouth.

His fingers threaded through her hair, his hands tightening against her head, but he allowed her to remain in control as she moved up and down his length. He was too big to fit all the way into her mouth, so she grasped the base of his hardness with one hand, stroking him with both her hand and her mouth while she used her other hand to fondle him below. When he groaned, excitement shot through her own body. Why had she been so reluctant to do this for him before today?

"Sarah, I can't… I'm going to finish."

He tried to move her head away from him, but she resisted. She wanted this, both for herself and for him. To show James that she accepted him.

He spent himself into her mouth with a guttural sound, and she swallowed all of it. She allowed him to pull her away from him then, watching in silence as he covered himself and buttoned the fall of his trousers. Then she stood to face him.

His eyes searched hers for several seconds. "Why?" he finally asked.

"Because I hate this distance between us, and…"

"And?" he prompted when she hesitated.

She'd come this far and she wouldn't allow fear to continue to silence her. She lifted a hand to caress his cheek. "I love you and I cannot continue to live separate from you. And since I'm being completely honest—perhaps for the first time since our marriage began—I'm afraid you'll find someone else to take my place."

He shook his head in disbelief. "I must have fallen asleep. Surely this is a dream."

He spread his arms and she moved into his welcoming embrace.

"You're not dreaming."

"In the face of your honesty, you should know that I'd wait forever for you. I love you, Sarah Hathaway, and no one else could ever take your place."

She would have wept with joy if her husband hadn't chosen to distract her then in another, more delicious manner.

EPILOGUE

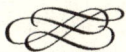

January 1814

ALL TOO SOON, James found himself pacing outside Sarah's bedroom again. Only this time, instead of worrying that she might be miscarrying, his wife was giving birth to their first child.

His mother had tried to drag him away, advising him that Sarah might be some time yet. James knew he wouldn't be able to stop obsessing over how Sarah and their child were doing. And so he planted himself outside her door and refused to allow anyone to draw him away. If he'd been allowed, he would have been in the room with her.

Her screams had him itching for a bottle of brandy, but he wouldn't dishonor her in that way. Sarah was going through the pain of childbirth… his part, by comparison, was easy. Still, he hated that he could only stand helplessly by and wait.

The door opened a crack and Lady Mapleton poked her

head out, giving him a strained smile that didn't quite reach her eyes.

"The baby is almost here," she said before closing the door again and disappearing.

He knew that Sarah's mother was only trying to be helpful, but her words did little to put him at ease. He'd been present for the birth of many foals, and he knew that the danger to the mother didn't always ease after the baby was born. Complications did arise. He personally knew two men whose wives had given birth to healthy children only to then succumb to death when they continued to bleed.

The sound of a baby's cry pierced the air, and James collapsed against the wall. He closed his eyes and prayed that Sarah would also be well.

A touch on his arm had him opening his eyes to find Emily and his mother standing before him. The expression on his mother's face told him that despite her attempts to calm his nerves, she'd also been concerned.

"It will be over soon," his mother said.

Emily's face was pale, and for once, she wasn't her normal jubilant self.

"I had no idea childbirth could go on for so long or that it was so painful. I'm glad now that I wasn't allowed inside the room with Sarah. As it is, I don't think I'll want to have children... not if the screaming is any indication of the pain I'll have to suffer."

Emily shuddered and his mother laughed. "You'll forget all about Sarah's screams after you've held the baby."

Emily looked doubtful, but the bedroom door opening prevented her from replying.

Mrs. Bryers beamed at him. "You have a healthy son."

"Sarah?" he asked, holding his breath.

"Her Ladyship is tired, but she, too, is well. She wants to see you now."

James needed no further prodding, brushing past the midwife and making his way to Sarah's side. His wife was gazing down at the baby in her arms, an expression of wonder on her face. After tearing his gaze from her face, he realized she was feeding the baby at her breast.

He lowered himself onto the bed beside her, ignoring the bustle of movement around him. "You look beautiful," he said, cupping her cheek.

Her laugh warmed his heart. "You are decidedly prejudiced. I'm sure I look a fright."

She looked down at their son and he followed suit. He couldn't resist moving his hand to cradle the baby's head, marveling at his warmth. His son continued suckling, ignoring his touch.

He had no words in that moment. He wanted to tell Sarah what she meant to him, but the words lodged in his throat—that he would never again doubt her or their life together. That he would do everything in his power to make her happy.

Fortunately, his wife knew him well enough that no words were necessary.

"I know," she said, leaning forward to brush a kiss against his lips.

The squawk of protest from their son had her leaning back, frantically trying to reattach him to her breast. James's heart swelled.

There, in front of him, was everything he'd ever need.

CAPTAIN HATHAWAY'S DILEMMA

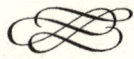

HATHAWAY HEIRS ~ BOOK 3

To fulfill his duty, he must forsake his chance at happiness.

When the man who saves his life during the Battle of Waterloo dies from wounds that were meant for him, Captain Edward Hathaway must live with the guilt of having survived and is determined to fulfill that man's dying wish.

Grace Kent only accepted her childhood friend's proposal of marriage so he wouldn't go off to war with a broken heart. But while she still grieves for her friend after learning of his death, she cannot resist her attraction to the handsome Captain Hathaway.

He is determined to discharge his duty at the expense of his own happiness. She wants only one taste of true passion.

Together, can they overcome the guilt that continues to haunt them both?

DEDICATION

To Neil, with all my love.

ACKNOWLEDGMENTS

This book would not have been possible without the encouragement of the other others in The Incomparables boxed set—Lynne Connolly, Cerise DeLand, Dominique Eastwick, Suzi Love, and Sabrina York.

Thank you!

CHAPTER 1

Mont-Saint-Jean Farm, Belgium
June 21, 1815

GAZING DOWN AT the shrunken figure lying on the hospital bed before him, Captain Edward Hathaway searched for signs of the perpetually happy young man everyone knew and loved. Why was it that men always looked so much smaller in stature when stretched out on a bed?

Or in a coffin.

His mind shied away from that image. He'd seen more than his share of death recently, but he'd also seen men survive worse wounds than the loss of a leg. And if anyone deserved to live, it was Private Freddie Reynolds.

It should have been him in that bed. Freddie had come between him and a bayonet aimed directly at his back during that final, bloody battle on the fields near Waterloo. The private had fended off that blow, but his heroism had been rewarded with a musket ball to the leg. Edward still didn't know what exactly had happened. They had managed to break through the front line of Bonaparte's infantry, but the enemy had been everywhere. Time had passed in a blur of blood and battle frenzy as every man fought for his very survival.

But he did know one thing. If not for this man, he would probably be dead.

He never knew what to expect each day when he walked into the field hospital that housed far too many of his men. The number of injured in the ward dwindled daily as men were discharged, transported, or succumbed to their wounds. But Freddie survived, and Edward clung to the hope that he would shake off the fever that seemed to plague him.

He was rewarded when the young man opened his eyes.

"The nurses told me you were awake earlier today. I was beginning to think you were pretending to be asleep to avoid speaking to me."

"Not at all," Freddie said with a strained chuckle as he drew himself up into a seated position on the bed. Neither of them said anything about his grimace of pain or about the visible absence of one of his legs underneath the blanket. "I was hoping to see you today, Captain."

Edward lowered himself onto the stool by the bed. "It eases my mind to see you up." He'd been thinking about what to say to this man, but how did one adequately thank someone for saving one's life? "I am forever in your debt," he said, having decided that the prosaic words would have to suffice.

"It has been an honor to serve with you, Captain."

It sounded as though the man was saying his farewells, but Edward shook off that morbid thought. "The honor has been mine. If there is ever anything I can do for you, you have only to ask."

Freddie looked him square in the eye, and in their depths Edward could see his determination. "In case there is no future, I do have a request to make of you."

"There *will* be a future," Edward said, refusing to believe otherwise.

Freddie looked away for a moment, struggling to form his next words. "I have written a letter to Grace. I'd like you to take it and deliver it to her personally. It is vital that she receive it." He pulled a folded square of paper from under the corner of his pillow. "I wrote it earlier today, and one of the nurses was kind enough to seal it for me."

Edward balked at the implication that the man before him would not be seeing his oft-spoken-about betrothed again. "I'm sure you will see her yourself soon enough."

Freddie tried to hand the letter to him, but he was weaker than he appeared. When Edward didn't take it right away, his hand sank to the bed. "I would consider it a personal favor."

Edward couldn't deny the request, but he hated that Freddie was even considering the possibility that he wouldn't recover. He took the letter from his hand.

"Promise me that you'll deliver it in person, Captain."

"You have my word, Private. But I won't be returning to England for at least another few weeks. I hope by that time to be delivering it to you and you can give it to your future wife yourself."

His promise seemed to put the young man at ease. His

shoulders visibly relaxed, and he could only nod in reply. Taking that as a sign that Freddie needed to rest again, Edward stood and took his leave.

When he reached the hallway, out of sight of Freddie and all the wounded men in the ward, he had to stop and gather the composure for which he was famous. Seeing Freddie in such low spirits had unsettled him more than he would have thought possible. The man in that bed was not the person he'd come to know. The Freddie he knew had buoyed the mood of every man in their regiment at one point or another. He was the eternal optimist who refused to give up hope even in the most dire of circumstances.

Edward had to struggle against the impulse to march back into that room and order the private to get better.

The sound of a single pistol shot came out of nowhere, unnaturally loud in the quiet hospital environment. Without thinking, Edward's hand flew to the hilt of his sword, but then he remembered where he was and that he didn't have the weapon that had seemed a part of him for so long.

He waited, listening for signs of a battle. But instead of hearing the clash of swords or the return fire he expected would come from the men stationed outside the makeshift hospital, a woman's cry of alarm came from the room he'd just vacated.

Dread settled in the pit of his stomach as he rushed into the ward. What he saw there affected him more than anything he'd seen on the battlefield.

CHAPTER 2

Somerset
July 1815

EDWARD WASN'T GOING to be put off another day. He had one last duty to perform—a personal favor for the man who had saved his life and subsequently lost his own—and he wouldn't fail.

He'd visited the modest estate and manor house in Somerset for the past three days and been turned away each time. Today was the fourth day he'd been denied entrance, but he wouldn't leave without speaking to Grace Kent in person. He suspected she'd been home on that first day. He'd been shown into the drawing room and told to wait before the butler had returned to tell him that his mistress was away from home. On his next three attempts, he'd been barred from admittance at the door. But it didn't matter if Miss Kent was home and refusing to see him or avoiding him by going out each day, he *would* see her today.

It was early afternoon, and he settled in for a long wait amid a small grouping of trees to the east of the house. He wasn't positioned so far away that he wouldn't be able to see the comings and goings of those within, but the cover provided by the trees would obscure his presence from those same people.

In retrospect, he realized it had been a mistake to send Miss Kent a note informing her of the purpose for his upcoming visit to Somerset. It would have been better to turn up unannounced and give her the letter her betrothed had asked him to deliver if he didn't recover from his injuries.

Edward didn't pretend to understand women. Freddie had confided that he'd known Grace all his life and that their friendship had blossomed into love shortly before he'd enlisted in the army. He would have thought the woman would welcome a final missive from her beloved, but he supposed it was possible her resistance to seeing him meant that her grief was too great to deal with the reminder of everything she had lost when Freddie died.

He hated times like this, when he had nothing to do but sit and wait. His thoughts drifted then, to past battles and all the horrors he had witnessed. Memories were the curse of those who'd survived. And now, more than ever, he couldn't forget the day he had failed the man who'd saved his life.

He'd lost track of how much time had passed when he spotted two figures riding toward the house. As they approached, he could see one of the riders was a woman and, from the way the second was dressed, guessed he must be a groom. They rode toward the stables where the man helped the woman to dismount before leading both horses inside.

When she turned toward the house, Edward jumped to his feet, intent on seizing the opportunity to corner the elusive Grace Kent. He cut across the grounds, his long stride eating up the distance. Miss Kent had avoided him thus far, but today he would finally discharge his duty and begin the business of trying to establish some sort of civilian life for himself.

He knew how to move quickly and quietly, and she didn't hear him approaching from behind. She was still several yards from the front of the house when he caught up to her.

"Miss Kent," he called out.

She stopped and turned to face him. She must have expected him to be the groom because her gaze darted from him to the stables before finally returning to him.

She took a step back, her face tightening as she waited for him to speak. But he found himself unable to do so for several seconds, struck silent by the beauty of the woman before him.

Golden hair tumbled from beneath the edges of a tall hat, her pale skin accentuated by the deep blue of her riding habit. The color of the garment had the odd effect of making her blue eyes appear an even brighter shade. Or perhaps that was the natural color of her eyes. He gave himself a mental shake when he realized he was staring. It was little wonder Freddie hadn't been able to stop talking about his future wife. At the reminder that he was here on Freddie's behalf, he experienced another stab of guilt at having been the cause of the young man's death. If the private hadn't intercepted the blow meant for him, he and Miss Kent would be reuniting right now.

"Please excuse my abrupt appearance. I only just arrived and didn't want to miss you again today."

"And you are?"

He frowned. Surely she wasn't going to pretend she didn't realize who he was. He'd play along, however, for Freddie's sake.

"Captain Edward Hathaway, at your service." He started to bow but hesitated when she began to shake her head in denial. "Am I correct in assuming you are Miss Grace Kent?"

She took another step back. "No... I'm sorry, but..."

She didn't finish, but he didn't need her to. Damn, this must be Grace's sister.

"I apologize. You must be Lady Trenton. I served with Freddie Reynolds and considered him a friend. He spoke of your sister, and of you, often."

Her forehead smoothed and she dipped into a curtsy. "I am pleased to make your acquaintance."

WHAT WAS SHE DOING? Needing something to do with her hands, she reached up and toyed with the locket she wore around her neck. It was bad enough that she'd been avoiding Captain Hathaway—thwarting what was no doubt an unpleasant task he hoped to fulfill before heading back to his own home—but now she was also lying to him. She hadn't intended to. She'd been shaking her head not in denial of her identity but because the very last thing she wanted was to be presented with one last letter from Freddie. She didn't think her conscience would be able to survive the guilt his words would no doubt cause.

But when Captain Hathaway immediately jumped to the conclusion that she was her sister Helen, she had taken the opportunity to avoid the inevitable pain for yet another day.

Now that her initial panic was beginning to fade, an uncomfortable realization began to take shape. As she stared at the stranger before her, she realized she was drawn to him in a way she had never been to Freddie. Taller, broader, more handsome, he was everything her betrothed had never been. But greater than his physical appearance, there was an indiscernible quality that drew her attention like no man she had ever met. She imagined that few women would be able to resist Captain Hathaway once he chose to pay them court. And unlike her feelings for Freddie, whom she had known since childhood, she could never imagine her feelings for Captain Hathaway being even remotely brotherly.

"Is Miss Kent at home today?"

It took her a moment to realize he had spoken. From the resigned look on his face, she could tell he didn't expect her to answer in the affirmative. And given the fact that she had all but said she was Helen, it was too late to correct his misconception.

"My sister has been away from home this past week."

He raised a brow in reply to her statement, making no effort to hide his disbelief.

"Upon my word, Captain, my sister is not in residence at the moment." The words were true enough, only they were about the wrong sibling.

"I don't suppose you could tell me where I might find her?"

The weight of Captain Hathaway's regard almost made her squirm, and she couldn't help but think he must see right through her pretense. "If you have something for Grace, you can leave it with me. I'll make sure she receives it."

She thought that was a good compromise. She wouldn't have to feign a pleasure she didn't feel at receiving a letter from Freddie. And more importantly, she wouldn't have to read it now. She could put the missive away and read it at a later date, after she had dealt with the grief of losing a good friend and the guilt she felt daily at the knowledge that she'd planned to break their betrothal when he returned from war.

But instead of handing her the letter, he shook his head. "I'm afraid I cannot do that. I was the last person to see Freddie alive, and he asked me to deliver his missive into her hands personally." He hesitated, as though considering whether to continue, before adding, "He saved my life, and honor demands that I fulfill his final request."

Grace faltered, her mind floundering for a suitable response. "I understand." She wanted to cringe at the banality of her reply.

The air lay heavy between them, neither saying anything for several seconds. Finally she had to look away from him.

She heard his exhale. "So, your sister? If you'll tell me where she is, I'll make sure to deliver the letter to her there."

She shook her head and braved another glance at him. "I… arrived after she'd left."

"Without telling anyone where she was going?"

"I think she wanted to avoid me." She warmed up to her

tale, recalling how many times her sister, who was the elder by only three years, often meddled in her affairs. "If she told the staff where she planned to go, she swore them to secrecy."

"People deal with grief in many ways." The flicker of anguish she saw on his face told her he was dealing with his own sorrow.

"We all knew and loved Freddie. News of his death hit us very hard." She had to close her eyes as another wave of guilt and sadness threatened to overwhelm her.

She almost jumped out of her skin when he reached for one of her hands and squeezed it.

"He was a good man, one of the best I've had the pleasure of knowing, and it was an honor to serve with him."

Her lips trembled, and she squeezed his hand back in acknowledgment of his own loss before releasing it. "Thank you."

He cleared his throat. "Do you know when she is returning?"

After their brief moment of camaraderie, she had to look away before voicing the lie. "I'm afraid not."

Captain Hathaway squared his shoulders. "I'll wait for her arrival, then."

"And if she doesn't return soon?" She hated the thought of wasting the captain's time. Perhaps she should tell him the truth. He'd be annoyed with her, but not as much as he'd be if he were to learn some days from now that she hadn't been honest with him.

A gleam entered his eyes as he stared down at her. "Then we'll have time to get to know one another."

A thrill shot through her at his words, along with the realization that he must know her sister was a widow. And in that moment, she knew she'd do almost anything to get to know this man better. It wouldn't go anywhere—it couldn't—but she'd never met a man who intrigued her even half as much as Captain Hathaway did.

She mentally asked Freddie for his forgiveness as she smiled back at the captain. "I'd like that very much."

CHAPTER 3

OTHING HAD CHANGED since he'd left on his mission earlier that day. Not really. Freddie Reynolds was still dead because he'd failed to see the signs that the young man was so dejected he'd actually take his own life. Edward still had to fulfill Freddie's final request—deliver his letter to the woman he'd loved and planned to marry. And Edward was still stuck in Somerset for the foreseeable future, the ever-present reminder of his failings weighing upon his conscience.

Yet as he made his way back to the small inn where he'd rented rooms for himself and Henry Gordon, his former batman while serving in the army and who now acted as his valet and personal servant, he felt decidedly more optimistic than he had in a long time—longer than he could remember —and that was all due to Lady Helen Trenton.

When he entered the small, dark room he'd been occupying since his arrival four days before, he found Gordon sitting at the small table in the corner of the room, reading. His valet placed the book on the table and stood as Edward closed the door to his room.

"You're in a better mood. I take it you've delivered the letter and want me to pack your belongings?" Gordon looked about the sparse room. They both knew the wardrobe standing next to the bed contained very little. He'd had the majority of his belongings, what little he'd allowed himself to keep while serving abroad, sent to his brother's estate in Gloucestershire.

Edward did want to quit the cramped inn, but they wouldn't be leaving Somerset. On his return, he'd given some thought to his plans for the immediate future and the first thing he wanted to do was to find alternative lodgings. He hoped to get to know Lady Trenton much better, but he certainly didn't expect her to visit him in a public inn. And he very much wanted her to visit him.

"Miss Kent is away and hasn't left word about when she plans to return. I've decided that since we must wait, we might as well make ourselves more comfortable."

His valet raised a brow. "I can inquire about moving to better rooms."

"Actually, I was thinking about leaving the inn altogether. I'd like you to look into renting a small cottage."

Gordon's brows almost disappeared into his hairline, and Edward could tell the man was questioning his sanity when he cast another eye about the room. To be truthful, while the chamber contained only the bare necessities of a bed, wardrobe, and small table to take meals, it was vastly more comfortable than sleeping on a cot in a tent in the midst of a battlefield. Since Gordon had served as a private under him, he knew the man's sleeping arrangements had been even more uncomfortable, having to sleep out in the open during a campaign. The beds at the inn were clean and, while a little lumpy, seemed luxurious in comparison.

Edward braced himself for the question he could tell the other man wanted to ask. But proving again that he had chosen wisely in deciding to employ the penniless young man when they'd both retired from the army, Gordon didn't give voice to his thoughts.

"If you'll give me a list of your preferences, Captain, I'll see to it right away."

Edward turned away and strode to the window. Out of a habit he'd developed since enlisting, he kept the other man in his peripheral vision. He couldn't help but feel exposed, as though he were placing himself and his actions on display with this request. While Gordon had served as his batman for the past year, Edward had never had a private life to scrutinize. And before enlisting he'd never had a valet, so he wrestled with the knowledge that he was revealing something very personal.

He almost laughed at his own melodramatics. Men had always pursued women, so it wasn't as though he was doing anything untoward or shocking in wanting to bed the tempting widow he'd met that afternoon. He turned his back to the window and faced Gordon.

"Some place quiet on the outskirts of town." He paused, considering how much to reveal, before adding, "Preferably where others won't see the comings and goings of any guests I may choose to entertain."

Gordon kept his curiosity in check with the aplomb of a man who'd been raised to serve, but he couldn't suppress his knowing expression that said he now understood the reason for his employer's sudden desire for comfort.

"I'd also like you to arrange a picnic lunch for tomorrow."

His servant didn't even pause before asking, "Will this meal be for yourself only?"

"No, I'm hoping to have a guest."

"Of course, Captain. I'll go down now and ask Mrs. Hillier to make the arrangements. If there's nothing else you require, I'll start making inquiries right away about cottages that are available for rent."

At his nod, Gordon retrieved the book he'd been reading, gave him a small bow, and left the room.

That small inclination of the other man's head struck Edward as being faintly mocking, but he attributed that perception to his feelings of self-consciousness. He couldn't help but think of his brother James who, as the new Viscount Hathaway, would now be surrounded by servants, and shuddered. It was bad enough having one servant who was aware of everything you did.

Thoughts of the beautiful Lady Trenton were never far, and now he allowed them to crowd his mind, unable to hold back the sense of anticipation coursing through his veins.

It was difficult to ignore the ever-present guilt that threatened to spring to life at any moment, but he refused to permit that emotion to dictate his actions. He wasn't courting Lady Trenton, so it wasn't as though he was headed for the wedded bliss that his friend had lost when he'd died in Edward's place. No one, not even Freddie, would expect him to live the life of a monk. All that mattered was that she wasn't an innocent. He'd make sure she understood that theirs would only be a brief liaison. In any case, he didn't have anything to offer a woman of her station and doubted she'd want more than that from him.

CHAPTER 4

A BREAKFAST TRAY was brought up to Grace's room, as it had been every morning since she'd returned home after learning about Freddie's death. Her father was very active in Parliament, and at her insistence that she needed time alone, her parents had remained in London. She'd been grateful for the opportunity to work through her grief away from their concerned presence.

But now her thoughts centered on her meeting with Captain Hathaway yesterday. She still suffered twinges of guilt at having lied to him, but when she remembered how he had flirted with her, she couldn't help but feel the thrill of anticipation.

After having breakfast and dressing, she made her way downstairs in search of something to occupy the long hours of the day ahead. She was at the base of the stairs when she saw the sealed note on the entrance table. Hoping it was from her parents to say they would soon be returning from Town, she crossed over to the table. Her heart stuttered when she saw that it was addressed to her sister.

It could only have come from Captain Hathaway.

She picked up the note and, her blood racing, made her way back to her bedroom. When the butler saw that it was missing, she knew he would assume she was holding it for Helen. Once safely behind the closed door, she broke the seal and unfolded the paper.

Lady Trenton,

I hope you will excuse my boldness, but I would like to invite you to luncheon with me.

In my brief time in your corner of Somerset, I have heard much about the beauty of the view from the hill to the west of the village—being native to the area, I assume you know the one. I thought a private picnic, far from gossiping eyes, would suit our purpose of getting to know one another better.

I will be there this afternoon at 1 p.m. If you do me the honor of accepting my invitation, you will find me at the top of the hill near what I'm told is an oak tree famous for its age.

I hope to see you there.

Capt. Edward Hathaway

She had to reread the note to make sure she'd read it

correctly the first time. Captain Hathaway had actually invited her to have a private lunch with him.

Aside from Freddie, whom she'd known all her life, Grace had never been alone with a man, and for a moment, she contemplated taking her maid as a chaperone. Doing so would send the clear message that while she enjoyed the captain's company, she was not the type of woman to indulge in private rendezvous with men she barely knew.

But as she considered the idea, she realized she was. There was no question that she would accept Hathaway's invitation, and she would be alone when she did so.

Excitement filled her as she refolded the note, her hands shaking, and hid it within the pages of a book of poetry that sat on the small writing desk in her room. She then placed the slim volume in the bottom drawer of the desk. She knew she should destroy the note—to keep it was to risk it being discovered. But this was the first time in her life an interesting man had shown her any attention, and she found that she didn't have the heart to throw the invitation into the fire. To do so seemed almost a sacrilege.

No one in her family liked to read poetry, and she doubted any of the maids would be interested, so it was unlikely anyone would open the volume even if they did stumble upon it.

Content that the invitation was safely hidden, she proceeded back downstairs.

The morning passed more slowly than she'd thought possible. Finally, when midday approached, Grace changed into her riding habit and headed out to the stables. She hadn't sent word ahead of time asking for her horse to be saddled because she didn't want to arrive before the appointed time. This luncheon wasn't like the balls she'd attended in London, but she knew arriving early was never desirable. The last thing she wanted was to appear too eager.

She watched the groom saddle her horse, her thoughts wandering to the man she was about to meet and how much he had affected her. She ruthlessly tamped down the guilt she felt about betraying Freddie. He'd placed her in a horrible position when he'd asked her to marry him, and she half suspected he'd timed the proposal to ensure she agreed even though she'd never considered him more than a good friend. She'd never intended to follow through with the marriage, planning to break the engagement when he returned from battle. Only he never had, and now everyone expected her to be heartbroken. She did miss him, and sometimes it hurt to breathe when she realized she'd never see his smiling face again, but she imagined it wasn't the same pain a woman felt when she'd lost her beloved.

When the groom moved to saddle a second horse so he could accompany her on the ride, she stopped him, telling him his presence wouldn't be needed. He started to protest, but she murmured something about riding to see a neighbor. Surely Captain Hathaway could be considered a neighbor if he was staying in the village, where she assumed he'd taken a room at the inn. The groom, of course, thought she meant to visit a friend who lived but a ten-minute ride to the south.

She allowed him to help her mount and headed off in the direction he expected her to go. When she was out of sight of the house, she turned east and rode across the field before finally arriving at the road that led north to the hilltop Captain Hathaway had mentioned in his note.

When Grace reached the base of the hill, her horse gave a small neigh of protest. She realized her nerves had led her to grasp the reins too tightly and forced herself to ease her grip. As the gelding began his climb, she looked up and spotted Captain Hathaway standing just where he'd said he'd be. His hands were in the pockets of his trousers, and he leaned casually against the trunk of the oak tree he'd mentioned in his note. Their eyes met, and when he smiled down at her, she couldn't keep an answering smile from forming on her own lips.

She hadn't even arrived at the top of the hill and already she knew she had made the right decision in accepting his invitation.

She drew the horse to a stop next to him and waited.

"Good afternoon, Lady Trenton."

She inclined her head in greeting and allowed him to help her down. She did this almost every day when her groom would assist her to mount and dismount, but having the captain's hands on her was decidedly different. When his hands settled on her waist, she noted immediately that they were much larger than those of the young man who normally accompanied her. And it had to be her imagination, but she thought she could feel their warmth even through the fitted jacket of her riding habit.

But what was most different was how his eyes fixed on hers when he touched her and how he maintained that contact as he lifted her from the saddle and lowered her to the ground.

They stood like that for several seconds... his hands on her waist, their gazes locked as she was powerless to do anything but stare up at him.

EDWARD FOUND HIMSELF in danger of drowning in the deep blue of Lady Trenton's eyes. When he came back to himself, he realized he was still holding her. He wanted nothing more than to lean forward and take her mouth with his, but it was too soon. And the heightened color staining her cheeks told him she wasn't altogether comfortable with the way he was manhandling her.

He forced himself to release her and took a step back. "I am so happy you consented to join me."

Clearly she was still embarrassed by his forwardness, for she looked away when she replied. "The day is lovely, and I admit I was curious."

Her color deepened as though she realized she had said too much, and he found himself charmed by her uncertainty. She might have consented to meet with him in private, but he could tell it wasn't something she did often.

He'd racked his brains the night before, trying but failing to remember how long it had been since Lady Trenton's husband had passed away. But he took the fact that the woman before him wasn't wearing black, nor had she the day before, as an indication she was no longer in mourning.

She turned to face the small village visible in the distance. "The view is lovely up here."

He took the hint. It appeared Lady Trenton was not about to just drop into his arms like ripened fruit, and he had to admit he liked that about her. It would make winning her even more satisfying.

"I thought it would be nice to lay out the meal in the shade of the oak."

"I am a little warm," she said. "I'd like that."

He retrieved from his horse the blanket and basket he'd brought with him—he hadn't realized how awkward it would be to carry the latter on horseback—and smiled his thanks at Lady Trenton when she took the basket so he could spread out the linen under what had to be the largest oak tree in all of England.

He offered her a hand, and she hesitated only briefly before placing her smaller one in his and lowering herself onto the blanket. When she released his hand and looked up at him, the expression in her eyes threatened to steal his breath. Reflected in their depths, he saw excitement and expectation. But not desire. Not yet.

He lowered himself next to her—far enough away to satisfy even the most disapproving of chaperones, but close enough that he'd be able to reach her without too much effort if she gave him even the slightest encouragement that she wanted from this meeting the same thing he did.

For now, she seemed content to make him work for her attention. He watched as she opened the basket the innkeeper's wife had packed for him not a half hour before. He tamped down his enthusiasm and took first the stack of plates Mrs. Hillier had included and then the wrapped packages as Lady Trenton removed each one and passed it to him.

When they were done, every inch of the blanket was covered with far too much food. Edward held back his sigh of disappointment as he reached for the remaining two plates and handed one to Lady Trenton. He waited for her to fill her plate before starting on his own. He feared awkward silence would descend once they began to eat, but that didn't happen.

"When we were much younger, my sister and I used to visit this same spot for hours to watch the comings and goings at the village," she said, ignoring the beef on her plate and taking a bite of plum cake.

He couldn't imagine what would have been so fascinating as to capture the interest of two young girls. "And what did you see?"

"Not too much. I admit that I used to hope we'd see a foreign prince or some other equally absurd nonsense."

"And did you?"

"We did see fine carriages on occasion, but more often than not they were just stopping at the inn so the occupants could eat and stretch their legs before continuing on with their journey."

"No foreign princes?" He was amused despite himself.

"Alas, not that I could tell. If a prince or two had been among them, they took great pains to disguise themselves as ordinary members of the gentry."

The wistful smile she gave him had Edward imagining that she still wished for such a sighting. They spent the rest of the meal in companionable conversation. When they'd both eaten their fill, Lady Trenton leaned toward him and he found himself holding his breath.

"Can I confess a secret to you?"

The expression on her face was a little sad and, in that moment, he wanted only to make her happy. He pushed aside the inner voice that asked him just how far he was willing to go to make that happen. He inclined his head in a nod, unable to voice any words as he imagined her confessing romantic interest in him. In his mind, he played out just how he would show her that he felt the same pull of attraction toward her.

Her voice was low and husky. "You must promise never to tell anyone."

He drew back a tiny bit in what he suspected was a vain attempt to hold himself in check. "You have my word."

She looked away from him, and for a moment, he feared she'd changed her mind about confessing her attraction. But then she straightened her shoulders and faced him again.

"Grace wasn't in love with Freddie."

Her words were so far from what he'd expected to hear that it took him a few moments to decipher what Lady Trenton had said.

"Miss Kent?" he said, his brow wrinkling. He'd been trying to forget the reason for his visit, had hoped the beautiful woman before him would offer him some respite from the guilt that had been pressing upon him, but now that emotion was back.

She nodded. "Grace loved him, of course, but that affection was similar to what she would feel toward a brother."

His frown deepened. "Many marriages are built on less than that. I daresay they would have been very happy together. From the way Freddie talked about her, I know he would have done everything in his power to make sure that happened."

Lady Trenton shook her head, the corners of her mouth turning down. "I'm afraid not."

He was about to protest, to say something about how his friend would have moved heaven and earth to ensure the happiness of his beloved, but her next words left him speechless.

"Grace was planning to break their engagement when Freddie returned."

She couldn't have surprised him more if she'd slapped him for the wayward thoughts he'd been having about her. He was powerless to stop the spark of anger that ignited within him.

"Because he'd lost a leg? Is she that shallow?" He scowled. "Are you?"

She shook her head, the vehement movement causing her curls to bounce. "No, of course not. To begin, we received word of his injury on the same day the second notice arrived telling us about his death."

She'd soothed his indignation on his friend's behalf, but her confession still made no sense. "Then why? Was there someone else?"

Lady Trenton's hands clutched at her locket. "Not then, no. But I think... I think she might since have developed an interest in someone else."

He had to fight back the urge to shake her for more information.

"I know this is none of my business, but Freddie Reynolds saved my life, and I find myself more than a little defensive about his memory. If your sister didn't know about the injury he sustained during that final battle, and if there wasn't another man at the time, why was she going to jilt him?"

She flinched at the harsh accusation but didn't try to deny its truth. "She never wanted to accept his proposal of marriage. She did love him, but not in the same way he felt about her."

He was about to ask why she would have accepted in the first place, but he didn't need to.

She continued as though he'd already voiced the question. "He asked for her hand right after telling her he had enlisted and would soon be leaving for the continent. I…" She gave her head a small shake before continuing. "What was she supposed to do? Send him off to war with a broken heart? She didn't wish to marry him, but she didn't want him in such low spirits that he wouldn't fight with everything in him to return."

He didn't want to feel sympathy for the faceless woman—the one who would have rejected his friend's love after he returned from war—but he did. If his own sister had come to him with a similar dilemma after receiving an unwanted proposal of marriage under the same circumstances, he probably would have advised her to do the same thing.

He nodded curtly and looked away. Somehow the information Lady Trenton had shared increased his feelings of guilt. It was absurd since this was something completely beyond his control—he hadn't even met the woman in question. But emotions weren't always logical.

When he looked back at Lady Trenton, she was staring at her hands, which were clasped tightly in her lap. He was surprised to see her shoulders were slumped in dejection, but then he remembered that she, too, had known Freddie and she must have also been feeling his loss. He wondered, in that moment, if she had loved her husband very much, and the thought caused a slight ache in his chest.

She had removed her gloves when they sat to eat, and he reached out to cradle one of her bare hands in his much larger one. Her skin was flawless, her hand tiny and delicate, and he couldn't hold back his need to lift her spirits.

When he raised his head to look at her, she was staring at him, her eyes wide with surprise. In their depths, he saw again the flare of her attraction to him. Leaning forward, his voice low, he said, "I'm going to kiss you now."

It wasn't a question, but she nodded her acceptance. He tugged on her hand to pull her closer. Their faces were now only inches apart, and her eyes had lowered to look at his mouth. When she drew her tongue along her plump lower lip, he wanted to groan. Instead, he moved slowly, afraid she would draw back at any moment, and pressed his lips against hers.

Her soft sigh was almost his undoing, but he kept the kiss light, moving his mouth gently over hers, noting how she leaned into him. He drew back then and stared down at her. When she finally opened her eyes, her expression was dazed and he had to fight against the urge to sweep her into his arms and make her his. He didn't understand why since she was a widow and would be no stranger to the physical act of love-making, but his instincts told him he needed to go slowly with her, and he always trusted his instincts.

They stayed like that for what seemed an eternity, gazing into each other's eyes without a word. Finally he could stand the wait no more.

"Helen…," he started, preparing to tell her just what he hoped would happen between them.

Her Christian name on his lips seemed to startle her, for she drew back and looked away. He couldn't understand why… Surely after meeting him in secret and allowing him to kiss her, she shouldn't be shocked.

"I need to return," she said, standing and shaking out her skirts. When she donned her riding gloves, he was surprised to see that her hands shook slightly.

He'd made a misstep somehow, but he couldn't pinpoint what had caused Helen—he could no longer think of her as Lady Trenton—to retreat so thoroughly. He stood and began to repack the remains of their lunch. She watched him in silence, and when he handed her the packages he'd rewrapped so she could place them in the picnic basket, he noted that she was careful to ensure their hands didn't touch. He was tempted to press the issue, to ask her what he had done to offend her, but seeing the stony determination in her expression, he decided it would be best to wait for another opportunity.

Together they walked to where she had left her horse to graze. She was studiously avoiding his gaze, so instead of helping her into the saddle, he waited for her to look at him. When she did, he could see the confusion in her eyes. No doubt it matched his own.

"I'd like to see you again," he said.

She swallowed with difficulty before replying. "I'm not sure that is wise."

"Hang what is wise. If recent events have taught us anything, it is that we must grasp these brief moments of happiness with both hands lest they slip away forever."

Her eyes softened. "I feel the same way."

"Good. Tell me where and when, and I'll make sure to be

there." She ran her tongue over her lower lip again, and the nervous gesture was almost his undoing. "Helen?"

She winced. "I don't know. You must give me time to think."

He wanted to protest, but he could tell from the way she held herself so tightly in check that she was becoming agitated. He lifted her into the saddle and took a step back.

"If I don't receive word from you tomorrow, I'll call on you the morning after." He was acting like a brute, but the thought of allowing this woman to slip through his fingers… the one thing fate had seen fit to gift him despite his recent sins… was more than he could stomach.

She nodded in reply. He took a step back and watched as she turned her horse back in the direction of her home and started down the hill at a trot. He waited, hoping she would turn back to look at him, but the wait was in vain.

CHAPTER 5

*G*RACE FOUND IT almost impossible to sleep that night. Thoughts of Captain Edward Hathaway, memories of their time together that afternoon, plagued her mercilessly. She wasn't experienced when it came to men, but she had a very good idea why he wanted to see her again, and it wasn't to court her.

He wouldn't be staying in Somerset long. In fact, he'd probably already have departed if she'd told him who she was and accepted Freddie's letter. No doubt his extended visit left him with too much time on his hands and he was bored. He thought her a widow, and women in such a position were known to take lovers. She'd never thought to find herself tempted by the idea of having a brief love affair, but heaven help her, she was.

She was already four and twenty. Not old enough to be considered firmly on the shelf, but with each year that passed, she got closer to that point. Her engagement to

Freddie hadn't been formally announced, but it was known that she wasn't free to entertain offers of marriage. That didn't mean there hadn't been gentlemen who'd flirted shamelessly with her. There had even been a few who'd hinted at a similar arrangement to what she suspected Hathaway was offering her now, but she'd never been tempted to accept them. She'd actually started to wonder if she should go ahead and marry Freddie when he returned—no other man had come even close to stirring her romantic interest, and at least she and Freddie shared a friendship and mutual respect for one another. She'd known they would have been content together.

Then she'd met Captain Hathaway, and suddenly all the things she'd read about in the horrid novels to which her sister had introduced her years earlier made sense. The long, meaningful glances, the way her heart seemed to beat more quickly whenever he was near. And heavens, it had threatened to stop beating altogether when he'd kissed her. It had been a chaste kiss, but if she'd read him correctly, he'd meant to continue. If he hadn't called her by her sister's name, reminding her of her deception, she wasn't sure she would have had the strength to pull away.

As the new day dawned, bright and clear, she had to face the truth—she wanted to experience more of what Captain Hathaway offered. This might be her only opportunity to know passion. But in order to engage in any type of love affair with the captain, she would have to keep pretending to be her sister, and she wasn't sure she could continue lying to him.

Somehow she made it through the day, though she couldn't say afterward what she had done to occupy her time. Looming ever present in her mind was Hathaway's warning that he wouldn't give up his pursuit of her.

She was no closer to reaching a decision when late afternoon approached. She only knew that one way or another, she would be seeing Captain Hathaway again. Would she be brave enough to reach for the pleasure he promised with every look and touch, or would she allow propriety to dictate her actions when he called on her? It wouldn't take much to end his pursuit—all she'd have to do was tell him she'd misled him and be honest about who she was.

Grace's room overlooked the front of the house, so when a carriage approached she saw it right away. For a moment, she thought her parents had returned earlier than expected, but as it neared she recognized it as belonging to her sister.

It would appear her dilemma was at an end. If Captain Hathaway was paying attention to the comings and goings in the area, and she believed him thorough enough to be doing just that, he would soon learn of her sister's arrival. He would think it was her returning from the fictitious trip she'd invented to keep him from discovering her identity. When he called on the morrow, he would discover the truth.

She wanted to believe she would have been honest with Captain Hathaway the next time they met, but wasn't sure she believed it.

She made her way downstairs and waited outside for the vehicle to come to a halt, watching as a footman helped her sister and then her maid down from the carriage. They looked alike, she and Helen. Like her, Helen had fair hair and blue eyes. They were only two years apart in age and had often been mistaken for twins by strangers meeting them for the first time. A pang went through her when she realized that if Captain Hathaway had, indeed, met Helen first, he would have been pursuing her instead.

"This is a surprise," Grace said as she embraced her sister. "Are you just visiting, or will you be staying?"

Helen linked her arm with Grace's, and together they moved into the house and headed for the drawing room. Over her shoulder, she asked a footman to bring tea.

"I'll be here for the rest of the summer. I've received word from London that Mama and Papa plan to return soon. They've been worried about you and wanted me to check on you, and since I had nothing to do at home..." Helen shrugged and dropped onto the settee. "It is so good to finally get out of that carriage."

Grace's thoughts returned to Captain Hathaway as she asked, "Did they say when they would be returning?" She chided herself even as she asked the question. She *knew* what would happen now. The captain would learn of her deception and, after giving her Freddie's letter, would leave long before her parents arrived.

"Papa still has some matters to attend to, but I know they hope to be back before the end of the month." Helen hesitated, examining her intently before asking, "How are you doing? I was devastated to hear of Freddie's death. I can only imagine how much worse it was for you. If I'd known you were here by yourself, I would have come down sooner."

Seeing the sympathy in her sister's eyes, Grace remembered, again, that day one month before when they'd received the news. It had taken her days to get over the initial shock and grief at having lost a good friend. But the guilt, the feeling that she hadn't been worthy of Freddie's regard, had never left her.

"It was difficult. I loved him, but..." She took a deep breath before admitting the truth to her sister. She had only told one other person about her true feelings before today. "I wasn't in love with him. I think it is safe to say that we both felt the same way about Freddie."

Helen reached out and grasped her hand, giving it a quick squeeze of understanding before releasing it again. "I suspected as much, but still I'd hoped to see you married and living together happily. Many marriages are based on much less than what you and Freddie shared."

Grace nodded and had to hold back the tears that stung her eyes. She'd confessed the truth about her feelings, but she wouldn't dishonor Freddie's memory further by admitting that she'd planned to end their betrothal when he returned. "Remember how he used to tease us mercilessly about how much we looked alike? Pretending not to be able to tell the difference between us?"

That was all it took for the two of them to fall into sharing memories of all the scrapes Freddie had dragged them into. When the footman arrived with their tea, Grace waited as her sister poured and handed her a delicate cup of the fragrant brew. It was always like this when her sister returned home. Helen fell into the habits that came with being the older sibling, and Grace allowed herself to feel comforted by the fact that her sister would always know what to do.

"I'm so glad you're here," Grace said.

Helen took a sip of her tea and smiled back at her. "Are

you going to tell me now what is bothering you? Aside from Freddie, of course."

Grace sighed. She shouldn't have been surprised. At times Helen knew her better than she knew herself.

"I've had a visit from the captain of Freddie's regiment. Freddie wrote me a final letter before he…" She couldn't say the words.

Helen was instantly alert. "What did it say?"

"I haven't read it yet. I did a horrible thing, Helen."

Her sister's brows drew together in a frown. "You didn't destroy it?"

"Oh no, never that."

Helen's expression softened. "Do you want me to read it first?"

Grace cringed at the sympathy in her sister's eyes and her guilt intensified. "I don't have it yet. When Captain Hathaway arrived, I had him turned away from the house at first. I couldn't stand the idea of reading a letter from Freddie telling me how much he was looking forward to returning home and about his dreams for our future." She couldn't face the censure she knew she'd see on her sister's face, so she occupied herself with pouring more tea into her cup. "When we finally met, we had something of a misunderstanding."

"What sort of misunderstanding?"

Grace braced herself as she blurted out the truth. "He thinks I'm you."

"Why would he think that?"

Helen's voice was surprisingly free of emotion, and Grace looked up to see her frown was back in place.

"When I refused to take the letter, he assumed and…" Her

shoulders drooped. "And I didn't correct that assumption."

"Oh, Grace."

"I know. I'm a horrible person. I'm doing a disservice to Freddie's memory, and I'm keeping the man here under false pretenses. I told him Grace was away, and he's waiting to deliver the missive. He says he promised Freddie he would do that."

Her sister placed an arm around her shoulders and drew her closer to her side. "You are not horrible. You have received a great shock, and I think anyone would understand why you cannot face the idea of reading Freddie's letter now that he is no longer with us."

Feeling unworthy of the comfort her sister was offering, Grace pulled away from her. "That isn't the worst of it."

"You like this Captain Hathaway."

Grace closed her eyes as misery flooded through her. "I *am* a horrible person. He invited me to a picnic lunch yesterday and he was so attentive... And now, since he thinks I'm a widow..."

"He wants more."

Grace nodded.

The silence in the room was almost deafening before Helen finally spoke. "Well, this is unexpected. I take it you don't want me to take your place from this point forward?" Her sister correctly interpreted the horror that spread through her at even the thought of Helen being with Captain Hathaway. "I thought not."

She knew that Helen was only teasing, but it did nothing to lighten her mood.

"You care for this captain." It wasn't a question.

"I don't know. I barely even know him."

"But…"

Grace slumped back on the settee. "He makes me feel things I never did with Freddie, nor with any other man I know."

"Is he attractive?"

"Oh yes." Grace sighed and realized she must look like a lovesick fool. Well, perhaps she was a fool. How else could one explain why she'd been acting so out of character? "But it isn't just his looks. I've met many handsome men in London since Freddie went away, and heaven knows more than a few of them have pursued me, but no one has ever made me feel the way Captain Hathaway has."

Helen, bless her heart, didn't condemn her. "Would it be so bad if he knew who you really were? Just tell him the truth. Explain that you couldn't handle the idea reading Freddie's letter yet and behaved badly."

Grace cringed. "I'm going to have to. But I know he won't feel the same way about me when he discovers who I am."

"That's a chance you're going to have to take. You can't continue to lie to him."

"I know," Grace said, a sense of finality settling in her bones. "It was stupid and cowardly, and now I must face his censure when he learns I've been wasting his time."

When Helen suggested that Grace send him a note asking him to call, she shook her head and explained he was already planning to visit tomorrow. But what she didn't tell her sister was that she planned to visit him later that night and tell him the truth in private. She'd acted the coward long enough, and she needed to do this on her own.

CHAPTER 6

*G*RACE MOVED SILENTLY through the house and exited by means of a window in her father's study. Helen had already gone to bed, exhausted from having risen early that morning and spending hours in a carriage. That left Grace free to slip out of the house shortly after the sun went down. She couldn't risk trying to saddle a horse herself and being caught, so she set out on foot in the direction of the village.

It took her three quarters of an hour to reach the cottage the captain had mentioned he'd be renting for the remainder of his stay in Somerset. When she finally arrived, her stomach was in knots. She could very well imagine what Hathaway's servant—surely he'd have at least one with him—would think when he found an unescorted woman paying a call after dark.

She almost sagged with relief when the door was opened by Hathaway himself. Surprise, then delight, lit his face when he saw her. He glanced over her shoulder and his smile turned into a frown.

"Please tell me you didn't arrive on foot?"

She couldn't resist the urge to dip into a deep curtsy, saying, "It is very nice to see you too, Captain."

For a moment she thought he was going to lecture her about safety, but in the end, his good humor won out. He opened the door even wider, and she stepped into the hallway.

"I'd offer you refreshments, but…" He gave a small shrug. "I only have my valet with me and he has gone out."

Hathaway's words set one small part of her mind at ease. At least he didn't have scores of servants who would immediately brand her a trollop.

They were alone in the house, and her pretense was now at an end. Grace took a deep breath to steady her nerves and met his gaze. There was no point moving to the small sitting room she spied on the right. Once he learned the truth, the captain would give her Freddie's letter, and she would be on her way again.

"I am here to let you know my sister arrived this afternoon." She hesitated, dreading what she must confess now.

Hathaway nodded. "I'll call tomorrow then."

Somehow she had to tell him the truth. "About that, there is something I must tell you. I—" She froze when Hathaway placed a finger over her lips.

"Let me speak first."

The way he was looking at her, the fact that his hand had moved and now he was cupping her face, rubbing his thumb over her lower lip, left her bereft of speech. She could only nod.

"Once my duty here is discharged, I will be leaving."

She waited, knowing he wanted to say more.

"I don't want to waste what little time we have together talking about your sister. I would much rather talk about you and me."

He stepped closer so their bodies were almost touching and she found it difficult to breathe. She could see the heat in his eyes as he gazed down at her, trying to tell her without words just what he wanted from her.

She wanted the same thing.

He seemed to be waiting for her reply. She knew he wouldn't press her, that the decision about what happened next lay with her. If she told him the truth now, he would step away from her. He wanted the experienced woman he thought her to be, not the innocent for whom he felt only duty. If she allowed that to happen, she would spend the rest of her life regretting her cowardice. This was her one chance to know passion. To experience the fulfillment of a desire only he seemed capable of rousing. Whether she ended up marrying someone who left her feeling lukewarm or spent the remainder of her days a spinster, she would at least have this one memory to look back on.

Before her nerves could get the better of her, she reached up and drew his head down. She saw the flare of satisfaction in his eyes before she closed her own and waited for his kiss. She didn't have to wait long. With a softly whispered endearment, he pressed his mouth to hers. This kiss was so different from the one they'd shared the day before. He drew her body against his, and when she opened her mouth in surprise, he took advantage of the opportunity to thrust his tongue within.

Heat suffused her at the intimacy. She'd never kissed a man like this—had only offered Freddie a peck on the cheek before he'd left—but somehow she knew what to do. Her fingers slid into his hair, and she twined her tongue with his.

When he lifted his head minutes later, a hint of red stained the top of his cheekbones. She was incapable of speech, but none was necessary. Hathaway took hold of her hand in his larger, callused one and led her toward the stairs.

It was only as she followed him that she realized the captain wore only a shirt and trousers, and she couldn't help but stare at the way his muscles shifted as he moved. He was so broad, and she'd felt how strong he was when he'd held her against him.

He opened the door to his bedchamber and waited for her to enter first. If she were going to change her mind, now would be the time to do it. But Grace had committed to this, she wanted it more than she'd thought possible. Anticipation filled her as she preceded him into the room.

Her gaze fell first on the large bed, then on the trunk placed at its foot. Resting atop was a sealed note.

"Let's not think of Freddie," he said, taking her hand again and turning her to face him. "Tonight there is only the two of us."

She nodded, relief filling her when he pressed her close and kissed her again. As his mouth devoured hers, his fingers touched her through the fichu she'd tucked into the bodice of her dress, and with a flick of his wrist, he removed it. She gave a helpless whimper, her excitement increasing. This was really happening. She was in Hathaway's bedchamber, sharing intimacies she had only imagined.

"Captain—" she started, drawing back.

He gave his head a sharp shake. "No, call me Edward. I want no reminders of war in here."

She licked her lips, and his eyes narrowed on the small movement. "You must show me what you want me to do, Edward."

Her words seemed to startle him, and she remembered he thought her a widow. She was supposed to know what to do.

Working only on instinct, trying to make him forget her careless mistake, she pulled his shirt from his trousers and burrowed her hands underneath. The feel of his hot skin under her fingers felt deliciously wicked. Her gamble had paid off. He made an impatient sound, turned her around, and started undoing the buttons of her dress. There were far too many of them, but finally he reached the last one. He pushed the fabric from her shoulders, and she felt a hint of alarm when it fell to the floor.

She had to remind herself that he thought her experienced, so of course he wouldn't feel the need to go slowly. When her stays followed next, she drew in a deep breath. He groaned in appreciation and cupped her breasts from behind through her chemise.

Now it was her turn to groan. His body was hard behind her, his hands insistently cupping and kneading her, and when he ran his thumbs over her nipples, heat spiked through her.

"I have imagined doing this to you." His voice was low against the skin of her neck and gooseflesh rose on her arms.

He turned her, again and, before she realized his intent, dragged her chemise down her shoulders. She should have been embarrassed when her breasts sprang free, but the way he looked down at her, as though she were the most beautiful woman he had ever beheld, made her only want more. She was lost to sensation as he caressed her again, and when he lowered his head to take the tip of one breast into his mouth, it fueled her desire.

Needing to feel his skin, she pulled at his shirt. He obliged her, drawing back to lift the garment over his head. She could only stare at him in appreciation.

"We're going too fast," he said. "I want to savor every inch of your body. Take all night to worship you."

She shook her head, her curls bobbing. She couldn't be away from home all night. With each hour that passed, the risk grew that someone would discover she was missing.

If he'd known who she was, she didn't think she'd be able to act in so forward a manner, but since he thought her a widow, she could touch him however she liked. Relying only on her instincts, hoping they would be sufficient to keep her from doing something wrong, she lowered her hand to the bulge in his trousers and stroked him. She was rewarded when his breath hissed out of him.

"You are more than I could have imagined, H—"

She cut him off with a kiss. It would spoil everything if he called her by her sister's name now.

When he lifted her in his arms and tossed her onto the bed a moment later, she knew she had succeeded in making him forget his vow to go slowly. She tilted her hips so he could remove her chemise completely.

She watched in silence as he stepped out of his trousers, then his smallclothes underneath. When he straightened, she couldn't take her eyes from his arousal. It jutted out from his body, and she felt the first stirrings of alarm at its size. She knew what was supposed to happen now, but found it hard to imagine that he would actually fit inside her.

"You're so large," she said.

His eyes heated, and she realized he'd taken her words as a compliment.

He joined her on the bed then. If she'd thought it wonderful to be held in his embrace before, the feel of his body now, all his warm skin sliding against her own, almost left her mindless with pleasure.

She thought he would enter her then, but instead he began to trail hot kisses down her body. Knowing how much he liked her breasts, she wasn't surprised when he spent some time caressing and kissing them. What she didn't expect, however, was for him to move even lower.

She was completely out of her element and had vowed she wouldn't protest, but one minute later, she did just that when he spread her legs wide and moved his head between them. "What are you doing?"

He answered her by setting his mouth over her intimately and stroking her with his tongue. Her hips jerked up off the bed.

This was too much. Did men actually kiss women *there*? They must.

The sight of him between her legs, coupled with the bliss spreading through her, was too much. She closed her eyes and gave herself up to sensation as he continued tormenting her with his mouth and tongue. When he thrust a finger inside her, her entire body tensed before a wave of intense pleasure, unlike anything she'd ever experienced, ripped through her.

When he moved to cover her body with his again, she was still struggling to recover her breathing.

"I never imagined…"

His smile was strained. "You feel tight. How long has it been?"

She shook her head, unable to voice yet another lie. He didn't ask again. When he lifted one of her legs, she realized he wanted her to clamp them around his hips. She did so, her breath hitching when she felt his hardness pressing against her.

She tried not to tense. She'd heard that some women, particularly those who were avid riders as she was, didn't feel much pain when they made love for the first time. Still, he was watching her too closely. When he started to enter her, she lifted her head and kissed him. He groaned against her mouth as he sank into her with a single thrust.

It appeared she wasn't one of those women who felt no pain. She stiffened at first, but when Edward would have moved to look down at her, she clung to his neck and deepened the kiss. He didn't protest, and after a few moments, the discomfort had receded.

He began a steady thrusting motion between her legs, and before long she started to feel the stirrings of desire rise within her again.

He tore his mouth from hers and she allowed it, feeling the need to try to catch her breath. But she couldn't, and then she was coming apart again, splintering into a thousand pieces. He stared down at her as he continued to move, but she was too caught up in what she was experiencing to be embarrassed by his scrutiny. Much to her surprise, she found she very much liked the fact that he couldn't seem to tear his gaze away from her.

He closed his eyes and jerked his hips away from her then, and she felt the warmth of his release against her inner thigh.

He rolled onto his side, taking her with him. They lay like that for several minutes, their bodies pressed tightly together as they struggled to right their breathing. She needed to remember everything about this moment. The way she could feel his heartbeat against her own chest, the solid feel of his warm skin against hers, the way he held her as though he never wanted to let her go.

Her heart was still racing several minutes later when she realized that nothing had changed. She still needed to tell him the reason for her visit.

She pulled away and rose to sit on the edge of the bed as she struggled with what to say. She couldn't blurt out the truth, not after what had just happened between them.

He made a funny, strangled sound that surprised her.

"What is the matter?" she asked as she looked over her shoulder at him.

But he wasn't looking at her. Her eyes followed his, and she froze when she realized he was staring down at her blood on his bedsheets.

CHAPTER 7

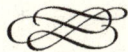

SURELY HE WAS imagining things. He stared down at what could only be blood on the sheets where Helen had lain, but his mind couldn't quite comprehend what he was seeing.

His gaze met hers. "But you're a widow…"

She closed her eyes, and he struggled to understand what was happening. How was it possible that she could still be a virgin? He tried to remember how long she'd been married, but Freddie had rarely spoken about Helen. He'd talked almost nonstop about Grace, the woman he'd planned to wed, but only about the rest of her family on rare occasions.

When she opened her eyes again, understanding dawned when he saw the guilt reflected there. "You're not Helen."

She shook her head.

He swore, and she flinched at his harsh language. Rising swiftly, he began to dress. After a few moments of silence, she did the same.

He tried not to watch her as he dragged his trousers back on, but he was only human and his eyes kept drifting back to her. He couldn't help but notice the way she struggled with her stays. Without a word, he moved behind her and, after a moment of hesitation, reached for the laces of the garment and helped her back into it. His fingers—no, if he was being honest, his whole body—struggled against the urge to remove it again even as he tied the final knot. The desire to tear the chemise she wore beneath it took his breath. Even knowing who this woman was, he wanted nothing more than to take her back to his bed. The only thing that stopped him was the memory of Freddie telling him how much he loved Grace and imploring him to deliver his letter to her. It had been his last request right before he took his own life.

He pushed away his desire and moved to where his shirt lay on the floor. He turned his back on the woman with whom he'd just made love and pulled it back over his head. When he turned back to face Grace, he was slightly relieved to find she'd finished dressing. But his torment wasn't over quite yet. She turned around, and he had to grit his teeth when he realized she needed his help to do up the row of buttons at her back.

He was in hell, and this was his punishment.

He crossed the much-needed space he'd managed to put between them and began the slow, arduous process of covering up the woman he'd taken such delight in disrobing what felt like only moments before. When he finally reached the last button, he dropped his hands and waited for her to turn around. It was several seconds before she did so, and she kept her gaze averted from his.

It almost hurt to look at her, and in that moment, he

understood why his friend had lost his heart to this woman. If he wasn't careful, he could very easily find himself following suit. But Freddie had died because of the despair brought about after receiving wounds meant for him. Freddie had saved his life, and Edward wouldn't shirk his responsibilities now. He wouldn't use the woman his friend had loved and then casually toss her aside.

When he spied the gauzy material of the fichu she'd worn when she first arrived, he bent to retrieve it. He handed it to her and watched in silence as she tucked it into the neckline of her dress, hiding her glorious breasts from him.

"We'll marry at once," he said. "I can leave tomorrow morning to procure a special license."

He expected her to agree or to nod her acceptance, but when she lifted her head to meet his gaze, her eyes were wide with confusion. "Why?"

He scowled. "Because I don't take advantage of innocents." When she flinched, he realized he'd spoken much louder than he'd intended.

"It was not my intention to force a proposal of marriage from you."

Her hand moved up to toy with her locket, and he remembered Freddie saying that he'd given it to her after she agreed to marry him. Ice ran through his veins at the thought of having made love to her while she wore it.

"Nevertheless, what's done cannot be undone, and I owe it to Freddie to behave honorably." He wasn't sure if he'd mentioned her former betrothed's name to convince her or himself of his responsibility toward her.

"You would have been content to bed me, believing I was a

widow, and quit Somerset without offering marriage. Does it really matter that I'm not?"

"Of course it does. You are not so innocent that you wouldn't know society has one set of rules for women who are or once were married and another, much harsher set of rules for those who have been ruined."

"I detest that term," she said, returning his scowl. "And I refuse to discuss this further."

When she turned toward the bedroom door, he blocked her path.

"I don't understand how you thought I wouldn't notice you'd never been with another man." Never mind that he'd been so consumed by lust that he'd only made the discovery after seeing the physical evidence of her innocence. "I will give you time to acquaint yourself with the idea, but we will be married."

She looked away from him. "I can't talk about this with you."

He wanted to press the issue, but the stubborn tilt of her head told him there was nothing he could say at that moment to make her understand marriage was the only course of action open to them. He'd give her the time he promised, but not too much of it.

Resisting the almost overwhelming urge to draw her into his arms and use other methods of persuasion, he moved aside and allowed her to brush past him.

He stepped into his shoes and followed as she rushed downstairs, trying to ignore his annoyance at just how anxious she was to leave. When she halted abruptly at the base of the stairs, he glanced over her shoulder and saw that Gordon was in the sitting room. He'd been reading but had risen when he saw Grace.

Edward jerked his head to the left and his valet bowed before excusing himself to go upstairs. Grace's color was high, and it was clear she was embarrassed at having been seen.

"My servant is loyal and won't say a word."

Her lips compressed into a tight line, but she gave her head a small nod. He followed, once again, as she left the cottage. He waited until they were outside, where Grace could be reassured that their conversation wasn't being over-heard, before reaching for her hand and pulling her to a halt.

"I must leave," she said, refusing to meet his gaze.

He allowed her to pull her hand from his, the movement leaving him feeling oddly bereft, but he wasn't about to allow her to go home on her own.

"I will take you home," he said. When she shook her head, he added, "I insist."

He resisted the urge to smile when she let out a long-suffering sigh and followed him to the small stable at the rear of the cottage where he kept his horse. When she saw he only had one, she visibly recoiled.

"I am not riding on that horse with you. I walked here and will return the same way."

The thought of her walking home alone in the dark made his blood freeze. He'd give Grace the time she needed to get used to the fact that they would be married, but he wouldn't allow her to put her life at risk.

"I'll either walk beside you or we can ride together. But if we walk, there is an increased likelihood that we'll be seen, and then you'll have no choice but to marry me." Not that she had a choice in any case, he added silently.

When she said nothing, he leaned forward and trailed a hand along the neckline of her dress. His fingers dipped inside briefly, and he didn't miss the way her breath hitched. Damn, he was getting hard again. Before he could give in to his selfish desire and compound his betrayal of Freddie, he tugged the fichu from where she'd tucked it into the top of her bodice and pulled it from around her neck.

"Cover your hair with this. If we see anyone on the way, you can turn your face into my shoulder and conceal your identity." He could tell that she wanted to protest, so he added, "Unless, of course, you want to be seen alone with me."

She yanked the fabric from his hand, making no effort to hide her annoyance, and tied it around her hair. He couldn't stop his gaze from drifting down to her bodice. The upper swells of her breasts were visible now, and they quivered with her quick, jerky movements. His mouth watered as he remembered with vivid clarity how they had tasted.

If she noticed, she didn't say anything. He saddled his horse quickly, noting how Grace kept glancing toward the open door of the stable. But she chose wisely to wait for him to finish because there was no way he was going to allow her to walk alone at night when anything could happen to her. While it was true that the surrounding area seemed quiet and safe, he'd seen enough to know that atrocities could occur anywhere.

When he was done, he led his mount outside, swung into the saddle, and held his hand out to her. He frowned when she hesitated, tamping down the urge to remind her that she hadn't minded his touch not a quarter of an hour before.

"The sooner you get on this horse, the sooner you'll be home and rid of me."

His words had the desired effect. She placed her hand in his and allowed him to help her up so she sat sideways before him. Her left arm was around his waist for balance, and he had to shift in the saddle so she wouldn't feel how he'd hardened again.

The ride to her parents' estate wasn't a long one, but it threatened to undo Edward's resolve to be circumspect in his behavior toward Grace until she agreed to marry him. Aside from the arm she braced at his waist, she tried to keep herself away from him, but her body kept swaying against his before she stiffened and pulled away again. She didn't need to lean against him though to drive him insane. Her scent alone reminded him of how it had felt to hold her, to kiss her and sink into her.

He kept his gaze fixed forward, determined not to leer at her cleavage, but it took all his willpower to do so. The worst of it was that he could tell by the way her breathing had quickened that she, too, was not immune to being this close to him.

He didn't take her right to the house but rode to the small copse of trees where he'd taken shelter on the day they'd met. When he came to a halt, she slid from the horse and left him without a word or a backward glance.

He supposed it was what he deserved.

CHAPTER 8

*E*DWARD DIDN'T EVEN try to hold back his intense relief when he heard the knock at the front door the following morning. It hadn't taken Grace long to come to her senses. He waved his servant away and opened the door himself, but it wasn't Grace standing on the threshold. Instead, he found his brother.

He wasn't surprised James had tracked him down. His brother wasn't a patient man at the best of times and wouldn't have been happy to receive Edward's letter telling him that his arrival in Gloucestershire had been delayed. But that didn't stop Edward from chastising him.

"Was there some emergency of which I wasn't aware?" He moved into the small sitting room and sank into an armchair, leaving his brother to close the door and follow.

"It isn't far," James said. "It wasn't a great inconvenience for me to come here."

Edward raised a brow as James took a seat in the other chair, which was all the prodding James needed to tell him the real reason for his visit.

"Fine. Mother insisted that I come and make sure all is well with you. I'm under strict orders to discover if there is anything that would prevent you from joining us at some point in the near future. She's afraid you'll disappear again and she won't see you for another few years."

Edward blew out a harsh breath as thoughts of just how complicated his life currently was assailed him. But the last thing he wanted to do was discuss Grace Kent with his brother, or how he had betrayed a friend, the man who had saved his own worthless hide. He hadn't just slept with the woman Freddie loved more than life itself, he'd taken her innocence. He was afraid to admit even to himself how much he wanted to give her his name, to be the one to take care of her. And he knew, deep down, that the fact he wanted her so much meant he shouldn't have her. Edward had failed Freddie when he'd needed him most, and he didn't deserve happiness in return. Certainly not with Grace.

He tried to push back his morose thoughts and concentrate on not betraying his inner turmoil. "I still can't believe you are actually the viscount now," he said, trying to shift the focus onto his brother. "And how is it possible that you already have two sons? Uncle must be rolling over in his grave."

James fixed him with an amused expression. "Of that we can have no doubt. But you won't distract me by changing the subject to my life. I'm not quite that self-absorbed."

Edward shrugged. "There isn't much to say. You can tell

our mother that I will definitely be returning, hopefully before too much longer."

"A woman is involved," James said.

Leave it to his brother to know immediately what was troubling him. "Isn't one always?"

"Is there anything I can do?"

Edward shook his head. "I doubt it. But you can help me take my mind off the situation."

James seemed to consider his request and in the end let the matter drop. "Mother was very unhappy when you enlisted. I'm sure she didn't say as much when she wrote to you, but in the beginning she could hardly sleep. Things got better when the months went by and we didn't receive word that you had died in battle. But when Napoleon returned..." He released a breath. "We were *all* concerned. I can't tell you how relieved I am to find you in one piece."

Their care touched him. He'd known, of course, that his family would be worried about him, but it had never been something that affected his thoughts. All that had mattered was that they were safe at home. In retrospect, he should have realized they would have wanted to say the same about him. "You can assure Mother that I have retired my commission, so she needn't fear that I'll be heading off to battle again."

"I've already told her as much, but you know how she worries."

Yes, he did. And while he would have chafed under the weight of her concern when he was younger, he now found the thought comforting.

"There's another reason for my visit," James said.

Edward knew his brother well enough to read his body

language. James leaned back in his chair, but the casual position was a little too contrived. And his brother had never been able to keep his eyes from glowing when he was excited.

"Well, get on with it. I can tell you're almost bursting."

James let out a small bark of laughter. "How I've missed you these last years." He leaned forward, bracing his weight on his knees. "It's about the horses."

Edward hadn't been expecting that. "I thought you'd moved the stables to Gloucestershire. And from what I've read in our sister's letters, you spared no expense."

James grinned. "Uncle's fortune was good for something after all."

Picturing the expression on the former viscount's face if he'd known a good portion of his wealth had gone toward embellishing the stables their father had founded, a venture he'd always disdained, Edward let out a snort of laughter.

"I know. It's been a couple of years now and I still find it amusing. At any rate, before you make other plans for your future, I wanted to let you know that there will always be a place for you at Hathaway Stables."

Anticipation surged through him at the thought of going back to his greatest passion—raising horses. But much as he missed it, the last thing he wanted was to accept charity from his brother. His income was sufficient for his own meager needs. *But not if he married Grace*, an inner voice argued. He did his best to ignore it.

"I'm not sure why you need me. Your instincts when it comes to horseflesh have no equal. You always had an excellent eye and few could do a better job raising and training them."

James frowned. "You do yourself a disservice. It's true that I usually jumped in before you when I saw the potential in a horse, but you know I've never been known for my patience. Before you enlisted, you were always by my side. I saw the gleam in your eye when we stumbled upon a horse that showed great promise. That's one of the reasons I was always so quick to act—because your reaction usually confirmed my own belief that we should do what we could to acquire the animal."

Edward hadn't known his brother had even noticed which horses he'd favored. But now that he thought about it, those were the animals he chose, even when they hadn't discussed the matter. He'd always assumed James relied only on his own instincts.

"Be that as it may, you've done well these past few years without me."

"Yes, and it's been deuced difficult. I've only managed because I've been neglecting some of my other duties, but I can't keep doing that. I need you, Edward. What do you say?"

His excitement started to grow as he considered the future. To be able to go back to breeding and training horses was more than he'd hoped for. He'd missed it in the past few years, more than he would have thought possible. And best of all, he'd be near his family again.

"I'd say you have yourself a partner."

"Excellent. And just so you know, I haven't forgotten that the original stables founded by Father belonged to both of us. I've been putting away your half of the profits while you've been busy elsewhere, so there's a tidy sum waiting for you. I even have a comfortable house I can give you."

Edward didn't even bother to protest. James had always been generous by nature, and he knew there would be no refusing the gift of a house. And to be honest, he didn't want to refuse. Now he just needed to see if that house would have a mistress in one Grace Kent.

CHAPTER 9

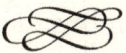

ONLY TWO DAYS had passed since she and Edward had made love, and he'd told her that he would give her time to think about the future. He hadn't mentioned it, but in the clear light of day the next morning she realized that she'd taken a great risk giving in to her passion. It was then that she understood she could be with child. If that were the case, she would have no choice but to accept the captain's suit. She'd often been accused of being stubborn, but even she wouldn't bring shame on her family merely because Edward wasn't in love with her.

When she awoke to discover her monthly courses had arrived, Grace didn't know what to feel. Uppermost was the thought that she should be relieved. There would be no baby and, therefore, no reason for her to wed. No doubt, the captain would be beyond happy to hear the news. There was a not-insignificant part of her that was disappointed, but she refused to dwell on the reasons for that disappointment.

She needed to tell Edward he was no longer obligated to marry her, and she felt compelled to do so right away. She set out earlier than normal for her ride that morning, wanting to escape the house before her sister woke and insisted on accompanying her. She thought she'd have to lie to her groom again, but apparently content with the fact that she had returned home safely after her last outing alone, the young man allowed her to leave without protest.

Her chest tightened the closer she got to Edward's residence. The cottage where they had made love. She wanted to turn around and return to the safety of her home. Instead, she pressed herself to keep going. She left her horse to graze and made her way down the path to the front door. Echoes of the last time she had been there kept playing in her mind. It had only been two days, but they had been two of the longest days of her life.

When Edward's servant opened the door, she had difficulty meeting his eyes.

"Captain Hathaway isn't expecting me, but I hope he will see me at this early hour."

If he thought her a strumpet, he gave no indication of it. In fact, he seemed almost happy to see her. "If you'd like to wait in the sitting room, I'll let him know you are here."

She didn't have to wait long. When Edward swept into the room not one minute later, she was grateful to be seated. He was so tall, so handsome… and the intense expression on his face when he looked at her, a mixture of surprise and satisfaction, left her weak in the knees. She knew then that she had committed the unpardonable sin of falling in love with him.

And after she explained why she was there, he would give her Freddie's letter and leave without a backward glance.

She tried to keep hold of her composure when he moved farther into the room and, instead of sitting in one of the chairs opposite her, lowered himself next to her on the settee.

They were both quiet for what seemed an eternity before he spoke. "I didn't expect to see you again so soon. I thought I'd have to storm your house and insist on being given entrance." He was aiming for levity, but his smile did not reach his eyes.

"I never wanted to deceive you," she said. In that moment, it seemed more important than anything else that he know she hadn't set out to trap him into marriage. "The last time I visited you, I intended to tell you the truth about who I was." He frowned, and she didn't need to hear the words to know exactly what he was thinking. "Yes, the fact that my sister had arrived forced my hand. I wanted to be the one to tell you, and I fully accept that I should have been honest with you right from the beginning."

The worst thing about lying, even if it was a lie only by omission, was that you inevitably risked having your honesty questioned when it mattered most. She hated that the man sitting next to her now had every reason in the world to think she was still being untruthful with him. She held his gaze, willing him to believe her.

"I don't understand why you lied in the first place."

She closed her eyes briefly and sighed, mentally preparing to be completely honest with him. "You assumed I was my sister and I..." She gave a helpless little shrug, knowing her excuse was feeble. "I allowed you to continue in that belief. But I never said I was Helen."

He frowned, and the disappointment in his eyes caused her to flinch. "I still don't understand why you didn't want me to know who you were."

She took a deep breath before admitting the truth. "I panicked. I knew you were there to deliver Freddie's letter—I think it's no secret that I'd been avoiding you for days—and when I ran into you... when you introduced yourself and I shook my head, I wasn't denying my identity. I was shaking my head because I didn't want you to give me his letter."

"And I immediately jumped to the conclusion that you were your sister."

"Yes," she said, nodding eagerly, grateful he remembered that moment. "It was stupid and selfish, but when you assumed I was Helen, I agreed even before I knew what I was doing. I didn't mean to deceive you, but I wasn't ready to accept that letter." She looked away then as she admitted, "I'm still not sure if I'm ready."

He didn't say anything, and she continued with her confession. If she expected him to believe her, she would have to be completely honest, and that meant revealing things she had never told another person. "I was so angry when I learned of Freddie's death, but mainly with myself. I'd known for some time before he enlisted that his feelings for me were beginning to change. From time to time I'd catch him looking at me in a way he never had before, and there were moments when I could have sworn he was about to kiss me. I should have dissuaded him, told him that my feelings for him would never be anything more, but I didn't want to hurt him. And in truth,

I didn't want to lose his friendship. I never imagined he'd enlist, nor that he'd propose marriage right before leaving. When word reached us that Freddie had died…" Her breath hitched, but she drew comfort when Edward grasped one of her hands. "I know he enlisted because he wanted to prove himself to me. I'd teased him for being sweet and kind natured, and I think he thought joining the war against Napoleon would show me he wasn't weak. But I never thought that about him. I would give anything if it meant he could be here with us again."

She didn't realize she was crying until Edward pulled her into his arms, and she went willingly. She'd been trying so hard to keep herself from falling apart—holding back her grief at losing a dear friend and trying to deny the guilt that whispered late at night, when she was alone in bed, that it was her fault Freddie had died. Her head told her she hadn't done anything for which she should feel guilty, but a small corner of her heart couldn't help but wonder if she could have prevented his death. If she'd asked him not to leave—to marry her right away instead—he would still be alive.

When she finally pulled away, she was surprised to see the haunted look in Edward's eyes. His voice was stark when he spoke. "If anyone is to blame, it is I."

She hated to see his pain and wanted nothing more than to comfort him the way he had comforted her. "I know he served under you, but you cannot hold yourself personally responsible for his death. That dubious distinction goes to Napoleon and the men fighting with him."

"Freddie received his injuries after saving my life." Edward gave his head a sharp shake. "He charged in like a damned fool

331

and placed himself between me and the bayonet that was aimed at my back. I never saw it coming. I heard the clash of swords behind me, and when I finally dispatched the devil intent on eviscerating me from the front, I heard his cry. When I turned to help him, it was too late. He'd taken a musket ball to his leg, but at least I stopped the blade that was aimed at his belly."

Grace's heart broke at the description of Freddie's bravery. Yes, she'd teased Freddie and called him too kindhearted for his own good, but she knew that when it came to those he cared about, he was fiercely loyal. She could very well imagine Freddie rushing in to save Edward without thinking of the danger he'd placed himself in.

"That wasn't your fault. Wasn't he doing the same thing he'd done in countless other battles? You protected each other as well as you could, and I'm sure the same could be said for every man in your regiment." He started to shake his head again in protest, but she continued. "His letters were filled not with stories about the battles he'd fought, but about the men he served with. He even mentioned how you'd saved his life a time or two."

Instead of comforting him, her words seemed to cause him further anguish. "I probably shouldn't tell you this, and you must promise never to reveal this to his parents. It would devastate them to learn the truth."

A shiver of foreboding crept up her spine, and in that moment, she wanted to tell him to stop. But her avoiding unpleasantness was what had landed them in this untenable situation in the first place, and she had made a vow not to indulge her need to escape.

She nodded and braced herself for what was to come.

"I was with Freddie right before he died. He'd just given me his letter to you after exacting my promise to deliver it in person."

The certainty that he was about to reveal something she very much didn't want to hear grew with each word he spoke, but it was clear that Edward needed to confide in someone. He'd borne whatever he was about to tell her for this past month, and she hoped that by sharing this confidence with her he'd gain a measure of peace.

"I was blind. Edward had lost his leg and he wasn't his normal happy self, but I never imagined…" He took a deep, shuddering breath before continuing. "I was still in the hallway outside his hospital room when I heard the blast from a pistol. When I returned to his room, it was too late. He'd taken his own life."

A sob escaped her throat, and if possible, his expression turned even grimmer.

"I failed Freddie twice already, the first time when I ignored his dejection and told myself he would soon come to terms with having lost a leg, and the second time when I took the woman he loved to my bed. I won't fail him again and leave you to suffer for my own selfishness."

Deafening silence followed his vehement vow, and when she spoke, her voice was barely audible. "I am not with child." She could see the protest forming on his lips and cut him off. "My monthly courses began this morning. So you see, there are no consequences to the night we spent together. You are free to go on with your own life." She mentally added the "without me," knowing that her voice would betray her feelings if she spoke them aloud.

She expected him to be happy at her news, but his posture didn't relax and he certainly didn't exclaim his relief. Confusion clouded her mind when he reached for her hand.

"It matters not that you are without child. You were an innocent, and I have betrayed Freddie's memory. Nothing has changed."

"No one knows about us—"

"*I* know, and I cannot live with myself knowing that I have dishonored both of you."

His demeanor was so cold. She wasn't so young that she still entertained romantic fantasies—any foolish notions she'd had of marrying for love had been dashed when she'd witnessed her sister's marriage to a much older gentleman— but it hurt more than it should have to hear the practical words coming from Edward's lips.

"Surely your own feelings should be taken into consideration? I know that Freddie wouldn't expect you to sacrifice your own happiness for him."

She spoke the truth, but even as she said the words she knew she was fishing for something to tell her she could marry Edward. She couldn't stop remembering the way he'd been when he'd thought she was Helen. Carefree, flirtatious, and above all he'd looked at her as though she were her own person and not just Freddie's betrothed.

He dropped her hand and leaned slightly away from her. "My feelings have no bearing on this."

His words hit her like a slap, and she needed to get away from him before she betrayed just how much his calm, practical manner had hurt her. She stood and took a step backward when he followed suit.

"I thank you for your offer, but I cannot accept it. As I have already mentioned, it was never my intention to trap you into offering for me. And as my reputation is still intact, we would both be better served if we said our good-byes and pretended this entire episode had never happened."

He crossed his arms over his chest and pinned her with a narrow-eyed stare. It took every ounce of strength she possessed not to squirm under that intense gaze.

He was so cold, so distant now. She couldn't help but remember the moment he'd changed from the charming man who wanted to get to know her better to this stranger. It had happened the moment he'd realized her true identity. The heat that had been in his eyes when he looked at her had cooled, and his entire demeanor had stiffened. In that moment, she'd known he would forever hold himself separate from her. It was as though Freddie had been right there in the room with them and he still hadn't left.

"I will take your reluctance as a sign that you require more time to accustom yourself to the idea of marrying someone you barely know."

Unspoken was the accusation that while she needed more time to accept his offer of marriage, she'd had no such qualms about sharing a bed with him. She wondered what he would say if he suspected that she denied him now only because she was terrified of just how much she wanted to say yes. This man, with his ability to cut himself off from his feelings—from her—was far more dangerous to her peace of mind than any potential scandal she might face if someone were to suspect what had happened between them.

"If you would be so kind as to give me Freddie's letter now, I will take my leave."

She thought he was about to argue with her, could almost see the words taking shape in his mind as he continued to stare down at her, but he never spoke them. Instead, he turned on his heel and left the room.

She let out a shaky breath as she listened to him climb the stairs and heard the sound of a door being opened upstairs. He was descending mere seconds later and moved back into the room.

When he extended the letter toward her, she knew they were both reliving the moment when he had first approached her and she had shaken her head and stepped away from him. The moment when he'd come to believe her to be someone else and they'd started down a path they never should have taken.

She was relieved her hand wasn't shaking when she took the letter from him. "Thank you," she said before moving around him.

When he let her leave the house without another word, she knew beyond any shadow of a doubt she was doing the right thing. Edward had convinced himself there could be nothing but duty between them, and she couldn't marry a man who would never allow himself to see her as something more than a responsibility. She would rather remain alone for the rest of her days.

CHAPTER 10

*A*LMOST A WEEK and a half had passed since she first rejected Edward's proposal. He'd been true to his promise, though, to give her time. Since that day when she'd told him she wasn't with child, he'd called on her daily to act the part of the perfect gentleman courting the woman he hoped to marry. She hated everything about the pretense. Every time he spoke to her with polite interest, without even a hint of warmth in his voice, she became more convinced she had made the right decision in rejecting him. She couldn't help but wonder if he had been disappointed in her when they'd made love, reinforcing her determination to keep holding him off until he finally gave up and returned home.

That day could not come soon enough. But despite everything, she didn't regret giving in to her passion even though it hurt more than a little that Edward only wanted to wed out of a sense of obligation.

She tried to imagine any of the other men of her acquaintance performing a similar sacrifice—insisting that they marry even though no one knew of their liaison and there was no danger she was with child—and couldn't do so. To a man, they all would have absented themselves as quickly as possible, relieved at how their near miss had turned out.

Edward Hathaway was far too noble, and she loved him for it. His daily visits, while frustrating in the extreme, were also a temptation to accept his offer of marriage, which still stood.

The first sign that he was serious in his intention of courting her was the bouquet of roses that arrived the morning after she'd visited him the second time. The simple but beautiful arrangement was not just an announcement to her of his intentions, but to the world at large. When it had arrived, she'd known it wouldn't take long for word to spread that she had an admirer.

Helen chaperoned them during his visits, and it came as no surprise to Grace that her sister was utterly charmed by the captain. What woman wouldn't be? That first afternoon, the tension between them had been high, their already awkward situation made worse by the fact that Grace kept looking for signs that Edward would have preferred to spend time alone with her sister. But even if he did, he showed no indication of it. When Helen had suggested they take a walk about the gardens, Grace had leapt at the opportunity to quit the stifling confines of the drawing room and their stilted conversation.

As the days passed, a different arrangement of flowers arrived each morning, followed by an afternoon of very proper, chaperoned visits. It didn't escape her notice that

Helen went out of her way to make sure she and Edward had some time alone together. But if her sister hoped that in doing so she was facilitating a love match, she was destined to be disappointed.

As the days passed, it got harder for Grace to see him and to be reminded about what could have been if they had met under different circumstances. Her despair was made worse when they returned from the most recent of their now-daily walks to find that her parents had finally arrived. As she and Helen stepped into the house and learned of their arrival, she was grateful Edward had taken his leave of them outside.

Grace turned to her sister, the stirrings of panic threatening to overwhelm her. "What do I tell them about Captain Hathaway?"

Helen shrugged. "They probably already know."

The words had barely left her sister's lips when a flurry of movement on the stairs told them their mother was descending.

"I was so hoping to see Captain Hathaway again," Lady Kent said. "Why didn't you invite him in?"

Grace couldn't have heard her mother correctly. "You know Captain Hathaway?"

"Of course we do, my dear. Didn't he tell you? He called on us in London because he had a letter from Freddie that he had to deliver personally. When we told him you had already returned home, he set out to visit you here."

"He never said anything." She looked at her sister, who shrugged to indicate that this was the first time she, too, was hearing about this.

"I assume he's given you the letter? I can't imagine how

hard it must have been to receive it so soon after learning about Freddie's death."

Grace didn't miss the look of concern on her mother's face. "I haven't read it yet," she admitted.

Her mother drew her into a tight hug. "You take all the time you need, dear." She pulled back and gazed down at Grace. "What is this I hear about the captain courting you?"

Grace groaned. "Not you too, Mama."

"It is not a crime to want to see one's daughter happy and settled," she said with a slight lift of a shoulder.

"Captain Hathaway is being very kind to me, but he isn't courting me."

Her mother raised a brow. "I heard he was sending you flowers?"

Her mother's ability to know everything that was going on never failed to surprise her. For a fleeting moment, Grace wondered if she knew about what had happened between her and Edward, but her mind shied away from that possibility. If her mother knew, she'd already be making wedding plans.

"How do you hear these things all the way in London?"

Her mother smiled in triumph. "I've decided to invite him for dinner tomorrow."

Grace resisted the impulse to beg her mother not to. She knew that once her mother's mind was made up, there would be little chance of her changing it.

"You have no objection?" Lady Kent asked.

Grace shook her head and resigned herself to an uncomfortable evening of intense scrutiny from her parents.

"Excellent," her mother said. "I will have a footman

deliver the invitation shortly. But first I must tell your father. He's been very worried about you."

Grace watched as her mother breezed down the hallway and entered her father's study without knocking.

"They're going to be so disappointed," she said, her voice barely above a whisper.

Helen had been watching their exchange in silence, but now that they were alone again, she dragged Grace into the drawing room. "Captain Hathaway cares for you."

Grace immediately shook her head. "No he doesn't." She hesitated, wanting to confide in her sister, but decided in the end just to tell her the base truth about her current predicament. "He and Freddie were friends and Freddie saved his life. He feels honor bound to take care of me because of that."

Helen looked at her as though she'd gone insane. "That man has not been visiting you every day out of a sense of duty."

Grace wanted to believe her sister, but the way he'd been treating her recently convinced her otherwise. "He doesn't love me. You've seen the way he acts toward me."

"Grace, the man can hardly take his eyes off you. And when he thinks neither one of us is looking?" She fanned herself with an exaggerated wave of her hand. "Trust me when I say that while he may be acting the gentleman, his thoughts are anything but proper when it comes to you."

Her foolish heart actually felt as though it were going to burst out of her chest at her sister's words. "I don't believe you."

Helen released a dramatic sigh. "Tell me, how do you feel about the captain?"

Her feelings were still too new, and his reception of them too uncertain, for her to admit she loved him. Even to her sister. "I am not indifferent to him."

Helen laughed outright at her sister's equivocation. "Lord, the two of you are a pair. Each one crazy about the other but neither one willing to admit it."

"I didn't say I had strong feelings for him."

Helen gave her an indulgent smile. "You didn't have to."

Grace winced. "Do you think Edward knows?"

Her sister's smile widened, and Grace could have cut out her tongue for slipping and using his first name. "I think he is as oblivious to the truth as you."

Grace had to consider the possibility that Helen was seeing only what she wanted to see. "What do I do? I'm not sure I believe you, but if there's even a slight chance that he does have feelings for me…"

"He does, but I suspect you'll have to pry them out of him."

"How?"

"Well, we can start with tomorrow's dinner. No more sensible outfits for you, dear sister. Tomorrow evening you are going to dress to dazzle, and then you are going to have to flirt with him."

Grace cringed. "In front of our parents?"

"Of course. How better to make him squirm than have him realize what you are doing and know he cannot reciprocate unless he wants Papa to pull out his dueling pistols?"

"And if he doesn't 'squirm,' as you so eloquently put it?"

"He will." Helen's expression could only be described as evil.

Grace considered her options carefully, but she really had no choice. If there was even the slightest possibility that Edward cared for her, she needed to find out. There would be no more running away for Grace Kent.

CHAPTER 11

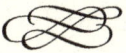

$\mathcal{T}$HE SOLITUDE GRACE had enjoyed before Helen's visit and her parents' return to their country estate for the rest of the summer had been a soothing balm to her soul after learning of Freddie's death. She still hadn't managed to make herself read his last letter—it seemed her guilt would always be a part of her—but now that the house was once again filled with people and with activity, she felt she'd soon be able to do so.

But not until after dinner that evening. She wasn't sure she'd find the courage to engage in a light flirtation with Edward, especially in front of her parents, if she had to read another letter from Freddie about how much he was looking forward to returning home and spending his life with her. He'd always been upbeat in his correspondence, and while she'd known he must have faced horrors on a daily basis, it had never really occurred to her that he wouldn't return. She'd always assumed he would somehow get over her breaking their engagement and they would find their way back to being friends. But he'd done the unthinkable and actually died. Edward's revelation that it had been by Freddie's own hand had horrified her. It was nearly impossible to reconcile the optimistic man she'd once known with the one who would sink so low in spirits that he would do such a thing.

No, it was better for now if she tried not to think about Freddie at all.

As expected, her father spent the day in his study meeting with the steward and catching up on all matters pertaining to the running of the estate. Her mother, as she always did after returning home from London, spent the day examining every room in the house before heading outside to do the same with the gardens. It was as though she expected everything to have fallen into a shambles during her absence and needed to reassure herself otherwise.

That left Grace and Helen to amuse themselves, and they did just that. Helen was determined that Grace look her best for dinner that evening and so embarked on a campaign to make over one of her own dresses so that it bordered on being scandalous.

Grace's mouth dropped open in shock when Helen ripped out the seams of the lavender gown's bodice and started pinning it quite a bit lower.

"Mama will never allow me to wear that in company," she said with a grimace. "And even if she did, I don't think I'd feel comfortable having so much of my bosom on display."

Helen gave a heavy sigh as she removed the pins and adjusted the neckline again so it would fall somewhere between the original shape and the scandalous one.

"I think this might suffice. And you're right, but it's Papa you need to worry about. He wouldn't care who was around—he'd send you right back upstairs to change. I've become so accustomed to living my own life away from them that I'd forgotten how protective they can be."

Grace didn't comment, but she did give silent thanks for that overprotectiveness. And she did insist on trying on the dress before her sister whisked it away to make the changes to the décolletage permanent.

Now, standing before the full-length mirror in Helen's old bedroom, the one she still used when she returned home, Grace could see that Helen had been right. But her sister hadn't just modified the neckline of the gown. She'd also narrowed the fabric that swept down from the bodice, making the dress skim over her figure in a way that was much more daring yet still on the proper side of decorum. Their parents, in particular Papa, wouldn't be happy, but they wouldn't put up too much of a fuss. Especially if she made sure to go downstairs after their dinner guest had arrived.

Helen's eyes shone with excitement. "You look beautiful, Grace. Captain Hathaway won't be able to hide his feelings from you tonight."

"I hope you're correct. If not…" She shuddered. "I don't relish the idea of making a fool out of myself."

"You won't," Helen said. "If you trust nothing else, believe that I know a few things about men."

Remembering how her sister had had half the *ton* eating out of her hand during her one season in London, Grace clung to the belief that Helen might just be right.

CHAPTER 12

*I*T WAS TOO LATE to take Lord Kent aside and ask the man's permission to court his daughter—he imagined word of his courtship would have already reached Lord Kent's ears since he hadn't been making a secret about his intentions. What he really wanted to do as he arrived for dinner was press Grace again to marry him, but if the way she'd been holding herself aloof from him was any indication, she wasn't any more likely to accept today than she'd been the first time he asked. He was frustrated with his lack of progress and couldn't fathom what more she wanted from him. They were compatible physically—there was no way an innocent could have faked her reaction to his touch—and before he'd discovered her true identity, their conversation had been free and easy. Why, then, was it so impossible for him to figure out what she was thinking? Worse, he was beginning to fear that his courtship was just as uncomfortable for her as Freddie's had been. He wanted Grace to come to him freely, but he wasn't sure he'd be able to wait for that. But the opposite—leaving Somerset without her—seemed equally impossible to him.

As he stepped into the drawing room, his eyes immediately sought out Grace, but he found only her parents and her sister.

He greeted them each in turn, somehow holding himself back from asking if Grace would be joining them. It occurred to him that she hadn't yet pled a headache to escape having to see him.

It was Lady Kent who gave voice to his concern. "I have no idea what is taking Grace so long. Perhaps I should go up and check on her."

"Oh, that is my fault," Helen said. "My maid was feeling unwell, so I sent her back to bed and used Grace's maid. I'm afraid I monopolized her terribly when I was getting dressed." She smiled at Edward. "I'm sure Grace will be down soon."

Her overly bright response had him suspecting she was hiding something, but he merely nodded. All that mattered was that Grace planned to join them.

He heard her step on the stairs before he saw her, and he was grateful for the moment to prepare himself for her arrival because when she stepped into the doorway of the drawing room, he almost swallowed his tongue. The gown she wore wasn't exactly risqué, but it showed far more of her than he was used to seeing. When she stood still, the fabric of her lavender dress fell in a straight line from under her bosom, but when she moved it molded lovingly to her curves—curves he was intimately familiar with—for a brief second before falling back into place.

But overshadowing the way her gown offered quick

glimpses at the lithe body beneath was just how much of her upper chest was on display. The neckline wasn't scandalously low—he'd seen far more revealing dresses during his time on the continent—but it showed more than enough to remind him what it had felt like to touch her there and rain kisses on her breasts. To suck one rosy-tipped peak into his mouth, then the other...

His trousers were starting to become too tight and he had to look away. He caught the twin expressions of surprise on Lord and Lady Kent's faces and he half hoped they would send her back upstairs to choose a different gown. Good Lord, how was he supposed to behave like a gentleman in front of Grace's parents when all he wanted to do was pull their daughter into another room and renew his intimate acquaintance with her?

When nothing of the sort happened, he crossed to where Grace stood and bent over her hand. He could feel every eye in the room boring into his back.

"You look lovely tonight, Miss Kent."

She returned his greeting with a slight curtsy. "It is so nice to see you again, Captain."

Was it his imagination, or was her voice warmer than it had been since the truth about her identity had been revealed? That might have been wishful thinking on his part, but he wasn't imagining the way she smiled up at him. Or that she wasn't wearing Freddie's locket.

He tore his gaze away from hers when Lord Kent remarked that he was famished and ready to go in to dinner. Grace's father rose and offered an arm to his wife and the other to Helen, while Edward did the same for Grace. As he waited for the others to precede them, he was powerless to stop his gaze from dipping to her neckline before he forced himself to drag it back to her face. Grace said nothing, but her raised eyebrow made it clear she had noticed his interest.

"You can hardly blame me," he said softly in reply to her unspoken observation before following the others down the hall and into the dining room.

Since theirs wasn't a formal dinner party, the numbers were uneven. He'd hoped to regain his composure by putting some distance between himself and Grace, but when he crossed the threshold, he saw that Lady Trenton had already seated herself on the side of the table with only one place setting. That left him with no other option than to help Grace into her seat and take the one next to her.

He expected that under the watchful eye of Grace's parents and older sister, he'd be able to regain control of his wayward desire, but it almost seemed as though Grace and Helen were conspiring to make that impossible. Whenever he tried to engage Lord or Lady Kent, one of them would drag the conversation back to something Grace knew much about. He couldn't ignore how much he missed her and the closeness they had so briefly shared when he had to look down at her where she sat beside him. Her décolletage beckoned at the edge of his vision, but for the most part, he managed not to let his eyes stray in that direction. It was bad enough that Grace had caught him staring at her breasts—he didn't relish the rest of her family witnessing his admiration of her charms.

GRACE WAS NO CLOSER to knowing if Captain Hathaway could ever come to love her, but her light flirtation with him at dinner had succeeded in showing her that he was not indifferent to her. For the first time since he'd learned her true identity, he'd behaved as though he actually enjoyed her company.

Gone was the stiff, formal demeanor he'd adopted when he'd decided to court her. She'd made every effort to engage his attention over dinner, and while she knew he'd found it almost impossible to keep his eyes from straying to her neckline, he'd also been attentive to what she'd said. It hadn't taken her long to go from forcing herself to act more open in his presence to feeling more than a little giddy at the attention he was showing her. Her spirits had lifted every time she'd caught a hint of heated promise in his eyes.

More than anything, she wanted to follow through on that promise with him.

She'd been allowing her pride to put up barriers where none were needed. If she hadn't rejected Edward's proposal of marriage, if she hadn't behaved as though she wanted nothing more than to be quit of his presence when he came to call, she knew now that she could have thawed much of his cool facade. She'd tried to push him away simply because he hadn't fallen prostrate at her feet and declared his undying love for her.

But she wanted this man like no other. He might never come to love her, but they did share a special connection, one that she had never felt with any other man. Not even Freddie.

When the meal ended and it was time for the ladies to leave the men, Edward moved behind her and drew her chair back. He took that opportunity to speak to her in a voice low enough so only she could hear. "I need to see you in private."

His words, together with his warm breath on her neck, caused a slight shiver to go through her. She met his gaze and nodded before leaving the room with her mother and sister.

"Well, that was interesting," her mother said as they made their way down the hallway to the drawing room where they would wait for the men to finish their port.

"Indeed," said Helen, her smile threatening to engulf her face as she beamed at Grace. "The captain couldn't take his eyes off you."

She'd hoped for just that outcome, had schemed with her sister to try to make him reveal his interest in her, but she couldn't rejoice yet. Before she could take that final step with the captain, she had to close the door on the guilt that threatened to suffocate her whenever she thought of Freddie. She needed to read his letter before she and Edward had that private conversation. Only then would she be free to contemplate a future with him.

"There is something I must do," Grace said when they reached the drawing room. "I'll rejoin you in a few minutes."

She didn't wait to see what Helen or her mother would say but turned and made her way upstairs. When she entered her bedroom, she walked over to her writing desk and opened the top drawer to retrieve Freddie's letter.

She lowered herself into the chair, took a deep breath, and broke the seal. Her resolve almost faltered when she spied her dear friend's familiar scrawl. Her heart told her to put the missive back in the drawer, but her head reasoned that she needed to do this. There could be no future until she had laid the past to rest.

She took another deep breath and began to read.

My dearest Grace,

You already know how much I admire you. I have made no secret of my plans for our future in my other letters, and bless you, you have said nothing to contradict them.

But what you don't know is that I realize I have done you a great disservice. I know you do not return the depth of my affection, but that knowledge did not stop me from putting you in an untenable situation in offering for you when I did. I knew exactly what I was doing... I knew you had no choice but to agree to marry me when, if I'd asked at any other time, you would have rejected my suit. I can only say I hoped that with time apart you would come to miss me and realize that your feelings were deeper than you'd imagined. But your letters in reply to mine, while balms for my soul, have made me realize that your affection for me does not go beyond that which comes after many years of friendship.

It is important that you know I had intended to release you from your promise when I returned home. I love you too much to live with the knowledge that I had trapped you in a marriage you did not desire. I would rather retain you as a dear friend than see you every day and know that you do not love me in the way that I crave. With any other woman, a marriage based on friendship would suffice, but never with you. I want more or, barring that, nothing at all.

I plan to entrust Captain Hathaway with delivering this letter to you, but I am asking you to tell him that I have kept something from him. He knows I have lost a leg and believes I will be returning home. But the doctor has told me there is no hope and the expressions of sympathy I see on the nurses' faces when they change my bandages underscore that progno-

sis. The wounds I received have festered, and I have been told that I will soon succumb to them. Even now I feel my thoughts beginning to cloud from the fever. I dare not tell the Captain and have sworn the doctor and nurses to silence because I know he is too good. If he suspected, he would prevent me from doing what needs to be done. Please do me this one last favor and put his mind at ease.

I am, as ever, yours in love and friendship,

Freddie

"Oh, Freddie."

Grace's heart clenched, and a new wave of grief at losing her friend engulfed her.

CHAPTER 13

"I've never been one to dance around an issue, so I'll come straight to the point and ask you about your intentions toward my daughter."

Edward had faced down many hostile enemies during his years of service. One concerned father was nothing in comparison. "If Miss Kent agrees, I hope to marry her. I'd like your permission, but we are both old enough that it isn't needed."

Lord Kent's brows drew together. "When you called upon us in London, you told us that you had a letter for Grace from the man she was supposed to marry."

"I did and I have delivered it to her." After much avoidance on her part, he added silently.

"Did Freddie put you up to this? Did he ask you to come here and pay court to Grace?"

"No, my lord." Edward hadn't expected that question, but he could see why Lord Kent would wonder. Of course, he wasn't giving his daughter enough credit if he thought that was the only reason he'd stayed in Somerset.

"Good," he said, leaning back in his chair. "Grace deserves better than that. I made a mistake when I allowed Helen to marry Lord Trenton solely because of his position in society and without any thought to his feelings for her. I have no intention of allowing the same thing to happen to Grace."

He wondered at the man's cryptic comments. Freddie hadn't told him much about Lady Trenton, only that her husband had died in some sort of accident. He couldn't even remember the details now.

Lord Kent was more at ease now that he'd settled his concerns. Their conversation shifted, naturally, to his time on the continent and that final battle. While Edward made sure to share the story of Freddie's bravery, he wouldn't reveal the truth about his last moments. He and Grace knew and that was enough.

Disappointment settled over him when he returned to the drawing room with Lord Kent and found only Lady Trenton and Lady Kent waiting. Despite what she had indicated, Grace must have decided to put off their private conversation. Seeing no point in prolonging the evening, he took his leave.

As he left the house, he tried but failed to make sense of Grace's behavior over dinner. He'd felt alive and invigorated when he realized she was flirting with him and wondered if he'd scared her away. He'd been careful to be circumspect toward her since that day she'd rejected him a second time, hoping that giving her time to get to know him better would ease her concerns about marrying him. And tonight he'd thought his patience was finally being rewarded when he saw signs of the spark that had drawn him to her the first time they'd met. With it had come the realization that he hadn't proposed to her only because he'd wronged Freddie's memory by taking the man's betrothed to his bed. He wanted her because of who she was, not who she'd been supposed to marry.

Grace was his and he meant to keep her. But juxtaposed against that belief was the doubt that told him he didn't deserve to be happy.

The thought of spending his life without her left him experiencing emotions he'd always been able to keep at bay. During England's involvement in the war against Napoleon, he'd been successful in his campaigns mainly because he'd always had the knack of pushing back his emotions, keeping them behind an imaginary wall, and doing what needed to be done. Freddie's death had left a crack in that wall.

And now Grace had taken advantage of that crack and caused the entire wall to crumble, leaving him open and exposed.

He couldn't help but wonder if he was destined to be unhappy. After all, why should he find joy in Grace's arms when Freddie had been denied that very thing? And if he was being completely truthful with himself, he had to admit he'd had doubts all along when Grace had hidden the truth of her identity from him. She'd wanted to tell him the truth that evening, before they'd made love, and he'd stopped her. He hadn't wanted to consider the possibility that his suspicions were correct and so had acted selfishly, convinced that by ignoring his reservations they would prove false.

Only they hadn't been false.

He was halfway to the stables, choosing not to wait at the house for a groom to bring his mount, when he heard his name called. Half expecting he had imagined it, he turned to find Grace rushing out of the house and hurrying toward him. He looked past her and saw that her parents had come to the door, no doubt wondering why their daughter was chasing after him. His blood began to pound as he wondered the same thing.

Lady Trenton moved into the doorway and spoke to them, but from this distance, he couldn't tell what she'd said. But he could see their obvious uncertainty before they stepped back into the house. Grace's sister smiled at him before closing the door.

When Grace reached him, his concern for her reputation warred with his desire to drag her into his arms. But he would not do what Freddie had done to her—force her into a marriage she didn't want.

"Your sister convinced your parents to go back into the house, but I think they're probably watching us from a window."

Grace had to take a moment to catch her breath before replying. "It matters not. I only care about you." She paused before adding, "Do you care for me at all? Beyond feeling bound to take care of me?"

He hesitated, his heart filled with a mixture of anticipation and dread, as he considered how to respond. He stared down at her and was momentarily overwhelmed not just by her beauty but by the fact that he sensed she was on the verge of baring her soul to him. Panic threatened to surface as he struggled with the certainty that he was the last man who should be accepting what she was offering.

"I can't love you," he said when he finally spoke. Although he hadn't answered her question, strictly speaking he hadn't lied. It was true that he shouldn't love her, not when his continued existence had come at the cost of another's life, but he hadn't said that he wasn't already in love with her.

"You know that Freddie was a very dear friend to me, but our engagement, for me, was a practical one, meant to last only so long as he remained at war."

She'd confessed her intention to break her betrothal to Freddie before and, in that moment, he could understand just how heartbroken the man would have been. "Freddie deserved better," he said.

Her eyes were filled with sorrow. "Yes he did. I wish I could have given him that, but in the end…" She struggled to regain her composure, and his heart ached for her. "Please, just read his letter."

He wanted to deny her request, but her earnest expression kept him from giving voice to the words.

She must have seen his hesitation, for she added, "He speaks of you in it. And he wanted you to know about that last day." She held the letter out to him. "Please?"

With sudden clarity, he could understand why she'd avoided him those first few days he'd been in Somerset and why she'd taken advantage of his misunderstanding when she'd shaken her head in denial. The very last thing he wanted to do in that moment was read the words of the man who had died in his place.

Wanting only to have the task finished, he took the letter

she extended to him and unfolded the paper. His eyes scanned the words before him. When he reached the end, he started over again at the beginning.

The revelation that Freddie had known he'd done Grace a disservice in leaving her with no option but to agree to his proposal astonished him, as did his friend's declaration that he'd intended to release her from her promise when he returned home. But what surprised him most was learning that Freddie had received news he was going to die and there was nothing the doctors could do for him.

He'd been correct when he wrote that Edward would have tried to prevent him from hastening that end.

He refolded the note and handed it back to Grace, his mind racing with the implications revealed by its contents. They stared at one another for several long seconds.

"I didn't know," he said when he finally broke the silence. "All this time I thought he'd acted precipitously, that he was in low spirits and would have recovered in time. I've been so angry at myself for not realizing what he planned to do and stopping him."

Grace shook her head. "You couldn't save him. Freddie could be quick to act, often jumping right into the middle of all sorts of madcap adventures when we were young. But this... what he did in the end... wasn't one of those times. He knew what he was doing."

He ached to draw her into his arms, but at that moment he couldn't be certain of anything. Not only had everything he'd believed about his duty to his friend been turned on its head, but he couldn't trust his instincts when it came to the woman before him. She'd refused him twice already but had been attentive to him all evening. Hell, he'd been half-hard whenever she'd looked at him. But now he didn't know how to act. Should he press his suit again, or would doing so place him in the same selfish category as Freddie?

In that moment, he knew exactly how his friend had felt about Grace because he felt the exact same way. In his letter, Freddie had stated that he loved her enough to want her to be happy without him, but Edward wasn't sure if he was capable of letting her go.

It felt as though they were on the edge of a precipice, the future fraught with potential. Should he go over the cliff with her, knowing he would not be able to hold back the need pulsing through his very soul, or draw back and allow her the freedom she'd craved now for so many years?

"Tell me what you want, Grace." He took one of her hands, half expecting her father to come bursting out of the house but willing to take that chance. He swept his thumb over the back of her hand, his blood beginning to heat when he saw her eyes widen and a shiver go through her body. The night was warm, so he knew that slight tremor couldn't be attributed to her being cold.

As he stared down at her, he tried to read her thoughts. Emotions flickered across her face—hope, doubt, uncertainty —but he was determined not to press her. He would give her the freedom to make this decision for both of them.

"I think..." She looked away and he tensed, waiting for her to pull away from him. When her gaze met his again he couldn't tell what she was thinking, but he noticed how her shoulders had straightened as though she, too, were bracing herself for another uncomfortable scene between them.

He loosened his hold, but instead of drawing her hand from his, she tightened her grip.

She took a deep breath and spoke quickly. "I want you. But I don't want you to marry me out of a mistaken sense of duty. Or because you feel honor bound because you believe you've ruined me."

His heart began to beat faster, but he allowed Grace to finish. She'd been holding herself aloof from him and was finally confiding in him again. He realized again just how much he'd missed this open side of her.

"I could have stopped you that evening I came to your cottage… I know you would have respected my wishes."

"Why didn't you?"

"Because I didn't want to. You make me feel things I've never imagined possible. Since Freddie went away, there have been a few men who made it known they wanted to engage in a discreet affair." He must not have hidden the anger that sparked at her admission because she rushed to add, "Nothing happened with those men. I wasn't looking to trap you and I wasn't with you because I was curious about the intimate side of male-female relationships. I didn't stop you because… Well, because it was you. I wanted nothing more in that moment than to be as close as possible to you." There was the barest of hesitations before she added, "I love you."

She humbled him with her confession. How had she gone from being a woman who hid from him so he couldn't deliver a letter that might cause her pain to the brave woman standing before him now, laying her heart open?

Hang her parents. Now that Grace had confided her feelings for him, he'd be damned if he let her go. And if that meant he could only have her because her parents forced a match between them, then so be it.

He drew her closer, and when there was only the smallest of spaces separating them, he clasped her face between his hands and lowered his head to hers. Somehow he kept the kiss gentle, but the fire that leapt through his veins at finally having her in his arms again had him using every ounce of self-control he possessed. He broke the kiss before that control could snap and he devoured her right then and there.

The last time he'd proposed to this woman—no, he thought ruefully, the last time he'd ordered her to marry him—he'd told himself he was doing it for Freddie. He realized now that all along he'd been thinking only of himself.

"I've been an idiot and have mishandled everything. But you should know that duty and honor are not what I feel when I look at you or hold you."

Her smile was tremulous. "Ask me again."

He needed no further prompting. This time he got down on one knee before reaching for her hand again. "I love you, Grace Kent." He enjoyed how her eyes had widened in shock at his proclamation and took heart in the fact that he was finally doing something right. "Will you make me the happiest of men and consent to be my wife?"

She yanked on his arm and he allowed her to pull him up. When she threw herself into his arms, he closed his eyes in relief and tightened his embrace.

"Yes," she said into his shoulder, her head nodding frantically against him, punctuating that single word.

She was grinning when she pulled back to look up at him, her face radiant with joy. The guilt he'd been feeling, his doubts about being deserving of happiness, all faded away, replaced with the certainty that he would spend the rest of his life making sure Grace would always be this happy.

"The ceremony will take place as soon as possible," he said. "I need to make love to you again… and this time I might even call you by the correct name."

She swatted playfully at his shoulder. "That is a terrible thing to say."

The front door to the house opened then, cutting off what he'd been about to say, and her family descended upon them. They made no pretense that they hadn't been observing his marriage proposal and Grace's acceptance, and a small part of him was glad of that fact. This time Grace would not be escaping him.

She shot him a glance then, her expression telling him she was done hiding from him.

He'd gone through much in his life to reach this point. War, bloodshed, the loss of many good men under his command, one of whom he considered a friend and whom everyone had loved. But to find this woman he would do it all again.

MISS HATHAWAY'S WISH

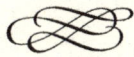

HATHAWAY HEIRS ~ BOOK 4

Emily Hathaway makes a special wish this Christmas...

Emily Hathaway wants to marry for love, but after three unsuccessful seasons she's given up on finding the same happiness her brothers found in their marriages.

Sir Jonah Stanton has returned to England after ten years abroad. A Christmas party at Hathaway Manor provides the perfect opportunity to ease back into English society. But one thing has changed since Jonah's been away. His friend's little sister is now a young woman, and he finds himself appreciating her in ways he'd never imagined possible.

As Emily becomes reacquainted with Jonah, she discovers the feelings she'd attributed to friendship run far deeper. Is it possible Jonah might be the man she's been looking for all along?

ACKNOWLEDGMENTS

I was very fortunate to be among a special group of authors in the *Winter Wishes* box set: Heather Boyd, Cheryl Bolen, Collette Cameron, Sasha Cottman, Donna Cummings, Bronwen Evans, Alina K. Field, Samantha Grace, Barbara Monajem, Wendy Vella, Lana Williams, and Bree Wolf.

And a special thank you to Heather Boyd for all the extra work she undertook to make this anthology a reality.

CHAPTER 1

December 15, 1816

EMILY HATHAWAY COULD BARELY contain her excitement as she made her way to the Hathaway manor house. She'd taken care to bundle up, so the cold air that nipped at her nose didn't dampen her spirits.

It was ten days before Christmas, and her eldest brother had agreed to host a ball the following evening. Some of the guests who lived far away would begin to arrive this afternoon, and Emily's thoughts had been filled with nothing else for the past month. The entire event would only last three days and two evenings, but it was, essentially, a house party. She'd never imagined such an event would take place under her brother's roof.

James had become Viscount Hathaway four years before, when their uncle died without an heir, but he'd never lost his preference for avoiding social gatherings. He attended only those events he felt were necessary and declined all other invitations. Of course, that only resulted in his favor being courted by all, his attendance at a soiree a prize many sought to claim.

Her brother had loathed every second he'd spent in London over the past few years. He and Sarah had escorted her for what had proven to be three very long seasons during which James had scowled at any man brave enough to approach her. That Sarah had somehow convinced him to host this gathering spoke volumes about how much he loved his wife.

Emily quickened her pace, looking forward to spending the morning with the two women who had made her brothers so happy. She imagined Sarah would already have things well in hand, but there were always last-minute details that needed to be taken care of.

When she reached the manor house, she didn't bother to wait for the butler to open the door and let her in. Nonetheless, he appeared instantly as she closed the door against the sharp breeze. She visited so often she might as well be living here. If Mama hadn't insisted on staying at the dower house when James first inherited the viscountcy, she'd be living in the manor house now. But she hadn't wanted to leave her mother alone when she was still reeling from the sudden change in their social status, and now Emily was comfortable with the arrangement.

She smiled at the older man as she removed her hat and cloak and handed him the garments. "It's a beautiful morning despite the cold, isn't it, Dalton?"

He inclined his head by way of response, but the corners

of his mouth lifted in an ever-so-slight smile. "Lady Hathaway is waiting for you in the library."

"Thank you," she said, then rushed down the hall to the room that was near the back of the house.

When she crossed the threshold, she saw that Grace was also present. Both she and Sarah were seated on a settee placed near the blazing fireplace, their fair heads bent together in conversation. She was grateful for the tendrils of heat she could feel reaching out across the room.

She'd known Sarah since she and James had wed four years before. She'd only been sixteen then, but they'd taken an instant liking to one another and had become friends from the start.

Grace was a newer addition to the family. When her brother Edward had returned to England the year before after serving in the war against Napoleon, he'd met Grace in Somerset and fallen in love. They'd been expecting Edward's arrival in Northampton and had been shocked to receive an invitation to Somerset for his wedding to a young woman named Grace Kent. They now lived in a small house bordering James's estate, and Edward helped with Hathaway Stables, continuing the business their father had started before any of them had been born.

Sarah turned to Grace as Emily made her way to the fireplace to warm her hands. "I told you she would be early."

"I may be new to this family, but I could have predicted that for myself," Grace said.

Emily only smiled in response as she waited for both women to stand so she could give them each her customary hug by way of greeting. It wasn't the first time they'd teased her about her exuberance, but who could blame her? They were about to host an event she'd thought would never take place in this house.

She pulled back after hugging Sarah and gave her head a slight shake. "I still can't believe James actually agreed to host a house party. Everyone can see that he loves you, but my brother has got to be one of the most stubborn men in existence." As far back as she could remember, James had always insisted he'd never allow himself to be forced to stay under the same roof with strangers who would expect him to dance attendance on them. He hardly tolerated a dinner party, and his behavior when in London was barely civilized. "You must share your secret."

Sarah laughed as she and Grace sank back onto the settee. She waited for Emily to join them before saying, "Well, to begin, don't call it a house party in his presence. We're referring to it as a Christmas ball and not mentioning the fact that some of the guests will be staying for two nights."

Emily fought the urge to roll her eyes. "Changing the name of the event doesn't change what it is."

"You and I both know that. But James is terrified we're going to have a snowstorm and all the guests will be trapped here for days on end. As for how I convinced him to host a ball in the first place..." She shared a look with Grace before continuing. "I shouldn't tell you this since it takes the shine off my accomplishment, but it was actually Grace's idea."

Emily lowered herself onto the settee next to Grace, barely managing to keep her expression even as all manner of unwelcome thoughts threatened to surface. She'd walked in on each of her brothers and their wives several times in what could only be called a heated embrace, and she now regretted asking the question. "If this has anything to do with what you get up to in the bedroom when you're alone with your husbands, I'd rather not hear the details."

Grace and Sarah laughed again, and she realized she hadn't been successful in holding back her slight grimace.

"If you really want to know, it involves you actually," Grace said when their amusement died down.

"Me?" Emily was now more confused than ever. James would never agree to host a ball—especially not so near to Christmas—for her.

"I'm almost afraid to tell you." Grace cast a sheepish glance at Sarah before facing her again. "You might not be happy when you hear this."

Emily waved a hand in dismissal at Grace's concern. "You might as well tell me straight away and get it over with. Even if I am annoyed, we all know I'll forgive you soon enough as long as your intentions weren't malicious."

"Oh no, never that. It's just that… Well, you'll reach your age of majority just before your next season starts."

This time Emily didn't even try to hold back her frown. She tried not to think about the fact that she'd already had three unsuccessful seasons and was almost one-and-twenty with nary a marriage prospect in sight. After this year she feared she'd be firmly on the shelf.

"Which means," Grace said with an arch smile, "that you will no longer need your brother's approval to wed."

Sarah jumped in to add, "I've assured Grace that James would never withhold your dowry to force you to fall in line with his wishes. He never approved of the way his father was cut off when he began breeding and selling horses, after all. James would never be so heavy-handed in dealing with his own family."

Grace nodded. "That means you'll be free to wed whomever you wish."

Emily couldn't see how her upcoming birthday had anything to do with hosting a ball, especially since she couldn't imagine running off with anyone, and said as much.

Sarah shook her head in exasperation, her blond curls swinging with the movement. "This will be the last opportunity James has to choose someone *suitable* for you. Or at least to have a say in whom you choose. When I pointed that out to him, he relented and agreed to host this party. Of course, he also insisted on providing me with a list of suitable candidates."

A sense of dread settled over Emily as she imagined all the staid, boring men who would be paraded before her like prized cattle over the next two days. She'd seen clearly enough the type of man of whom her brother approved, and none had held even a faint interest for her.

What had once seemed like an enjoyable occasion had now become a vain attempt to find her a husband. And the last thing she wanted was another reminder that she was destined to remain a spinster since she refused to settle for anything less than the happiness her brothers had found for themselves.

Emily leaned back against the cushions of the settee and closed her eyes. "I know you meant well, but the two of you have done me no favors."

"Don't fret," Grace said, reaching over to pat her hand.

"Sarah and I might have slipped in a few invitations about which our husbands know nothing. There will be several men here who never show their faces in London during the season. You'll have the opportunity to meet someone new."

"And," Sarah added, "there will be no expectation placed upon you—or on these men—to circle each other, looking for a potential marriage partner. You can be yourselves without all those constraints."

Emily opened her eyes and stared right at the woman who'd just spoken such nonsense. "Clearly you don't know my brother as well as you think you do. He *loves* constraints. He's always trying to rein in my 'indiscriminate enthusiasm.' And won't it seem a little odd if it's just us and a whole house filled with men?"

She had to close her eyes again as the awfulness of the situation settled over her. How humiliating. Everyone present would know exactly what Sarah and Grace were trying to do. Find a spouse for their almost-spinster sister-by-marriage whom no man wanted.

Although that wasn't strictly true. Plenty of men had wanted her, but they'd wanted her generous dowry more. Anyone with enough wealth that the money to be settled on her when she wed wouldn't be the main enticement was either already wed or utterly boring. Or old. She didn't want to think about all the men who'd already buried wives and were looking for another young woman to take their place. And now she'd have to deal with them under this roof.

Thank the heavens she resided at the dower house with her mother. At least she could escape there when the situation became too insufferable at the manor house.

She realized it was too quiet and opened her eyes to see what Grace and Sarah were doing. She found them staring at her, twin expressions of exasperation on their faces.

"There will be plenty of women here as well—both wed and unwed. You needn't worry about being uncomfortable."

Emily could feel the heat creeping up her face. "You can hardly blame me for my reaction. You could have assured me this wouldn't appear to be a gathering put together to rid yourselves of me before you mentioned all the men you plan to parade me before."

Grace gave Emily's hand another brief squeeze. "You can hardly blame us for wanting to secure for you the same happiness we've found."

"And as you recall," Sarah continued, "I was forced into this marriage with James and wasn't at all happy about it. But it turned out well for everyone involved."

"If you say so," Emily said, trying her best not to allow her dismay to cloud her former enthusiasm. Things wouldn't be so bad if she made sure to stay close to her family or members of her own sex during the ball.

Sarah was quiet for several moments, and Emily knew she wanted to reassure her again, but instead she stood and moved over to the table that acted as her desk. Three chairs had been placed around it, and she settled into one and lifted a page from one of the neatly separated piles. "The menus have been planned, but I haven't been able to make up my mind about what activities should be made available for this afternoon and tomorrow before the guests who are staying here return to their rooms to dress for the ball. This might be the shortest house party any of them have ever attended, and while they might not expect much, I'd like to ensure everyone isn't bored to tears."

Guilt settled over Emily when she saw the way Sarah's brows had drawn together as she dropped the page she was holding and concentrated on a second pile. Pushing aside her doubts about any embarrassment she might suffer, Emily stood and, together with Grace, joined Sarah to give their opinions and to reassure her everything was well in hand.

CHAPTER 2

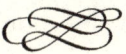

JONAH STANTON WASN'T SURE how he'd allowed himself to be talked into attending this ball. But after spending the past ten years away from home and earning his fortune, he supposed his attendance at such events was inevitable now that he was back in England. All it had taken was one disappointed look from his mother before he'd readily agreed to accompany her to this house party. He might be twenty-eight, but it was clear he was sorely out of practice when it came to holding out against maternal guilt.

Of course, there was also the fact that he was trying to make up for his absence when his father died the year before. By the time he finally learned of his father's death, several months had already passed. It had taken another six months before he was able to return home.

He told himself this would be a good opportunity to become acquainted again with English society. He'd been away for so long he wasn't sure anyone would remember him.

It was late morning when they finally arrived at the Hathaway estate. The carriage deposited them at the dower house where his mother would be staying with her good friend Mrs. Hathaway. Or would she now be considered the dowager Lady Hathaway? Could one be a dowager when they'd never held the title of Lady Hathaway?

So much had changed since he'd left. James now held the title of Viscount Hathaway, and the entire family had moved from Newmarket, where they'd been neighbors, to Northampton. They'd grown up together, however, and Jonah was looking forward to the upcoming reunion.

After seeing his mother settled, he made his way on foot to the manor house where he would be staying with the other guests. He could have settled back into the carriage for the short distance, but he'd already been cooped up in its interior for the past day minus the few hours they'd spent at an inn along the way. Despite the cold, he welcomed the opportunity to stretch his legs and breathe in the fresh air. It was decidedly brisker than that to which he was accustomed after spending the past ten years in India. Still, he was back in England to stay now and would need to become reacclimated to cold winters and to the damp weather the rest of the year.

He was about halfway through his walk when he noticed a small figure approaching. He'd been told Emily Hathaway lived with her mother in the dower house, but since the woman coming toward him was bundled up against the cold, it was difficult to tell if she was the young girl he'd once known.

He did a few quick calculations in his head and realized Emily would now be a young woman.

The approaching figure was covered from the neck down

in a voluminous cloak that was sky blue in color, and her hair was tucked away beneath a dark-colored hat that could only be called practical. A few strands of dark hair had escaped to frame her face, adding an allure to her appearance that sparked his interest.

As she neared and looked up at him with sparkling blue eyes, he could see this was none other than Emily Hathaway. It was almost impossible to believe she was all grown up.

The way her head tilted to the side and her face scrunched up as she tried to place how she knew him reminded him of the lively child he'd once known. It wasn't difficult to tell when she recognized him, for a large smile spread across her face and her eyes lit with happiness.

"Jonah? What are you doing here? Aren't you supposed to be away in India?" She gave her head a slight shake as though to remind herself to curb her tendency toward exuberance. He'd almost forgotten that about her. "No one told me you were coming."

"Actually, it's Sir Jonah now. It seems that when one comes from an old family with ties to nobility and becomes personally responsible for ensuring the royal kitchens are equipped with enough exotic spices to satisfy the regent's palate and impress all manner of visiting dignitaries, the crown can be very generous."

"You'll have to excuse me for my ignorance, *Sir Jonah*," Emily said before dipping into a deep curtsy. He didn't miss the twinkle in her eye when she straightened. "I am but a humble woman. Tell me, do you possess a ring I should be kissing? I wouldn't wish to offend you by not offering you all the courtesies you're owed."

"I see you're as precocious as ever," he said, his tone dry.

Her laugh still had the ability to make him smile, and he found himself doing so now as she let forth a peal of delight.

"James and Edward will be so happy to see you! I'm going to have to box their ears for not telling me to expect you."

She turned and headed back toward the manor house, and he fell into step beside her.

"Well, in the interest of saving them a little pain, I should confess that they didn't know I was coming."

She glanced sideways at him, and her eyes narrowed. "Did Sarah invite you?"

"Would it be a problem if she had?" He couldn't understand why her jaw tensed at that. "Actually, it was Lady Hathaway—your mother—who extended the invitation. I don't believe she was aware I'd returned when she invited my mother. Mother, of course, wrote back, and together they decided that she shouldn't travel so far alone. *Et voilà*, you now have to endure my company."

"That's nice. Mama did say something about Mrs. Stanton coming to stay with us over Christmas." She stopped and looked up at him. "Oh, that means you'll be staying as well. We'll be able to become reacquainted properly after the ball when the guests leave."

"Yes, it's all been settled," he said as they resumed their walk.

"I wonder why Sarah didn't mention it?"

"She probably has a lot on her mind with the ball being so close to Christmas. Mother will be staying at the dower house with you and Lady Hathaway, and I'll be at the main house with the rest of the guests."

"Mama really doesn't like being called Lady Hathaway. She's still struggling with just how much our lives have changed since James inherited."

Jonah gave her words some thought, but in the end shook his head. "If I'm to adjust to being back here again, I have to practice my manners. I've become lax over the past few years, so I'm going to have to insist on formality so I don't embarrass myself—or your family—around others."

"I suppose that means I'll have to call you Sir Jonah now, and of course you'll insist on calling me Miss Hathaway."

They'd reached the house and Emily stopped again. Jonah took a moment to admire the sheer size of the manor, marveling at just how much his friends' lives had changed in the past few years. Their former home was large, but certainly not anywhere near the scale of the house before him now.

He turned to face Emily, detecting a slight frown on her face that had him wondering as to its cause. "Is something the matter?"

"Oh no," she said, giving her head a vigorous shake and smiling at him. "I was just thinking how strange it is that I feel as though I know you so well when I don't. Not really. You're my brother's friend, and it's been ages since I last saw you."

"It's been ten years since I moved to India and you were… ten years of age, was it?"

"Heavens, I feel so old now. Mama always goes on about how time goes by more quickly as one ages, and now I understand what she means. It doesn't feel as though ten years have passed. I was still a child the last time we spoke."

"I must admit, I find it difficult to imagine you're all grown up, especially since I can't see what you look like under that hat and cloak."

Emily laughed again, no doubt thinking he was jesting, but he was completely serious. She was taller than the last time he'd seen her, but at over six feet in height, he still towered over her. She'd always been outgoing and loved tagging along after her brothers, much to their chagrin. He hadn't minded since he didn't have any brothers or sisters and had enjoyed her penchant for trying to make them all laugh. But he found it almost impossible to picture what she'd look like when she removed her cloak and hat. From what he could tell, her personality hadn't changed much from that outgoing girl he'd once known, although he had to admit she'd developed a sense of wit that he found charming.

"You'll have to wait a little longer to sate your curiosity," she said, giving him a small push toward the door.

"What? You're going to leave me here all alone?"

"Hardly alone," she said. "My brothers are home. You can become reacquainted with them and meet their wives. Enjoy the quiet before most of the male population of England starts arriving later this afternoon. I'll be back then to help greet them."

He raised a brow at that. "Just the male population?"

"Well, my sisters-in-law insist that won't be the case, but I'm afraid they're matchmaking."

He gave a sympathetic wince, knowing he'd soon be facing the same thing next year when the season began. Only he wanted to get married, he told himself.

"At any rate, enjoy the peace until then. I'll return with

Mama and Mrs. Stanton this afternoon and will stay through dinner."

With a small wave, she turned and walked away. Jonah watched her for a full minute, allowing his curiosity about what she looked like under that cloak to take hold of his imagination. Catching himself, he gave his head a shake to clear his thoughts and turned back to the house. Emily wasn't wrong that he was looking forward to the relative peace before the other guests arrived. The ball tomorrow evening would be his official return to society.

CHAPTER 3

$\mathcal{E}$MILY WAITED FOR the carriage door to open, impatient with the formality of having to take the conveyance when the manor was only a mile from the dower house. She didn't complain, however, because she knew it was important to her mother that they keep up appearances. Despite the fact they'd all settled into their elevated station in society, it was something about which her mother still worried.

"Emily…"

The note of warning in her mother's voice brought Emily out of her reverie. She hadn't even realized she was tapping her foot.

"Oh, leave the poor girl," Mrs. Stanton said with a fond smile. "She's excited, and who can blame her."

Mama gave her head a small shake. "I'll never understand where she gets her energy and her love for all manner of social events. It certainly wasn't from her father or me."

The carriage door swung open, and Emily let out a sigh of

relief. She waited as the young footman—a new member of her brother's staff whose name she hadn't yet learned—helped her mother and Mrs. Stanton out of the carriage. And then, finally, he was handing her down as well.

Even though she was wary about her family's match-making efforts, Emily couldn't deny that her mother had been correct. She was still excited about the upcoming ball.

They'd scarce entered the manor before Sarah descended on them. She greeted them warmly and waited while Mama introduced her to Mrs. Stanton.

"Thank goodness you're here," she said, her voice low. "A number of guests have already arrived, and I'm afraid I'm being run ragged."

"Is something the matter?" Mama asked, her lips tightening in concern.

"I don't believe so. It's just that it's much more intimidating than I imagined, overseeing the well-being of houseguests with whom one has only a passing acquaintance. I can't imagine why I thought this was a good idea."

"Nonsense," Emily said, drawing her arm through Sarah's. "Now that we're here, you can delegate and we'll help you. Tell me, has my brother gone into hiding yet?"

Sarah gave a small laugh, but Emily could sense the tension behind her composure. "Not for lack of trying. The first guest arrived one hour ago, and I've already caught him trying to sneak away to his study three times! As punishment, I've set him up in the drawing room where he is now surrounded by would-be friends whose names I'm sure he can't remember."

Emily wasn't surprised, especially since she still couldn't

believe her brother had agreed to host this event. But not only had he agreed, now he was engaging in polite conversation with strangers? He must be desperate to see her settled. But despite her unease, she vowed to enjoy this once-in-a-lifetime experience. After all, it wasn't entirely outside the realm of possibility that she'd meet her future husband over the next two days.

CHAPTER 4

*J*AMES FOUND HER in the library several hours later, browsing the bookshelves for a distraction.

He came to a stop next to her. "We seem to have switched personalities. Why is it I'm out there and you're hiding away in here?"

She glanced toward the doorway, and when she saw the door was open, she crossed the room to close it. She leaned against it and let out a breath. "Lord Kirby has been relentless. Every time I turn around, he's there. I just needed ten minutes to myself before it's time to head in for dinner."

James lifted one hand to rub at the back of his neck. "About that…"

Emily narrowed her eyes. "What did you do?"

"He's a good man. You should give him a chance. Everyone speaks very highly of him."

Emily sighed, telling herself that her brother meant well. But she couldn't help cringing as she imagined the conversation he and Lord Kirby would have had that led the latter to believe he was her brother's choice of a husband for her.

"Getting to know him is one thing, but he's scarce given me a moment to breathe since we've been introduced."

"That's a good thing, is it not? It means he likes you."

James looked so confused. Emily wanted to tell him that she felt no spark of interest for Lord Kirby, but perhaps her brother was right. His own wife had been in love with another man when they'd wed, and look at how well their marriage had turned out.

She nodded and took his arm, allowing him to lead her back to the drawing room. The moment Lord Kirby spotted her, he started in her direction. The man was fair-haired, and she had to admit he was attractive, even if his pale blue eyes were a little unsettling.

Emily took a deep breath and greeted him with what she hoped was a warm smile. Then she spotted Jonah entering the room and no longer had to pretend to be happy.

"Sir Jonah," she called out in greeting. "Please join us."

Jonah's head swiveled in her direction, and she watched as his dark eyes swept over her. She remembered their earlier conversation and how he'd joked about not being able to imagine what she looked like under her cloak.

She took the opportunity to examine him as well. He'd been slimmer all those years ago, but now he filled out his navy-colored jacket in a most becoming manner. His hair was the same sandy brown, the lightened ends just touching the edge of his cravat. She remembered how his hair had always been a wild mess and felt the urge to tousle the strands from their current immaculate state.

One corner of his mouth tilted up. "Miss Hathaway," he said when he reached the small group. He gave her a formal bow before greeting her brother and Lord Kirby.

"It is *so* good to see you," she said. "Where have you been hiding?"

"Lady Hathaway introduced me to her and James's sons, and I've been keeping them company in the nursery. I'm afraid I might have bored them with tales of India."

Emily laughed. "That's highly unlikely. I'm sure William and George talked your ear off and barely allowed you to get in a word."

"You've caught out my lie." His mouth turned down in an exaggerated grimace as he turned to James. "Were we that rambunctious as youths? It's a wonder our parents survived."

"We were worse," James said.

"Well, I for one would love to hear about your adventures abroad," Emily said, ignoring the small frown that appeared on Lord Kirby's face before he excused himself and turned away from the group.

"Emily." James's tone told her he didn't approve of her silent dismissal of the other man.

She lifted one shoulder. "I haven't seen Jonah since I was ten! We have so much to talk about."

She took Jonah's arm and he led them to one of one the new settees Sarah had arranged for the comfort of the guests.

"Where would you like me to start?" he asked.

She considered his question for a moment but didn't know what to ask. She couldn't imagine visiting such an exotic location, let alone living there for ten years. "Tell me everything."

CHAPTER 5

*J*ONAH FOLLOWED THE SOUND of laughter down the path to what he was told would be a small pond.

It was deuced cold that morning—certainly too cold for him to be outside—but that hadn't deterred Emily from deciding to go ice-skating. The activity wasn't on the approved list of entertainments for the guests, but that hadn't stopped her from volunteering to take her two nephews outdoors to work off some of their excess energy.

Jonah had almost decided against the outing, but when Mrs. Hathaway mentioned over breakfast that she expected Lord Kirby would want to join her daughter, he'd wasted no time donning his outerwear and searching them out.

He'd watched Kirby fawning all over Emily the evening before during dinner, and the display had bothered him more than a little. Kirby was far too boring for Emily, and it irked him to no end that James seemed to be pushing for a union between the two. It was also clear it was a match Emily didn't want, and he could hardly be considered a friend if he didn't help her avoid being alone with the man.

He paused to take in the sight before him when he rounded the last bend. He scanned the area and felt his tense muscles loosen when he didn't see Lord Kirby. The boys' nurse—an older, matronly woman—stood off to the side, watching the group with what looked like trepidation. Jonah couldn't blame her. He himself had never participated in this particular sport.

William—who had taken great pride in telling him the day before that he would be three in a month's time—was already gliding over the smooth surface of the pond with a casual confidence that indicated this wasn't his first time skating.

George—the younger of James's two sons—wasn't as successful. Emily was skating backward while holding both of his hands in hers. He watched as she released one hand, only to grasp it again when the boy lost his balance atop the slim blades that were attached to his boots.

William glided to a stop beside Emily and George and placed his hands on his hips. "Hurry up and learn how to skate so we can have a proper race. It's no fun racing Aunt Emily. She never lets me win."

Emily laughed. "When you're all grown and have surpassed me in height, I'm sure you'll have your revenge. I need to win now while I still can."

She glanced up and caught sight of where Jonah was watching them from off to one side. Her eyes lit and her genuine smile made him revise his misgivings about braving the cold.

"Well, this is a rare treat. Have you come to join us, Sir Jonah?"

William and George turned to look at him. William's eyes lit up at the prospect of having another playmate while George pressed closer to Emily's side.

"You seem to have things well in hand. Besides, I don't have any skates."

He couldn't tell who was more crestfallen by his statement... William or Emily.

"I'm not very good," a little voice called out from amid Emily's skirts.

"Oh, George, you'll learn. William wasn't very good the first time I took him skating last year, but now look at him!"

George didn't look as though he believed her, and it was obvious from the aghast expression on William's face that he didn't either.

Jonah crouched down near the edge of the lake and met the youngest Hathaway's eyes. "Do you want to know a secret?" He glanced at William and could see he'd caught the older boy's attention as well.

George nodded.

"I never learned how to skate. Your grandmother told me I could borrow a pair of blades to attach to my boots if I was coming out here to join you, but I didn't want to embarrass myself by falling."

George loosened his grip on Emily's skirts and stood straighter. "I fell a few times."

Jonah nodded and kept his tone serious. "Everyone falls when they first learn how to skate."

"Aunt Emily can teach you," William said. "Nurse says she has the patience of a saint."

George nodded. "She said William was awful when she taught him, but I don't believe her."

"I'm a natural," William said, his chest puffed out with pride. "But I know George will be too."

"Yes, they are," Jonah said with a smile as he rose to stand. "Then it seems I'll be the only one who doesn't know how to skate."

"You don't actually need blades to slide around on the ice," Emily said.

His gaze caught hers, and he could see the mischievous twinkle she wasn't even trying to hide.

"That's how I started," George added. "I'm good with my boots."

Jonah narrowed his eyes at her. It wasn't bad enough that he was going to freeze to death out here—and why wasn't everyone as bundled up as he was?—but now she had to humiliate him.

"I'm sure it will make George feel better if he's not the only person learning to skate." Her innocent expression vanished, her voice taking on a decidedly evil lilt. "I'm sure you wouldn't want to disappoint the boys."

Well, this was really his fault. He should have stayed indoors. He didn't know why the thought of Kirby being out here with Emily had bothered him so much, but he should have ignored his urge to race out and make sure they weren't alone together.

"Besides," Emily added, "you're so well padded, I'm sure it won't hurt if you do fall."

Jonah couldn't hold back his bark of laughter at her witty observation. Living in India for the past ten years had left him with zero tolerance for the cold. Emily and her nephews were wearing coats and mittens but no scarves or hats. He'd once been impervious to England's cooler weather, but that had been a lifetime ago. He wasn't sure he'd ever get used to it again.

"I'll do my best," he said, stepping onto the ice with exaggerated care and smiling widely at the two boys when he didn't immediately fall. He wasn't sure how long he'd be able to hold on to his dignity, but in that moment he didn't really care.

He watched as Emily resumed her careful guidance of George. This time when she released one hand, he wobbled only once before straightening and continuing to skate next to her. He wasn't sure whether George or his brother was more excited by the feat.

"See, I told you that you could do it!" William said.

Feeling foolish standing rooted to the spot while everyone else was having fun, Jonah pushed off, ignoring the warning bells in his mind that told him this endeavor wouldn't end well. It might have been a decade since he'd last had to navigate ice, but surely his body would remember how it was done.

He'd underestimated how difficult it would be to stop and found himself windmilling his arms to keep his balance as he made for the edge of the pond. He counted it a win when he stumbled onto firm ground again before his feet slid out from under him.

Emily's laughter trailed after him. He turned to glare at her but couldn't hold his expression of mock indignation when he saw how beautiful she looked. Her cheeks were flushed from the outdoor activity and the cold, her blue eyes dancing with amusement. And he realized that he wanted to kiss her.

He looked away from her lest he betray his inconvenient discovery and watched as William came to a stop beside his aunt.

"I'm hungry," he said.

"Me too," George added.

The boys' nurse stepped forward at that, but she was careful to avoid the slick surface of the lake. "I'll help you with the skates and we can head back."

Emily helped George skate to the woman's side and started to kneel to unstrap the blades from his boots, but the woman shooed her away.

"I'll help George. Can you ensure William doesn't cut himself with his blades again?"

Jonah winced imagining that.

Emily nodded and lowered herself onto a log next to her older nephew.

"I can do this myself," William said, a hint of stubbornness in his voice.

Emily began to work on the straps that tied her skates to her boots, but Jonah didn't miss the way she watched her nephew out of the corner of her eye. "Of course you can. But it's Miss Abigail's job to worry about you, so you can understand why she'd ask me to watch you."

"I suppose." William's tongue poked out of the corner of his mouth as he worked at undoing his straps, and soon enough he'd removed both blades. "See?"

"You're such a big boy," Emily said, snatching the blades away from him and passing them to the nurse.

"Thank you, Miss Hathaway," the woman said as she took both pairs of skates.

Emily made no move to join the group when they turned to head toward the house.

The older woman's brows drew together and she glanced between Emily and Jonah. "Are you joining us?"

"You go on ahead, Miss Abigail. Jonah and I will follow shortly." The woman looked like she was about to protest, so Emily added, "It will give Jonah and me time to catch up. We grew up together back in Newmarket, but Jonah has been away from England for a few years. He's almost another brother to me."

The woman looked as though she wanted to argue, but instead gave a curt nod and started after the boys who were already racing toward the manor house.

Jonah waited for her to disappear around the bend in the path before speaking. "I'm like a brother?"

Emily shrugged. "That depends on how overbearing you are. I'd like to think we're friends, but I know Miss Abigail wouldn't want to leave me unchaperoned. In fact, I wouldn't be surprised if she sent my maid out as soon as she reaches the house."

Emily lowered herself onto the log again, and Jonah took a seat next to her, careful to leave a respectable distance between them.

"You can't blame her. The house is filled with strangers, and as you told William, it is her job to worry."

Emily rolled her eyes. "You'd think I was still a child the way she fusses. The way they all do."

"They care about you. That isn't a bad thing."

"No, I know it isn't. Please excuse me, I'm just feeling a little disappointed."

Her statement surprised him. Emily had always been outgoing and loved meeting people. "If memory serves, there was never a stranger you didn't want to turn into a friend. Don't tell me you've developed James's hatred for social events."

Her sigh had him imagining that that was exactly what had happened, but then she confused him by saying, "I *love* balls."

"Are you afraid this one isn't large enough? I can assure you that while you've been out here, a steady stream of guests have been arriving. I'm surprised the manor has enough bedrooms for everyone."

Emily shook her head. "No, it's just that what I thought was to be a lovely event—one I never imagined James would ever agree to host—has turned into another attempt to find me a husband. And after three unsuccessful seasons, I'd like to enjoy one ball without everyone in my family watching me to see if I'll find a suitor."

Jonah couldn't hold back his laughter.

"You find my dismay amusing, *Sir Jonah?*" Emily folded her arms across her chest and glared at him. He could tell she wasn't genuinely angry, however.

"I imagine there is no end of men lining up to court you."

She sighed and relaxed her arms so they were resting on her lap again. "You're correct, of course. Who wouldn't want to court a passably attractive young woman with a sizable dowry?"

He could only shake his head in bewilderment. "I imagine

your dowry might be an inducement for some, but trust me when I say it isn't the only thing they want."

Wanting to put an end to this conversation, Emily reached down for her skates, which were resting behind the log, and stood. "We should head back before my maid arrives to chaperone us."

He fell into step beside her, and they walked in companionable silence for a full minute before Emily spoke again. "How did you know to find us here?"

He didn't want to ruin the morning by mentioning the real reason he'd come out, so instead said, "Your mother mentioned it. I'll admit I was worried you might be overdoing it in the cold. Speaking of which, I feel as though I should be offering you my coat, but I'm afraid I'd freeze on the spot if I removed it."

"Poor Jonah. Has India ruined you for England? Are you planning to return once this party is over?"

Jonah shook his head. "My days living abroad are over. I'm here to stay now."

His heart lightened at the look of relief on her face.

"I'm glad. I'd hate to have to say goodbye again to a friend. At least now you can visit and we'll see each other often."

Jonah didn't reply, but he knew that wouldn't be happening if she met someone at the ball later tonight. When she married, she'd be spending her days with her future husband's family and wouldn't have time for him.

He pushed aside his disappointment at the thought.

CHAPTER 6

*E*MILY'S DANCING SLIPPERS were beginning to pinch her feet. Unless she was mistaken, she'd danced with every man at the ball once, but she was far from tired. She'd have to find a proper way to thank Sarah and Grace for keeping true to their word. While there were several eligible men present—many of whom would never be seen in London during the season—there wasn't that same air of desperation surrounding this event. All in all, she was enjoying herself more than she'd thought she would.

That didn't mean she hadn't noticed the looks of interest from some of the men. But when she didn't encourage their attention, they moved on readily enough.

Unfortunately, the same wasn't true of Lord Kirby, who seemed oblivious to the fact she was avoiding him. Bolstered by the knowledge that James was clearly in favor of a match between them, he'd been relentless in his pursuit.

The man was becoming a problem. His confidence that

he'd win her hand despite the fact she'd been careful not to encourage him was beginning to annoy her as the evening wore on. She'd taken to moving from group to group when she spotted him approaching her, unable to spend more than a few minutes in one place.

She'd just taken refuge with Sarah when James joined them.

"Have you been avoiding Lord Kirby?" His voice was low, but Emily glanced at those around them to ensure they hadn't overheard. "I thought we'd agreed you would get to know him. He's smart, titled, and well-off. And from the way several of the other women are looking at him, quite handsome. You don't want to miss your chance with him."

Emily didn't want to have this conversation on the edge of the ballroom floor where anyone could overhear them. She cast another look around them before replying. "If you're so enamored, maybe you should pursue a relationship with him."

James's mouth dropped open in shock, and Sarah's amused laughter broke the tense silence that followed her statement. Sarah sobered soon enough, whispering, "Speak of the devil…"

Emily turned to find Lord Kirby fast approaching. Her gaze went back to her brother, who was grinning at her in satisfaction. She found that she much preferred James when he was glowering at any man who dared approach her.

Lord Kirby greeted them with what she imagined, for him, was great enthusiasm since the man rarely showed even a hint of emotion.

She glared at James when he took his leave, dragging Sarah onto the dance floor with him.

"Is something the matter?" Lord Kirby asked.

"Oh no," Emily said, managing a polite smile. "My brother was just teasing me. You know how siblings can be."

"I'm afraid I am an only child."

That explained so much. If ever there was a man in need of a sibling to shake up his unflappable reserve, it was the one standing before her now. Although Jonah was also an only child, he wasn't quite so unemotional.

Lord Kirby's arms were clasped behind his back, and he looked down at her from his greater height, his pale blue eyes sending a shiver through her. When he cleared his throat, she knew what was coming. He was going to ask for leave to court her. She frantically searched for an excuse to put him off, but nothing came to mind. She stood there, frozen, as he began to speak.

"I'm so glad to have caught up with you. There was something I wanted to discuss—"

"Emily, there you are. I wondered where you'd been hiding."

Lord Kirby frowned at Jonah's familiar use of her given name, but Emily couldn't find it within herself to care. In fact, at that moment she wanted nothing more than to embrace him.

CHAPTER 7

*J*ONAH COULD SENSE Emily's relief and so pressed on. "After our dance together, you promised me a turn about the room. I've come to collect."

He ignored the way Kirby glared at him, instead offering Emily his arm. She clutched it with a little more enthusiasm than was seemly and took her leave of the man who'd been hovering over her moments before.

"Thank you," she said when they were out of Lord Kirby's hearing. "I think he was about to ask for leave to court me." The way her brows drew together told him she wouldn't have welcomed the man's interest.

"You didn't seem to be enjoying yourself, so I decided to intervene."

"Oh no," she said. "Do you think he noticed? I don't wish to hurt his feelings."

He wasn't surprised the young woman he'd once known as a sensitive, carefree child was more concerned about someone else's feelings than her own. "I'm sure he's fine. If he realized you didn't care for his company, he wouldn't have been hovering over you."

The words left a sour taste in his mouth, but he tried to ignore his displeasure at the thought of Kirby—or any man—courting Emily. He'd known her since she was a child, so it was natural he'd feel protective of her. He didn't wish to see her unhappy.

"Of course," she said with a soft sigh.

She didn't say anything else, and neither did he when he realized she was leading them out of the room. It was a pity it was too cold for the doors to the garden to be open. Instead, they'd have to wander along the hallway where others had also sought escape from the crowded confines of the ballroom.

He knew his next question was overstepping the bounds of propriety, but he couldn't hold back his curiosity. "Is there already someone for whom you have a *tendre*? I can't imagine a young woman as beautiful as you doesn't already have an understanding with an equally handsome young man."

She cast a sideways glance at him, an odd expression on her face. "You think I'm beautiful?"

One corner of his mouth tilted up. "As do most of the men here. I'm hardly alone in that thought."

Emily winced at the reminder of her would-be suitor. "To answer your question, no, there isn't anyone."

He ignored the surge of pleasure her admission brought since he was certain it wouldn't be true for long.

"Do you wish to return to the ballroom?" He didn't want their brief time together to come to an end, but she had told him she loved balls earlier that morning. He could have taken her into one of the other first-floor rooms that were open to guests but found himself reluctant to release her to the company of yet another man who was eager to capture her attention. He'd seen clearly enough that Kirby wasn't the only man interested in getting to know Emily better. The thought shouldn't have bothered him as much as it did.

Being with Emily was comforting. He knew he'd have to begin his own search for a bride soon. That was, after all, one of the reasons he'd decided not to return to his life abroad. But first he needed to readjust to society here. Yes, he'd been surrounded by Englishmen and women while in India, but things were decidedly different there. Freer. He'd almost forgotten all the constraints that were placed upon one here in his home country.

Even this brief stroll would cause tongues to wag despite the fact there was nothing untoward between them. They were friends, their comfort in one another's company aided by long familiarity.

Emily nodded toward the end of the hall and he hesitated, thinking she was going to lead him into James's study, the one room on this floor that wasn't currently open to the public and was sure to be empty. She cast him a curious look and he began moving again.

Unable to stop himself, his thoughts went to what sort of mischief they could get up to behind those closed doors. What shocked him most about the wayward direction of his thoughts was the fact he wasn't disgusted with himself. No, he found he *wanted* to be alone with Emily.

Her brothers were going to beat him to a bloody pulp, but

as she led him the rest of the distance, he couldn't bring himself to care.

He was so distracted, so intent on his own imaginings about what was going to happen, that he almost didn't stop when she tugged him over to the side. Only then did he see that chairs had been placed in the hallway for those who wanted a moment of relative, but not true, privacy.

Disappointment crashed over him.

He'd been away from polite society far too long if he believed Emily Hathaway was leading him away for a romantic assignation. But in that moment he realized he wanted more than friendship from her.

Emily withdrew her hand from his arm and lowered herself onto one of the chairs. After she was settled, he did the same.

"My family means well. But between James pushing me toward a staid, respectable union and Sarah and Grace going to great lengths to ensure there were a few eligible men present, I feel as though I am something of a disappointment to them."

He could understand not wanting to be pushed into a union one didn't desire, but surely Emily didn't wish to remain a spinster. He chose his words with great care when he asked her just that.

"You don't wish to wed?"

"Oh no, it's not that. It's just that I never thought it would be so *difficult* to find someone."

He raised a brow at that but didn't have to ask the obvious question.

"Yes, well, perhaps it isn't quite that difficult to find a husband. But I want what my brothers found. I want love."

He had to hold back his impulse to laugh. Of course Emily would be stuck on such a romantic notion.

"Sometimes love comes later. From what James told me, he didn't expect Sarah would ever come to care for him."

"That may be true, but he was smitten with her from the start and willing to take the risk that their union would come to mean more. But I haven't felt that emotion for *anyone*. Oh, I like many of them well enough, but I don't feel a spark of interest, let alone anything that approaches love. The closest I've come to feeling any heat are the moments my anger is sparked when I realize they care more for my dowry that they ever would for me."

"I hate to tell you this"—and he found that he really did —"but there are more than a few men here who have absolutely no need of your dowry."

Emily blew out a breath. "They may not need it, but you can trust me when I say they want it nonetheless." She shook her head as if to clear her mind of the current subject and smiled up at him. "Well, now that you've learned my secret Christmas wish, you have to share yours. Tell me, *Sir* Jonah. What is it you're hoping to receive this Christmas?"

What was he hoping for? He couldn't shake the feeling that there was something missing in his life, but he ascribed that to the sensation of being unmoored now that he was back in England. He didn't know what he was going to do to fill his days, and that thought unsettled him.

"I don't know yet."

Emily laid a hand over his and gave it a brief squeeze

before releasing it again. He was surprised at the unguarded show of compassion, but what unnerved him more was his desire to reach for her hand again, peel the glove from her fingers, and clasp it within his.

Emily stood then, saving him from doing something foolish, and he followed suit. "Come," she said. "We should head back now before tongues start wagging."

"If you want to start a few rumors, you should dance with me a second time."

He'd been joking, but Emily leaped at the suggestion. "Maybe Lord Kirby will think you're courting me. You can do that, right? Feign interest in me to keep him at bay?"

Jonah felt a strange sensation in his belly at her words. He ascribed it to nerves at the reminder that soon he'd be entering the marriage mart himself. He wasn't sure about the wisdom of Emily's suggestion, but he found himself powerless to disappoint her. "I think I can manage that."

He held out his arm and Emily took it, smiling up at him in a way that had him feeling ten feet tall as they made their way back to the ballroom.

CHAPTER 8

*E*MILY COULD FEEL the tension in the air when she entered the breakfast room to find the only occupants were Jonah and Lord Kirby. It was almost midday, and she'd hoped to avoid her would-be suitor by arriving after he'd departed, but clearly she hadn't waited long enough.

Jonah was leaning casually against a wall, his arms folded across his chest and an expression of extreme boredom on his face. Lord Kirby, on the other hand, was glaring at her partner in crime from his seat at the table. She could see that Jonah hadn't been exaggerating after they'd returned to the ballroom when he told her the other man hated him. He'd suggested it was because of their pretend courtship, but Emily couldn't help but wonder if there wasn't more to the story than he was willing to share.

She only had a moment to take in Jonah's appearance, her foolish heart giving a small leap at how handsome he looked in his maroon coat and waistcoat and buff breeches, before he noticed her. The corners of his mouth lifted and a spark of mischief danced behind his eyes. She almost pitied Lord Kirby in that moment and suspected Jonah was doing everything in his power to stir up the other man's temper.

Lord Kirby leaped to his feet when he realized he and Jonah were no longer alone. "Miss Hathaway, I am so happy to see you this morning," he said, greeting her with a cautious smile. "I was afraid the time would come for me to depart before I had the opportunity to bid you adieu. Or to tell you how beautiful you look."

"That would have been a tragedy."

Jonah's interruption caused Lord Kirby to clench his jaw, but the unwelcome audience didn't deter him from his task. Lord Kirby closed the distance between them and gazed down at her.

Emily could almost see the wheels turning in his mind. She'd avoided this moment the night before when Jonah had come to her rescue, but it was clear the man wouldn't be deterred.

She managed to keep a polite smile on her face when Lord Kirby reached for her hand and dropped a kiss on the back. She'd been through this same situation enough times now to ensure she always wore gloves as a barrier.

He released her hand with reluctance. "Will you be in town this coming spring?"

She took a discreet step back, allowing her smile to widen the tiniest fraction so he wouldn't take offense at her retreat. "I believe that's the current plan." She didn't offer him any encouragement, but she knew he would take her polite response as an attempt on her part at coyness.

"I look forward to seeing you there then. Perhaps you'll spare me a few moments of your delightful company when your attention isn't quite so consumed by old acquaintances who make unwelcome demands of your time."

She said nothing to that, knowing full well he was referring to Jonah. But the only acquaintance who was pressing upon her time was him and all the others who saw her only as a means of attaching themselves to a wealthy family.

She dipped into a brief curtsy, making sure to break eye contact, and sighed with relief when he took it as the dismissal it was meant to be. He stepped back but didn't depart just yet.

She chanced another glance at his face and noticed the slight crease that had formed between his brows as he glanced in Jonah's direction. She knew then that he'd learned Jonah and his mother would be staying with them through Christmas and the beginning of the new year. Longer, perhaps, if it snowed and the roads become impassable.

If it wouldn't be a breach of decorum, she suspected Lord Kirby would have pressed for a longer stay himself. She was grateful that the house party hadn't been planned for the actual Christmas holiday as Emily had originally wanted before she learned it would become yet another attempt by her family to find her a husband. No doubt that was James's doing, and for once Emily was glad her brother avoided society whenever possible.

She glanced at Jonah and wasn't surprised to see what could only be called a self-satisfied smirk on his face. He appeared to be taking an inordinate amount of pleasure in Lord Kirby's distress. It was too bad, really, that his show of triumph over the man was merely an act. What would it be like to have two men fighting for her attention—especially if one of those men was Jonah?

"Yes, I've enjoyed our opportunity to become reacquainted," Jonah said, his tone rife with insincerity. Emily was glad Sarah wasn't there to witness it since she was so concerned about ensuring each of their guests enjoyed their stay. "But if those heavy clouds are anything to go by, we'll soon have snow, and we'd hate for you to be stuck here with us over the holidays. You really should leave now if you want to make it home. It would be a shame to find yourself stranded at an inn on Christmas morning."

Emily managed not to laugh at the frown that crossed Lord Kirby's face before he gave them both another bow and turned to leave. She counted it a tremendous feat of restraint when she held back her mirth for a full ten seconds after the man left the room.

"You are so evil," she said when she managed to catch her breath again after her amusement died down. "The poor man looked as though he wanted to strangle you."

A corner of Jonah's mouth tilted upward in a more genuine smile. "I'm quite certain that's exactly what he wanted to do. If you hadn't arrived when you did, I'm sure he would have called me out merely for the offense of existing."

Emily gave her head a slight shake, wincing slightly as she wondered whether Lord Kirby had heard her laughter. Oh well, it was too late to worry about it now.

"Kirby was right about one thing," Jonah said. "May I say that you look lovely today, Miss Hathaway? Of course, you always do."

At his formality, Emily glanced toward the doorway to see

who was witnessing their exchange. When she realized they were still alone, she cast a sideways glance at him and made her way to the sideboard.

"You can save your teasing for others, *Sir Jonah*. These past few days have been trying enough."

She expected him to join her as she reached for a plate. When he didn't, she realized he must have already eaten. "You needn't stay to keep me company. I'm sure someone else will be along shortly."

She'd given him permission to escape but was glad when he didn't take the opportunity. Instead, he waited for her to finish loading up her plate—she felt a sense of relief that she could eat her fill without worrying about appearing gluttonous —and followed her to the table.

"There is no place I'd rather be," he said, lowering himself into the seat next to her.

How was a girl to keep her thoughts from scattering in the presence of such a formidable opponent? With his classically handsome features and wit, Sir Jonah Stanton would have no difficulty finding a bride this upcoming season. He was going to have to carve his way through the crowds of hopeful young women vying to capture his attention.

Needing to divert her thoughts from their current path, she grasped for the one subject she knew would unsettle him. "Tell me more about Lord Kirby."

Jonah's frown told her she'd succeeded in distracting him from his teasing. She had to look away lest she betray her amusement.

"I thought you weren't interested in knowing more about him."

She lifted one shoulder but kept her gaze averted. She hoped he'd take it as shyness on her part, but in truth she feared she would burst into laughter again. It appeared Lord Kirby's dislike of Jonah wasn't one-sided.

"You and he are of an age, are you not?"

"Yes." Jonah's reply was curt.

She met his eyes and somehow managed to keep a straight face. She raised a brow, and Jonah folded his arms across his chest.

"You are not going to entertain his suit. He's far too annoying and dull for someone like you."

"Someone like me? James seems to think we'd make a good match, and he is not one to give his consent lightly."

"You know what I mean. You are far too full of life to saddle yourself with someone so stolid."

"It sounds like I'm just what he needs then. Someone to show him the joy life has to offer."

Jonah scowled at that. "I sincerely hope you're joking."

Emily could no longer hold back her laughter. "I wish you could see the look on your face." She attempted to arrange her features into a similar scowl but gave up and chuckled when his frown deepened.

"To set your mind at ease, I'll admit that I won't be entertaining Lord Kirby's suit. My interest in him stems solely from my curiosity about the animosity between the two of you. Were you rivals at school?"

Jonah shook his head, and Emily was glad when his expression softened. "Nothing quite so dramatic, although we did know one another back at Eton. We've never been anything more than acquaintances, but I've always found him to be a little too full of himself."

"So you weren't onetime friends who had a falling-out?"

"Definitely not. I told you this last night, but apparently you didn't believe me. Kirby means to have you for himself, and he can't abide the sight of me because he thinks I'm standing in his way."

Emily took a sip of her tea as she contemplated Jonah's words. Lord Kirby wasn't the first man to have set his sights on gaining her hand in marriage.

"So I take it his fortune is limited and he needs my dowry?"

Jonah hesitated, and for a moment she didn't think he was going to reply. Finally he shrugged. "I don't think so. Really, Emily, you must see that you hold a great deal of worth beyond the amount James will be settling on you when you wed. You are smart, generous, have a lively wit, and you brighten every room you walk into with merely a smile."

Emily found herself at a loss for words. It almost seemed as though Jonah admired her. But no, she was letting her imagination get away from her.

"It's too bad you won't be able to be my protector during the upcoming season," she said when she could speak again. "Although it shouldn't be too difficult to convince my brother to forgo the affair entirely. I'll just have to figure out a way to keep Sarah from changing his mind again."

"I remain ever at your service, Miss Hathaway." He grinned at her, and Emily felt her foolish heart lighten at his obvious good mood.

She had to force her thoughts back to reality instead of

allowing herself to get caught up in foolish daydreams. "You forget that I know you're planning to look for a wife. You can hardly do that while pretending to court me to keep unwanted suiters at bay."

Jonah held her gaze for several seconds before speaking. "I don't know. If my luck holds, I may not need to worry about that. But only if you promise to come to London in the spring. How else would I be able to court you properly?"

Emily's stomach did an odd little flip at his words. She had no witty comeback and could only watch, struggling to keep her jaw from dropping open, as he rose and strolled from the breakfast room.

It wasn't possible he'd spoken in earnest. No, he was teasing her again. Jonah didn't need her fortune, and they'd known each other much too long for him to be interested in her romantically.

That thought shouldn't have depressed her as much as it did.

CHAPTER 9

*D*ESPITE HER BEST EFFORTS, Emily couldn't stop thinking about her conversation with Jonah. No matter how hard she tried, her thoughts kept circling back to what it would be like to have Sir Jonah Stanton court her.

He'd woo her with flowers and drives through Hyde Park, but he wouldn't be content to follow the traditional path quite so strictly. He'd find moments to take her aside and kiss her whenever he could. No, not just one kiss but several. Whenever the opportunity presented itself.

Emily had to give her head a sharp shake to keep from getting carried away with her fantasy. Her feelings for Jonah were being muddled by the role he'd played during the ball the night before. And after his teasing that morning, it was becoming difficult to separate fantasy from reality.

It was possible Jonah was also caught up in the same trap. But come spring he'd be over any inclination he might have had to court her.

She made her way to James's study, wanting to thank him properly for agreeing to host the Christmas ball. He might have had ulterior motives, but in the end she'd enjoyed herself tremendously. Perhaps he'd like to go for a ride. It seemed an age since the two of them had gone riding together, and she needed to distract herself from thoughts of Jonah.

She let herself into the study after a quick knock. "It's safe to come out now, James—"

She stopped abruptly when she realized her brother wasn't alone. In fact, he and Sarah were in the midst of a heated embrace.

He spun them around, his broad back shielding his wife so Emily couldn't see what was happening, something for which she was infinitely grateful.

"How many times have I asked you to knock first, Emily?"

Fumbling for the door latch, she let herself back out with a hurried, "I didn't see anything. In fact, I wasn't even here."

She released a shaky chuckle once she'd escaped the room. Well, it appeared James had found another way to celebrate his newfound freedom from unwelcome houseguests.

Never mind—there was always Edward or Grace. Setting out in search of them, she made her way to the library and cautiously opened the door.

And stood frozen in shock for several seconds when she realized Edward was lying over Grace on the settee, his mouth traveling down the column of her throat while his wife let out a little sound that spoke volumes about how much she was enjoying her husband's attentions.

They hadn't noticed her entrance, so when she could move again, Emily closed the door as quietly as possible. She leaned against the wall and closed her eyes, unable to forget that little sound.

More than anything, she wanted the type of relationship her brothers had both found. Maybe she should take Jonah up on his offer and allow him to court her in earnest before he changed his mind.

She decided the safest course of action was to return to the dower house since she was unlikely to run into anyone engaged in a heated embrace there.

CHAPTER 10

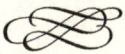

ITH THE WAY HER day was going, Emily wasn't surprised to find Jonah at the dower house. His mother was staying there, after all, so it made sense he would visit. But she couldn't help wondering if the universe was conspiring against her that morning, going out of its way to dangle before her everything she would never have.

Jonah, who was seated in a comfortable armchair, stood when she entered the morning room, which was her mother's favorite room in the house. She wasn't sure why they called it that since it faced south and was filled with natural light for most of the day. Mama and Mrs. Stanton were sitting together on the settee, both engaged with their needlework.

"We didn't expect you back so soon," her mother said, lowering the square of fabric onto her lap. Mrs. Stanton looked up from her embroidery as Emily moved farther into the room.

"Everyone was busy at the manor." She really didn't want

to explain what they'd been so busy doing, so she turned the conversation to them. "What were you discussing? I heard laughter from all the way down the hall."

"Jonah was just telling us about some of the adventures he had while in India." Mrs. Stanton gazed fondly at her son. "He has the most amusing stories—I'd almost forgotten how he could entertain his father and me for hours."

"I'm sure he does," Emily said in reply, grateful for the change in subject.

"What was everyone busy doing?" Jonah asked.

Emily was going to kill him. She turned to meet his questioning gaze and didn't miss the amusement lurking there, as though he knew exactly what was going on at the main house. Now that she thought about it, maybe that was way he'd chosen to visit his mother. "Certainly nothing that required my attention."

She narrowed her eyes slightly, promising retribution if he pursued the current subject. Fortunately, he understood her unspoken threat and didn't say anything further.

"You're welcome to join us," Mama said. "I can call for some tea to help warm you. I know how cold it is out. Thank heavens we won't have to make the trip back and forth to the main house after today."

Emily lowered herself onto the settee next to her mother. From the look on both her and Mrs. Stanton's faces, it was clear they were holding something back.

"Are you going to make me beg, or are you going to tell me what has you both so happy?"

Mama laughed and gave her a pat on the knee. "I never

could keep anything from Emily. She's far too adept at reading my expressions."

Emily merely waited, not bothering to comment on what they could all see for themselves. Her mother was terrible at keeping a secret, a trait that Emily knew she shared. Her mother's eyes danced with delight, and it was obvious to everyone that she was excited.

Jonah took his seat again and answered her question. "It appears you're going to be moving to the main house for the week leading up to Christmas."

"I thought it would make a nice change of pace to spend the Christmas season together, especially since Jonah will be there. And I'll admit I'm looking forward to seeing George and William every day."

Somehow Emily kept from bouncing in her seat. She gave her mother a quick hug. "Really? Oh, I must tell my maid what to pack. Although if I forget something, it won't be too onerous a task to fetch it."

When her gaze moved back to Jonah, she noted the fond smile on his face as he took in her excitement. Anticipation shot through her when their eyes met. They were going to be seeing much more of one another in the next week, which would give them both the opportunity to discover whether their pretend courtship could develop into something more.

And in that moment, Emily knew what she had to do. She needed to discover whether she and Jonah were physically compatible. Some might say she was acting with ill-advised haste, but there was only one way to learn what a marriage to Jonah would entail. They were already friends… Could they be more?

Logically she knew she might come to regret her hasty decision, but she'd always trusted her instincts and they'd never led her astray. And the more she got to know him, the more she began to believe that Jonah might be the man she'd been looking for all along.

"Actually, I just remembered that there was something I needed to discuss with *Sir* Jonah."

Jonah raised a brow at the way she emphasized his title. "I am ever at your disposal, Miss Hathaway."

The hint of amusement in his voice reminded her of all the reasons they were good together. They shared a sense of humor, and Jonah understood her in a way many others who'd sought her favor hadn't. Surely it wasn't too much to hope that perhaps they could have more than friendship.

She looked directly at her mother, doing everything in her power to keep her expression impassive.

"This is something we need to discuss in private, Mama."

Her mother gave her a penetrating stare, and for a moment Emily feared she'd be able to read her mind. She forced herself not to look away lest she betray the fact that she had ulterior motives for wanting to have a private conversation with Jonah.

"May I inquire as to the subject of this discussion?"

Emily didn't want to lie to her mother, so she opted for evasion instead. "It's the week before Christmas and I need his assistance with a few matters."

Strictly speaking, both statements were true. Hopefully her mother would think she wanted to talk to Jonah about a Christmas gift for Mrs. Stanton.

Jonah's mother caught Mama's eye, a strange look passing

between them, before she turned to her son. "Of course. You and Emily are practically siblings, so I know there won't be anything untoward happening."

Emily tried her best to conceal her displeasure at Mrs. Stanton's characterization of their relationship. Did everyone see them as such? She certainly didn't see him in the same light as her brothers.

Jonah followed her into the hallway. They'd scarce crossed the threshold when he spoke, his voice low so their mothers wouldn't overhear. "I most definitely do not consider you a sister."

Emily's heart soared, and she couldn't hold back her relief. "Well, that's good. I find that two overprotective brothers are more than enough."

She didn't say anything else until they reached the drawing room, which was far enough away from the morning room that they could speak freely. To ensure none of the staff would interrupt them, she pulled the door until it was almost closed.

Jonah stood in the middle of the room, waiting for her to sit. Instead of doing so, she came within a few feet of him and took a deep breath.

"There's a matter I need to discuss with you, but I don't know how you'll take it."

CHAPTER 11

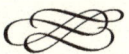

*J*ONAH'S THOUGHTS LEAPED to scenarios too unpleasant to contemplate, the foremost of which was that, despite her protestations to the contrary, her affections were already engaged elsewhere.

"You're secretly betrothed to another."

"What?" Emily's nose scrunched at his statement. "No, of course not. Why would you think that?"

"What else would you have to tell me that I won't like? Unless… Did Kirby return? He didn't press his unwanted attention on you, did he?" He frowned as it occurred to him that perhaps Kirby's courtship wouldn't be quite as unwelcome as she'd led him to believe.

"No, nothing like that. You saw him take his leave. He was already on his way before you disappeared yourself." She tilted her head. "Why didn't you tell me you were planning to visit your mother?"

Jonah didn't know how to reply to that. He wasn't about to

tell Emily that he'd shared his desire to court her with their mothers, who'd both been delighted by the news. He wasn't quite ready to share that information with James or Edward—not until he knew whether Emily reciprocated his feelings—but he'd wanted their mothers' support. He needed to approach this with care, for it had suddenly become far too important to him that Emily see him as more than just an old family friend. Or as a brother.

"Why don't you tell me what you wanted to say before I jump to any more conclusions? I assure you, my imagination can be very fruitful."

He'd hoped to elicit a laugh from her, but instead Emily gave a sigh and looked away. He waited, resisting the urge to press her.

"Has Edward told you about his courtship of Grace?"

Now she had him truly confused. He could in no way imagine how her brother's relationship with his wife had anything to do with him or Emily.

"I know they met when he was delivering a letter to her written by a friend who passed away at the end of the war."

She examined him closely for several seconds. "Nothing beyond that?"

"No, of course not. Edward is hardly the type to share the details of his relationship. I do know, however, that he cares for her a great deal."

Emily sighed. "He does. And James also loves Sarah."

He remembered her Christmas wish that she also find love and felt a pang when he realized he wanted that as well. He'd told her he didn't know what he wanted for Christmas, but that was no longer true. He wanted Emily.

He didn't reply and Emily continued.

"Sarah didn't want to wed James. Their union was agreed to by her father, and for reasons she's never shared with me, she agreed to it. But she'd imagined herself in love with someone else at the time."

He winced, imagining the disappointment that knowledge must have cost James. "But they moved beyond that."

"Yes. But they were lucky."

"Many find happiness with their spouses when presented with similar circumstances."

"Yes, and many despise one another, while others merely tolerate their husband or wife."

"What do you know of such marriages? I was under the impression your parents were happy as well."

"They were," Emily said with a sigh.

She sank onto the settee, and Jonah hesitated only a moment before taking a seat in one of the armchairs. He wanted to sit next to her, but it was too soon for that.

"What is bothering you?"

He'd almost asked her if she was worried about his declaration that he wanted to court her, but something held him back. Was it possible the beautiful, lively young woman seated before him felt none of the same emotions currently plaguing him? Was she trying to convince herself that a practical union with him would be enough? While he'd expected to enter into such an arrangement when it came time to wed, he found that was the last thing he wanted with Emily. Still, the knowledge that James and Sarah's love had come after they'd wed gave him some hope.

"During my time in London, I've seen too many people

who are unhappy in their marriages. Sarah has pointed out to me every married woman who has approached James about engaging in an affair. He never would, of course—he turns them down and has told Sarah whenever it happens—but his unavailability seems to make him all the more attractive in their eyes."

Well, good for James that he could share that information with his wife. It went a long way toward confirming that his friend had chosen well in his marriage despite their unsteady beginnings.

"It happens, but that's not the type of marriage I want either. My own parents were happy together before my father's death."

Emily's gaze softened as she gazed at him, and he had to hold back his desire to bridge the distance between them and kiss her. Before he could do anything, she had to tell him why she needed to speak to him in private.

"James and Sarah were very fortunate, but I'm not willing to risk my future happiness on luck."

"Not even if you consider your future spouse a friend? Surely that weighs the odds more favorably."

Emily shook her head, and Jonah felt that denial like a blow. Still, the battle for Emily's heart wasn't over yet, and he refused to concede before he'd even entered the fray.

"I think Grace had the right of it."

She stood and he followed suit, gazing at her with confusion as she crossed to the door. For a moment he thought she was going to leave without telling him the reason for this conversation.

Emily opened the door slightly, and he realized she was

checking to make sure no one was present to overhear what she was going to say.

"And what was this idea of hers?"

Emily approached him, but this time she didn't sit. "She and Edward had a tryst before they were wed."

Jonah's heart began to race as he realized what she was suggesting. Still, he wasn't going to assume. He wanted—no, he *needed*—to hear her say it.

"Go on."

"I think we should do the same, you and me. That way we'll know if a future marriage between us has the potential to be as happy as what my brothers have found."

His heart screamed yes at the suggestion, but his head cautioned him otherwise. If he hadn't missed his guess, Emily was a maiden. What if their first time together was filled with more pain than pleasure? It was entirely possible she'd renounce him completely if that happened.

He also knew that her brothers wouldn't be pleased with Emily's plan if they learned of it.

"And how exactly would we enact this plan of yours?"

Emily waved a hand. "That's simple enough. The manor house is quite large. I'm sure we could find a quiet corner. Or we could come here since Mama and Mrs. Stanton won't be in residence."

He wanted to agree, but still he hesitated.

Emily took a step closer. "I need to know if we can find the same happiness in our own marriage. Given how happy James and Edward are, I don't want to settle for mere friendship. I like you, Jonah, a great deal. I believe we have a chance at happiness together, but I need to be certain."

Jonah didn't really want to fight her on this anymore, not when it was what he wanted too. "Your brothers are going to kill me. I foresee that I won't live to see our wedding day if we go through with this plan of yours."

"You'll do it?" Emily's eyes lit up.

"Was there ever any doubt?"

"There was some doubt." Emily looked away for a moment before meeting his gaze again and continuing. "I feared you might have been teasing me earlier when you said you wanted to court me."

He smiled down at her. "I would never tease about something like that. What would be the point?"

"It was such a surprise. And, well, I found I liked the idea more than I thought wise. Thank you, Jonah."

She reached up to place a hand on his arm but stopped short. Her uncharacteristic awkwardness had him reaching out to take her hand in his. As he dropped a kiss on the back of her hand, he noticed she'd removed her gloves and remembered that another man had made the same gesture earlier that morning. He took heart from the fact she didn't remove her hand from his and enjoyed the feel of her skin under his own.

Emily gave her head a small shake. "I don't know what to say now. I hadn't planned this far ahead."

"Well," Jonah said, running his thumb along the back of her hand and taking pleasure in the way she shivered at the contact, "I think I can take it from here."

"I'd like that," she said with an eagerness that touched him deeply.

"I'm going to show you exactly what you've been missing,

Emily Hathaway. But first you must agree to my suit in earnest."

Emily tilted her head to the side. She glanced at him from under her lashes. "That depends on what you show me, doesn't it?"

Jonah gave her hand a sharp tug, and with a small squeak of surprise, Emily fell against him. "Should we seal our pact with a kiss?"

Emily searched his expression before giving a wordless nod.

Jonah needed no further encouragement and lowered his mouth to hers. He still held her hand in his as he tried to keep from advancing too quickly, too soon. His mouth moved softly against hers, but he couldn't hold back his groan when she threaded the fingers of her other hand in the hair at his nape.

He didn't even realize he'd thrust his tongue into her mouth until he heard her small gasp of surprise. He tried to pull back, but then she was returning his kiss in earnest. He released her hand and brought her body flush against his as he explored her mouth. He fought the urge to take their embrace further, and it was with great reluctance that he slowed the kiss and stepped back.

Emily's breathing was as shaky as his when she looked up at him, wonder in her expression. "In the interest of full honesty, I should tell you that wasn't my first kiss. But it was by far the best."

He said nothing in reply, not wanting to ruin the priceless moment by calling attention to his own past experiences. But he realized the same was also true for him.

CHAPTER 12

*E*MILY'S MAID WAS pinning her hair up with quick, efficient movements when her two sisters-in-law entered her bedroom.

"Am I late?" Emily asked.

Tonight was to be their first dinner together, just the Hathaways, Jonah, and Mrs. Stanton. She couldn't help thinking that if things went well between her and Jonah, they'd soon be one large family.

Grace shook her head. "No, we're a little early. Although the men have already gone downstairs."

While they waited for the maid to finish, the two women perched on the edge of her bed and chatted about how it was infinitely more difficult to host a house party than to be a guest.

Her maid tucked the last few pins in her hair and took her leave. When Emily turned in her seat at the dressing table, she saw that Sarah and Grace were looking at her with great interest. She had to hold back her sigh.

Hoping to forestall further speculation on their part, she said, "No, I will not be encouraging Lord Kirby."

Sarah tilted her head to one side, her gaze sharp. "Forget about Lord Kirby. I know James wants to see you settled with someone solid, but to him that means boring. Lord Kirby would smother the very life from you."

Why did everyone think they knew her so well? "Perhaps I'd liven him up, make him more outgoing."

"Perhaps," Grace said. "But it's been my observation that men rarely change once they've reached adulthood."

Grace met Sarah's gaze. The two of them had a plan in mind, and she was almost afraid to find out what it was.

"Perhaps we should go down—" Emily started.

Sarah continued as though she hadn't spoken. "How do you feel about Sir Jonah?"

Grace nodded in agreement. "We know you've been acquainted with him since you were a child, but he's been away for so long. Edward thinks you consider him a brother, but perhaps there could be something more?"

Emily sighed. These two were relentless in their desire to find her a husband. She knew their meddling came from a place of love though and couldn't be angry with them. And if she was being completely honest, she wanted to share her secret with them. But she couldn't tell them what she was planning. They wouldn't tell her brothers if she asked them not to, but she was loath to ask them to do something that would anger their husbands.

"I'll consider it." She laughed when she saw the twin expressions of disbelief on both Sarah's and Grace's faces. "Come, let's not keep everyone waiting."

"You can't just say that and leave," Sarah said following her to the bedroom door.

Grace was right behind her. "I never realized before today that you have a mean streak. Surely you're going to tell us more."

"I'll tell you more when there's more to say." That wasn't strictly true, but Emily didn't know what to think about the current situation herself. How could she talk about her feelings when they confused her so much?

She'd relived her conversation—and kiss—with Jonah over and over in her mind. But before she shared any details with the two women who'd come to mean so much to her, she needed to explore her newfound feelings. Given her lack of luck when it came to finding love, she was afraid speaking of them would somehow jinx her and Jonah's relationship before it even started.

The three of them entered the drawing room together to find everyone else already present. The men were standing by the fireplace, discussing something in low, earnest tones while Mama and Mrs. Stanton sat on the settee, equally engrossed in conversation.

It took all of Emily's self-restraint not to stare at Jonah lest she betray her interest to the other occupants of the room. James had already cornered her before she'd gone upstairs to change for dinner to ask her how she felt about Lord Kirby. He hadn't been surprised when she replied that he seemed pleasant enough and that she was sure he'd make some *other* woman a fine husband. The last thing she wanted was to draw his attention to a potential alliance with the man who'd remained behind.

She wondered if it had ever occurred to James to consider a match between her and Jonah. They'd been friends for most of their lives since the Stantons' estate bordered their former home in Newmarket. She was so much younger than Jonah and couldn't be considered a contemporary, not with an eight-year age gap between them. But what seemed unthinkable at ten and eighteen would scarcely be considered much of a difference now that they were twenty and twenty-eight.

Despite Emily's attempt to appear casual in his presence, it was impossible to ignore how handsome Jonah looked. He was slightly taller than her brothers, and of the three anyone would agree he was the most handsome. He was dressed in deep blue, and it occurred to her that since she also wore blue, they matched.

She watched her brothers move to greet their wives, telling them how beautiful they looked. Really, you'd think they hadn't seen one another in a month, but Emily knew what they'd been up to earlier in the day after the last guest had departed.

Emily wanted that type of relationship so much it almost hurt.

She was so taken by the display of marital affection displayed before her that she didn't notice Jonah approaching until he was standing next to her.

"How is it possible that you grow more beautiful each time I see you?"

His voice was low, for her ears only, and Emily felt her heart skip. She would have thought he was teasing her—poking fun at the display her brothers were giving them—but the intensity of his expression told her otherwise. She hadn't forgotten he'd called her beautiful and wasn't ashamed to admit she'd dressed to capture his attention, the bodice of her dress lower than what she normally wore.

She gave a slight curtsy, trying to hide the effect his words had on her. "Thank you, kind sir." She was about to pay him a compliment as well, but she became aware of other eyes on them and chose to remain silent.

"It is so good to have everyone gone." The relief in James's voice was almost comical. "I haven't been able to enjoy a meal properly in days."

Sarah wound her arm through her husband's. "Not even when you snuck away and locked yourself in your study? I'm sure I saw at least one of the footmen bring you some food."

Emily tilted her head, the picture of innocence, and asked, "Was there anyone here who *didn't* expect that to happen?"

James replied with a shrug. "I may have agreed to host the thing, but I never said I'd dance attendance on the guests every hour of the day. That's why the rest of you were here."

"Well, for once, I actually agree with my brother." Emily gave an exaggerated shudder. "I thought Lord Kirby was going to call out poor Jonah."

"Whose idea was that?" Edward asked. "To have Jonah pretend to be a suitor?"

Emily felt a twinge of annoyance at the unvoiced implication that Jonah would never be interested in her but ignored it. It *had* started as pretend after all.

Jonah replied for her. "It was Emily's, of course."

She shrugged. "You can hardly blame me."

James expelled a breath, but in the end he gave her a nod. "*Touché*. You cleverly outmaneuvered us all."

He cast a speculative glance at Jonah, and Emily held her breath, wondering if he suspected there was something more than pretense behind their actions. Fortunately, the dinner bell rang and he turned away from them to lead his wife from the room.

Jonah leaned down and said softly, "I hope you don't mind that I'm going to escort my mother in."

"Oh no, of course not. We don't want to risk everyone asking questions if you didn't."

"I'm not going to keep my interest in you a secret forever, Emily."

She knew that if anyone was watching them now, the soft smile she gave him would betray her growing feelings for him. "We'll discover very soon if there's something real between us."

Jonah looked as though he wanted to argue, but instead he gave a small nod and started to turn away.

Emily hesitated but decided it was better to be seen handing Jonah a note than to be caught passing him one in secret. James and Edward had already led their wives from the room, and before Jonah could reach his mother's side, she called his name.

He turned back to her, one brow raised.

"I wanted to give you that list I promised you."

She took a small, folded note from where she'd stashed it in the palm of her glove and handed it to Jonah. To his credit, he said nothing, simply tucking the note in an inner pocket of his tailcoat.

"What was that?" Mrs. Stanton asked as she placed a hand on her son's arm.

"Emily's playing matchmaker. She knows I'll be in London in the spring," he said before leading his mother from the room.

He hadn't lied, she'd give Jonah that. But the note she'd given him had nothing to do with his search for a bride, containing instead the location where they'd meet later that night.

It was just her and Mama alone in the room. Emily had started to follow the others when her mother laid a hand on her arm. And just like that, she knew her mother hadn't been fooled.

"I trust you and Jonah, but please be careful."

Emily stared at her for several seconds, then nodded silently in reply. Arranging what she'd hoped would be a secret encounter with Jonah was hardly a topic she wanted to discuss with her mother, after all.

When she entered the dining room, her gaze met Jonah's. She said nothing when the footman pulled out the empty seat next to him, and she found herself wondering if everyone realized there was something more than friendship between the two of them.

Her gaze swept over the group. She believed every woman present knew, or at least suspected. She was certain James had no idea, and Edward was an enigma. But when the younger of her two brothers gave her a half smile that told her he was vastly amused and looked to Jonah, then her, she almost groaned aloud.

Hoping to draw attention away from her and Jonah, she turned to James as the footmen began serving the soup. "What were the three of you discussing when we came down to dinner? It seemed serious."

James's brows drew into a frown. "I think we're going to have to sell the old stables."

Mama gasped, and Emily felt a small pang of loss. Papa had established those stables, and they'd always been a part of their lives. But when her brother inherited and moved to Northampton four years before, he'd moved their primary horse-breeding establishment here. He and Edward ran it together, with the latter taking control when James was too busy with estate matters. They'd kept the old stables running, however, with help.

"Fraser feels he's getting too old to run the Newmarket stables," Edward said. "He plans to retire soon, and we can't run it ourselves. Frankly, we're loath to trust it to someone we don't know. It would be better to sell it outright while it's still successful."

"Your father loved those stables." Mama's voice was so small. She wouldn't berate her brothers for their decision since she trusted their judgment, but it was clear she was disappointed.

"I might know someone who can run the stables for you."

All eyes turned to Jonah.

"Well, don't keep it a secret," James said.

Jonah chuckled. "Me."

Emily felt her heart give a small leap. Jonah had said he

wasn't planning to return to India, and while she'd wanted to believe him, she realized a part of her had been unsure about his commitment to remaining in England. He'd been actively involved in trade for the past ten years and wasn't the type of man to enjoy a life of idle leisure.

But if he helped run one of their stables, that would keep him engaged. It also meant she wouldn't have to worry about leaving England if they wed. Emily hadn't even realized a small part of her had worried about that happening until it was no longer a concern.

Her gaze swung to James and Edward. They were looking at each other, smiles tugging at the corners of their mouths.

"It's been many years since you used to visit us at the stables and help out," Edward said.

"But you always did have a knack for handling horses," James added.

Emily was almost bouncing in her seat. "And his work for the past few years means he has experience running a business."

James's eyes narrowed at Emily's staunch endorsement of his old friend. Fortunately, Jonah's next statement distracted him.

"I'd be willing to purchase the stables outright, but we all know the Hathaway name has undeniable weight when it comes to the business of breeding and raising horses."

Emily watched as her brothers looked at one another again. She had no idea how they did it, but they'd always been able to communicate with few—or even no—words. When she glanced at Jonah again, his expression betrayed no doubt. He already knew how this would go.

It was Edward who broke the silence. "James and I will discuss the details with you after dinner, but I think we can come to an agreement."

Jonah's eyes flickered to hers before he looked away, but in the second their gazes had met, she could see their entire future.

CHAPTER 13

*J*ONAH GLANCED DOWN at the note Emily had given him one final time to ensure he'd memorized its contents before tossing it into the fireplace. He watched the edges of the paper begin to darken and curl before it caught flame. When it was nothing but ashes, he stooped to bank the fire.

He left his bedroom and started along the route Emily had laid out for him. Given how protective her brothers were, he wasn't surprised she'd thought of everything. His route would take him near the kitchen, giving him an excuse if he should run into anyone since he could always claim he'd lost his way in a quest for something to eat.

Just before reaching the stairs that led down to the kitchen and servants' quarters, he veered left down another hallway, his goal the last room on the right. He hadn't been in this wing of the house before, and he suspected it was normally kept closed.

He was surprised when he opened the door and found he was in what appeared to be a storage room filled with bedroom furniture. Old, ornate furniture that was heavily covered in gilt.

He closed the door and when he turned around, Emily popped out from behind a wardrobe. She was a vision. Her dark hair was down, but she still wore the blue dress she'd donned for dinner. He turned back to the door and locked it.

"Where are we?"

Emily closed the distance between them. "This was the furniture in James's bedroom when he first moved in. You should have seen the house. There was gold everywhere. I imagine it would have rivaled the palace of Versailles."

Jonah could imagine how his friend had taken that. He wasn't one to swan about, and he would have hated the ostentation Emily described.

"You made sure you weren't followed?"

Jonah reached for her hand and drew her close. "No one saw me. And if they did, they probably thought I was heading to the kitchen for some food. Although given how much we ate over dinner, they would have to think I possess a bottomless pit for a stomach."

Emily's mouth twisted into a delightful little pout at his teasing. "It was the only thing I could think of to ensure we weren't discovered."

"Speaking of which… Were you hoping to get me killed by passing me that note in front of our mothers? What if one of them said something to your brothers?"

Emily hesitated, a hint of worry creeping into her eyes. "I think everyone knows about us. Everyone except James,

454

that is. I believe even Edward suspects, but I can't be certain."

He resisted the urge to jump back and place some distance between them. "About tonight?" He could just imagine the chaos that would ensue if her brothers decided to break down the door he'd just locked. He could hold his own against James or Edward, but against the two of them together? It was too gruesome to think about. "Maybe we should postpone our little experiment. I can still ask James for permission to court you properly first."

She tried to draw her hand back, but he didn't release it. "You don't have to stay if you don't want to."

"I haven't changed my mind, Emily. I just don't want you to be forced into something you don't want. I don't care if the entire household storms through that door and demands we wed tomorrow, but I know that isn't what you want."

He took a deep breath when she closed the distance between them and pressed her body against his. His hands settled on her waist, and he reveled in the anticipation that surged through him when she grasped his upper arms.

"I wanted to tell you earlier how handsome you looked, but I didn't want to attract more speculation. But I must say, I enjoy seeing you in just your shirt and waistcoat." Her hands roamed up and down his arms while her eyes remained on his. "You're very muscular. I find that I like that."

Jonah was done with words. He claimed her lips in a kiss that rivaled the heat of the one they'd shared earlier. Emily's arms went around his neck as she threw herself into the embrace.

His palms itched with the need to draw up her skirts, but

first he needed to know just how much restraint he should show.

He broke their kiss. She followed the backward movement of his head, trying to keep their mouths pressed together, but he had the advantage of height on his side.

"I don't want to stop," Emily said, her breathing ragged.

Jonah was powerless to deny her. "I have no intention of stopping, but I need to know… Have you made this offer to other men?"

A little *V* formed between her brows. "And if I have? Would that be enough to make you change your mind about me?"

He dropped a quick kiss onto her forehead, hoping to erase that crease. "That would be the height of hypocrisy on my part. I don't care if I'm your first as long as I'm your last. But I do need to know whether I should be careful. Often there's pain the first time a man lies with a woman, and I would spare you as much of that as possible."

Emily raised a hand to his cheek and met his eyes, a slow smile blossoming on her face. "I haven't lain with anyone else —I haven't wanted to before you. You'll be my first and hopefully my last."

Jonah closed his eyes for a moment. It turned out he was a hypocrite after all, for her admission pleased him more than it should.

He nodded toward the bed that was jammed into the corner of the room. From the haphazard piles of objects strewn on the floor next to it, he imagined Emily must have cleared the surface of the bed before he arrived. "Do you think that will hold our weight? It looks very insubstantial."

Emily lifted one shoulder. "I have no idea. Want to test our luck?"

James laughed. "I'm feeling like the luckiest man in the world right now."

Emily squeaked, then clapped one hand over her mouth when he lifted her into his arms and tossed her onto the bed.

CHAPTER 14

*E*XPECTATION ROSE WITHIN HER when Jonah followed her onto the bed. Emily inched backward, making room for him. She'd thought she'd be filled with nerves when this moment finally arrived, but instead she felt nothing but anticipation. The way Jonah stared down at her as he braced himself over her on his elbows set her heart racing.

She'd seen similar looks on other men's faces, and now she knew what the expression was… desire. Perhaps Jonah had been correct when he told her that other men wanted her for more than just her dowry. But that knowledge changed nothing, because there was only one man she wanted, and he was here with her right now.

She reached for him the same moment he lowered his head. This time he moved with care, his mouth exploring hers slowly, but somehow that only made her want him more. When he settled the length of his body over hers, most of his weight braced on one arm bent by her head, a delicious heat consumed her.

This was what she wanted, what she needed. This surfeit of emotion and sensation that threatened to overwhelm her. She'd never imagined Jonah would be the man to call it forth. She'd always liked him, but now she felt so much more.

She needed to let him know.

When he moved to kiss along her throat, she was surprised at how good it felt to have his lips pressed there. She'd never realized just how sensitive her neck could be.

Somehow she managed to speak. "We don't have to do this."

He lifted his head and looked down at her. She didn't miss the way he lifted his body so it was no longer pressed against hers, and she wanted to weep at the loss.

"Have you changed your mind?"

She shook her head. "No, I find that I want to continue more than I'd thought possible."

He searched her eyes, trying to decipher the truth behind her words. "Then why do you want to stop? If you're not ready—"

"No, it's not that. I need to tell you something first."

He shifted so he was lying on his side next to her, leaning on one arm. The other rested on her hip as though he too needed to maintain that connection with her. He said nothing, waiting for her to continue.

She shifted onto her side so they were now facing one another and brought her hand up to his face. Running her fingers along his jaw, she marveled at how Jonah was now so dear to her. "I've been very picky when it comes to men because I wanted to ensure I had the same type of marriage as my siblings found."

Jonah shifted his head and pressed a kiss in her palm. "Something for which I am infinitely grateful."

She smiled as she ran a thumb over his lower lip. "I approached this as a sort of test, but I've realized I don't need it. I know you're the only man for me."

He captured her hand and rolled so he was over her again. His gaze was intense as he stared down at her. "I love you, Emily Hathaway. But please don't tell me I have to stop now and ask for permission to court you first."

Emily didn't hold back her delighted laughter. She knew Jonah would wait if she asked him to, but that was the last thing she wanted.

"I love you too, Sir Jonah. Now please compromise me so my family will have no choice but to agree to your suit."

Neither of them believed that would be necessary. Her brothers were protective, yes, but they liked Jonah a great deal. Still, if that lie was needed to overcome any qualms he might have about continuing, she'd tell it again and again.

He answered with a smile that could only be called wicked, one that had all her senses on high alert.

"Your wish is my command," he said before kissing her again.

They continued to kiss, and she had to concentrate to undo the buttons of his waistcoat. When she succeeded in tugging open the material, she made a small sound of satisfaction and placed her hand on his chest over the lawn shirt. That sound turned into a surprised moan when she realized he'd used the hand on her hip to inch up her skirts.

He drew back and slid his hand along her outer thigh. "Are you fine with this?"

In reply, she tugged his shirt from his trousers. When she burrowed underneath and ran her fingers over his abdomen, he let out a small hiss.

"I'm going to take that as a yes."

He rose onto his haunches, and Emily watched with wonder as he removed his waistcoat and dragged his shirt over his head before tossing both garments onto the floor. When he lowered himself over her again, she took great satisfaction in running her hands over the exposed skin. He was harder than she'd expected, and his skin gave off enough heat to compensate for the lack of a lit fire in the room.

She stiffened in surprise when he moved his hand to her inner thigh but then forced herself to relax. She wanted this, after all. It was normal to be a little nervous about what was to come, but she most definitely did not want to stop.

She wasn't wearing any smallclothes, which Jonah clearly liked from the look of surprised wonder on his face.

She yelped in surprise when he rolled them over again so she was lying on top of him. He used his legs to spread hers farther apart, and she didn't resist. When his mouth clasped the peak of her breast through her dress, a bolt of pure sensation streaked through her. It only intensified when he moved his hand between her legs.

"Jonah…" His name was a long, low moan on her lips. When she thought about the intimacies that took place between a man and a woman, she'd expected to feel embar-

<label>462</label>

rassment, but instead she felt only eagerness to experience more.

His touch was pure magic, and the pull of his mouth on first one breast then the other had her making sounds that were decidedly unladylike. She allowed herself to sink into the world of sensation she was experiencing through Jonah's touch. There would be time later for her to bring him to equal heights, after he showed her what to do.

Once she stopped worrying about what she should be doing, it took little time for her to reach crisis. One pure, unexpected moment where all thoughts left her and she could only feel.

When she called out his name, it was louder than she'd expected, but Jonah covered her lips and silenced her cry of pleasure.

His movements slowed and she sagged on top of him, her head on his chest and her breathing ragged. It took her a minute before she found her voice. "I can see now what all the fuss is about."

Jonah chuckled, but the sound was cut off with a strangled moan when she reached down and cupped his manhood. She was shocked at how hard he was.

Jonah dropped a kiss atop her head. "I'd ask you if you want to stop now, but I'm afraid you'll say yes."

She lifted her head to meet his gaze. "I don't want to stop. I want to experience everything with you."

He shifted their positions so he was over her again. "Good." His brows drew together. "This might hurt at first."

"I know." But given how much Sarah and Grace seemed to enjoy their husbands' company, she also knew that it would pass. If not tonight, then the next time they were together.

She'd worn a dress with a low bodice and a half corset, thinking only to entice Jonah. It hadn't occurred to her that it would take just a quick tug for him to expose her breasts before he captured one peak in his mouth again. The feel of his warm, silken mouth on the bare skin of her breast was infinitely better than when he'd teased her through the fabric of her dress.

She was determined to give him as much pleasure as he was showing her. Her fingers had gone to his hair, where they combed through the thick sandy-brown strands. Needing to touch every inch of him she could reach, she lowered her hands first to his shoulders, then stroked the heated skin of his upper back. When he lifted his head and began to kiss her again, she was able to reach his waist and she dipped her hands beneath the fabric that still covered his hips.

He groaned and tore his mouth from hers. "I'm not sure how much longer I can wait."

"I'm ready now, Jonah."

He searched her face as if to assure himself she wasn't just saying the words to give him what he wanted. In response, she started to unbutton the fall of his trousers. He remained unnaturally still, as though he were afraid to move, but when she reached to encircle his manhood with her hand, he let out his breath with a stuttering exhale.

Jonah took over then, positioning her legs so he could brush his hardness against her folds. Then he moved forward, entering her with great care.

She'd expected pain, but she was so slick with desire it

didn't hurt beyond the initial pinch at his invasion. Still, Jonah stopped his movements and gave her time to adjust to him, concentrating again on kissing her. Emily would never tire of the feel of his mouth against hers, but soon the ache where they were joined had her lifting her legs to encircle his hips. A spark where Jonah had touched her earlier had her gasping in pleasure, and she started to thrust her hips against him, chasing the earlier sensations.

He gazed down at her, one corner of his mouth tilted upward. "I take it this isn't unbearably painful for you?"

From the tight set of his jaw, Emily guessed that his determination to be careful was costing him dearly and her heart expanded.

"Is this all there is?"

In response, Jonah pulled out and then moved back in. The smooth glide of his body within hers had her releasing a small "ooh" of surprise and delight.

There were no words after that. When Emily reached her second peak, she stifled her moans against his shoulder. Jonah gave a small grunt and pulled out of her, spilling onto the sheets. She knew it was prudent, but a small part of her could hardly wait until they wouldn't need to worry about preventing a pregnancy.

Jonah rolled to one side and took Emily with him. They lay together, the only sound that of their mixed breaths for several minutes.

It was Jonah who broke the silence. "How soon do you think we can wed? After all, once I declare my intentions, James will no doubt have a footman guarding you. We might not get another opportunity to be alone together."

Emily laid a hand along his cheek, savoring the knowledge that when the day of their wedding arrived, she'd be able to touch him whenever she wanted. "Then we should make proper use of tonight."

His smile was wicked. "I like the way you think, Miss Hathaway."

EPILOGUE

Christmas Day, 1816

𝒩O LONGER CONTENT to hide his feelings, Jonah asked James for permission to court her the day after their tryst. They wouldn't need her brother's blessing once she turned twenty-one in the spring, but they both wanted it anyway.

Once James granted it, Emily took great joy in being able to show her affection openly. But Jonah had been correct when he said her brother would have someone watching him like a hawk at all times to ensure he didn't overstep the bounds of propriety with her. Fortunately, she'd earned the affection of most of the household staff, and they were willing to look the other way when she and Jonah wanted to be alone together for brief periods of time. It also helped that Sarah was more than willing to distract her husband.

At Jonah's insistence, they didn't make love again. He

wanted to wait until they were wed, and Emily was currently in negotiations with her family about how soon she and Jonah could marry without stirring gossip about unseemly haste.

It was Christmas morning, and Emily's patience was starting to wear thin. She managed to grab a seat next to Jonah in the breakfast room, where they'd all gathered before they would go into the drawing room to open their gifts. James's brows drew together when Jonah reached for her hand, which was resting on the table next to her plate. She was relieved when her brother didn't say anything.

"What do you think about a March wedding?" Sarah didn't look up from the task of buttering her toast.

Emily's heart leaped. Her preference was for Jonah to fetch a special license so they could be wed soon, but she realized that wasn't going to happen. And calling the banns over the next three weeks had also been vetoed. Fortunately, March wasn't so far away.

"I don't see why we need to rush." James's voice was a petulant grumble, suggesting he and Sarah had argued about the matter and he'd lost.

Emily frowned. "First you wanted to throw me at Lord Kirby, a stranger, and now you have reservations about my marrying someone you know, whom you respect and call a friend?"

James had the courtesy to look abashed at her rebuke. "I have no reservations about Jonah. It's just difficult for me to think of you as a grown woman who will be leaving us soon."

"The distance between Newmarket and Northampton isn't that far," Jonah said. "Besides, we're also going to be business partners, and I've always found it preferable to conduct business in person rather than relying solely on correspondence. Have no fear, James. We'll be here so often you'll soon tire of seeing my face."

James made a small harrumph. "That's a gruesome thought."

Everyone broke into laughter since they all knew that of the three men present, Jonah was the only one whose features could be considered classically handsome.

Jonah squeezed her hand and she met his gaze. "It's only three months."

Emily released a soft breath. "I've never been very patient. But I've already waited three endless seasons to find the love of my life. What's three more months?"

She knew the smile she gave Jonah would be considered overly sentimental, but she didn't care because she meant every word.

"With that settled, we should head into the drawing room," Sarah said. "I'll go collect the boys so we can open presents. I'm sure they're driving their nurse crazy."

"Well, I already have my gift," Edward said. All eyes turned to him as he dropped a kiss on the back of his wife's hand. "Grace and I are expecting our first child."

Emily leaped from her chair to congratulate her brother and his wife but had to wait her turn to offer them each a hug since the other women had done the same.

They were making their way to the drawing room—minus Sarah, who'd gone up to the nursery—when Mrs. Stanton spoke. "Perhaps by next Christmas Emily will be able to give me a grandchild as well."

That was all it took for James to position himself between

her and Jonah. "Just make sure there are no surprises before then," he said with a low growl.

Emily couldn't hold back her laughter, and soon everyone else was joining in.

When Sarah returned with her two nephews several minutes later, Emily found her heart was full. Jonah had already fulfilled her Christmas wish. Anything else she received that day would pale in comparison.

THANK YOU

Thank you for reading! I've had a lot of fun with the Hathaways and I hope you did as well.

If you enjoyed this book, you can share that enjoyment by recommending it to others and leaving a review.

To learn when I have a new release, you can sign up for my newsletter at:

https://www.suzannamedeiros.com/newsletter/

BOOKS BY SUZANNA MEDEIROS

Dear Stranger

Forbidden in February (A Year Without a Duke multi-author series)

Anthologies

The Novellas: A Collection

Hathaway Heirs: Books 1-4

Landing a Lord series

Dancing with the Duke

Loving the Marquess

Beguiling the Earl

The Unaffected Earl

The Unsuitable Duke

The Unexpected Marquess—coming soon

Hathaway Heirs

Lady Hathaway's Proposal

Lord Hathaway's Bride

Captain Hathaway's Dilemma

Miss Hathaway's Wish

For more information about Suzanna's books, please visit her website:

https://www.suzannamedeiros.com/books/

ABOUT THE AUTHOR

USA Today bestselling author Suzanna Medeiros was born and raised in Toronto, Canada. Her love for the written word led her to pursue a degree in English Literature from the University of Toronto. She went on to earn a Bachelor of Education degree, but graduated at a time when no teaching jobs were available. After working at a number of interesting places, including a federal inquiry, a youth probation office, and the Office of the Fire Marshal of Ontario, she decided to pursue her first love—writing.

Suzanna is married to her own hero and is the proud mother of twin daughters. She is an avowed romantic who enjoys spending her days writing love stories.

She would like to thank her parents for showing her that love at first sight and happily ever after really do exist.

To learn more about Suzanna's books, you can visit her website at https://www.suzannamedeiros.com or visit her on Facebook at https://www.facebook.com/AuthorSuzannaMedeiros.

To learn when she has a new release available, you can sign up for her new release mailing list at https://www.suzannamedeiros.com/newsletter.

Made in the USA
Monee, IL
19 May 2021